Cougar

by

Christine Davies

Cougar

Cover Art by *The Wild Rose Press, Inc.*

The Wild Rose Press, Inc.
PO Box 708
Adams Basin, NY 14410-0708
Visit us at www.thewildrosepress.com

Publishing History
First Edition, 2025
Trade Paperback ISBN 978-1-5092-5973-1
Digital ISBN 978-1-5092-5974-8

Published in the United States of America

The sacred black mountain lion roams the mountains of New Mexico. It is said that those who are protected by it are destined to find True Happiness.
Cady Grayson is one of the fortunate few.
Cougar is the legend incarnate.

Prologue

She struggles against the ropes, crying out as the thick cords slice her skin. Her wrists and ankles are slick with blood. Panting from her desperate efforts to free herself, her breath mists in the frosty air.

The sun has not yet made an appearance and dark clouds scurry across the steel-gray sky. A cold wind whistles through the trees, the sound highlighting her terror. She shivers as it covers her with its icy breath.

Bound to a tree, she looks longingly at the fire, its warmth just out of reach. A shout of laughter draws her attention to two men huddled by it, their faces twisted, their features hideous in the fire's light. She stiffens when one of them rises to his feet, grabs his rifle, and saunters into the forest. He is swallowed up by the trees. The other man pushes himself to his feet and, with measured tread, walks toward her. His dark shaggy hair hangs past his shoulders like shredded twine; his nose looks as if it had been broken and left to rot.

He stops just steps away, his dark eyes glazed with lust, his sick smile of anticipation revealing black, rotted teeth. His image dances before her, undulating against the flames. Her flesh crawls, and clammy rivers of sweat trickle down between her breasts, soaking her tattered dress.

Her captor leers as his large hands stretch toward the opening in his pants. She opens her mouth to scream, but only a hoarse croak escapes, scraping painfully against her dry throat. She increases her struggles, fighting the terror threatening to send her over the edge of sanity. As he leans toward her, she shrinks back against the tree, desperately wanting to melt into the trunk. Without warning, the horses begin to move restlessly against each other, stamping their hooves and snorting loudly, their ears pressed flat against their heads. The man looks over his shoulder at the nervous beasts, his hand inching toward the knife at his belt. He scans the area, shrugs his shoulders, and turns back to her. When he reaches down and grabs a handful of her dress, a low growl reverberates throughout the glade, the sound blending eerily with the wailing wind. He jerks back as if burnt, and stands rooted to the ground, paralyzed with fear.

The sun begins to peek over the horizon, casting threads of light through the trees, dappling the forest floor. The wind dies down, and the air is still, the glade quiet. Her gaze sweeps the nearby boulders, and, with a gasp, she cowers against the tree. She holds her breath, willing herself to remain motionless.

A black mountain lion, crouched on a rocky ledge, is watching her, its mouth slightly open and revealing its pink tongue, its amber eyes glowing with an inner fire. She is mesmerized by their hypnotic quality. The cat breaks the spell and swings its head toward the man. Her heart pounds, her eyes widen, and, fighting the urge to scream, she awaits the beast's next move.

At her expression, the man comes alive, and fumbles for his knife. In his haste, the blade drops harmlessly to the ground. With a bone-chilling hiss, the huge animal rears back on its haunches, and springs forward—its front paws extended, claws bared, preceding its large, sleek black body.

The man screams and falls to his knees, covering his head with his arms in a futile attempt to ward off the cat's assault. The mountain lion's powerful jaws sink into the man's neck, severing the life-sustaining veins and silencing his scream of horror.

The mountain lion gives one powerful shake of its head and releases its victim. The man crumples to the ground, his mouth a hideous abyss, forever silent.

The cat swings toward her, its black head cocked to one side, his amber gaze piercing her to the tree. The flames from the fire outline its lithe silhouette in a ghostly aureole. Her breath catches in her throat as she clenches her bound hands into fists, certain she will meet the same horrible fate as her captor. She is helpless, at the mercy of the raven-black, amber-eyed mountain lion. The animal takes a step toward her bound, quaking body, then stops, its gaze never leaving her face. It takes another step toward her…

Cady screamed and sat bolt upright in bed.

Chapter 1

Santa Fe, New Mexico Territory, Spring 1871

Flames danced in the grate, throwing serpentine shadows against the wall. The man sitting behind a massive oak desk wrote furiously, his fountain pen skimming over the single sheet of paper, his hair shining like freshly fallen snow in the steady glow of a lone candle. He laid down the pen, took a last look at what he had written, then folded the letter and placed it inside a brown envelope. Retrieving the pen, he scrawled across the front of the envelope before placing it on the corner of the desk.

He rose to his feet, stretched his arms toward the ceiling, and crossed over to the fireplace. With a contented sigh, he settled himself in one of the high-backed leather chairs facing the hearth and looked up at the portrait. He nodded, satisfied, and dropped his gaze to stare into the fire, a broad smile on his face. He leaned his head back against the supple leather and, with another sigh, closed his eyes.

Across the room a window slid open, silently. The curtains parted and a tall, somewhat lanky silhouette joined the undulating shadows on the wall. A floorboard creaked beneath a booted foot and the silhouette froze as the man reposing in the chair became instantly alert, sitting up and looking around the shadow-filled room. A gust of wind blew in from the open window, billowing the curtains and disturbing the papers on the desk. The brown envelope, lifted by the wind, fluttered to the floor and slid under a tall set of shelves set against one wall. The candle flame flickered and died, plunging the room into near-darkness.

The sound of a single gunshot shattered the silence.

****

St. Louis, Missouri

"I tell you, Frederick, I can't take it! I won't take it! Cady Grayson has been nothing but trouble since the day she landed on our doorstep. She is defiant, spurns everything decent—" Mildred shook a bejeweled finger at her husband. "She has got to go!"

Frederick cringed beneath his wife's tirade. He opened his mouth to respond but she wasn't finished venting her rage.

"I want her gone! I don't care where she goes, just get her out of this house!"

When she paused for breath, Frederick took the opportunity to plead his case. "But, Mildred, she's Melinda's only child. I can't just turn my back on her."

"It is not my fault your sister up and died. And her husband too! It was inconsiderate of them to do so. Imagine, leaving us saddled with an undisciplined brat like Cady!" She narrowed her eyes at her husband. "And by no choice of my own, I might add."

"But Mildred—"

"If you hadn't allowed your brother to talk you into taking her in, she would still be *his* problem," she complained, taking a seat in her favorite chair by the window.

"Mildred, you know Sebastian has five children.

After his wife died, he just couldn't take care of Cady too."

"Hah! So he said!"

"Aren't you being unduly harsh?" He shrank beneath her quelling look and added weakly, "We're all the family she has left."

"That's not true. There's her grandfather."

Frederick nodded slowly in agreement. "Yes, perhaps he still wants her."

"Fine. He can have her."

"I will telegraph him in the morning." Frederick rubbed his bald head with long, even strokes.

Cady had just opened the front door and stepped into the house but paused at the sound of her aunt's voice raised in anger. With a grimace, she quietly closed the door, knowing instinctively she was the reason for her aunt's tirade. She need not know what was said—she was often the cause of her aunt's displeasure.

When Frederick walked into the foyer, calling out for her, Cady quickly ducked into his study, wanting to compose herself before the confrontation. She wiped her damp palms against her legs and, feeling the coarse material, glanced down and groaned. Denim trousers and a white cotton shirt were not Aunt Mildred's idea of suitable attire for a young woman. Cady bit her lip, suppressing a flash of apprehension, and shrugged her shoulders in resignation. Her attire would cease to matter once her aunt heard of her wild ride through town. That would certainly push her over the edge. Hadn't she been told repeatedly that young women did not ride astride and unescorted? But how was a girl to ride with the wind, her hair billowing behind her, the sun warm on her face, if not astride and at full gallop? She sighed. *Such inane rules women had to follow. Rules no doubt made up by men or spinsters. I will never agree with my aunt's view of being blessedly born a woman.*

"Cady! Will you come in here, please?" Frederick's voice echoed in the foyer.

Cady glanced at the stairs but knew she didn't have time to change into something her aunt would approve of. Not that she wanted to. The dresses her aunt handed down were not only ill-fitting but fashioned from the most distasteful fabrics—purple muslin with small green polka dots, dull beige linen with yellow stripes...

Cady composed her features and strode from the study, mentally preparing herself for her aunt's anger and her uncle's timid disapproval. Before making her presence known, she paused in the parlor doorway. Just how angry were they?

Frederick Letton stood beside his wife fingering his gray mustache and looking absently out the window. His thin gray brows were lowered over dull brown eyes, his mouth turned down at the edges. Mildred Letton sat in a high-backed embroidered chair. Even seated she was nearly as tall as her husband. Her hands were folded in her lap, her lime-green-and-pink skirt arranged perfectly around her legs. Her forehead was creased, her nose pinched, giving her the appearance of someone assailed by a rotten odor. From their demeanor, Cady surmised that the matter was indeed dire. She thought back over the past couple of days. Other than her outing this morning, which her aunt couldn't possibly have heard about yet, she had kept herself out of trouble.

"Did you wish to see me, Uncle Frederick?" Cady took a step into the room, fervently wishing the floor would magically open and swallow her whole. The air was oppressive and, refusing to be intimidated, she fought the urge to run.

"Come and sit down," her aunt commanded, eyeing her with disdain. "Really, Cady, I do abhor those clothes. For heaven's sake, you are a woman. Dress like one!" She rolled her eyes as if seeking answers from a higher source. "Why can't she be more like my Adelaide?" she lamented with a shake of her blonde head.

Cady perched on the edge of the gray-and-white-striped sofa, struggling to keep her expression composed. She had heard those words so often they were burned in her brain. She placed her hands in her lap and looked up at her uncle, not a shred of emotion on her face, while she waited for them to dole out punishment for whatever offense she had committed.

She had no idea of the picture she created, one that tore at her uncle's heart. Her hair, a tangle of unruly coal-black curls, floated around her shoulders and tumbled down her back; her eyes, an interesting mixture of violet and blue, were now wary as she waited for him to inform her of her latest transgression.

"Cady, you have been with us for several years now," her uncle said slowly, as if carefully weighing each word. "You know I loved your mother dearly and would have done anything for her. That is why I opened my arms, and my home, to you when Sebastian could no longer take care of you. Unfortunately…" He glanced at his wife. At her imperious nod, he turned back to his niece, clearing his throat. "I plan to telegraph Chas Grayson—your grandfather—in the morning. I think it best for everyone if you went to live with him. I tried to do right by your mother, but I believe you would be better off—"

"Yes, of course," Cady interjected, masking her joy behind a façade of disinterest. Oh, to live with her grandfather would be heaven indeed! It was a fact she didn't remember him well, except that he had been kind. But she could not let them see how much she welcomed this news. No, her aunt would be quick to snatch it away. She reached for an errant curl and began to wrap it around her finger as the doorbell sounded in the distance.

"Please let me know of his decision." The doorbell sounded again as Cady stood up preparing to leave. She wanted to relish this unexpected, glorious news alone.

"Where is that Tillie?" With a sigh of exasperation, Mildred pushed herself to her feet and marched from the parlor, calling out for the maid as the doorbell sounded once again.

"Cady, I'm truly sorry it has to be this way. But your aunt…" Frederick raised his hands in supplication.

"It's fine, Uncle," she murmured, continuing to hide her elation.

"These past years have been hard on you," he continued sympathetically and reached out to brush an ebony curl off her shoulder.

Cady stiffened and suffered his gesture of solace. "Frankly, I'm surprised you and Aunt Mildred took me in," she said without a shred of self-pity. "I thought for sure when Uncle Sebastian said I had to leave, I'd find myself on the streets."

"Well, you do make it difficult for anyone to like you," Frederick countered, becoming brave in his wife's absence. "You lack discipline, defy—"

"I know, I know," she stopped him, not wishing to hear it again. Tilting her head to one side, she asked bluntly, "How would you behave if you felt you didn't belong? That you were a burden to bear, with no one giving a damn about you?"

Frederick sighed at her expletive but knew chastising her would do no good. He never had been adept at reprimanding his wayward niece. Now his wife… "You are such an angry child, Cady. You would fare better if you learned to deal with your bitterness. Or at the very least, hide it. Not everyone gets what they want out of life," he added with his own sigh of regret.

"If my parents hadn't died, none of this would have happened."

Frederick reached for her hand. "Your parents' death was indeed unfortunate, and tragic, but that is no reason to hate the world. You are young and quite lovely and have your whole life ahead of you." He shook his head at her stubborn expression. "I'm truly sorry it has to be this way."

Cady snatched her hand away. "I'm not."

Frederick gave her a searching look before adding, "You should learn to believe, Cady."

"*Believe*? Believe in what?"

"Believe that you will find happiness." He ignored her snort of derision and continued, "Learn to trust in others. Perhaps if you were more—"

"Stop coddling the girl, Frederick," Mildred snapped, having come back into the room. Brushing past him she sat again in the high-backed chair. "This house is falling apart. It takes three rings before Tillie answers the door," she said with a weary sigh.

Cady, thinking herself dismissed, made to leave. Her aunt spoke out, stopping her before she could escape.

"And another thing, missy. Leona Smitton told me

you nearly trampled her to death this morning. Said you were riding through town like a woman gone mad. It's just not done," Mildred declared with a frown. "I am becoming a laughingstock. And it's all your fault!" She glared at her niece, noting with satisfaction her downcast eyes and subservient expression.

"Now go and change for dinner—in a dress, if you please," Mildred ordered, dismissing her with a wave of her hand and a quick pat to the impeccable bun fashioned at her nape. Cady observed the action with a covert roll of her eyes. Never, in all the time she lived here, had she once seen a single strand of hair out of place. Like everything in this house, it too was rigid.

Mildred spied Tillie standing in the doorway and motioned the maid into the room. "Yes? What is it?"

"This just came for Mr. Letton," Tillie said, holding out a yellow envelope. Frederick took it from her, tore it open, and quickly scanned the contents. His head snapped up and he looked at his wife in disbelief.

"It seems our problem is solved."

"What do you mean?"

He waved the slip of paper, casting a guarded look at his niece. "It's from a Mr. Doswell, Chas Grayson's lawyer. Your grandfather is in a coma and not expected to survive the week. According to his will…" He took a deep breath before blurting out, "you are the sole heir to his fortune."

Mildred's mouth dropped open in shock. "What? Why in heaven's name would he make that idiotic decision?" Her expression registered genuine bewilderment. "Why would anyone in their right mind bestow anything on her?" She scowled at her niece, who had since dropped back down on the sofa, appearing just as astonished.

"There are some conditions, of course, and it will be necessary for you to travel to Santa Fe," Frederick continued, studying his niece. Her complexion had turned quite pale, emphasizing her vivid indigo eyes. She was furiously twisting a strand of hair around her finger and staring at the piece of yellow paper in his hand.

"He doesn't even know her," Mildred interjected, still amazed at the news.

"He does indeed know her," Frederick reminded his wife. "After her parents died, before she went to live with Sebastian, Cady spent some time with him after the funeral."

Mildred snorted and turned back to Cady. "Then it's lucky for you he's in a coma. If he knew you now, I'm sure he would change his will."

Cady ignored her aunt's verbal assault, squashing the overwhelming desire to strike out at the miserable old witch. Instead, she sat quietly and listened to her uncle.

"According to Mr. Doswell, you are to travel to Denver by train. There, someone will meet you and escort you to Santa Fe." He peered at his niece. "Cady…"

"What's all the commotion?" a voice asked from the doorway.

"Come in, Adelaide," Mildred bade her daughter. "Come hear this ludicrous news."

Adelaide, stroking the long blonde braid hanging over one shoulder, glanced around in curiosity. "What news?" she asked as she moved into the room, her cream-colored silk dress rustling with each step.

"It seems our Cady stands to inherit a fortune." Her aunt's tone was just this side of contemptuous.

Cady watched her cousin's confusion turn into one of utter disbelief. She stared wide-eyed at Cady. "Who left you a fortune?" she demanded, settling herself in the matching chair next to her mother.

"Her grandfather," Mildred announced before Cady could answer. "He actually made her his sole heir." She shook her head in disbelief. "The man must be insane."

"No!" Adelaide gasped. "His *entire* fortune?"

"It's true," Frederick interjected. "Cady is going to Santa Fe."

"Where's Santa Fe?" Adelaide asked, flipping the braid over her shoulder.

"In the territory of New Mexico," he answered absently, glancing back down at the telegraph.

Adelaide sat back, glanced slyly at Cady, and whispered, "Why, that's in the middle of nowhere."

Cady continued to wind the long strand of hair around her finger as Adelaide's well-placed barb found its mark. She swallowed past the lump in her throat as she began to comprehend the reality of her situation. She was going to an unknown territory—possibly set upon by Indians and renegade outlaws! Lord, everyone knew how uncivilized the West was! This realization somewhat altered her earlier elation. She flinched at the sudden pain in her scalp and eased the tension in the taut curl around her finger.

"There's nothing to worry about," Frederick said, trying to allay the anxiety flickering in his niece's eyes. "Your grandfather is quite wealthy. He has a huge spread with a thriving cattle business. I am sure everyone will welcome you with open arms. And, too, there is every possibility he will recover."

"How did it happen?" Cady asked, her voice hoarse

with unshed tears.

"Mr. Doswell doesn't say."

"I can't fathom his reasons," Mildred declared. "Cady's nothing but a worthless brat." She narrowed her eyes at her niece. "You have caused nothing but trouble since day one. You have contributed nothing to this family—except misery. We'll be well rid of you!"

Cady did her best to ignore her aunt's cruel words, her eyes burning with unshed tears at the thoughtless words spoken at this time of sorrow.

"You'll be perfectly safe," Adelaide reassured her, with a smirk. "I'm sure not all Indians are hot-headed savages."

"Oh, shut up, Adelaide," Cady snapped, sparing her cousin a mere glance.

"Well!" Adelaide huffed, sitting back in her chair, arms crossed.

"Do not speak to her that way," Mildred snapped. "She deserves more respect than that from you!" She took a deep breath and, narrowing her pale brown eyes, arched a brow. "I have only one question, missy. Just what are you going to do for us?"

Cady looked at her wide-eyed, utterly perplexed by her question.

"Now that you're rich, we expect you to return our kindness."

"Your what?" Cady asked, incredulous. "Since when have you shown me one speck of kindness? Since the day I arrived, you have treated me like an unwanted, unwelcomed visitor."

"If it had not been for us taking you in, you would have been left on the streets to fend for yourself. Heaven knows what you would have turned into if we hadn't opened our home to you. I would think that constitutes kindness." She patted her bun. "And I believe that calls for compensation."

"You have to be out of your—" She stared at her aunt in disbelief. "To think I owe you one damn thing is—" Cady sputtered to a stop, too stunned to continue.

"Please," Frederick whispered. "I'm sure we can settle this without arguing."

"It's only fair that she shares the wealth with her kin. Or at the very least reimburse us for what we've spent on her over the years," Mildred declared, with a wave of her hand.

Cady jumped to her feet, skirted her uncle, and rushed from the room, ignoring his plea to stay. She could no longer stomach his sympathy nor her aunt's contempt. Her cousin's look of pure pleasure while trying to terrify her was most telling. She ran into her bedroom, slammed the door, and dropped onto the cushioned window seat, her thoughts banging into each other.

Was she truly leaving? Leaving this house? To never again feel the bite of her aunt's viciousness nor suffer her cousin's air of superiority? *This was too good to be true!* But to the wilds of New Mexico? Why, it wasn't even part of the union!

She shuddered, recalling her nightmare with vivid clarity, and her elation dimmed a bit more. Weren't there mountain lions out West?

Tears blurred her vision, and she became engulfed in a deep sense of loneliness. Being an only child and an orphan, she was virtually alone in the world. She brushed angrily at her tears, knowing it would do no good to cry. Tears hadn't helped in the past, and they wouldn't help now. She would just have to make the best of it like she had done with every other upheaval she's faced in her young life.

Cady was nothing if not resilient. She had survived the shock of her parents' death, weathered her misfortune from that tragic event, and endured her time with the Lettons—all accomplished with only slight injury to her soul. She didn't remember her grandfather that well, but how sad to think that now she wouldn't get the chance to know him better, if what Mr. Doswell predicted came true.

She studied the tree limb scraping lightly against the window. A bird chirping a gay trill perched on the branch among the newly sprouted, pale-green leaves. Recalling her uncle's advice, she scoffed. How could she believe happiness could be hers? And trust in others? Hah!

Well, maybe I could—right after I capture the moon in the palm of my hand!

Chapter 2

Cady was startled awake by the train whistle's loud shriek. She sat up, brushed the hair from her eyes, and glanced around the car. It was cast in shadows, most of the other passengers still asleep. The wheels clacked rhythmically on the tracks, taking her to an uncertain future. She looked out the window. The monotonous view of flat grassland, stretching seemingly forever, was unchanged from the previous day. In the early morning light, she could just make out the mountains in the distance, giant purple peaks silhouetted against a sapphire-blue sky.

Cady stretched her arms over her head and winced at the sharp pain that knifed through the back of her neck. She rubbed the sore area to ease the hard knot, compliments of her uncomfortable sleeping position, and moved her head from side to side until she had worked out the kink.

She couldn't wait to get off this train. She was not used to inactivity, and being forced to sit for hours on end with nothing to do but read or look out the window had made her irritable. She reached for her handbag and pulled out the letter she had received years ago from her grandfather. In it he had written that he was sorry she couldn't live with him, but it had been mutually decided that at her tender age she needed a woman's influence. She wouldn't be getting that living with him, widowed as he was. At the time, Cady had thought it was just his way of getting out of an obligation. But under the present circumstances, and the arrival of his more recent letter, she no longer believed that.

His second letter had arrived the day after Mr. Doswell's wire had come with the startling news of his near-death state and the request to come to Santa Fe. Chas had simply written that it was time she came to live with him. He had not elaborated. She had been surprised by his invitation, for she hadn't heard from him since that letter years before, but it had pleased her no end. She had prayed, fervently, he would recover. At night, while abed, she had fantasized about their life together. He would welcome her with open arms, shower her with love. She would belong.

Well, she was on her way to Santa Fe, but not to live with her grandfather. He was dead. That sad news had been delivered the day before she was to leave St. Louis. Chas Grayson had died in his sleep. It was now imperative that Cady travel to Santa Fe, Mr. Doswell had wired.

The initial shock had abated, but Cady was still numb with disappointment and grief. She had glimpsed a chance at happiness only to have it vanish, leaving her doubting its very existence. Could she ever hope to get another chance? A feeling of profound sadness welled up inside her. Now, she would never know her generous grandfather, the one person, it seemed, who had truly wanted her.

The day Cady was set to leave, she had wavered between excitement and apprehension. She had taken only the necessities—a few items of clothing, her mother's silver hairbrush and matching comb, and her mother's brooch, a beautiful gold pin embedded with pearls. It was her most precious possession, for her father had gifted her mother with it on the occasion of Cady's birth. Before secreting it inside her valise, Cady had lovingly wrapped it in a strip of linen. From under her bed, she had pulled out her treasured secret possessions—her dime novels. They had gotten her through many a hardship. Deciding to take just one, her favorite, she had left the others inside her bureau drawer.

While packing her valise, she had suffered through a visit from Adelaide. Her cousin had sashayed into her room—without knocking—and sunk down on the bed. Cady had sat back on her heels and eyed her warily, waiting.

Adelaide leaned back against the bedpost and studied her trimmed and polished fingernails. "Perhaps you'll be happy there."

"What's it to you?" Cady asked, rising wearily to her feet and crossing over to the window seat.

"Well, for one, you'll be gone." She stroked her blonde braid. "But do be careful," she said, her voice dropping to a whisper. "The West is so uncivilized. I understand people shoot each other over the least little offense. And don't forget about the Indians," she added with a dramatic shudder. "I hear the most horrific stories—"

"That's not funny, Adelaide," Cady snapped, twirling a strand of black hair around her finger.

"What?" she asked, her tone innocent, her eyes round. "You're not scared, are you?"

"Of course not."

Adelaide laughed and tossed her head. "Perhaps one of your heroes will rescue you—should you find yourself in trouble."

Cady cringed. Not for the first time did she berate herself for revealing a secret fantasy to her cousin, mistakenly thinking her an ally when she had first come to St. Louis. Cady had turned to her dime novels to escape the unhappiness in her life and had foolishly confessed to her cousin that she hoped to be whisked away by a strong, handsome man on horseback. He would take her in his arms and— Of course, she had set aside those dreams long ago. Life was cruel, that was reality. It was futile to think it otherwise.

Adelaide sat forward, blue eyes glittering, and asked, "You do plan to give us some, don't you?"

"Some what?"

"Money."

Cady turned away from the greed twisting her cousin's face. "No, I do not."

"Why, you ungrateful little witch. We took you in…"

"And made my life a living hell."

"For heaven's sake, Cady! You're rich! You can afford to be generous and spread the wealth around."

The screech of the train whistle pulled Cady abruptly back to the present. She shook off the disturbing feelings that nasty scene with her cousin had evoked and looked out the window. *It is true, I am indeed a wealthy woman.* Even now, she carried more money in her handbag, compliments of Mr. Doswell, than she had seen in all her nineteen years. But infinitely better was the fact that she would be free of her aunt's cruel and oppressive nature and her cousin's spite.

No, she was not sorry to leave. She had no regrets, no misgivings. Her time with the Lettons had thankfully come to an end. It was time to look forward to a new life in New Mexico. Her stomach tightened in anticipation, and she was suddenly filled with a sense of excitement for the future and all the possibilities it held.

Cady had no way of knowing her adventures would begin well before her arrival in Santa Fe.

****

Late in the afternoon, the train pulled into Denver amid clouds of black smoke belching from its huge smokestack. When it came to a screeching halt, Cady gathered her valise, smoothed her wrinkled blue-and-green calico dress, and followed the other passengers out the door.

She stepped into the bright sunshine and blinked, momentarily blinded by its brilliance. After a few moments, her eyes became accustomed to the glare, and she glanced around the crowded platform searching for someone who might be waiting for her.

People bustled around the platform; some moved off, appearing to have a definite destination in mind, while others were welcomed by family and friends. She waited until the last person had left and still no one approached her. Had the person Mr. Doswell sent to meet her mistaken the date of her arrival? Had she? *What to do now?* Cady spied the stage office located not far from the train station and came to a quick decision. She grabbed her valise and made her way toward the small wooden building. With her shoulder, she pushed open the door, entered the small, airless room, and approached a window where a man lounged against the wall. He was dressed in a black-and-green plaid shirt and a black string bowtie, a cigar clamped firmly between his teeth.

"I would like to purchase a seat on the next stage to

Santa Fe," Cady said, rifling through her handbag for the fare. After taking out the necessary coins from her change purse, she placed them on the counter.

The man reached for the money, counted it, then handed her the ticket.

"What time does it leave?" she asked, tucking the ticket into her handbag.

"Day after tomorrow," he said, chewing on the end of his cigar.

"Day after tomorrow!" She had not counted on spending the night in a strange town, alone, much less two. Looks like she didn't have a choice. "Can you tell me where I might find a room?"

"The Hotel Colorado," he said, jerking his thumb over his shoulder.

Cady nodded her thanks, grabbed her valise, and left the stuffy office, the door slamming shut behind her. She retraced her steps back to the train station and left a message with the station master that if anyone came looking for her where she could be found.

The town was bustling with activity. Its raised sidewalks, made of rough wooden planks, were crowded with pedestrians, and all manner of conveyances vied for space on the narrow dirt street. Shops lined both sides of the thoroughfare, selling everything from mining equipment to ladies' hats. The buildings were set close together and sported boldly painted signs advertising their wares. Cady continued down the sidewalk, her valise banging annoyingly against her leg, until at last she saw a sign painted in large red letters proclaiming the Hotel Colorado.

The hotel was a three-story edifice boasting a façade of intricate molding and silver filigree. The lobby was large and, at that time of day, nearly deserted. The floor was covered with a large rug woven in colors of red-and-blue. On the walls hung paintings of landscape vistas depicting various scenes particular to the West. Overhead, a chandelier cast a soft glow over the entire lobby. Cady headed to a long, black counter where two men, both dressed in red-and-blue uniforms, stood talking together.

Cady placed her valise on the floor and gained the attention of one of the men. He had straw-blond hair, a thin blond mustache, and a pasty complexion. Cady wondered if he ever saw the light of day.

"I would like a room, please," she said, reaching inside her handbag for her change purse.

"We don't cotton to that here," he said, his tone priggish, and looked insolently down his nose at her.

"Cotton to what?" Cady asked, looking up at him in confusion.

"We don't want your kind here," he added, his brown eyes narrowed with disdain.

"What kind?"

"Go on with you, missy. We're a family establishment."

Cady had always thought of herself as a patient person, it was, after all, a most fortunate quality to possess when living with an abusive aunt, a timid uncle, and a malicious cousin. But she was tired, grimy with dust, and hungry for a decent meal. The clerk's rudeness stretched her patience paper-thin.

Putting on her best Aunt Mildred impersonation, she settled a frown on her face, leaned forward, her hands flat on the counter. "I have just arrived on the train from St. Louis. I'm taking the stage out day after tomorrow.

All I want is a room for these two nights," she snapped, her eyes flashing fire.

"Sorry, ma'am,' he drawled in a voice tinged with sarcastic regret, obviously not the least bit intimidated by her display of assertiveness.

"Do you not have any rooms available?" At his blank stare, she burst out furiously, "What is wrong with you?"

"Try Fannie Morrison's at the edge of town. I'm sure she'll put you up for the night." He turned and winked at his companion who snickered in response.

"Fine," she answered, exasperated. The desire to strangle the man was so overwhelming she had to stop herself from crawling over the counter and doing just that. Although it would be highly satisfying, she had no desire to land in jail for assault.

A man standing by the door in the lobby of the hotel had been watching the scene with interest, an unwilling smile tugging at his mouth. He had followed the lovely young woman down the crowded sidewalk, admiring the gentle sway of her hips as she made her way through town. She was petite in stature and carried herself with a grace he found lacking in many women. But the hideous blue-and-green dress she wore hung on her body like a burlap bag, hiding from view what he imagined to be a fine figure.

Now watching the scene unfold, he admired the girl's tenacity but had heard just about enough of the clerk's rudeness. He stepped up behind the woman, his forbidding presence immediately drawing the clerk's attention. That one's eyes widened at the sight of the tall, imposing man whose gaze pierced him like a knife.

"Is there a problem?" the stranger asked.

Cady jumped at the sound of the man's voice—deep and rich. She whirled around and slammed into a body chiseled from stone, her nose nearly pressed flat against his chest, a very broad chest. Her heart in her throat, she lifted her gaze to his face, and leaning back to get a better view, she nearly fainted. Lord, one of her dime novels' heroes had come to life! He was magnificent!

Struck speechless, too busy taking in his handsome features to realize she was gawking, she continued her perusal. He was tall and endowed with a lean muscular build. He had swept his wide-brimmed hat off his forehead, affording her a full view of his face. His long, black hair was pulled back, and his strong, square jaw was covered with a thick stubble of black whiskers. He looked like he spent every waking moment in the sun—his skin tanned a warm golden-brown, highlighting the unusual color of his eyes, amber, with just a hint of brown in their depths. They were mesmerizing.

"Is there a problem?" he repeated, his voice low and even, his expression inscrutable.

Cady blinked twice and stepped back. The sharp edge of the counter dug into her back, bringing her abruptly to her senses. She blushed with embarrassment and, clearing her throat, managed to find her tongue.

"No, no problem," she answered, sounding harsher than she had intended. She cringed inwardly when one of his dark brows shot up at her tone. "Please," she whispered, raising her hands, and motioning him back. His larger-than-life presence was so—so intimidating!

Granting her wish, he stepped back, allowing her enough room to lean down and grasp the handle of her valise. She turned back to the clerk and instantly regained her temper.

"Since you won't take my money, perhaps Miss Morrison will." She spun on her heel, sidestepped the intriguing stranger, and headed for the door.

"Fannie Morrison?" he asked the clerk. Cady, curious by his incredulous tone of voice, paused in her stride and glanced back over her shoulder.

The clerk had already come to the realization that this awe-inspiring man was the young woman's champion. He suddenly began to doubt his wisdom. He swallowed hard and nodded slowly, taking a step back from the heat of that amber glare.

"Are you full up?"

"N-no," the clerk stuttered, nervously brushing a lock of hair from his eyes.

"Then why is she being denied a room?" He pushed back his cinnamon-brown duster and rested his hand on the butt of his gun nestled in a holster strapped around his hips.

The clerk's eyes followed his movement. He paled visibly and beginning to fear for his life, turned back to Cady, who had stepped back up to the counter and was listening with interest to their exchange.

"My apologies, ma'am. You see, you're alone and, well, we thought, that is…here." He pushed the hotel register across the counter.

Cady signed the black book, took the key from the clerk's shaky hand, and turned back to the stranger. She looked up at him, trying unsuccessfully to calm the erratic pounding of her heart. His striking good looks, vibrant sherry-colored eyes, and deep rich timbre of his voice had captured her wits. After several awkward moments had passed, she mentally shook herself. *Stop staring at him!* She opened her mouth, hoping words would come out.

"Thank you, ah…?"

"Cougar, ma'am."

"Cougar? What kind of name is that?" she asked, melting beneath the smooth warmth of his voice.

"Mine." He settled his hat back on his head.

"Oh, well, then thank you, Mr. Cougar."

"Just Cougar, ma'am." His mouth curled into a half-smile as she unabashedly continued to stare. "Ma'am?" he drawled.

She started and nervously smoothed back her hair. "Yes, well, thank you again." Ignoring the clerk, she skirted Cougar's tall frame and followed the young boy who had grabbed her valise and was now headed toward the wide staircase in the back of the hotel.

Cougar watched her walk across the lobby and didn't look away until she had disappeared up the red-carpeted stairs. He turned back to face the clerk.

"Would you like a room, too?" the clerk blurted out, pushing the register toward him.

Cougar started to decline, preferring to sleep under the stars. His gaze swept the register, and returned sharply to the small, neat lettering on the last line. *Cady Grayson.*

He had found her. The image of her oval face, framed by coal-black hair, her eyes the color of the sky before a storm, floated before him and suddenly what he had agreed to do didn't seem so bad—despite the risks. He nodded, took the fountain pen from the clerk's outstretched hand, and signed his name beneath hers.

"If I hear of any more problems…" Cougar glanced at the name tag pinned to the clerk's shirt, "Simpson…you won't be happy I did."

"Yes, yes, of course," Simpson stammered, relieved he had merely received a warning for his stupidity. He watched the imposing man stride across the lobby before quickly sending up a prayer of gratitude.

Chapter 3

Cady was unaware she had been found. She followed the boy up the stairs and into her room. Looking around, she took in the somewhat gaudy décor. Red was certainly a favorite color. The room was small and offered a narrow bed covered by a red-and-white-striped quilt, a commode with a matching flowered pitcher and bowl upon it, and a small bureau with an oval mirror hanging above it. A red-and-black area rug covered the wooden floor and red velvet curtains framed the single window that looked out onto a narrow alley.

She plucked a silver coin from her handbag, tipped the boy for his assistance, and closed the door behind him before stepping over to the bed and falling face down on the mattress, her arms flung wide. The bed was soft, unmoving, and she savored this little bit of heaven. Too soon, she'd find herself back in a moving conveyance. She rolled over onto her back and stared at the stark white ceiling. Mentally tracing the intricate design carved into the wood, she went over in her mind the scene downstairs.

Why had she been refused a room? Had the clerk thought she was a thief or—? She sat up, blushing hotly as an incredible thought pushed through her confusion. Had he thought she was a—? Oh, she had heard about those kinds of women. There was an area in St. Louis Aunt Mildred had forbidden her and Adelaide to go near.

Naturally, Cady had defied her aunt's dictate and ridden there anyway, seeing for herself the gaudily painted women who strolled up and down the street looking for customers. No wonder the clerk had been so rude. She was surprised he hadn't tossed her out on her ear, despite the stranger's interference. If she weren't so mortified, she could laugh at that nonsense.

Cady turned her attention to the stranger. With an uncharacteristically dreamy sigh she laid back against the pillows. Just thinking about his ruggedly handsome features made her shiver. And his eyes! They were a most unusual color and reminded her of the wine her aunt occasionally enjoyed before dinner. She knew she had never seen the likes of them before, but they had an air of familiarity. Yet taken as she was by his looks, she had sensed in him an innate wildness, an edge of danger.

She covered her face with her hands. Lord, how she had gawked! He must have thought her an utter fool—behaving like the village idiot. But, despite that, he had been kind enough to secure her a room, even though he didn't know her. Perhaps, like a dime novel hero, he was coming to the aid of a damsel in distress?

Resolutely, she pushed him from her mind. She was being silly and had more important things to do than daydream over a man she would most certainly never lay eyes on again. She still had to meet up with the person who had been sent to escort her to Santa Fe. Certainly, they would check at the train station and learn she was at the hotel. If they didn't show, well, she would just travel on alone. After all, she was perfectly capable of taking care of herself. Hadn't she proven that all these years?

The familiar anger began to well up inside. There was a time when she had been happy, touched by love, before cruel fate stepped in and shattered nirvana. She was nine years old when a freak accident took her parents' lives, leaving her alone, despondent, and dependent on others. Because she'd had no trade to ply nor money of her own, she was left to the mercy of relatives.

She'd been comfortable living with Sebastian and his family, but her contentment had been slowly smothered with the Lettons. Her Aunt Mildred thought Cady defiant, but she wasn't—not at first. That came later, after enduring life with the hateful woman.

She had laid a hand on Cady—once. Cady struck back and so astonished the woman she had never again raised her hand against her niece. Yet her aunt's heartless words were often more cutting than physical abuse.

Because of this, Cady found it hard to trust anyone and her pain, over the years, had turned into blame. She blamed her parents, she blamed fate. She bit her lower lip to still its trembling. If only they hadn't died!

Cady's stomach growled, protesting its lack of nourishment. She quit her self-pity, rose from the bed and walked over to the commode to wash away the dust she had collected on her travels. She yanked off the hideous calico dress and pulled a cobalt-blue linen one from her valise. It had a square neckline and long, tight sleeves that flared at the wrists. She would forget the bustle—frankly she thought them unsightly even though they were the fashion.

The blue linen was her best dress, not one of her aunt's shabby hand-me-downs. When she had learned she would be moving to Santa Fe, she had used some of the money Mr. Doswell had sent to purchase it, wanting to make a good impression when she arrived at her destination.

She donned the dress, smoothing out the wrinkles as best she could, and pinned her mother's gold-and-pearl brooch to the bodice. Before heading downstairs, she took a look in the mirror and smiled, nodding her head in approval.

Cady entered the hotel's dining room. Like the rest of the hotel, red was the dominant color. Red-and-gold-flecked paper covered the walls, a red rug sprinkled with gold dots was underfoot, and the tables were spread with white linen coverings. Since most of the tables were empty, she had her pick of where to sit and chose one near the front windows overlooking the street.

After ordering her meal from a short, dark-haired woman, Cady leaned back, sipping a glass of red wine, and watched the passersby stroll by the hotel. Her attention was soon drawn to a man standing across the street. He was leaning against a post, one booted foot crossed over the other, his hat pulled low over his eyes. He appeared oblivious to the activity around him, but she sensed, despite his nonchalance, he was acutely aware of his surroundings.

She straightened, knocking the table in her haste, catching the glass of wine with both hands before it toppled over. *The stranger from the lobby!* Alarmed at the sudden rush of warmth stealing over her, she wondered frantically if she was becoming ill with the fever. And what was that flurry of movement in her belly? Like a bee trying to escape.

There was something about him that made her act most unlike herself. When she had faced him in the lobby, her heart had pounded so hard she thought she would faint. She had to subdue the urge to touch him, to run her fingers over his whisker-stubbled jaw. Never had she been so affected by anyone. But she had sensed in him a nuance of danger that was unsettling.

Why was he watching the hotel? Was he following her? She took a deep breath trying to calm her sudden apprehension. Perhaps he was merely waiting for someone; there was certainly no reason to be alarmed. He had been nothing but kind, and had succeeded in securing her a room. But what an odd name—*Cougar*.

She averted her gaze and glanced around the dining room, pausing on two men seated at a table, deep in conversation. She started to look away when one of them glanced up and caught her eye. Their gazes held for just a moment before he pulled his hat lower down his forehead and turned back to his companion. A shiver went up her spine at the cold, calculating look she had seen in his dark, beady eyes.

The woman arrived with her dinner, and after thanking her, Cady set to her meal, pushing all thoughts of Cougar out of her mind. She was on her way to a very uncertain future, and to waste her time thinking about him was not something she had a mind to do. Despite her good intentions, her glance kept straying to the lone figure across the street.

****

Cougar made sure Cady had reached her room, after leaving the dining room, before returning to his own. He sank into a red-and-black-striped chair, stretched his long legs out in front of him and, with a weary sigh, dropped his head back.

Despite his fatigue, his nerves were stretched taut, his every sense heightened. He was uneasy being in a territory where he was wanted. Men hungry for blood or money never listened to reason. He would relax once he had crossed back into New Mexico and left Colorado behind.

If only he could trap the one responsible for branding him a wanted man. But the culprit was a wily son-of-a-bitch, with friends in high places, and it would be futile for Cougar to speak out against him—he wouldn't be believed.

A smile curved his mouth. Cady Grayson was one hell of a beautiful woman—stop-and-stare beautiful. He had been prepared to like her—no reason not to. What a shock it was he wanted her.

He'd been physically affected by her silent, yet flattering, once-over in the lobby. His stomach muscles had tensed, and he'd had the overwhelming desire to sweep her up in his arms and kiss her. Either that or drop to his knees at her feet in awe. He had seen many fine-looking women in his life, but this one took his breath away. Her eyes, an interesting mix of blue and purple, commanded attention. They were large and surrounded by thick, black lashes. Her ivory skin fairly glowed in the light from the chandelier, contrasting sharply with her glossy black hair. Her mouth was full and lush—just made for kissing.

And what a temper! She had fairly blistered the hotel clerk's ears. Of course, the man had deserved it—and more. But Cougar was not here to make trouble. He was simply fulfilling a promise to a friend, and fulfill it he would, regardless of the possible consequences if he were to be spotted in Colorado.

Cougar put aside his musings of the delectable Cady Grayson and drifted into a light sleep, the chair facing the door, his hand resting on the butt of his gun.

Chapter 4

It was the muffled voices that pulled Cady from sleep. She blinked at the ceiling, trying to remember where she was, as the voices penetrated her sleepy confusion. She threw off the blanket, jumped from the bed, and crept to the open window. Pushing aside the curtains, she leaned out the window and looked down into the alley behind the hotel. A hazy circle of light from a lone gas streetlight illuminated two men standing beneath her window. They were whispering loudly and gesturing with their hands as if trying to convince each other of something. There was an air of familiarity about them that was too elusive for Cady to grasp in her sleep-addled state.

She made her way back to the bed, stumbling over the edge of the rug and landing face down on the mattress. She slipped beneath the quilt, pulled it up under her chin, and drifted back into sleep.

The door to Cady's room opened, was quietly shut, and locked. Two shadows drifted across the wall as the figures made their way to her bed. She stirred, stopping them in their tracks. With a sigh, she turned over onto her side. A breeze blew in through the open window, moving the curtains and caressing Cady's cheek. Her eyes fluttered open and she blinked, trying to determine what had disturbed her this time. When her eyes focused in the dimly lit room, she saw the two shadows. With a smothered gasp, she sat up in bed, flinging her heavy braid over her shoulder.

The men rushed toward her and before Cady could react one had grabbed her shoulders, pinning her to the bed. His fingers bit painfully into her shoulders. The other man jumped on top of her, straddling her body. With one hand clamped over her mouth, he fumbled with a bandanna. Cady bit down on the restricting hand and bucked, twisting her body back and forth.

"Ouch! Keep her still, damn it!"

"I'm trying to! Hurry up!"

Cady succeeded in dislodging the miscreant off her body and dumping him to the floor. She took a deep breath and let out an ear-splitting scream, struggling against the man who still had her pinned by her shoulders. She reached up and grabbed his wrist, twisting it until she heard his pained curse and felt his grip loosen. The other man leapt from the floor and tried to quiet her, grappling with her flailing arms. She screamed again, the sound bouncing of the walls, and tried to free herself from the quilt twisted around her body.

A pounding on the door stopped the two men. They exchanged startled glances and fled to the open window. They looked down at the ground, hesitated, and with a muttered curse, one flung himself out the window, quickly followed by the other. Their howls of pain drifted up amid the persistent pounding on the door.

"Cady? Cady, open the door!"

It took her a moment to recognize the voice and when it finally penetrated her scare, she jumped from the bed and ran to the door. She stopped halfway, surprised that she was willing to open the door to a total stranger, albeit a helpful, handsome one. She stood in the middle of the room in indecision.

"Cady!"

Hearing the concern in his voice, she came to a quick decision, and rushed to the door and pulled it open. There, in all his magnificence, was the man who had occupied her thoughts since meeting him in the lobby. He was clad in the same clothes as before, but his shirt was unbuttoned, exposing a large expanse of golden-brown skin.

Cougar stepped into the room and looked around.

"They jumped." She pointed to the window.

Peering down into her face, he asked, "Are you hurt?"

"No."

Cougar reached the window in two long strides. He looked down into the alley and found it deserted. He turned up the oil lamp on the bureau and returned to her side.

"What happened?"

"There were two men," Cady told him, closing the door, and turning back to him. "Their voices woke me." She tilted her head. "How did they even get in? I locked the door."

"They picked the lock." Cougar studied her face. She appeared to be in shock. Her eyes were as round as full moons, and her face was pale and drawn.

"What did they want?" she asked, unable to suppress a shudder.

"Among other things, I'd say that fancy pin you were wearing."

"Among other things?" He saw understanding dawn in her eyes. "Oh my," she whispered brokenly. "They wanted *me*." And if possible, her face went a shade whiter.

"Oh, hell," Cougar muttered, pulling her over to the bed and pushing her down onto the soft mattress. "Wait here," he said over his shoulder before leaving the room and returning shortly with a small bottle of reddish-brown liquid.

"Drink this," he ordered, handing her the bottle. "It will take the edge off."

Cady sniffed it, her nose wrinkling at the potent smell, then tipped the bottle to her lips and took a sip. It tasted bitter, the fiery flavor burning her tongue.

"What is it?" she asked.

"Whiskey."

She took another sip, feeling the liquid heat dousing her scare. "Thank you, Mr. Cougar," she said and handed him the bottle.

"Just Cougar." He took a swig of the whiskey before replacing the cap and placing it on the bureau. "So, what happened?"

"I woke up and found them in my room. One of them grabbed my shoulders and the other tried to gag me, but he had trouble with the bandanna. I knocked him off the bed," she finished weakly yet with a proud tilt of her chin. She suddenly remembered. "I saw them earlier—in the dining room."

She looked up at him, his presence seemed to fill the room. From her viewpoint, seated on the bed, he seemed to touch the ceiling. A mantle of uneasiness settled about her and, acutely aware of her barely dressed state, she crossed her arms over her chest, clenching the cotton material between her fingers. She rose to her feet, not wanting him to know how much he unsettled her.

"How did you know my name?"

"I was sent here to take you to Santa Fe." When her eyes widened in disbelief, he added, "Your grandfather asked me to meet you, before he—"

"Why didn't you say so earlier?"

"I didn't know who you were until I saw the hotel register."

"Who are you?"

"Cougar."

"Yes, I know your name. But *who* are you?"

"A friend of your grandfather's."

"Hmm," she murmured uneasily. He seemed awfully young to be a friend of her grandfather's. Perhaps he was the son of a friend. That was a bit more reassuring…and believable.

"I'll give you a few minutes to dress and pack."

"Why?"

"We're leaving."

"But the stage—"

"We won't be taking the stage."

"Why not?"

"We can't afford to wait. It's obvious what they wanted—"

"They're gone now," she pointed out.

"They may come back," he countered.

"I will take my chances and wait for the stage," she said stubbornly. "But don't let me stop you. You may leave—"

"You don't seem to understand," he admonished, his tone stern. "You're in danger. What if I hadn't arrived when I did? What if I hadn't even been in the hotel?" He cocked his head, arching one brow. "Can you honestly believe they won't try again?"

She started to refute his logic, but her earlier scare

returned, sapping her of the strength to argue. She sank to the bed, torn with uncertainty. If he spoke the truth, her grandfather had trusted him enough to escort her to his ranch in Santa Fe, so she should be able to trust him as well. If he lied…well, time would tell. And she most certainly did not want to be here if those ruffians did come back.

"All right, I will go with you."

Cougar sat down next to her on the bed, wanting to comfort her. It wasn't at all like him, but he'd heard the uncertainty—or was it anxiety—in her voice. He put his arm around her shoulders and drew her up against his side. He pushed her face against his chest and stroked her hair, unintentionally stirring up the scent of violets. The fragrance awakened something deep inside, a feeling altogether new to him.

Cady allowed herself to be comforted and relaxed in his embrace. It had been so long since anyone had treated her with kindness, and hungry for it, she was more than content to accept what he offered. After a moment, though, her body was again suffused with warmth, the fluttering in her stomach returned, and flustered, she pulled away.

"I'm fine, truly," she told him, her voice trembling.

Without thinking, Cougar did what he had wanted to do since he had first laid eyes on her. He kissed her. Nudging her chin up with one finger, he brushed his mouth lightly across hers. The contact was electrifying, surprising them both, and sending a powerful current running through them at lightning speed. They gazed into each other's eyes, as if trying to understand what had just happened. When none dawned, he bent down and captured her mouth, settling his lips on hers and pulling her in closer. Several long minutes of pure bliss passed.

Cougar broke contact first and looked into her face, watching her closely. He ached to kiss her again but thought better of it when he saw clarity beginning to dawn.

She jumped to her feet. "What was that for?" she demanded, completely out of sorts, and asking the first question that popped into her head. When he just tilted his head and looked at her oddly, she reached for a tendril of hair that had come loose from her braid, and coiling it around her finger, looked around the room, taking in everything but him.

Cougar rose to his feet. "Do you have anything besides dresses to wear?"

"I have denims," she answered, uneasy at his surly tone. *Why was he being disagreeable? One would think he had been pounced on.*

"Wear them," he ordered over his shoulder as he left the room, pulling the door shut behind him.

Cady stared at the closed portal, too shocked to move. When he had wrapped his arm around her shoulders, holding her close, she had felt a flurry of activity in her stomach—the bee was back. Then he kissed her—and it was powerful. But when he captured her mouth in a soul-stirring kiss, an unfamiliar, yet pleasant, sensation blossomed—and it scared her.

She lifted her hand and with one finger gently rubbed her lips. She had never been kissed that way before—actually, it was her first kiss ever. She had to admit she liked it. But her stomach ached, and she was so warm she just knew she was ill with the fever.

She didn't want to go with him. His fierce frown coupled with his mere presence could make a girl uneasy. Yet his incredibly good looks, warm mouth, and comforting embrace caused quite a different reaction. Never had she encountered these out-of-control, clashing feelings and she was completely unnerved. What should she do?

After what had just happened, how could she possibly spend the next few days *alone* with him? She glanced at the window and shuddered. What if the ruffians did come back? She was alone in a strange city, at the mercy of men who thought nothing of entering a woman's hotel room to do God knows what. And, surely, Grandfather wouldn't have sent a bad man to bring her to Santa Fe. *I have no choice. I will go with him.*

She dressed quickly in denims, a blue-and-white-striped cotton shirt, and boots, all the while wondering how her grandfather and Cougar had come to be friends. She remembered her grandfather as quiet, kind. Cougar was—she wasn't sure. She straightened up with a gasp. *What if he tries to kiss me again?* Her entire body overheated. Well, if he did, she would simply tell him not to.

She found Cougar waiting for her in the hallway, leaning against the wall, his arms crossed over his chest, saddlebags on the floor at his feet. He had on the same blue denims and cinnamon-brown duster but had changed into a honey-colored cotton shirt. Wordlessly, he slung his saddlebags over his shoulder, took her valise, grabbed her arm, and escorted her down the stairs.

They ignored Simpson, the clerk behind the counter, who watched them cross the lobby with a wary eye, and stepped out into the smoky darkness. Low-hanging clouds drifted lazily across the charcoal-gray sky and the sliver of moon barely illuminated the quiet town. Several gas streetlights were still glowing, so they were not in total darkness.

Cady glanced up at Cougar's closed expression and couldn't suppress a feeling of uncertainty. She wondered which was worse—take her chances and wait for the stage or travel with him—a virtual stranger? She had only his word that he was who he said he was, after all. She bit her lip in indecision. Her sudden disquiet overrode her previous decision to go with him.

"I'd rather wait for the stage," she said, grimacing at the tremor in her voice.

"We can't wait. Besides, the fewer people around the better." He looked down the deserted street. When she jerked her arm from his grasp, he glanced at her in surprise.

"Better for what? Just what do you plan to do with me?" she demanded, settling her hands on her hips.

"Take you to Sante Fe," he replied, his tone edged with exasperation. "I thought we resolved the issue. I want to get you out of here before whoever snuck into your room decides to come back. I can't take any chances." Her expression was still set, but not quite as stubbornly. "We'll make better time on horseback."

"Well..." She paused at his expression. He didn't look at all like he wanted an argument. "Much of what you say makes sense. But I'm not at all happy about this." She lifted her chin, ignoring the uneasiness creating knots in her stomach. "If you think I'll kiss you again, you're mistaken," she blurted out, regretting it immediately when his brow shot up along with one side of his mouth. She nearly died from embarrassment. Could she be any more moronic?

She spun on her heel and walked over to the two

horses tied at the hitching post. One, a large beautiful black-and-white stallion with the most unusual markings—she'd never seen the likes of before. The other, a small chestnut-colored mare with white stockings and a splash of white on her forehead, stood next to it. She reached out and rubbed the mare's soft muzzle, as she suffered through her self-induced humiliation.

"I really don't need your help, you know. I'm perfectly capable of getting to Santa Fe by myself," she said over her shoulder.

"I'm sure you are," he agreed. "But I made a promise to Chas."

When she turned back, she found him emptying her valise into his saddlebags. "What are you doing?"

"This won't fit on your horse," he answered, then flung her valise under the sidewalk. "And I just have the one set." He picked up her dime novel, creased and dog-eared, and turned it over in his hand. With a chuckle, he placed it with her other belongings.

Ignoring his ridicule, she scrambled under the sidewalk and dragged out the valise. She retrieved the brooch, wrapped in a square of linen, from the secret inner pocket. Glaring at him for his thoughtlessness, she shoved the pin into the pocket of her pants.

"I'd like to be off before sunrise," Cougar drawled, mounting his stallion. He stared down at her, one brow elevated impatiently. Sighing at his lack of manners, she dragged her horse over to the raised sidewalk and, fitting her foot in the stirrup, grabbed the saddle horn and pulled herself up onto its back. She gathered the reins, nudged her horse with her heels, and followed Cougar down the street, glaring at his broad back and mentally listing all the reasons why she should not go with him. He was a stranger, despite being a friend of her grandfather's; he emanated an edge of danger that made her uneasy; he made her appear foolish, though, to be fair, she managed that on her own; and he kissed her without permission. No, she was most assuredly not happy about this turn of events. But she was forced to go with him or suffer the consequences.

****

Governor Thornwilde handed his agent a thick black envelope. "Make sure you put this in Chas Grayson's hands—nobody but Grayson's." He waited patiently for acknowledgment of his dictate.

The agent nodded and placed the envelope in his brown leather satchel. With his middle finger, he straightened the metal spectacles perched on his nose and looked expectantly at the Governor.

"If it falls into the wrong hands, there will be hell to pay. I owe Chas a favor, and since I have at last learned the truth of the events of that day, I am more than happy to oblige. However, there are some who may try to prevent it from happening," he warned.

Williams tugged on his shirt collar and nodded again. "Right, sir. I will see that Mr. Grayson gets it posthaste." He glanced up at the clock. "I had better be on my way, sir. The stage departs soon."

Governor Thornwilde watched him leave his office and with a slow shake of his head wondered why he kept a man like Williams on his staff. He hoped he wouldn't botch this assignment like he had others in the past. But since he was the only man he could spare to make the trip south, he could only hope for the best.

After all, what could possibly happen?

Chapter 5

Cougar had to alter his earlier opinion. Cady was nothing like he had expected. Not once had she complained at the grueling pace he had set, riding beside him with grim determination, and the few times he had glanced over at her, she had refused to look at him. They had ridden through the night and most of the morning yet still had not traveled as far as he'd have liked. He had led them in a wide circle and backtracked several times so as not to leave a noticeable trail. He wanted to make it as difficult as possible for the intruders to find her, if they chose to follow.

Toward early afternoon, Cady was slumping in the saddle. Cougar took pity on her and pulled up into a small clearing to rest. He watched her dismount and place her hands on the small of her back, lean backwards, then with a lusty sigh, bend over at the waist only to straighten again and reach her hands to the sky. The wide-brimmed hat he had given her had kept most of the sun's burning rays from her face, yet even so, her skin was sun-kissed, a smattering of freckles dancing across her nose. His gaze drifted to her mouth. He scowled and quickly looked away, squelching the remembered feel of it beneath his own.

Cady, unaware of the turmoil she was causing, heard Cougar growl, and glanced at him in alarm. He had his back to her, tending to the horses, and seeming to ignore her. With a small shrug, she strolled around the clearing, trying to work out the kinks in her muscles. Lord, she was sore. Never had she ridden so hard for so long. She was determined, however, not to complain. She would not be a burden—even if it meant enduring this torture in silence.

She had felt his gaze on her more than once while they rode, and the constant frown he sported was disconcerting. She thought back to what she might have done to provoke his ill-humor and realized that his demeanor had changed after that kiss. Before that, he had been, well, amiable. She sighed, discouraged. She must be awful at kissing.

She looked askance at Cougar. Just how did he know her grandfather? Determined to get some answers, not caring if he was in a bad mood, she strode across the clearing and planted herself behind him. She pulled off her hat and shook her head, releasing the ebony mane to fall around her shoulders. She reached up to touch him on the shoulder and saw that she had already caught his attention, for he had turned and was watching her.

"How do you know my grandfather?"

"I told you—he was a friend."

"How do I know you're telling the truth?"

"You don't," he said with what could have been a grin.

She stared at him in surprise and found herself smiling back despite her apprehension. There was something about him that was intriguing, a magnetic quality pulling her to him, lessening her suspicions.

"Will you tell me about him?"

"What do you want to know?" Cougar leaned his shoulder again a tree and crossed his arms casually over his chest.

"Well, what was he like?"

"He was…" He paused, as if searching for the right words. "A blessing."

Cady thought about that, but before she could comment, he added, "He was looking forward to you coming to live with him."

"He was?" Her grin went from ear to ear.

"He beamed like a little boy on Christmas morning."

Cady suddenly felt very loved. He *had* wanted her!

"You have his eyes."

"I do?" Then nodding, she continued, "Yes, I remember we share that feature." Sobering, she asked quietly, "How did he die? I mean, I know he lapsed into a coma, but how? What happened?"

"You don't know?"

She shook her head. "Do you?" When he didn't answer, she prodded, "Cougar?"

"Oh hell," he muttered and turned away, busying himself with the horses.

"What?" she whispered, a feeling of unease rearing its head. She grabbed his arm and spun him around. Not an easy task—like turning a tree.

"Cougar! Answer me! What happened?" They shared a long look—hers frightened, his enraged, with pain buried deep in his eyes.

His words came fast and furious. "Your grandfather was murdered. Someone crept into his house and shot him. He was in a coma for several days and then he died."

Cady stared at him in disbelief, numb with shock. "Murdered?" Tears blurred her vision. "Do you know who killed him?"

"No."

She looked around the empty wilderness, suddenly feeling vulnerable. She was in a strange land with a strange man, trying to lose two men who had attacked her, who may or not be following them, and on her way to an uncertain future. She took a deep breath, trying to keep hysteria at bay. Her gaze lit on his gun, and she wished she had one of her own.

She looked up to find Cougar watching her expectantly as if awaiting her next move. They shared another long look before she averted her gaze and, using a small rock, swung up on her mare. After he had mounted, she followed him out of the clearing, and they continued south to Santa Fe.

As they rode, Cady tried to latch onto just one thought swirling around in her head. She was shocked to learn that her grandfather had been murdered. Murder was always tragic, whatever the circumstances, and never easily accepted. But to lose a loved one to murder? It was true, she hadn't known him well, but he had certainly thought enough of her to leave her his entire legacy. That spoke volumes. And, too, he had wanted her to live with him. That missed chance of being with him, gaining a sense of belonging, was heartbreaking, indeed.

And what about Cougar? When they spoke of Chas's murder, she had glimpsed the pain in his eyes. That was something one couldn't hide—or fake. And that thought further refuted any remaining doubts she'd had about his relationship with Chas.

Cady dismissed her depressing thoughts and looked around, taking in her surroundings. The trail was sandwiched between a sea of short grass and tall jagged mountains, peaks still clad in wintery snow, piercing the azure sky and creating a dramatic backdrop for the blue spruce pines, mountain mahogany and majestic white oak trees. Interspersed were stands of quaking aspen that towered over short juniper trees and other vegetation in the foothills, all vying for room to thrive.

As they galloped down the sunbaked road, the miles quickly covered beneath their horses' hooves, the trail cut through the rugged mountains and dipped down into a valley, a lush grassy flatland where cattle and sheep were grazing. Colorful wildflowers dotted the enchanting meadow—yellow violets and delicate wild crocus mixed with blue columbine and white daisies. A shimmer of water snaked down the mountainside, providing needed nourishment for flora and fauna alike. The view was foreign to Cady but held such an untamed beauty she was soon captivated.

As the sun began its daily descent, they stopped to make camp in a small glade beside a narrow river. Cady smiled upon spotting the small tributary, the sparkling water luring her to its edge with the promise of cool delight.

"Don't stray too far," Cougar warned as she ran toward the river.

She acknowledged his advice with a wave of her hand and made her way to the water's edge. Tall cottonwoods bordered the river, their trunks dark gray and deeply furrowed, their branches spread wide and casting cooling shade. Shiny green leaves dangled from the branches, rustling softly in the breeze, and protecting drooping clusters of small, round green seeds, wads of cotton-like fluff surrounding them.

She knelt on the bank unmindful of the mud, and took off her hat, allowing her hair to cascade down her back. She leaned forward, cupped her hands, and filled them with the clear, cool water. Splashing her face, she sighed in pleasure as it trickled down her cheeks, moistening her parched skin and leaving clear streaks through the dust on her face. She wet her bandanna and mopped at the sticky moisture on the back of her neck, then freed the top buttons of her shirt and ran the wet cloth around her throat and down the base of her neck.

A rustling sound from behind drew her attention and she glanced over her shoulder to find a deer had made its way to the river's edge to share in her bliss. It dropped its head, and its dainty lips drank the cool water. She smiled at the beautiful creature and turned back to the river, content to stay there the rest of the day. She looked back up as the deer bounded away.

When she heard another sound, she looked up smiling, expecting to see the deer again. But there was no deer. Her gaze swept the stand of trees bordering the river, and her eyes widened in alarm as her pulse began to race out of control. She screamed and jumped to her feet, clutching her throat in terror. She took a step back, slipped in the mud and nearly toppled into the water. She stood motionless, glued to the ground, as her worst fear became a frightening reality.

She was cornered, trapped like a defenseless animal, by three tall, copper-skinned men. Two were on horseback, one had dismounted and was standing not four feet away. They watched her, without a shred of emotion on their rugged faces, with steady dark brown eyes. Their long, black hair hung past their shoulders and colorful feathers sprouted from the backs of their heads. Odd designs were painted on their faces. Their chests were bare, save for thick leather straps that crisscrossed the reddish-brown expanses, and they wore only fringed buckskins and moccasins.

The soothing sounds of nature, that only a moment before had been sweet music, now bordered on the macabre. The rushing water was magnified to an ear-splitting roar and the birds' trilling was piercing in its intensity. She should have run screaming through the trees, but she was just too scared to move. Everything she had ever read or heard about Indians raced through her mind, drowning out all coherent thoughts of escape.

The Indian closest to her stepped up and reached out to finger a black tress. She flinched, feeling the cold sweat trickling between her breasts and down her belly. Weak-kneed and wobbly, she had trouble breathing with terror, a dead weight on her chest, making each labored breath painful.

She heard a rustling sound and her heart lurched. Too afraid to take her eyes off the Indian, she could only pray it wasn't more. From out of the corner of her eye, she saw Cougar striding toward them, his expression impassive, but eyes flashing with golden fire.

He planted himself between Cady and the Indian and pushed her behind his back. He began to speak rapidly to the Indian in a strange, somewhat guttural, language while gesturing wildly with his hands.

She moved out from behind Cougar and listened to the stilted exchange, her heart in her throat. She could not understand a word they spoke and became more unsettled each time Cougar pointed her way. And each time he did, the Indian glanced at her. She stood nervously by Cougar's side and waited with bated breath for the outcome.

During the conversation, the Indians on horseback

glanced between Cougar and her, their expressions unchanging. One of them widened his eyes at something Cougar said and turned to look at her, as if considering his words. When their conversation came to an end, the Indian nodded his head and after briefly resting his hand on his chest, mounted his horse, signaled to the other two, and all three turned and melted into the trees.

Cougar looked down at her. "Are you all right?"

She nodded slowly, staring at him with wide eyes. "What did they want?"

"You."

Cady gasped and put her hand to her chest. "Me?" she managed to ask past the lump in her throat. She looked around, frantic. "Are they coming back?" Her nerves, already stretched taut, were near the breaking point

"No." He shook his head and stared into the copse of cottonwoods where the Indians had disappeared.

"How can you be so calm? We're out here in the middle of nowhere. What's to stop them from coming back and killing us in our sleep?"

"I know them."

"You know them?" Her voice had risen sharply, high-pitched and shrill.

"They are my friends."

"Your friends?" she echoed, not sure she had heard him correctly. "How can you possibly be friends with Indians? They're horrid, ruthless savages!" She took a step back at the hard glint darkening his eyes.

"Not all of them," he muttered, and spun on his heel.

"Wait!" she called out, running toward him and stopping him by grabbing his arm. With the danger now past, she felt the need to make amends. "I didn't mean to insult your friends. It's just that I've read such horrible stories of raids, torture—"

"Don't believe everything you read, darlin'," he said, his words cutting across her apology.

Cady blushed with shame. She had no right to criticize his friends, even if they were Indians. Cougar had been more than kind and didn't deserve that. Besides, he had made them leave—and she was still in one piece.

"How is it you know their language?"

"I learned it a long time ago. Circumstances…"

"What?" she prompted, now thoroughly intrigued. When he didn't respond and just stood staring off into the distance, she knelt down beside the river and dipped her bandanna into the water. Absently, she moved it around with her fingers watching the ripples widen into a large undulating circle.

Still unnerved by the encounter, she wondered if perhaps, like Cougar said, she had been too hasty in believing what she had read and heard about Indians. They had seemed more curious than threatening. Well, maybe in the case of these three—she couldn't possibly dismiss everything she'd heard after just one encounter. And Cougar had said they had wanted *her!* Lord, what was she to think about that? And how in the world had Cougar become friends with Indians?

She could feel him behind her, could feel his powerful aura. She took a quick peek over her shoulder and saw him withdraw a slim cheroot from his pocket and lean against a tree, obviously intending to stay. She turned halfway around, twisting her body.

"I'm fine," she told him, her tone suggesting he could leave. If he grasped her meaning, he ignored it.

"What?" she demanded as he continued to watch her with an odd, almost searching, expression on his face. "They are gone, aren't they?" Cougar nodded. "Then...?"

"Well, there are wild animals around these parts," he drawled, pulling on the end of the cheroot. "Bear, coyotes, mountain—"

She jumped to her feet, looking wildly around the wooded area. *Mountain lions!*

Cougar whistled through his teeth at the erotic picture she unknowingly created. Her sharp movements sent her black curls dancing around her shoulders. The front of her shirt was damp and clung seductively to her breasts, their fullness outlined, their nipples hard. Engulfed in a blaze of aching desire, he tossed the cheroot to the ground with a low growl.

Cady glanced at him, her eyes narrowing in suspicion when she glimpsed the light in his eyes. Misreading his desire for humor, she snapped, "Stop trying to scare me!"

She had no way of knowing that he was thoroughly bewitched and had lost all rational thought. When he gave her a funny little smile, she took a step back, suddenly feeling like his next meal.

Her mouth was his downfall. Without taking his eyes from its lush fullness, he stepped toward her, grasped her upper arms, and pulled her up against his hard length. Ignoring her gasp of surprise, he wrapped his arms around her slim body and kissed her. Her mouth, open in astonishment, received his flawlessly. She tasted like the sun and the wind, and the flavors made his senses reel.

His mouth was at first warm and tender, then it

became possessive, demanding. He sucked gently on her lower lip, drawing it into his mouth. When he began to nibble on it, indescribable pleasure shot through her naïve body, the tingling sensation radiating to her toes, while more of her sanity dissolved.

She felt his hands glide down the curve of her back and up again, cupping the sides of her breasts, kneading the soft mounds with his strong fingers. As if in a trance, she not only allowed this blatant trespassing of her body but, wrapping her arms around his neck, she pressed into him, molding her body to his. His whiskered chin scraped roughly against her soft skin, and a ripple of excitement moved through her. She ached with longing—for what she didn't know, but instinct told her that what she craved she would find with him.

A bird flying overhead called out to its mate, the sound slicing through the sensuous cloud surrounding them. She started, sudden realization of where she was and what she was doing—and with whom—dousing her like a bucket of icy water. She jerked out of his embrace, placed her hands flat on his chest, and pushed. He loosened his grip, and she was able to twist free. She looked up at him in confusion, not understanding what had just happened—how she could so easily lose control over her body, her actions, her mind.

"Cady," he whispered, reaching out for her.

She held out her hands protectively in front of her and stumbled back. Cougar reached out for her again. She took another step back and, losing her footing in the soft mud, tumbled backwards into the river, emitting a very loud shriek. The last thing she saw before breaking the surface was the comical expression on Cougar's face. She disappeared, but a moment later bobbed up, sputtering between strands of wet hair clinging to her face. She brushed them out of her eyes and, glaring hotly at him, beat the water with her fists.

"You—you savage!" she shouted. "Look what you've done!"

Cougar, mentally grimacing at her choice of epithets, suppressed his laughter and reached out to help her from the river.

"Go away," she muttered, ignoring his outstretched hand. She scaled the riverbank, her wet clothes impeding her progress and leaving her to ultimately crawl on her hands and knees to reach solid ground. When free of the river's grip, she rounded on him, hands clenched into fists. Her angry words died on her lips. She was alone. He had disappeared as quietly and swiftly as a wisp of smoke.

With a shout of exasperation, she shoved her hat back on her head, spun on her heel and headed back to their camp, picking at her wet shirt where it clung persistently to her skin. Cougar was squatting in front of a small fire, staring into the growing flames, his expression inscrutable. He looked up when she approached.

"Enjoy your swim?"

"I want to go back to Denver."

"No."

"No?"

"No."

"Well, then...don't think you'll be kissing me again," she blurted out angrily.

"I won't," he said, a slight edge to his voice, and turned back to gaze into the fire.

"Why? Didn't you like it?"

His head snapped up, one brow arched, and looked at her like she was insane.

"Oh, damn," Cady muttered. *What is wrong with me? Could I be any more ridiculous?* She glimpsed his incredulous expression, couldn't even guess at his thoughts, but when she heard his chuckle, she cringed. She had just succeeded in making a fool of herself— again. She tossed her head, and stomped off to retrieve his saddlebags, which also contained her belongings.

Digging through his possessions, she found her comb half wrapped in a red bandanna, or the remnants of one. Removing the comb, she wrinkled her nose at the smell. It reminded her of the horrid, scented packets Aunt Mildred scattered around the musty attic. She threw the bandanna back into the saddlebags and pulled the comb through her hair, gently disentangling the knots while trying to understand the feelings Cougar could so easily awaken. She had no explanation for her wanton behavior. Lord, she was becoming as loose as those painted women in St. Louis! Of course, in all honesty, she was angrier with herself than with him. He had not forced her shameless response. No, he had merely aroused hidden desires with his mouth, with his hands. *I have got to stop his kisses!*

Cougar disappeared into the trees and returned shortly with two fat fish. He drove two saplings into the ground, one on either side of the fire, made a rack out of small branches, and balanced it over the flames, using the saplings as props. While the fish fried on the rack over half the fire, he made a batch of cornbread in a small black iron skillet and brewed a pot of coffee.

When the meal was ready, Cady accepted a plate of fish and cornbread from him and settled herself against a tree to eat. Doing her best to ignore him, her chin set at a stubborn angle, she cleaned her plate. She watched him from the corner of her eye as he ate his meal in silence, not once glancing her way. He looked upset. But he had no reason to be—it was she who had taken a tumble in the river. She shrugged, and scooted closer to the fire. The night air had cooled, and she was still clad in her damp clothes.

A ribbon of moonlight slipped through the tree branches and slithered across the ground. Cady lay back against her bedroll, pulled the blanket up under her chin, and looked up at the star-studded sky. Would she ever understand Cougar? He was so like the strong, handsome heroes in her dime novels, men she had often dreamed about rescuing her from her miserable life and living with happily ever after. She'd just never imagined them being as ill-mannered.

She rolled onto her side, thoroughly exhausted from the day. The physical activity in the saddle, the shock of confronting Indians, the emotional upheaval Cougar evoked with his kisses, had all taken their toll. Her eyelids fluttered closed and, with a deep sigh, she drifted into sleep. Her last thought being how to get him to kiss her again.

Cougar leaned back against a tree and watched her sleep. The moonlight touched her face with silver fingers, caressing her mouth. He stared at it, clearly remembering the feel of her pliant lips. Their intoxicating kiss had fired his passion—a passion he had never felt for any other woman. She made him feel more alive, more sensitive to touch, than at any other time in his life. He wanted her—it was that simple. If she knew just how much he wanted her, she'd run away and never come back.

It was apparent she didn't feel the same. Oh, when they were in the middle of a kiss, she surrendered to the moment, enjoying every second of it. But when it ended, she'd become mad or scared. But was she afraid of him? Or of the passion he had awakened?

It didn't really matter. Nothing would come of it—nothing could come of it. He stood and moved to his blanket to lay down. Tucking his hands beneath his head, he stared up at the stars twinkling brightly in the midnight sky. They seemed so close, close enough to reach out and capture one in his hand. He would give it to Cady. He rolled his eyes. *Where in the hell had that fancy come from?* He closed his eyes and tried to capture sleep instead, shutting out the cursed stars.

Chapter 6

The next morning Cady woke to an empty camp. Cougar's horse was still there so he hadn't abandoned her. Not wanting to be alone in case the Indians returned, she pushed the blanket aside and rolled to her feet. Thinking he might be by the river, she made her way there and, upon discovering him in the water, she sat on the bank and waited. After a few moments, he rose from the river like some erotic deity, clad only in a loincloth. In the early morning light, his long, wet hair glistened, and when he shook his head water droplets sailed through the air like sparkling drops of dew. Mesmerized by the vision, she watched him approach, her belly knotted in anticipation. As he walked by, he paused, and, placing his forefinger under her chin, gently closed her mouth.

"Time to go," he said as he continued toward camp.

Cady clamped her lips together, gave her head a little shake, and tried to cool her burning cheeks. Mortified at having been caught gawking, once again, she jumped to her feet, and keeping a wary eye out for Indians, hurried back to camp.

She found Cougar kicking dirt on the smoldering fire. He did not acknowledge her return except to hand her a sourdough biscuit. Since the scene at the river yesterday, he had not been exactly friendly toward her. Of course, shouting names and then ignoring him would not have endeared her to anyone. She accepted the biscuit with a whisper of thanks.

Munching on the hard bread, she strolled around the glade, enjoying the mild temperature and fresh mountain air. She was reluctant to get back on her horse. She had always loved to ride, and jumped at every chance to do so, but this trip wasn't enjoyable—it was torture. She eyed Cougar surreptitiously as he moved around the campsite, loading the gear on the horses. He moved with the grace of an animal, and, because he had not yet donned his shirt, she was afforded a view of the play of muscles beneath his warm brown skin as he moved this way and that. She frowned when she saw the long red welts crisscrossing his back and wondered how or why it came to pass. As if sensing her scrutiny, he looked over his shoulder and arched a brow.

She blushed scarlet and, with a groan of humiliation, turned abruptly and walked straight into a tree. A bit of the biscuit lodged in her throat, and she began to choke. Flushed with panic, she clutched her throat, trying to get air past the clump of hard bread. She heard Cougar race up behind her before she was slapped hard on her back. She coughed up the biscuit and with her hand on her chest, she took in deep gulps of air as her erratic heartbeat returned to normal.

"Thank you."

"You're welcome." He hesitated before turning away. "You really should pay more attention to your surroundings." His grin was crooked. "To keep from tumbling into rivers and walking into trees."

"Oh!" she gasped, annoyance quickly replacing gratitude. Ignoring his ill-placed humor, she stuck her bruised nose in the air and strode toward her horse. Why she found him so attractive was beyond her. He was insufferable!

They continued their trek south, crossing through terrain that seemed to change with each passing mile. They travelled through a wide expanse of desert, the sun bouncing off the dun-colored ground. The horizon shimmered in the distance, giving the illusion of a vast expanse of water. Cacti dotted the land, sprouting from the arid earth among clumps of white and purple sagebrush, their prickly green arms stretching unevenly to the sky. Large rock formations rose from the ground like giant fists, surrounded by hardy green plants. Windswept sand dunes undulated across the land, decorated with an abundance of prairie sunflowers, their yellow petals fluttering in the breeze.

Leaving behind the stretch of rocky, arid desert, they wandered over forested hills and into a valley filled with colorful wildflowers. Tall, slender aspens, their rich green leaves quivering, swayed in the wind, towering over an occasional sparkling stream that meandered down the mountainside from the snow-capped peaks.

Cady felt as if she were in a world of her own, surrounded by miles of untamed wilderness and a beauty beyond imagination.

By late afternoon they crossed into New Mexico. The sun was obscured by dark ominous clouds hanging motionless in the sky, seemingly too laden with moisture to move. A flash of lightning streaked across the horizon, answered by a resounding clap of thunder. The temperature dropped dramatically as the wind picked up in intensity.

Cady buttoned her jacket against the wind, as it whipped her hat from her head and tumbled her coal-black curls around her shoulders. She left the hat to dangle down her back from the cord around her neck.

"Do you think the storm will be upon us soon?" she shouted to Cougar who rode just ahead of her on the narrow shrub-lined path. She saw him nod before his words were carried back to her on the wind.

"We'll take shelter up ahead. There's a cave big enough for us and the horses."

When the first fat raindrops fell, Cady dug in her heels, urging the mare to a faster gait. She was caught completely unprepared when her horse suddenly reared up on its hind legs with a loud snort, its ears flat against its head. She lost her grip, the reins slipping through her fingers, and was thrown from the saddle. She sailed through the air and landed with a jolt on her backside. She quickly rolled into the brush to avoid the horse's flailing hooves and shook her head to clear it of dancing stars.

Cougar heard the commotion and pulled up on the reins. He glanced over his shoulder, his body stiffening at the imminent danger. His keen vision had spotted the snake, camouflaged in its natural surroundings and ready to strike. It was coiled in an open loop, its forebody elevated, its neck curved in an s-shape. Cougar slid slowly from his horse and crept toward Cady, pulling his knife from his boot.

"Lie still. Don't move."

Cady, alarmed at his somber expression and tone of voice, obeyed. The subtle rattling penetrated the ringing in her ears at the same time she saw the snake strike. It lunged forward with considerable speed, embedding its long, curved fangs in the soft skin of her lower leg just above the top of her boot.

Cady screamed and curled her fingers into the ground as instantaneous white-hot pain shot up her leg. She glanced down in horror and screamed again. The writhing reptile still clung to her leg, unable to withdraw its fangs entangled in her clothing.

Cougar leapt forward and with one quick swipe of his knife sliced the snake in two. As he gently removed the curved fangs from her calf, Cady fainted. He gathered her in his arms and sprinted up the hill to the cave, the horses jogging dutifully behind him.

The rain had become a torrential downpour, and they were both quickly soaked to the skin. First laying Cady on the ground, Cougar used his knife to hack away the dense brush covering the entrance to the cave. He grabbed a rolled blanket from behind his saddle, lifted Cady into his arms, and ducked inside the dank interior. With one hand, he shook out the blanket and laid it on the floor of the cave, then gingerly set her upon it.

At the mouth of the cave he gathered brush and twigs. Piling them in the center of the cavern, he soon had a small fire going, blowing on the tiny flame until it began to crackle and illuminate the cave, chasing away the chilly dampness.

That done, he concentrated on Cady. First, he tugged off her boot. Then, using his knife, he slit open her denims, ripping apart the material and baring her leg. He turned it toward the light of the fire to examine the snake bite. It was ugly. Her skin was a portrait of red, blue and black and had already swollen around the two holes made by the snake's fangs.

Cady's eyes fluttered open, and she focused on Cougar, who squatted beside her, bent over her leg. His face was set, his beautiful mouth drawn into a grim line.

The firelight accented the hard planes of his features.

"Cougar?" she whispered. "My leg—it hurts." She started to shake uncontrollably, her eyes glazing over with pain.

He glanced up, took in her pale complexion and the sweat beading her brow, and knew he had to work quickly. "The venom has to come out," he said, pushing his knife into the glowing embers of the fire.

"Venom?" Cady felt lightheaded, unable to comprehend what he said. She swallowed as a wave of nausea swept over her.

"The snake bite," he reminded her calmly.

Cady rubbed her forehead in confusion. Her leg throbbed in unbearable pain, and she was covered in a cold sweat. She moved slightly and winced at the ache in her lower back. Suddenly she remembered the fall from her horse and the snake striking her leg. She shuddered, her entire body shaking from the force.

"This is going to hurt," Cougar warned her before retrieving the knife from the fire and with careful precision cut a deep incision across the two holes in her leg. Cady bolted upright, screaming in pain, and grabbed his arm. Her short nails dug though his shirt and into his skin. He stuck the knife back into the embers and, placing his hand on her cheek, took a moment to comfort her. Caressing her skin, he gazed deeply into her eyes.

"I'm sorry I had to hurt you. I'll work as fast as I can," he promised. "Do you trust me?"

She nodded weakly and collapsed back against the blanket as he took her leg gently in his hands. He dropped his head, covered the snake bite with his mouth, and sucked, turning his head aside to spit out the venom. He did this over and over for several long minutes.

Cady gripped the blanket until her knuckles were cramped and stark white against the dark material. She tried to ignore the pain shooting up her leg by concentrating on her surroundings. The cave was large, the walls coated with grime and damp mold. Small black lumps hung from the ceiling—she didn't dare venture a guess as to their identity. Thunder crashed outside the cave and rain pounded the ground. The horses stood at the mouth of the cave, stamping their hooves and whinnying nervously.

When Cougar was sure he had sucked out all the venom, he sat back on his heels and looked at Cady, wrapping his hand around her wrist. She was pale and her pulse had dropped to a fluttery, thready beat.

"It's done," he said. "The venom—" She fainted again. He took a long pull of water from his canteen, rinsed his mouth, and spit it out. From the leather pouch at his belt, he selected a few plants and herbs. In the palm of his hand, he mixed them with water, making a poultice which he packed tightly around the snake bite. He removed his shirt, tore it into long, thin strips, and used them to securely bandage her leg. He brushed her damp hair from her forehead and laid his hand against her cheek. Her skin was cool to the touch. With his thumb, he brushed away the tears. She opened her eyes, tried to focus on his face, then closed them again and fell asleep. He lifted her upright, and with what remained of his shirt, he dried her hair and laid her back down on the blanket.

Something stirred in his heart as he looked down at this brave young woman. She had never once complained of the long hours spent in the saddle, had taken the encounter with the ruffians who'd trespassed in her room in stride, hadn't fainted or run screaming into the woods when confronted by Indians, and other than a few pained screams had endured this latest ordeal quite stoically. Chas would have been so proud of her. She wasn't much help, though, not knowing how to cook or even start a fire. He grinned. But she sure could kiss.

He rose to his feet and crossed to the mouth of the cave, grabbing the horses' reins to lead them to the rear of the cave. After stripping them of their gear, he rubbed them down and gave each a handful of oats. He returned to the fire with a bottle of whiskey and another blanket which he laid over Cady's inert body. He stoked the fire to a roaring blaze and sat close to keep watch.

The storm continued its fury; night fell and still it raged. Cougar sat by the fire, keeping his silent vigil, sipping whiskey from a tin cup, telling himself he had nothing to worry about. He felt certain he had removed all the venom, and the poultice would fight any that may have escaped into her blood. It would also help to heal the wound.

He took a deep breath to ease his taut muscles. She was his responsibility; he had promised to deliver her safely to Santa Fe, and if anything happened to her, he would never forgive himself. He was a bit surprised by this unfamiliar protective feeling but shrugged it off as the promise he had made to his friend. He was also mighty relieved to have put Colorado Territory behind him.

He leaned back against the wall of the cave, heedless of the dampness, and closed his eyes, telling himself she would come through this unscathed. She just had to.

****

Cady jerked awake, gasping for air. The blanket was twisted around her body, and she was covered in a cold sweat. She looked around with wild eyes. The cave was cast in shadows that in her frenzied state took on lives of their own. She flinched when a loud crash of thunder reverberated in the cave, the cold damp floor seeming to shake beneath her. Her gaze landed on Cougar, who was leaning back against the wall of the cave, his eyes closed, and reality slowly pushed through her panic. *It had only been a dream.*

Cougar opened his eyes and, seeing that she was awake, jumped to his feet and strode to her side. His smile faded when he saw her frantic expression. "Are you in pain?"

She shook her head. "No, not overly much."

"Then what is it?"

"I had a—nothing," she murmured, brushing away her tears.

Cougar knelt beside her. "Then why are you crying?"

"It was horrible!" she blurted out.

Cougar sat back on his heels and eyed her thoughtfully. "Your leg will heal," he said, slowly.

She shook her head vehemently. "No—no, not that."

"Then what?" His tone was soft, his touch gentle as he began stroking her hair.

"A dream—a horrible nightmare!"

"What was it about?" he asked, trying to keep his tone calm. It was obvious she was still quite frightened. "Cady?"

She looked up at him, uncertain. His expression was troubled, yet his eyes shone with compassion. Taking a deep breath, she began to tell him, her voice shaking. "Someone was after me. I was running so fast, trying to get away—but he was right behind me. I could feel his breath on the back of my neck. There were these—ah—white things, like cobwebs, clinging to me and slowing me down."

"Could you see who was chasing you?"

"No. All I knew was that I had to get to—" She stopped, horrified at what she almost revealed.

"What did you have to get to."

"I don't know," she mumbled, and averted her gaze. Lord, how could she possibly tell him?

"Go on," he encouraged her, taking note of her rosy cheeks.

Cady sighed and gazed into the fire. "I freed myself from the cobwebs and—and found myself in a clearing. There was a campfire blazing, but otherwise empty. I heard a rustling noise and spun around to see an animal emerging from the trees. A huge black beast. It crept toward me then leapt high into the air. I screamed and fell to the ground, covering my head with my arms. I thought for sure it would tear me to shreds." She shivered and looked up at Cougar. "I felt its arms go around me. But they weren't savage or brutal, they were warm and comforting. When I looked at its face—" She stopped, her blush deepening, and looked at Cougar in wonder. "It was you."

Cougar tilted his head to one side, his expression not giving anything away. He didn't speak and seemed to be thinking about what she'd told him.

"It was only a dream," he said after a while, rising to his feet and fetching the canteen of water. "But I'm sorry it scared you." He handed her the canteen. "You're safe now."

Cady sipped the cool water, keeping her head bowed, trying to shake off the lingering nightmare. She peered at him from beneath her lashes and studied his face. It was covered with a heavy layer of black whiskers, but even so she could see the deep lines etched around his mouth. He was gazing into the fire, the dancing flames reflected in his amber eyes, his expression thoughtful. *Should I have told him?*

She looked down at her leg. Her denims were slit from hip to hem, her leg tightly bandaged. She moved it and was relieved to feel only a slight throbbing pain. She was also feeling more clear-headed, and her pulse had returned to normal.

"Did you get out all the venom?"

"I think so. How do you feel?"

"All right, I guess." She moved and winced in pain. "My back's a little sore from being tossed to the ground. How long have I been asleep?"

"Several hours." He continued his contemplation of the blue-and-yellow flames.

"When will we reach my grandfather's ranch?"

"Tomorrow, late. If the storm lets up," he added.

Cady became silent as she too watched the fire. Her stomach was a ball of anxiety. She had no idea what to expect when she arrived at her grandfather's home nor the reception she would receive. It would most likely be as before. She would be an outsider, unwanted. She stiffened her spine and told herself it didn't matter.

She looked back at Cougar. She was still not completely at ease with him, but at every turn he had taken care of her. Of course, if he hadn't been there, she could have handled everything just fine. Well, maybe not the snake bite. But it felt good to let someone else take over. She was suddenly glad her grandfather had sent Cougar. It was odd, but despite his mood changes, and his sometimes-fierce frown, she was happy he was near.

Though it wasn't like her to take to someone so readily, especially a virtual stranger, his quiet strength gave her a sense of peace, of well-being. She lay back, snuggled under the blanket, and fell back asleep, feeling protected and safe with Cougar watching over her.

Chapter 7

As they neared Santa Fe, they crossed a high desert plain, then descended into a spectacular valley carved into the plateau. Cady, beyond exhaustion, was more than ready to get to her grandfather's ranch—her new home—despite being doubtful of her welcome.

The sun was a fiery ball perched on top of the mountains when Ponderosa Pines, her grandfather's ranch, came into view. Cady's stomach tightened in anxious anticipation, and she prayed she would be greeted with at least a modicum of kindness.

Chilled by the cool evening air, she huddled beneath her jacket for warmth, still amazed how the burning heat of day dropped with the sun. As they approached Ponderosa Pines, she took a deep breath, hiding her apprehension behind a serene façade. To divert her insecurity, she took a moment to study the hacienda. The house was two stories high with a wide front porch that wrapped around three sides of it. Tall leafy-crowned trees, silhouetted against the magnificent yellow-and-orange sunset, towered over either side of the house. As they jogged down the drive, she spotted several buildings set apart from the main house, situated near the stables. There, several horses milled around the large corral that encompassed the stables, and a group of men lounged together talking among themselves.

When they reined up on the front lawn, Cady slid

from her horse and gazed up at Cougar, battling her fear of the unknown. Before they left the cave, he had secured her belongings in a blanket which he now tossed to the ground. He tipped his hat in a sign of farewell and started to wheel his horse around.

"Cougar!" He turned back, one eyebrow arched. "Aren't you coming in with me?" She cringed at the quiver in her voice. "I mean—"

He shook his head. "I've done what was asked of me."

"But—" She stiffened her spine. She certainly didn't *need* him to stay. With a twist of sadness in her heart, she watched him gallop out of the yard and disappear down the drive.

On their journey, an unspoken bond had developed between them. It was not easily explained, and despite his occasional surliness, she had come to enjoy his company. If she were prone to fancy, she could almost believe he cared for her. His actions certainly said as much. And all that kissing! So why then did he abandon her now?

She stood fidgeting nervously with her hat and looked around the wide front lawn. Her attention was drawn to the front of the house when the door flew open, and a caramel-skinned woman rushed out onto the porch. She was clad in a simple dove-gray dress with a bright green apron tied around her ample waist. She had short black hair and black eyes, and a broad, friendly smile. She hurried down the front steps, but when she neared, she stopped abruptly, her eyes widening.

Cady grimaced, knowing she must look a fright. She was sunburned, travel weary, and limping from the snake bite. She self-consciously ran a hand through her hair and tried to straighten on her injured leg.

"Señorita Cady? We did not think you would arrive this soon! I am Maria Santora, Señor Chas's housekeeper. Welcome to Ponderosa Pines." She held out her hand.

Cady clasped hands with Maria. "Thank you," she said. "It's nice to finally be here, Mrs. Santora."

"Please, you must call me Maria," she insisted kindly.

"All right—Maria." Cady gazed into dark eyes that sparkled like polished coal. She could find no resentment there, only genuine warmth and friendliness. But before Cady could digest this, she was enveloped in a bone-crushing hug, her face smashed against Maria's generous bosom. She smelled nice, an appealing mixture of flour and spice.

"It is good you are here," Maria said, grabbing the blanket containing Cady's belongings.

"Yes," Cady agreed as she followed Maria across the lawn toward the house. Her leg, still swollen from the snake bite, made walking difficult, and she limped alongside the housekeeper. Maria stopped and peered at her in concern.

"Are you hurt?"

"I was bitten by a snake."

"Oh, dear. I will send for Doc Flint right away."

"Is he the doctor who tended my grandfather?"

"*Si.*" Maria took Cady's arm, guided her toward the front steps, keeping her pace slow. "Did you have a good trip? Any problems—other than the snake bite?"

"None to speak of. Well, I did encounter some Indians," she added with a shudder.

Maria looked at her in alarm. "Did they harm you?"

"No. Cougar talked to them, and they left me alone. He said they were his friends."

"Cougar?" Maria asked, her head tilted to one side.

Cady nodded, fiddling with her hat and missing Maria's smile. "I thought the same thing."

"What?"

"His name." Cady's eyes widened in surprise at Maria's amused expression. "Don't you find it an odd name?"

Maria chuckled and helped her up the front steps. "*Si*, I do."

"He is the most, most—"

"Handsome?" Maria supplied with a twinkle in her eye.

"I was going to say infuriating," she quipped. She stared at Maria with arched brows. "You know him?"

"*Si*, yes."

They both turned at the sound of a rider coming down the drive. Cady's heart leapt into her throat. He had come back! But as he neared, she saw that it wasn't Cougar and stifled a keen sense of disappointment.

The man reined up in front of the house and dismounted from his brown-and-white dappled horse. He was tall and wiry, with curly brown hair and friendly gray eyes. He wore a white cotton shirt and a pair of black pants with leather chaps. He was easy on the eyes but did not possess Cougar's dark, rugged handsomeness.

"Cady Grayson?" he asked and, at her nod, pushed his hat back off his forehead and said, "I'm Randy Brown, the foreman here at Ponderosa Pines. We weren't expecting you for another couple of days. Was the stage early?"

"I didn't take the stage." He cocked a brow at her. "Ah, Cougar brought me." She started to elaborate but Randy just nodded—obviously, it was all the explanation he needed.

"Welcome to Ponderosa Pines. I'll be in to see you shortly." He tipped his hat and, taking her horse's reins, led it to the stables.

A short, rotund man with black hair and a thick black mustache rounded the corner of the house. He came up beside Maria and tipped his hat to Cady. Maria slipped her arm through his and smiled.

"This is my husband, Carlos," Maria said. "Carlos, this is Señor Chas's granddaughter, Señorita Cady."

"A pleasure, Señorita Cady," Carlos replied with a broad grin. Cady smiled back, her trepidation all but dissipated by their more than kind reception.

"Come, you'll find it warmer inside," Maria said, helping Cady up the front steps and leading her into the front hall. It was long and wide and extended to the back of the house. They turned into the first room off the passageway—the parlor—that Maria explained was used as a family room as well as for informal business meetings.

Cady paused in the doorway and stared in awe at her surroundings. The room was a profusion of warm earth tones. The walls were covered in green and gold striped wallpaper that reflected the colors of the sun and grass. Two rust-hued sofas with matching brown and gold textured pillows strewn on either side, were positioned in an L-shape, a square table centered in front of them. Two comfortable-looking chairs of forest-green sat in front of a stone fireplace bookended by two small round-topped tables. A small pine writing desk and matching chair were in one corner of the room next to a long oak sideboard. The large floor-to-ceiling window was framed by dark gold curtains and opened onto the front lawn.

The muted colors were brought together by a large tribal rug of green, rust and gold that covered most of the floor. The room was filled with the scent of pine and smoke from wood that crackled cheerfully in the fireplace, banishing the early evening chill.

Cady perched on the edge of the sofa, relishing the softness of the cushions beneath her sore backside. She held her dusty hat in her hands, unsure of where to place it. She looked down at her feet and was dismayed to find her leather boots coated with dust. In fact, she was covered from head to foot with a thin layer of dust from her long ride on the trail. Maria took her hat and pressed Cady back into the sofa.

"Do not worry yourself, Señorita Cady. Señor Chas would sit in here conducting business covered in more dust than you," she said with a smile. She turned to the sideboard that held a variety of bottles and glasses.

With a contented sigh, Cady leaned back into the pillows and accepted a short-stemmed glass of sherry from Maria. Cady smiled gratefully, and waved her hand to the empty space on the sofa beside her.

"Please, Maria, won't you sit?"

"*Si, gracias*, Señorita Cady." Maria sat down and folded her hands in her lap. She looked at Cady suddenly teary-eyed. "You have the *patrón*'s eyes." She dabbed at her own with a white handkerchief. "Your grandfather would have been so happy today. He was looking forward to you coming to live with him." She shook her head. "He was sad he would not live long enough."

"He was sad—but I thought he didn't wake from the coma."

Maria averted her gaze and picked at her apron. "*Si,* this is true," she said slowly with a small nod of her head.

"Then—"

"Ah, Señor Randy," Maria interjected, as the foreman strode into the room. He removed his hat and stopped in front of the two women.

"Miss Grayson, after you've settled in, I will be pleased to answer any questions you might have, about the ranch or—your grandfather," he added with a sympathetic smile.

"Thank you, Randy. Perhaps tomorrow. And please call me Cady."

"Yes, ma'am."

After he left, Cady turned back to Maria. "He seems like a very nice man."

"He is. He has been here for quite a few years. Señor Chas thought very highly of him."

"He has a lot of responsibility for one so young," Cady remarked aloud. He couldn't be more than a few years older than she.

"He is a good foreman. He runs this ranch with a firm hand and a smooth touch. The men like him very much, they respect him."

"And how long have you and Carlos been here?"

"We have been with Señor Chas for longer than I can remember. We also have a son, Raul, who helps his father around the ranch. Ponderosa Pines is a wonderful place to live."

While Maria chattered on, Cady could feel the tension in her muscles begin to relax. Perhaps her worries were unfounded. Everyone she had met so far had been more than kind.

"Would you like to see your room? Maybe take a bath and a *siesta* before supper?"

"Yes, that would be wonderful." Cady stood and immediately groaned as her wounded leg buckled under her. She reached back and grabbed the arm of the sofa for support, grimacing at the pain shooting up her leg.

Maria was quick to note her suffering and, patting her arm, said, "I will send Carlos for Doc Flint. Your leg should be looked at right away."

"Cougar was sure he got out all the venom, but I'm afraid it still hurts quite a bit."

On their way to Cady's room, Maria gave her a quick tour of the hacienda, after first being assured that Cady was able to walk. The center courtyard off the back parlor and dining room was filled with fruit and pine trees, low bushy green shrubs, and flowers in full spring bloom. The blossoms were a vivid splash of color and filled the air with a sweet fragrance. Beneath the shaded area of the tree branches were two wrought iron benches, a refreshing place to sit in the midday heat, with a small matching table between them.

Back inside the house, the two women went up the wide staircase to the second floor and down the hallway to a room in one corner of the house.

"This is my room?" Cady asked in wide-eyed disbelief. Never had she seen anything so lovely. It was a sunset—richly varied in color. Decorated in mauve, the dominant color, with touches of orange and yellow mixed in, the colors melted together, creating a warm ambiance.

While Maria unpacked her meager belongings from the blanket, Cady glanced around in wonder, hardly able to believe this exquisite room was hers. A large bed covered with a butter-yellow quilt dominated the room, a spindly-legged table with a brass oil lamp and a vase of fresh-cut flowers beside it. A washstand holding an orange-and-white-striped pitcher and matching bowl stood between two long narrow windows framed by deep mauve curtains that overlooked the courtyard. A third window, also sporting deep mauve curtains, in one corner of the room, overlooked the stables and corral. A dressing table with a variegated tapestried bench and an oak wardrobe shared another wall with a small fireplace. A screen depicting a lively scene of wild horses against a backdrop of snow-capped mountains stood in another corner of the room beside a tall mirror. A plush, mauve-colored carpet was soft underfoot.

Cady turned toward the door when Carlos and a young boy entered the room carrying large buckets of water, the steam rising in ribbons to the ceiling. They nodded to Cady, then emptied the buckets into a tub hidden behind the screen.

Maria grabbed the boy's hand and pulled him forward. "Señorita, this is my son, Raul. Raul, say hello to Señorita Cady, Señor Chas's granddaughter. She is our new *patróna*."

"Hello, Raul," Cady said, bending down to shake the young boy's hand. He nodded shyly and stood staring at her with something close to adoration in his dark brown eyes. His father mumbled an apology and, grabbing his son's hand, dragged him from the room.

Cady laughed. "What an adorable little boy! How old is he?"

"Nearly ten. I think he has taken an instant liking to you, Señorita."

"Maria, will you please call me Cady? I don't want to stand on formality."

"*Si*, if that is your wish. Now, after your bath, you rest. I will bring you a tray later this evening." She closed the door behind her, leaving Cady alone in paradise.

After divesting herself of her dusty travel clothes, she carefully removed the bandage from around her leg, then stepped into the tub and slid down the smooth side until the water covered her breasts. She breathed a contented sigh as the hot water soaked her battered body, soothing her aching muscles. A small shelf on the wall next to the tub held a variety of glass bottles. She selected one, a violet-scented bath oil, and poured a liberal amount into the water. She grabbed a small round sponge and a bar of handmade soap from the shelf and scrubbed her skin until it glowed pink. She washed her hair twice relishing the feel of the squeaky-clean tresses between her fingers. After drying her body with a fluffy yellow towel, she donned a blue velveteen robe she found in the wardrobe and, humming a gay little tune, limped to the bed and sank down onto the soft mattress.

In search of a handkerchief, she dumped the contents of her handbag on the bed. Picking up a piece of paper she recognized it as the unused stage ticket. "Cougar," she whispered, flooded with emotion. *Will I ever see him again? Do I even want to?*

After wrapping a large cotton handkerchief around her wound, she stuffed the various articles, including the stage ticket, back into her handbag, tossed it on the floor and snuggled beneath the quilt. She fell instantly asleep filled with the hope that she would find happiness here, a place to belong. Her one regret was that she'd not be reunited with her grandfather.

****

Cougar turned his horse toward the mountains. He had waited in the trees until Cady was welcomed at Ponderosa Pines. She had not been too happy when he just left her on the doorstep, and, frankly, he didn't know why he had acted so thoughtlessly. But he knew she would be welcomed with open arms. When Maria embraced her and took her into the house, after speaking with Randy and Carlos, he knew his task was done, his promise fulfilled. Cady was safely in Santa Fe.

He had done what was asked of him and had no reason to seek her out again. If she wished to follow Chas's last request, then she would contact him. He doubted she would, though, not when she learned the truth.

He nudged his horse to a gallop, but hearing his name called from across the pasture, he pulled up on the reins and turned to see a young woman atop a small bay mare racing toward him, her hair a dark brown cloud billowing out behind her. He waited patiently for her to reach his side.

"Austin! I thought that was you," she said breathlessly, pulling her mare to a prancing stop.

"Cougar," he corrected with a warm smile.

"Oh, all right—Cougar," she said with an exaggerated sigh. "Where have you been? I thought you would have attended Chas's funeral."

"I had to go to Denver."

She gasped, her eyes widening in alarm. "You know it's not safe to cross the border."

"I had to collect Chas's granddaughter," he said absently, staring at her face. He reached out and touched the discolored spot on her cheek. "Cassie, what happened?"

"What? Oh, this?" She laughed nervously and touched the bruise. "I fell against the corral fence the other day. Clumsy of me, huh? It's nothing to worry about," she said quickly, averting her gaze from his sharp amber one. "What's she like?"

"Who?"

"Chas's granddaughter," she said with a laugh.

"Willful, suspicious, defiant, beautiful—"

Cassie stared at him in confusion, stunned by the contradiction as well as the sudden softening of his features. "Beautiful?"

"A brat, really," he growled and settling a scowl on his face looked over her shoulder at the snow-capped mountains.

"Is she awful, then?"

"No," he answered truthfully. "She's not so bad." He noticed Cassie's perplexed expression and realized how odd his description sounded. Hell, it only went to show his own conflicting sentiment.

"Well, either way, it is good to see you. Pa—"

"Don't start," he warned, holding up his hand.

"I'm sorry. It's just that Terence continues to bad-mouth you, and I just hate it. Renee is no help. She merely sits in her chair with a serene smile and doesn't say a word. Of course, Pa spends most of his time by himself now—with a bottle." She placed her hand on his arm and asked softly, "Why won't you do something?"

"And just what am I supposed to do?" he asked with an impatient lift of one black brow.

"I don't know. You could—"

"Drop it, Cassie. Webb settled things a long time ago when he turned me out. I have ceased to give a damn."

The young woman stared hard at him, her chocolate-brown eyes searching his for any lie to his words. But, as usual, she was unable to see beyond what he wanted seen. Troubled by his change in mood, she turned the subject and asked lightly, "How is Rose?"

"Distraught over Chas's death."

"Oh dear, of course she is. I will visit her."

"She would like that."

"Is that where you're headed now?"

"Yes."

"Give her my love and tell her I'll see her soon."

"I will," Cougar promised, his face relaxing again.

"I love you."

"I love you, too. Now be a good girl and get home. Looks like we're in for a storm."

"Bye, Austin, er, Cougar," she corrected herself with a laugh and, waving, she wheeled her mare around and galloped away.

Cougar waited until she had disappeared, a frown settling between his brows. It was not the first time he had seen her bruised. He'd bet his life she didn't fall against the corral. He swore under his breath, vowing to get to the bottom of this latest mishap and berating himself for so readily accepting her excuses in the past. He kicked his heels into his horse's sides and shot forward, heading toward the snowy mountains rising majestically in the distance. The wind whipped his long, black hair as the powerful steed quickly ate up the turf.

Chapter 8

Cady woke the next morning refreshed and eager to start the day. Last night, Maria had brought her a tray— a bowl of delicious beef stew and freshly baked rye bread. After eating every morsel, Cady had fallen back to sleep, only waking when Maria came in the next day with her morning coffee.

"Señor and Señora Taylor are here. They are in the parlor."

"They are? So early?" Cady instinctively reached for a strand of hair and twisted it around her finger, unable to stem her nervousness.

"I guess they are eager to meet you. I'll let them know you'll be down shortly."

Cady waited for Maria to close the door behind her, then set aside her cup of coffee. Webb Taylor, her grandfather's oldest and dearest friend, and his wife, downstairs waiting to meet her!

Cady was not a coward, but the urge to run was overwhelming. Maybe she should just pack up and leave and save them the trouble of asking. She wished she had met with the lawyer first and, therefore, armed with the knowledge of what was truly to be.

She swung her legs over the side of the bed and winced as sharp pain drew her attention to her swollen black-and-blue leg. Doc Flint had paid a call while she was supping last night, and after careful examination of the snake bite had declared, with a lift of his bushy gray brows, that it was healing quite nicely. At his obvious surprise, she had explained that Cougar had sucked out the venom and packed it with a poultice. Doc Flint had merely nodded, as if that was reason enough for the quick recovery. He informed her that the discoloration would darken with time then disappear, but the swelling wouldn't abate for several weeks. She should have no other lasting effects except for some lingering pain, a dull ache, and maybe suffer a bit of lameness until it completely healed. He had told her how quickly people die from snake bites if not promptly, and properly, treated. Cougar had done well, he surmised.

When she had questioned him about her grandfather, he had told her, with a sad shake of his head, that there was nothing more he could have done for his friend. The bullet had lodged in his head, and he had lapsed into a coma, never to recover. Tears had filled his blue eyes, and she had found herself comforting the old man. Unfortunately, he was unable to answer any of her questions as to the culprit.

Cady limped over to the washstand and washed the sleep from her eyes. She opened the wardrobe where her meager clothing hung neatly in a row, and stared at the pathetic dresses. Even in her limited fashion sense, she knew ugly clothes when she saw them. Rifling through the dresses, she settled on one the color of oatmeal. She held it up in front of her and eyed the bland color and out-of-date style. She made a moue of disgust and tossed it on the bed.

After donning a cotton chemise and the sorry-looking dress, she sat down at the dressing table and reached for the silver brush. She pulled it through her mane of midnight-black hair, the curls springing back as if they had a life of their own. She found some ribbons coiled in a jar and after selecting a bright yellow one, she braided her hair, weaving the ribbon into the long single plait. There were several crystal bottles of perfume on a silver tray and, choosing one that smelled of violets, she dabbed a little of the attar behind each ear. As a final touch, she pinned her mother's brooch to the bodice of her dress, adding a touch of elegance to her otherwise pitiful attire.

Cady made her way downstairs and paused in the parlor doorway before making her presence known, taking a moment to study her guests.

Webb Taylor was seated in one of the forest-green chairs by the stone fireplace, legs crossed, a full glass of dark amber liquid in his hand. He was a husky man with chestnut-brown hair threaded with an abundance of gray at the temples. There were deep creases around his mouth and eyes.

Renee Taylor sat on one end of the sofa next to him, her hands folded in her lap. She was quite pretty, slender, with wheat-blonde hair piled high on her head. She wore a sea-green dress with a high ruffled neck and long straight sleeves that flared out at the wrists. Cady self-consciously ran her hands over her dress, feeling quite dowdy in the elegant woman's presence, and taking a deep breath, stepped into the room. With a nervous smile, she said, "Hello, I'm Cady Grayson."

Webb looked up and, placing his glass on a round table beside the chair, rose to his feet. His size made her pause. Not only was he burly but tall and looked as solid as a tree. But his smile was friendly, and his brown eyes were warmly lit like burnished wood, somehow at odds with his towering frame.

"I'm Webb Taylor," he said. "This is my wife, Renee."

Renee had also risen to her feet and, smoothing the fine material of her dress, moved toward Cady with a welcoming smile. Her eyes were blue and shone with friendliness.

"It's so very nice to meet you, my dear. We've been looking forward to your arrival. Isn't that right, Webb?"

"Yes, indeed," Webb agreed with a nod.

"Thank you, Mrs. Taylor. It's a pleasure to meet you both." She felt some of her trepidation diminishing.

"Please, my dear, you must call me Renee. And my husband—Webb."

"All right—Renee," she murmured, moving further into the room and over to the sofa. Renee resumed her seat. Maria entered the room carrying a tray with a colorful ceramic pot of coffee and three matching cups. She placed it on the table in front of Cady and after slanting her a reassuring smile left them alone.

"We didn't expect you for another couple of days," Webb commented as he settled himself in the chair and reached for his glass.

"We arrived early."

Renee laughed, a smooth tinkling sound. "I've never known the stage to be on time, much less early."

"I didn't take the stage."

Renee glanced at her in surprise. "Then how did you get here?"

"Cougar brought me," Cady said, pouring a cup of coffee for Renee. She carefully handed it to her, grimacing as her trembling hand caused some of the coffee to spill over the sides. She handed her a napkin.

Webb sat forward and opened his mouth to speak, but Renee placed her hand on his arm. She shook her head, throwing him a warning glance.

"I met him in Denver," Cady added as she poured herself a cup of coffee, unaware of the stir she was creating. She looked up and said, "My grandfather asked him to meet me there, before—" She stopped talking at the expression on Webb's face. "Is anything wrong?" she asked, unsettled by his frown.

"I can't believe your grandfather—"

"Webb, your glass is empty," Renee observed, stepping smoothly into his anger. "Cady, be a dear and pour Webb another whiskey."

"Of course," Cady said, jumping to her feet and taking Webb's empty glass to the sideboard. She heard Renee speaking softly behind her back.

"Now, Webb, there is no reason to get upset," she whispered, sounding more like she was talking to a child than to her husband. "No harm was done." She glanced back at Cady, who had turned and was watching them. "I'm afraid your grandfather and Webb didn't exactly see eye to eye on your escort."

"Why not?" Cady's stomach tensed with uneasiness. "I mean, he was a friend of my grandfather's…wasn't he?"

"Yes, he was," Renee answered, sounding as if the very idea was absurd. "But Webb, well, it's not something we like to talk about."

Cady glanced nervously at Webb and handed him the replenished glass. He accepted it without a word. "I'll admit that he could be frustrating at times, but he was kind." She moved back to the sofa and sat down, averting her gaze from Webb's incredulous expression.

Renee glanced at her sharply, taking in the rosy blush staining Cady's cheeks. Webb swore under his breath.

"Are you aware that I am executor of your grandfather's estate?" he asked, abruptly turning the subject.

"No, I wasn't." Her back stiffened and her heart began to pound. *Here it comes. He will now order me to leave.* She looked at Renee, who was watching her, a thoughtful expression on her face.

"Which means I have authority over you."

"No," Cady said. "You have authority over the estate, not me." She returned his stare, reminding herself he had no real power over her. If he threw her out, well, she would just find somewhere else to go. The problem was, she was running out of relatives. Her posture rigid, her chin tilted at a stubborn angle, she listened quietly as he continued his edict.

"Until you are twenty-one, you live here under my good graces. Mr. Doswell can explain everything to you," he finished with a wave of his hand.

Cady, struck speechless by his overbearing attitude, wanted to scream at him—at fate. She would *not* be under anyone's thumb again! She started to stand when Renee leaned forward and laid her hand lightly on Cady's wrist. "Is there anything you'd like to know?" she asked.

Cady pulled her stunned gaze from Webb's grim expression and turned to Renee. Seeing the kindness in her eyes, she relaxed and sat back against the cushions.

"Is it true Chas was murdered?"

"Yes," Renee replied with a sad shake of her head. "It was truly tragic."

"Do you know who did it? Or why?"

"No," Webb growled. "But the son-of-a-bitch will pay."

Maria bustled into the room just then, interrupting their discussion. "Will you be staying for lunch?" she asked, directing the question to Renee.

"No," Webb grumbled, rising to his feet, and slamming the half-empty glass on the table.

"No, thank you, Maria. We must get back to Fallen Tree." Renee rose, grasped Webb's arm, and turned back to Cady. "We will see you again soon. In the meantime, I suggest you talk with Mr. Doswell. He will fill you in on the details of Chas's will."

After they departed, Cady watched from the window as their buggy disappeared down the drive, her heart heavy. Webb did not like her. He had been friendly when she first entered the parlor, but his demeanor had changed during their conversation. Renee had remained kind but the tension in the room was tangible. What had gone wrong? Was it something she said? Or had the tone changed after she had mentioned Cougar?

Maria came back into the room. "Does Webb dislike Cougar?" Cady asked curiously. "Neither you nor Randy became upset when I mentioned his name, neither did Doc Flint, for that matter. But Webb nearly exploded when he learned Cougar had brought me here."

Maria began to clear away the empty cups. "I do not know, Señorita."

Cady eyed Maria's reticence with confusion. "How does Cougar know my grandfather?"

"Señor Chas loved his mother."

"Did she return the love?"

"Oh, *si,* very much. But something happened that

prevented them from being together."

"What?"

"Please, Señorita. I do not like to talk about those no longer living."

"But—"

"It all happened a long time ago. There were no bad feelings between them."

"Hmm," Cady murmured, disturbed by Maria's displeasure. She reminded herself that she was an outsider here and to alienate the woman would not help to remain welcomed. She sat down on the sofa, leaned back against the cushions, and stretched her injured leg out in front of her.

"Will you tell me about my grandfather?" Cady asked, seeking to change the subject but also out of genuine interest.

Maria's face brightened and the furrow between her brows disappeared. She joined Cady on the sofa. "He was a wonderful *patrón*. He was kind and generous and he loved life."

"He sounds like a wonderful man." Tears welled up at the thought that she'd lost him before really even knowing him.

Maria reached out and patted her hand. "Señor Chas was a fine man. We will all miss him very much." She pulled a handkerchief from her apron pocket and dabbed her own teary eyes. "Do not let Señor Webb upset you, he is a bitter man and carries demons on his back."

Cady, curious about that remark, waited for Maria to elaborate. When she didn't, Cady let it go thinking to address it later. "Where is my grandfather buried?"

"You want to visit him? The family cemetery is on the west side of the property. It is easy to find. His headstone has been ordered but you will find your grandmother's marker. Your grandfather is buried next to her." She rose to her feet. "Raul will saddle up that little chestnut mare for you."

Cady changed into a long blue-and-yellow skirt that had been altered for riding astride, and a blue cotton shirt, before heading for the stables. Raul had her horse saddled, and minutes later, she was jogging out of the yard. Once away from the hacienda, she kicked in her heels and galloped over the grassland, the sun warm on her face, the wind caressing her skin. She had a clear view of the mountains where the sun cast shadows on the peaks and valleys, their craggy tops still glazed with snow. The ride was exhilarating—the sun and fresh air successfully lifting her spirits.

She found the family cemetery nestled in a forest of tall piñon pines. The grass was dappled with shade where the sun wove its way through the tree branches. A ring of wild iris and yellow yucca flowers encircled the small cemetery. She dismounted and approached where her grandfather was interred. She knelt, bowed her head, and whispered a prayer. *How I wish I had known you!* If he were anything like her father, she knew she would have loved him, dearly. Tears rolled down her cheeks at the loss of what might have been. She glanced at her grandmother's headstone, weathered by time, and noted her dates of birth and death. Cady had never met Anna. Her grandmother died before she was born. Cady's parents, wishing to rest side by side for eternity, were buried in Louisville, her mother's birthplace.

Feeling a presence behind her, she stole a quick glance over her shoulder. Her breath caught in her throat. Cougar stood there silently watching her. She rose slowly to her feet and turned, drinking in the sight of him. It had only been a day, but she had missed him.

They shared a long look before she broke eye contact. She waved her hand toward the fresh mound of dirt. "I wish he were alive," she whispered, wiping away her tears.

Cougar nodded and, taking her hand, led her over to a small wrought iron bench nestled in the wild iris. He pressed her into it and knelt by her feet, watching her closely.

"You are no longer afraid of me."

"I'm sorry, I wasn't aware it showed." She shook her head. "But, no, I am no longer afraid." The hard lines around his mouth softened.

"How is your leg?" he asked, pushing her skirt up over her knee, and peering beneath the bandage, examined the snake bite. "Still swollen, but it's not nearly as colorful." He rested his hand on her knee, the contact sending electric shocks up her leg.

"Doc Flint looked at it," she murmured distractedly, becoming uncomfortably warm from his touch. She pushed her skirt down, forcing him to remove his hand.

He glanced up at her, a small smile curving his lips as if he knew what his touch had done. He chuckled and moved to sit beside her on the bench.

"Have you settled in?"

"Yes," she answered, scooting over to make room for him. Having not expected to see him again, after the way he had just deposited her on the front lawn and disappeared, she wasn't sure how to behave.

"Is there anything you want to talk about?"

"No, not really," she answered, wondering where he was going with his questions. "Why are you here?"

"To make sure you are all right. Chas would've wanted that," he said as if he had rehearsed the words. He reached for a lock of her hair that had escaped her braid and rubbed the silky strand between his fingers. The subtle fragrance of violets wafted to him, soft and sweet. With a muttered curse, he rose to his feet, and stepped back. Why *was* he here? She hadn't mentioned Chas's last wish. Had she not read the letter?

He turned and asked brusquely, "Is there anything you need?"

Yes—you. That thought was so unexpected, she blushed. "No, everyone has been more than kind." She looked up at him curiously ignoring the flutter in her stomach. "Why are you being so nice to me? I thought when you left me—"

"Because you're Chas's granddaughter," he answered succinctly and turned his gaze toward the mountains, an indiscernible look in his eyes.

"Yes, of course," she said hating herself for thinking it might be something more. When he turned, she glimpsed a flash of pain in his dark golden eyes. "You miss him."

"Yes. He was the only one—"

"What?"

He shook his head and headed toward his black-and-white mottled stallion.

"I met Webb and Renee Taylor. Do you know them?"

"Yes." He waited for her censure, certain they had enlightened her.

"I don't believe Webb likes you."

"That's an understatement."

"I don't understand."

"Forget it."

"But—"

"I said forget it. It doesn't concern you."

"Cougar…" She sagged against the bench, not a little confused.

"If there's nothing more you need—" He swung up on his horse, looked down at her as if memorizing her features, then wheeled the stallion around and disappeared into the trees.

He was gone before she could ask him to stay.

Chapter 9

Dawn lit the sky with morning glory. Bands of pink and orange streaked across the ice-blue sky, highlighting the clouds with bursts of color. Birds greeted the day, their melodious tunes mingling with the sound of men leaving the bunkhouses and heading out to the range.

Cady had decided it was high time she did a little sleuthing of her own. Her grandfather had been murdered and the culprit was still out there, free to strike again. First, she would find out who would want him dead and why. Second, if there had been any witnesses to the crime. She would start with the sheriff. Then, since she had not heard from her grandfather's lawyer, she would pay him a visit as well.

She had already been in her grandfather's study, where the shooting had occurred, but had been so overwhelmed with a sense of loss she had quickly left. She could feel his pain lingering in the room.

Cady donned her best dress, the blue linen, and, trying to imitate Renee's elaborate coiffure, she piled her hair on top of her head and pinned it in place. When finished, she glanced in the mirror and gasped in horror. Her hair resembled a bird's nest, perched precariously atop her head. With a sigh of exasperation, she crammed a blue-and-white bonnet on her head, trying in vain to cover the mess she had created.

Before going downstairs, Cady went into her

grandfather's bedroom. The windows were wide open, allowing the early morning breeze to blow in, sweetening the room with its dewy fragrance. The sun danced across the floor, sprinkling the gray carpet with beads of light. She trailed her fingers along the top of the oak bureau and stopped before the bed, staring at the large four-poster and envisioning her grandfather taking his last breath there, alone. She swallowed the lump of tears in her throat, filled with deep sorrow for what was never to be.

She turned to leave, pausing when something shimmering from beneath the bed caught her eye. She knelt, peered under the bed and reaching in, withdrew a ring—a heavy, wide gold band, a flat surface on top. On closer inspection, she could make out the image of an animal carved on the face of the ring. She turned it over in her hand, admiring the delicate etching, and wondered if it had held some special significance to her grandfather. She placed the ring on the bureau and thought to ask Maria about the mysterious piece of jewelry.

****

Carlos expertly tooled the buggy down the narrow, winding streets. The streets were lined with adobe houses with tiled roofs and shaded patios. They were set close together and boasted elaborately carved doorways, each one different in color and design. The town built around a central plaza, the large public square bordered by trees and lined with a multitude of shops. Among the shops were two banks, a hotel and, built at one end of the square, a large church, its tall white spire piercing the azure sky. The town was flanked by adobe-colored hills that shimmered in the sun, painting the entire area with a blush of rose.

"I shouldn't be long," Cady told Carlos when they pulled up in front of the sheriff's office.

"*Si*, Señorita, I will wait here," he said, assisting her from the buggy.

She climbed the two steps to the sidewalk and pushed open the door. The sheriff's office was small and airless and cluttered with furniture. The walls were papered with wanted posters, some yellowed by time, others not. The sheriff was seated behind a desk, smoking a pipe, a pile of papers at his elbow. He looked up when she entered and laid his pipe in a glass bowl on his desk.

"Sheriff Bosler?"

"Yes," he answered, gazing at her in curiosity. "What can I do for you?"

"I'm Cady Grayson. I'd like to talk to you about—"

"Of course, Chas's granddaughter. Heard tell you were in town." He rose to his feet and extended his hand. "Glad to make your acquaintance, ma'am."

"It's nice to meet you, Sheriff." He was portly, with a thick brown mustache that curved up and around his cheeks. Black suspenders held up his trousers, and his plaid shirt strained over his protruding belly. A shiny silver star was pinned to the front pocket.

"Have a seat, ma'am," he offered, waving his hand toward an empty chair in front of his desk. He waited for her to take a seat then sat back down, picked up his pipe, and leaned his chair against the wall.

"I'm truly sorry that you arrived under such wretched circumstances," he said before relighting his pipe. The smoke curled around his head and drifted in lazy gray ribbons toward the ceiling.

"What can you tell me about my grandfather's death?"

"Well, it was no accident. He was brutally shot in the head and lapsed into a coma. Sorry, ma'am," he added quickly, having noticed her pained expression. "Anyway, he never did come to. Died in his sleep."

"Do you know who killed him?"

"If I knew that, he'd be in there," he said with a jerk of his thumb over his shoulder toward a closed door in the back of his office.

"I'm sorry, Sheriff. I didn't mean to imply that you were remiss in your duties. It's just that—"

"It's all right, ma'am. I can understand your frustration. It's a damn shame. Chas Grayson was a decent man." He smiled in memory, fingering his mustache. "Helped me settle in when I first arrived back in '58."

"Do you have any clues?" she asked, bringing him back to the matter at hand.

"There is one thing," he said as he rose to his feet and headed over to a tall cabinet in one corner of the room. He opened the top drawer, reached in, and pulled out what looked to be a torn bandanna. "Found this on the ground outside the window. Where Chas was shot," he clarified. "Only trouble is, red's a common enough color around here. Plenty of men wear them. As a matter of fact, most do."

"I see," Cady said, staring intently at the bandanna. She wrinkled her nose in distaste. "What is that awful smell?"

"Cologne, I think." The sheriff sniffed the bandanna. "Cheap cologne." He replaced the pungent bandanna in the drawer and slammed it shut.

"We are following one lead. A man was seen riding away from the house. Got his description." He shook his head. "Course, nobody has seen him in a long time. He's real good at keeping a low profile. Used to live around these parts years ago, before the scandal, that is. Then all hell broke loose."

"Who?"

"Don't like to say, ma'am, not until I'm sure."

"Sheriff, we're talking about my grandfather's killer. Surely, I have a right to know."

"Begging your pardon, ma'am, but it's my policy not to tell tales until I'm sure of the facts." He patted her hand. "Leave it to me, Miss Grayson. We'll catch the son-of-a—"

"Sheriff! It's mornin'! You gotta let me outta here!" yelled a surly voice from behind the closed door. It was accompanied by the sound of metal clanging against metal.

"Sounds like Brody's sobered up. Brought him in last night drunk as—" He looked apologetically at Cady. "Sorry, ma'am. If you'll excuse me?"

Cady stood and shook his hand. "Thank you for your time, Sheriff."

"I'll let you know when I have positive proof. In the meantime, if there's anything I can do, you just let me know—anything at all." He opened the door that led to the cells and shouted, "Pipe down, Brody! I'm comin'!"

Cady stepped out into the bright sunshine, fighting her disappointment. She had hoped the sheriff would have more information. And what he did know he wouldn't share—which was utter nonsense. She had a right to know who he suspected, but apparently, he was a closemouthed sort of man.

"Carlos, will you please take me to Mr. Doswell's office?" she asked as she climbed into the buggy.

"*Sí*, Señorita." Carlos clicked to the horse and the buggy moved forward.

The lawyer's office was situated in a small, nondescript house a few streets off the plaza. Carlos waited in the buggy while Cady went up the front walk and knocked on the door. A short gray-haired woman appeared in the doorway.

"I'm looking for Mr. Doswell. Is he here?"

"Yes, ma'am. Please come in. I'll let him know you're here."

"Thank you."

"And you are?"

"Cady Grayson."

The woman showed her into a room off the narrow hallway. Cady perched on the edge of a small navy-blue sofa, placed her handbag beside her, and folded her hands in her lap. Her palms were damp, her throat dry, as she nervously waited to meet with the lawyer. To distract herself from the coming meeting, she looked around the room. It was brightly decorated in blue and white and seemed a bit flashy for a man of the law. She glanced up when a man materialized in the doorway.

"Miss Grayson? I'm Hank Doswell. It's nice to finally meet you."

"How do you do?" She grabbed her handbag and rose to her feet. Hank Doswell was thin and nearly bald, except for a few strands of brown hair he had carefully combed over his head in an attempt to give the illusion of more.

"Fine, fine. Please come with me." He led her down the narrow hallway to a room at the back of the house.

Cady stopped in the doorway and looked around in shock. Never had she seen such disarray. Paper was littered everywhere, scattered across the desk, stacked in piles on the floor and on every available chair cushion. The walls were paneled in wood and two of them were lined with shelves filled with dark leather tomes and even more stacks of paper. The room smelled of leather and stale cigar smoke.

Mr. Doswell waved her to a squat, maroon-upholstered chair, removing a stack of papers before she sat down and settled himself in a large tan leather chair behind his desk. He pulled a sheaf of papers from his satchel and placed them on the cluttered surface of his desk.

"I'm sorry I haven't been out to see you, Miss Grayson. You weren't expected for a few more days. I, ah, also wanted to get everything in order before we met."

"Yes, of course," she murmured, wondering if that was even possible.

"Well, now that you're here…" He settled his metal spectacles on the bridge of his nose and peered at her over the rims. "First of all, let me extend my condolences. Chas Grayson, gunned down in the prime of his life. Such a shame. Most unfortunate—"

"Thank you, Mr. Doswell."

"Yes, well…" He picked up a sheet of paper that had drifted to the floor. "He recently altered his will—just before he sent for you. You are aware that you are his only heir?"

"Yes, you stated that in your wire. But I'm not sure I understand. What about my father's older brother? Surely, the inheritance would go to him."

"Your Uncle Cal is dead."

"Oh, I didn't know." Cady reached for a lock of hair that had escaped her coiffured nest and absently twirled it around her finger as she waited for Mr. Doswell to continue. She didn't feel anything but mild disquiet for her uncle's death. As far as she could remember, she had never met the man.

"Now, Cal's wife is also dead," the lawyer continued. "But he does have a son and daughter still living. Now what are their names? Oh, yes, Wiley and Lucinda."

"Then won't his children want the property?"

"Maybe, but it's not theirs to have."

"It's not?"

"Your grandfather disinherited your Uncle Cal a long time ago, to include his wife and children. You see, Chas believed Cal was indirectly responsible for his mother's death, your grandmother."

"Why? What did he do?"

"I don't know the details. Whatever Chas suspected died with him. Naturally, it was not my place to discourage him from what he believed." The lawyer retrieved a cigar half hidden beneath a stack of papers, waited for Cady's permission, and bent to light it. "Cal was kicked out of the house and told never to return."

"Is that why I never lived with him after my parents' death?"

"I suppose so, yes. I understand your father didn't have any contact with his brother after Chas disowned him."

"How do you know all this?"

"I have been your grandfather's lawyer for many years. In addition to that, we were friends."

"But why would he leave his inheritance to me? I only met him once. And I was very young at the time."

"According to his will, upon his death, Chas Grayson instructed that his property, and all that it entails, be left to his second son—your father. In the event of Neil's death, it goes to his children—you." He searched through the sheaf of papers and pulled out several sheets bound together. "Of course, if something should happen to you, it reverts back to Cal's children." Mr. Doswell pulled on the cigar, then blew the smoke in a single stream toward the ceiling. "Until you turn twenty-one, Webb Taylor is executor of the estate."

"Yes, he's already made that perfectly clear. However, he seems to think he has authority over me as well."

The lawyer nodded. "To some extent, he does." He cleared his throat and leaned forward. "However, Chas added a codicil to his will that overrides Webb's authority, if adhered to, that is."

"May I see it?"

"Of course," he said, flipping through the papers. "It's not here," he mumbled to himself and then aloud, "I could have sworn I put it with these other papers."

"I'm sure you'll find it," Cady reassured him, looking at the mass of papers with a touch of skepticism. "Do you know what it said?"

"Yes—yes, of course. After all, I drew it up and witnessed it." He glanced at her and said simply, "He wanted you to marry."

"Marry?" Cady nearly shouted.

"Yes, in order for you to inherit the property."

Cady wanted to cry. To be foisted on yet another person was unthinkable. She had spent the last ten years of her life thrust upon people who didn't want her. She felt pain and looked down at her hands. She was clasping them so tightly they had turned white, her nails making half-moon indentations in the skin. She loosened her grip, took a deep breath, and looked up at the lawyer, determined to set him straight.

"Mr. Doswell, I will not be forced upon another person, especially in marriage."

"But, Miss Grayson, you have to!" He straightened his spectacles. "I know for a fact that Mr. Grayson did not want certain people to inherit his estate. Leaving everything to you, with the stipulation that you marry, was the only way he could ensure it would not fall into the wrong hands."

"Wrong hands? Like whose?"

"Well, for one, Wiley Grayson. Chas did not want him to get one dollar of his money. I remember when he came here several years ago berating Chas for disowning his father and demanding to be put back in the will." Mr. Doswell shook his head, clicking his tongue. "It was a horrible scene. Then a while back he returned to Santa Fe. It was after that visit, your grandfather added the codicil to his will. You either marry the man he's chosen or lose the inheritance. If you refuse, then it would revert to Wiley and Lucinda."

"Why, that's blackmail!"

"Why do you say that?"

"I either marry someone I don't know, much less love, or lose the inheritance to a man my grandfather despised?"

Mr. Doswell nodded. "Yes, I suppose you could look at it that way, but it was also for your own good."

"How so?"

"Because once married, you'd be safe."

Safe? From whom? "And just who is it I am supposed to marry?"

He suddenly looked very uncomfortable, tugging on his shirt collar as if it choked him. Then, removing his spectacles, he laid them on his desk. "That's just it. I can't remember."

She stared at him, wide-eyed in disbelief. "You can't remember? Do you mean to tell me that you signed an important legal document and can't remember the most important part?" Her voice was becoming louder with each word. "Why, that is absurd!"

He grimaced sheepishly. "I know. And, please, accept my apology. I'm not usually this disorganized."

Cady seriously doubted that. If he could find anything in this mess he called an office, it'd be a miracle. She calmed, and said quietly, "Mr. Doswell, perhaps you're mistaken."

He drew himself up like an offended peacock. "Miss Grayson, I am a lawyer. I am never mistaken!" Just then a knock sounded on the door. "Yes," he snapped, and the door opened. The gray-haired woman appeared in the doorway.

"Your next appointment is here, sir."

"Thank you, Pearl." He glanced at Cady. "I'm sorry, Miss Grayson. You'll have to excuse me. I'll let you know as soon as I locate the codicil. It's got to be around here somewhere." Cady could only nod, still stunned by the news. "In the meantime, follow Webb Taylor's advice," he continued, rising to his feet. "He and Chas were very close, you know, and he'll know what's best for you."

Cady bid the lawyer farewell and blindly made her

way outside. She climbed into the buggy, her emotions in turmoil, and barely noticed that Carlos had maneuvered the buggy onto the main thoroughfare and had stopped in front of the post office.

"I need to get the mail, Señorita. Will you be all right by yourself?" Carlos asked. "Señorita Cady?"

"Yes?" She turned to Carlos with a blank stare.

"You are pale. Did you get bad news?"

"No. I'm fine, Carlos."

He nodded and hopped out of the buggy. After watching him disappear into the building, Cady idly watched a stagecoach barrel down the street, the horses' hooves kicking up a cloud of dust. *Marry!* How could this be? She had been so sure that she'd finally be in control of her own life.

"Good afternoon, ma'am," a voice spoke from beside the buggy, startling Cady. She whirled around, lifting her hand to shield her eyes from the glaring sunlight, and eyed the stranger. He swept his hat from his head and smiled. His dark blond hair was slicked back and left to curl around his ears. He was tall and thin with a solid build, and dressed in black pants, a white ruffled shirt, and a black-and-gray-striped vest.

"You're new in town, aren't you?" he asked, peering at her with friendly curiosity, his blue eyes bright with interest.

"Yes, I am."

"Where do you live?"

"Ponderosa Pines."

"Of course. You must be Cady Grayson."

"Yes," she said, not that surprised. It seemed as if everyone in town knew who she was. "And you are?"

"Terence Taylor, ma'am. I own the Fallen Tree

Ranch outside of town."

"Webb Taylor's son?"

"That's right."

"I thought it was Webb's ranch."

"Well, yes, for now." Turning the topic, he said, "I understand he and Ma were out to meet you."

"Yes." She subdued a small frown.

"Webb upset you, did he?" Terence asked with a laugh.

"Well, yes. Is he always so, ah, forceful?"

"Sometimes, depending on the topic."

"And are you like him?"

"Heavens, no!" Terence said with a wide grin. He spied Carlos coming out of the post office with a bundle of mail. "May I call on you sometime?"

"I suppose so, yes." He seemed pleasant enough and perhaps would be a future friend and ally.

"*Hola*, Señor Terence. How are things at Fallen Tree?" Carlos asked as he approached the buggy.

"Fine—fine," Terence answered absently, his attention fully occupied with the indigo-eyed beauty. He slipped his hat on his head, tipped the brim, and stepped back as Carlos jumped into the buggy and gathered the reins.

"Good afternoon, Miss Grayson," Terence called out, watching the buggy disappear down the street before turning on his heel and whistling a gay tune, strode into the Buckhorn for a quick drink before setting out for home.

Chapter 10

Cady bounced along in the buggy as they headed toward the ranch, watching the countryside go by with blind eyes and a heavy heart. Why was she *again* being forced upon someone? Didn't anyone understand that she needed no one? That she could make it on her own? Of course, she could always refuse. She could leave and make her own way in the world. But how would she survive? She had no money nor skills to earn it.

No, she would stay and see this through. It wasn't so much that she coveted the inheritance, but her grandfather had loved her enough to bequeath it to her. It would be a slap in the face to turn her back on it. So, she would want for nothing, inheriting a fortune—a fortune that included the ranch, fifty thousand head of cattle, and a wealth of gold at the bank—provided she marry.

Cady took a deep breath of fresh air. She was becoming physically ill from her inner turmoil so decided to do nothing until she had seen this codicil. Mr. Doswell had to be wrong!

Carlos pulled the buggy to a stop in front of the hacienda. With a wave of thanks, she went into the house pulling off her bonnet as she made her way to the kitchen. It had quickly become one of her favorite rooms in the house. It was large, airy, and filled with the most enticing aromas. The upper walls were whitewashed, the lower walls covered with variegated tiles of cactus-green and adobe-brown, a natural extension of the vista visible through the large window that nearly covered one wall. The floor was stone slab. A large mahogany table was in the center of the room, a wood-burning stove on the opposite wall.

As Cady neared the kitchen, she heard women talking, punctuated with an occasional burst of laughter. She paused in the doorway and found Maria had company, a striking young woman with long, dark brown hair. She was dressed in a simple pink-and-white calico dress. A slight discoloration on her cheek marred her otherwise flawless complexion. When she spotted Cady, she jumped to her feet and rushed over, clasping her hands in hers.

"You must be Cady. I'm Cassie Taylor, Webb's daughter." Her chocolate-brown eyes were warm and friendly.

"It's nice to meet you, Cassie."

Both girls returned to the table, Cady taking a seat opposite Cassie, and brushing aside an errant lock of hair that had fallen over her forehead. She smiled at Maria, who placed a cup of coffee in front of her.

Cassie glanced at Cady's upswept hair, and the tresses that were not, and smiled knowingly. "Renee?"

Cady nodded, self-consciously smoothing it, to no avail.

"I tried it once. Couldn't master it, so didn't try again."

The two girls shared a laugh as another curl escaped the nest.

"I just met your brother, Terence."

"So now you've met us all!" Cassie took a sip of her

coffee. "I must admit, I was very curious to meet you. When I heard you had arrived, I wanted to rush right over, but Pa said I should wait until you had settled in." She leaned forward. "So, are you settled in?"

"I am," Cady said with a laugh, enjoying her guest's candor.

They both heard a faint whimper coming from underneath the table. Cady looked down and spied a straw-covered basket moving across the floor. She grabbed the handle and lifted it onto the table.

"Oh, your gift! I nearly forgot!" Cassie jumped up and ran around the table.

"I brought it for you—to keep you company," Cassie said, lifting the lid.

Cady cried out in delight when a small fuzzy head appeared, followed by a round furry body. The golden-haired puppy leapt from the basket and into her arms. She giggled as its small pink tongue darted out and licked her cheek. "Oh, how delightful!"

Maria rubbed the top of the puppy's head. "He is the color of *oro*."

"*Oro*?"

"Gold."

"Then that shall be his name," Cady declared, setting him on the floor. Oro ran around the kitchen, yapping in delight, his wet nose to the floor.

"He will be great company for me," she agreed. "Thank you, Cassie."

"So, how do you like our part of the country?"

"It certainly is beautiful. Wild and untamed," she said. "I think I will like it here."

"Oh, I know you will! It's just so wretched you didn't know your grandfather. He was such a wonderful man." She tilted her head. "You know, you look a little like him. Especially your eyes."

"*Si*, she does," Maria interjected with a smile. "And just as sweet."

Cady laughed and leaned back in her chair. "I'm afraid my aunt would disagree with you, Maria."

"We will all miss him." Cassie reached for a sweet molasses cookie from a pretty ceramic platter. "Pa says his death wasn't an accident."

Cady nodded her head and took a sip of her coffee as another tress escaped and slid down her back. "I just met with the sheriff to see what he's done about it."

"And what did he say?"

"Not much, I'm afraid. He is following one lead, but he wouldn't elaborate. A man was seen riding away from here the night Chas was shot."

"Do they know who it was?"

"He wouldn't tell me—until he was sure of his identity. But he has a description." Cady peered at Cassie over the rim of her cup. She had paled, her eyes as round as moons. "Cassie, what is it?"

"Nothing, nothing at all. I guess I'm still upset about your grandfather's death. Oh, dear, look at the time! I must be getting home!"

Before Cady could comment, Cassie jumped to her feet and was already halfway out the door when she turned back as if suddenly remembering something. "Pa wants you to come over tomorrow. Will you come?"

"I'd love to, thank you, but—"

"You'll have Randy bring you?"

"Of course."

With a wave of her hand, Cassie disappeared.

Cady turned to Maria in confusion, wondering what

had caused Cassie's strange behavior and abrupt departure. "What was that all about?"

Maria pulled two golden-brown loaves of bread from the oven and placed them on the table. "I do not know, Señorita. Perhaps she is still upset about the *patrón*'s death. They spent time together." She reached for a knife. "She is a sweet girl. She will be a good friend." She looked up at Cady with a smile. "She has a crush on Randy."

"Ah, so that's why she asked!" Cady exclaimed. "Then I will be sure to bring him with me to Fallen Tree." She watched Maria bustle around the kitchen, keeping a watchful eye on her puppy as it staked out its new territory. Her thoughts turned inward and the distressing news she had heard from Mr. Doswell. *How can I sit and wait for that disorganized lawyer to locate the codicil in that mess he calls an office? I'll go mad first.*

****

Night had fallen and with it the warm temperature of day. Moonbeams illuminated a man sprawled beneath a tree. He began to stir, groaning loudly as he came fully awake. His temples throbbed, the pain making him nauseous. He struggled to sit up, rubbing the back of his neck, shivering as the chilly night air penetrated his clothing. He glanced around in a daze, wondering where he was and how he had come to be here.

Suddenly, he scrambled to his knees and began to frantically pat the ground around him. It was gone! He sat back on his heels and rubbed his eyes, engulfed in a cold sweat. Governor Thornwilde would be livid when he learned he had lost it. The governor's words echoed in his head. *If it falls into the wrong hands, there will be hell to pay.* But wait! Chas Grayson was dead! Perhaps he wouldn't have to start looking for other employment just yet. Perhaps the governor would forgive him for losing his satchel since the man he was supposed to deliver the envelope to was no longer alive.

Williams rose unsteadily to his feet and looked around for his horse. It, too, was gone. With a heavy sigh, and ignoring the pain knifing through his head, he started to walk. Not knowing where he was nor the way back to town, he could only hope he would eventually come across a ranch house.

He collected his thoughts as he ambled in the dark, piecing together the events preceding his waking in the cold night. He remembered stopping for a drink at the local saloon after arriving in town and, after quenching his thirst, had sidled up to two fair-haired ranchers who leaned against the long wooden bar talking together. He waited until he had gained their attention, then asked, "Can you tell me where I might find Ponderosa Pines? Chas Grayson's place?"

"Why?" The taller of the two asked, sipping his whiskey and looking at Williams with narrowed eyes.

Williams clutched his satchel tighter to his chest. "I have an important missive for Mr. Grayson. From Colorado," he added, becoming intimidated by the man's unrelenting stare.

"Chas Grayson is dead."

"Oh, dear." Williams thought about this for a moment then shrugged. "Well, it should be delivered nonetheless."

The rancher drained the last of his whiskey and flipped a coin to the barkeep. "I'd show you myself, but I have an appointment in town."

"I can show you where it is," the other one offered.

"I need to get home anyway. So long," he called out to his friend and motioned for Williams to follow him from the saloon.

And that was the last thing Williams remembered— the stranger from the saloon pointing him in the direction of Ponderosa Pines, then riding off in the opposite direction. A little while later, when he had stopped to relieve himself, Williams had been set upon from behind and knocked unconscious.

As Williams wandered aimlessly in the dark, the moon arced toward the horizon as the sun began its ascent, swallowing the stars in its wake.

Chapter 11

Cady laid the book on her lap, disillusioned. *It was too much.* Oh, at one time she had wished for a strong, fine-looking man to rescue her from her wicked relatives, carry her off on his great white steed to somewhere she'd be forever loved. She scoffed. Even if it did come to be, he'd just abandon her like everyone else in her life. Cynical, perhaps, but true, nonetheless.

The sound of excited voices pulled Cady from her musings. She leapt from the bed, rushed across the room to the corner window and looked down at the corral. The large dirt enclosure, surrounded by a split-rail fence made of thick wooden stakes and poles, was the center of the action. Several men hung on the fence, their feet resting on the bottom rung, avidly watching the activity in the corral and shouting encouragement.

Curious, Cady leaned out the window to better see what had captured their attention. She saw a tall man circling a large white mustang, swinging a long length of rope above his head, one end of which was fashioned into a noose. He wore black pants and a black shirt, the sleeves rolled past his elbows revealing tanned, muscular forearms, black boots and a wide-brimmed hat that obscured his face. The only splash of color was a red bandanna knotted loosely around his neck. Cady's stomach clenched in excitement, having caught the men's fevered enthusiasm as the cowboy tried to capture the wild horse.

She watched, her heart in her throat, as he succeeded in roping the bucking and kicking horse and managed to lead it over to a post. He quickly secured the rope, then yanked the bandanna from around his neck and attempted to blindfold the mustang, jerking his arm away when it tried to bite him. When he had accomplished that feat, another man crept forward and threw a saddle over its back, quickly strapping it into place and cinching up the girth, all while avoiding its flailing hooves. He moved away as the man in black swung up into the saddle. He pulled the blindfold from around the horse's eyes as a third man untied the rope from the post, setting the mustang free.

The horse snorted and began to buck wildly, its hooves kicking up clumps of dirt as it tried to rid itself of the unwanted weight upon its back. The rider yanked on the reins, jerking the horse's head up, and quickly wound the leather straps around the saddle horn. He took a firm grip on the saddle and began the long struggle of breaking the wild beast's will. Using his spurs, the rider prompted the horse to behave and obey his commands.

Cady unconsciously twisted a lock of hair around her finger, admiring the horse breaker as he maneuvered the wildly bucking mustang. She felt unusually giddy, awed at the power struggle between man and beast, muscles of both straining at the task.

A triumphant snort rang out as the mustang succeeded in unseating the rider. With a grunt, the man went limp and hit the dirt ground, rolling to escape its hooves. His hat landed with a splash in the water trough.

When he lay motionless on the ground, Cady thought for sure he was dead. She released her breath when at last he sat up, shook his head, and climbed to his feet. He slapped the dust from his pants and accepted his wet hat from one of the other cowboys.

When he turned toward the house, Cady's heart plummeted to her stomach. She gripped the windowsill so tightly her knuckles turned white. *Cougar!* She took a deep breath, smoothed her hair, and ran from the room, down the stairs and out the back door. When she reached the corral, Cougar was nowhere to be seen. Disappointment washed over her in waves.

She turned from the corral and strolled into the stables. It was littered with saddles, bridles, and a variety of equestrian gear. Fleece saddle blankets were folded in one corner and shiny stirrups hung from hooks on the walls. The hayloft was filled with sweet-smelling hay. Inhaling the fragrant aroma, she moved down the passageway, passing the row of stalls. She stopped in front of the last stall where she heard the soft sounds of munching. She peeked in and saw a golden-colored horse with ivory mane and tail, its muzzle buried in a bucket of oats. The floor of the stall was covered with straw and a door cut in half, the top half open, separated it from the passageway. Cady leaned over the half-door, admiring the Palomino.

She whistled. The horse looked up, nickered softly, and returned to the bucket of oats. She whistled again and smiled when it abandoned its snack and wandered over. She reached out and rubbed its velvet muzzle, laughing out loud when it nudged her hand looking for a treat.

"Good afternoon, Cady," a familiar voice drawled from behind and she nearly jumped out of her skin. The blood rushed to her head and her knees buckled. She grabbed the door for support before turning to face him.

"Cougar! What are you doing here?"

"Horse breaking."

"Yes, I saw you. It looked dangerous."

"It is if you don't know what you're doing." He leaned his shoulder against the wall opposite the stall. "You're looking well," he drawled, chewing on a piece of straw.

"Thank you," she answered distractedly. He was staring at her so intently, his eyes glowing with inner fire, she wondered frantically if she was naked.

"And your leg?"

"Doc Flint said it's nearly healed."

"That's good to hear. And how are things here?"

"Fine." She took a step back from his heated gaze, now centered on her mouth. "Did Chas want you to continue horse breaking?"

Cougar nodded and moved toward her but hesitated, his eyes darkening. Then apparently coming to a decision, he reached out and pulled her into his arms. His mouth captured hers in a fierce kiss—hard, almost punishing in its intensity, in its passion.

Cady found it exciting. She pressed up against him, fired with longing. She looped her arms around his neck and stood on her toes, her mouth clinging to his. She lost herself in his touch, as his hands caressed her body, the smell of horses and hay mingled with his own manly scent nearly driving her wild. A slow heat began to burn, and she leaned into him, kissing him with heated enthusiasm.

Without warning, he stopped and pulled away. With a muttered curse, he slipped her arms from around his neck, opened his mouth as if to speak, but closed it instead.

"Why do you always do that?" she demanded breathlessly, dazed by his kisses.

"Do what?"

"This!" She waved her hand. "Kiss me. Stop. Disappear." He didn't answer. With a shake of his head, he spun on his heel and strode from the stables.

"You're doing it again!" she shouted at his retreating back. She fell back against the stall door and covered her mouth with her hand. Her body felt as limp as a cloth just wrung of moisture. Why did he keep drifting in and out of her life? Had Chas asked him to look out for her? The thought had merit—he did keep popping up out of nowhere. But had Chas's wishes included kissing her until her senses reeled and her body ached with want? *I think not. But I must be getting better at kissing—he keeps coming back for more.*

She felt a nudge against her shoulder. The Palomino was staring at her with soulful black eyes. She reached out and stroked its velvet muzzle. "What am I going to do with him?" she whispered to the horse. "I don't seek out his bold advances, yet he makes me quake like a leaf in the wind, leaving me wanting more." She shook her head, unsettled by her strange fascination with him. "I know nothing about him except what he claims to be—a friend of my grandfather's. I know there is more. But what?" She had no answer for that and, oddly enough, neither did the Palomino.

She headed back to the hacienda, berating herself. She had to stop thinking about Cougar. He would never be a part of her life. She had to marry someone else. She stopped in her tracks. Was it Cougar? Her heart did a little flip. Could he be the one her grandfather had stipulated she wed? After all, he had trusted him enough to send him to Denver for her. But, if so, why hadn't he said something?

She continued walking, quickly dismissing the thought. She wasn't entirely sure she'd want to marry him. He was a chameleon, with his unpredictable mood changes, and she didn't understand his habit of appearing and disappearing, leaving her world spinning out of control.

I think my life with him would be a never-ending match of wits—in between kisses.

Chapter 12

Cady was nervous. She had no idea what to expect nor how she would be received. Her first meeting with Webb Taylor had ended badly. But since he had invited her to his home, he couldn't be that angry, could he? Renee had been pleasant enough with her warm smile and kind eyes. She had calmed Cady's uneasiness when Webb had gotten so angry. Cassie would be there, too, and possibly even Terence. She liked Terence. He was handsome and agreeable and, more importantly, he didn't play havoc with her emotions like a certain other man did—constantly.

Cady crossed to the wardrobe and stared at the dozens of outfits Maria's sister, Carmen, a seamstress by trade, had spent hours creating. Gone were the pitiful clothes she had arrived with, in their stead was a vast array of colorful, fashionable clothing suitable for her age and circumstance. She chose a chocolate-brown, flowing skirt and a golden-yellow blouse with short, capped sleeves and a square, ruffled neckline. She fussed nervously with her hair and, not wanting a repeat of the disastrous bird's nest, she simply pulled it off her face and secured it with a handful of pins and a red ribbon, leaving a few silky tendrils to frame her face.

She grabbed a red-and-yellow shawl and raced down the stairs and out the back door to the stables. Randy was standing by the corral talking with several of the hands who had just returned from the range. He turned to greet her with a smile as she hurried across the lawn toward him.

"Miss Grayson," Randy said, tipping his hat. "I'll be right with you."

"Certainly, take your time." She nodded to the other men and crossed over to the corral to wait. Staring into the dirt enclosure, she saw again the image of Cougar atop the mustang, his powerful muscles straining with his efforts to tame the wild animal. She blushed from the memory. At a touch on her shoulder, she spun on her heel.

"Are you ready to go?" Randy peered at her with concern. "Are you all right? I mean, you look a bit flushed."

"Yes, yes, I'm fine," she murmured, embarrassed by his astute observation. She waved her hand toward the sleek golden-colored Palomino prancing around the corral. "She's a beautiful horse. Who does she belong to?"

"She's yours."

"Mine?"

Randy nodded. "Mr. Grayson picked her out especially for you. He thought you would like her."

"Oh, I do! I saw her in the stables earlier," she said, admiring its graceful lines as it loped toward her. The mare nickered and nuzzled her hand looking for a treat. She accepted a cube of sugar from Randy and fed it to her horse. "What's her name?"

"Dream."

"How wonderful! I can't wait to ride her!"

Randy smiled at her enthusiasm, then noted the time. "We'd best get a move on." He assisted her into the one-horse buggy, jumped in beside her and gathered up the reins. Turning out of the yard, they headed toward Fallen Tree.

Cassie was waiting for them on the front porch, dressed in a blue-and-white gingham dress with a long full skirt, and a blue shawl draped around her shoulders. Her hands were folded in front of her, and she wore a big smile. The discoloration on her cheek had dissipated to a pale-yellow patch.

"Hello, Cassie!" Randy called out as he helped Cady from the buggy.

"Randy," she rejoined shyly then glanced at Cady. "Welcome to Fallen Tree, Cady." Her gaze slid back to Randy as they ascended the front steps.

"Thank you," Cady said, waiting patiently for Cassie to welcome them in, taking note of the rosy blush tinting her cheeks.

Cassie, remembering her manners, stepped aside to allow them entry. "Please, do come in," she said, waving them into the house. Randy stepped back and allowed Cady to enter first. Cady caught the glance they shared before Cassie led them into the parlor.

Cady took a moment to admire the room. Done in shades of blue and gold, it held an air of coziness. Webb sat in one of two blue-and-gold striped overstuffed chairs placed on either side of a large picture window. A dark-blue sofa lined one wall, and two high-backed gold-and-white tapestried chairs were by the large stone hearth. He looked up when they entered the room and set his glass on a table. He stood, nodded to Randy and grasped Cady's hand. His smile was friendly.

"Cady, it's good to see you again. Renee will be along shortly. Terence is out in the south pasture checking on the cattle, but he'll be back soon. I understand you met him in town."

"Yes, I did." Cady took a seat next to Cassie on the sofa berating herself for her fanciful worries. Webb didn't seem at all angry. In fact, he was quite cordial. He sat back down while Randy settled himself in one of the high-backed chairs near the hearth. Just then, Renee strolled into the room. She was fashionably dressed in a stunning cranberry-red dress with a square neckline, short sleeves, and a small bustle supporting the back of the skirt. Her hair was piled elegantly on top of her head.

"Hello, Cady, Randy." She waved Cassie aside and took her place on the sofa next to Cady. Without a word, Cassie moved to the other chair next to Randy.

An old man, dressed entirely in black, shuffled into the room. He was stoop-shouldered, his bulbous nose the same color as his bald pink head. He placed a tray of refreshments on the low table in front of the sofa.

"Ah, Ebbitt, thank you," Renee murmured with a warm smile for the old man. "Ebbitt came with me when I moved here from Boston," she explained, pouring whiskey for Randy and red wine for the women. She passed Cady a plate of deep-fried triangles of bread drizzled with honey.

"And when was that?" Cady asked, reaching for one of the sweets.

"I moved here after Belle died. Webb, however, came out with your grandfather." Renee nodded encouragingly at Webb, leaned back, and took a sip of her wine.

"We were just young pups then," Webb said with a chuckle. "Chas and Anna, Belle and me." He sighed and a faraway look came into his eyes. "We built our ranches from the ground up. Nothing but Indians and empty grassland when we arrived." He lapsed into a detailed accounting of their trip west and soon he and Renee took turns regaling Cady with an amusing story or two about life in Santa Fe. Cady enjoyed the lively conversation and found herself relaxing. She noticed that Cassie and Randy were having trouble keeping their eyes off each other and they both wore silly grins. How she longed for a man to look at her like that! Like she was the most important person in the world—*not* his next meal.

"Can you shoot a gun?" Webb inquired, startling Cady from her thoughts.

"No," she replied, her hand landing on her chest. "Why?"

"Now, Webb, do you really think that's necessary?" Renee asked, her brows pulled down in a frown.

"It's important to know how to protect yourself," Webb insisted, refilling his glass from the decanter of whiskey.

"She should at least know the basics, don't you think?" Randy asked, agreeing with Webb.

"Fine," Renee said with a sigh. "Although, it certainly isn't very ladylike."

"Neither is getting shot," Webb muttered into his glass.

Renee ignored his remark and waved her hand through the air. "Then by all means…"

Having heard many stories about the turbulent West, Cady felt certain she would feel safer if she knew how to protect herself properly. She grinned, imagining her Aunt Mildred's reaction if she were to amble into her parlor, a gun slung low on her hips.

"Did you meet with Mr. Doswell?" asked Webb,

bringing her back to the present.

"Yes. He told me that you are indeed executor of my grandfather's estate until I turn twenty-one." Webb gave her an arrogant nod. "But that he also wrote a codicil to his will."

"Codicil? I don't know about any codicil!"

"I have to marry in order to inherit his property."

Webb narrowed his eyes and snapped, "Where did you get a fool idea like that?"

"From Mr. Doswell. He told me that Chas had written it just before he died—when he sent for me."

"I'll get to the bottom of this."

"No, *I* will." Cady said with a frown, not liking his attitude at all.

"Just who are you supposed to marry?"

"I don't know. Mr. Doswell couldn't find the codicil while I was in his office."

"Didn't he remember what it said?" Renee asked.

"No."

"No?" Webb repeated in disbelief. "Well, can't say I'm not surprised, with that mess of an office. I often wondered why Chas kept him around."

"You know, at one time Webb and Chas talked about you and Terence marrying," Renee offered, lifting an elegant brow. "Perhaps that's what this is all about. A merging of our ranches."

"Could be," agreed Webb, taking a sip of his whiskey.

"I don't think so. Chas didn't much—" Cassie, quelled by Renee's disapproving look, sputtered to a stop.

"Ah, Terence, here you are!" Renee watched her son stride into the parlor. He smiled, his glance taking in the gathered group, and headed straight for Cady.

"We meet again," he said, grasping her hand and giving it a slight squeeze. He turned to acknowledge the others in the room before pouring himself a whiskey and sinking into the chair next to Webb. He sighed, stretched his long legs out in front of him and leaned back into the soft cushions.

"Everything all right in the south pasture?"

"Yep. I left Red to round up a few strays." He sipped his whiskey, peering at Webb over the rim of his glass. "I spotted Austin in town," he said, dropping his gaze to study the dark amber liquid in his glass.

"So? Ain't no business of mine."

"Just thought you'd want to know."

"I don't."

"Pa, you're entirely wrong about him," Cassie declared, a stubborn tilt to her chin.

Webb stared at his daughter as if she had lost her mind. "How can you defend that damned half—"

"Pa…" Cassie pleaded with an embarrassed glance at Cady.

Webb yielded to his daughter and clamped his mouth shut. He turned to stare out the window, a frown settling between his brows.

An uneasy silence fell over the room. Cady glanced at Webb. Whoever this Austin was, the mere mention of his name had him seething just below the surface.

"I think we should avoid any distressing topics. After all, we have guests," Renee suggested smoothly, looking pointedly at her son. Cady followed her gaze and found Terence hiding a smile behind his glass.

"Ma would be very disappointed in you," Cassie muttered.

"Cassie, that's enough," Renee admonished with a shake of her head.

"Don't you dare bring up your ma. She has nothing to do with this," Webb spat out between gritted teeth.

"Who's Austin?" Cady asked, curiosity winning out over trepidation of Webb's mood.

"Chas liked him," insisted Cassie, pulling Webb's attention back to her, who had ignored Cady's question.

"Chas was so starry-eyed over Rose he couldn't see straight," Webb said with a derisive snort.

"Who's Rose?" Cady asked, curiosity most definitely winning out over trepidation.

Webb's hand sliced through the air. "She has nothing to do with this either."

"But—"

"You don't know the first thing about it," he said, tossing back his whiskey.

Cady looked over at Cassie who was staring at her father, her chin set at a stubborn angle.

"Who's Austin?" Cady asked again, observing the faces around her. How could one man elicit such a host of emotions?

Cassie turned to Cady. "He is my—"

"Cassie…" Renee warned, reaching out and curling her fingers around Cassie's wrist. "You're upsetting your father."

"I don't like the way he…" Her words trailed off and she flinched in pain.

"Enough!" Webb's booming voice rattled the glasses on the sideboard. "He is no relation to us! Understand? The subject is closed!" He glowered at his daughter.

Cassie pulled her arm free from Renee's grasp,

jumped from her chair, and rushed from the room, one hand covering her mouth, tears spilling down her cheeks. With a concerned frown, Randy leapt to his feet and took off after her. The thunderous expression on Webb's face scared Cady into silence and she clasped her hands in her lap to keep them from trembling.

Renee rose to her feet. "Will you walk with me?" she asked Cady, taking her lightly by the hand. She led her out into a pretty little courtyard and sat down on a small wrought iron bench. She patted the empty space next to her in invitation, brushing aside her skirt.

"I can see you are confused by that distasteful scene in the parlor. I'm afraid Cassie wasn't on her best behavior. She has the uncanny ability to cause dissension between herself and her father."

Cady thought that remark odd since it was Terence who had opened the subject and started the argument. She kept silent, though, curious to hear what Renee had to say.

"If I may, I would like to explain." She took a deep breath. "You see, at one time Austin lived here with Webb and Cassie—when Belle was alive. Belle was my sister, you see, and after she died, Terence and I came to Fallen Tree. I had recently lost my husband and had no reason to remain in Boston. Webb was the only family I had left. Except for Terence, of course. Webb had already sunk into deep despair, and it seemed the only company he craved was a bottle of whiskey. He doesn't drink nearly as much as he did. I like to think I brought him back to life," she added with a small smile. "It was not easy, of course. He loved Belle so much. But ultimately, we fell in love, perhaps out of loneliness and shared grief. It seemed only natural that we marry."

She hesitated as if gathering her courage to continue. "One night, Austin—how shall I put it?" she shuddered delicately. "Attacked me," she said simply, nodding when Cady gasped. "I remember it well. It was a very hot night, and I was having trouble sleeping, so I decided to come out here for a stroll," she said, indicating the courtyard with a wave of her hand. "Austin was waiting in the shadows. You see, he fancied himself in love with me," she said, patting her blonde upswept hair with a perfectly manicured hand.

"He declared his love and tried to kiss me. I, of course, rebuffed his advances. He became quite angry and jumped on me, pressing his mouth to mine, and ripping my nightdress down the front. I screamed, to no avail. When I thought all hope was lost, Webb strode into the courtyard. I didn't say anything, of course. I didn't want Webb to know his son had attacked me."

"His son? Austin is his son?" Cady interjected incredulously.

"Well, not exactly, but he raised him as his own."

"Hmm," Cady murmured, trying to take in everything she had just heard.

"Even in his inebriated state, it was obvious to Webb what had happened." Renee glanced at Cady and noted with satisfaction that she was duly horrified. "Webb had him horsewhipped and banned from the ranch." She gave another delicate shudder. "It was all so horrible! You can understand now why Webb becomes furious at the mere mention of Austin Taylor."

"Of course," Cady agreed with a nod, stunned at her story.

"He vowed to get his revenge."

"You don't suppose—"

"What?"

"Could he have killed my—"

"I hate to say it, but yes. Austin knew how close Webb and Chas were. I think it's entirely possible he killed your grandfather out of revenge. I wouldn't put anything past him." She rose gracefully to her feet. "Now, shall we join the others?" she asked as if she had already set the distasteful memory aside. She slipped Cady's arm through hers as they strolled back into the house.

The tension in the parlor was thick. Webb and Terence sat quietly together, sipping their whiskey, each lost in their own thoughts. Cassie was conspicuously absent, as was Randy. Cady knew the visit had come to an end. "I think it best I get home."

"I trust we will see you soon," Renee said, placing a kiss on Cady's cheek. "In fact, I was thinking of having a party in your honor. Would you like that?"

"Yes, of course. Thank you, Renee, for everything." Cady looked at Webb. He nodded once and turned back to contemplate his drink.

Terence escorted Cady outside where Randy waited beside the buggy. She turned to Terence. "Will you please tell Cassie I hope to see her soon?"

"Of course. I hope that includes me, too."

"Certainly." Cady smiled. "Goodbye, Terence."

The horse kicked up a cloud of dust as it jogged down the drive. Renee's story replayed itself in her mind. What a horrid man! And if this Austin had killed her grandfather, she would see him hanged!

"What have we here?" Randy said, pulling Cady from her thoughts. She glanced around, noticed they had crossed into Grayson land, and followed his gaze to a man standing beside a horse, waving them down. Randy tooled the buggy beneath a stand of pine trees and, pulling on the reins, called out to the stranger, "What's the problem, mister?"

"Horse has gone lame. Must have picked up a stone." He reached down, lifted the horse's leg, and examined the bottom of its hoof. "Yep, there it is."

Randy jumped down from the buggy and peered over the man's shoulder. "In there pretty good?" At the man's nod, he offered, "Can I give you a lift somewhere?"

Cady had stayed in the buggy under the cool shade of the trees. She saw the stranger straighten, and in a move too fast for her to follow, he lifted his hand and brought his gun down on the back of Randy's head. Cady watched in disbelief as her foreman crumbled to the ground. Before she could react, a man jumped from a tree branch, a bandanna pulled over the bottom half of his face, startling Cady into action. She fumbled with the reins as he rushed toward her, his gun drawn.

"Hold it, lady," he said, his voice muffled by the bandanna.

Cady swallowed around the lump of fear in her throat, the reins slipping from her numb fingers. She saw the other man drag an unconscious Randy behind a tree and quickly tie him up.

"Get outta the buggy. You're comin' with us," the masked man ordered, his pistol trained on her chest. Her heart sank to her stomach. She had no choice but to obey. As soon as her feet touched the ground, she was spun around, her hands bound tightly behind her back, and a blindfold tied around her eyes. She struggled against the bindings until she felt the barrel of his gun stuck in her ribs.

"Quiet, missy," he hissed in her ear. "You about ready?" he called out to his cohort. "Somone might come along."

"Yep," came the answer, "all set."

Cady felt herself picked up and tossed onto the back of a horse. She was quickly joined by one of the men, who mounted behind her and wrapped his arm around her waist, keeping her in the saddle. He smelled—the odor tickling her memory, but in her present state of panic she was unable to place it.

She had no idea how long or how far they rode. Yet with each passing minute, her anxiety grew. Who were these men? What did they want? And poor Randy—left bound and unconscious. She prayed he was not seriously injured and that someone would find him and realize she had been taken.

The sun beat down on her, beads of sweat merging with the river of fear trickling between her breasts. Feeling the sun's warmth on her legs, she cringed, realizing her skirt must have twisted up around her knees, baring her legs. With her hands bound behind her, she was unable to lessen her humiliation and pull the skirt down.

With each step, she was jolted against the man mounted behind her. The first time, she stiffened and lurched forward, but his arm wrapped around her waist tightened painfully, keeping her in place.

Cady was close to her breaking point when, at last, the horse slowed to a stop. She felt the man dismount before she was dragged off the horse. She was shoved forward, and she stumbled, her legs long ago having gone numb. Pushed again, she began to walk haltingly forward with a sense of vertigo from the blindfold and the unsettling feeling of colliding into something. Her hands bound behind her back made her unsteady, and when she stumbled again, someone grabbed her arm and with a muttered curse dragged her forward and up two steps.

The heat of the sun disappeared, and she assumed she was no longer outside. She felt someone fumbling with the bonds around her wrists, and when freed, she was shoved roughly from behind. She lurched forward, automatically reaching for the debilitating blindfold around her eyes. She whirled around as the door slammed shut. She heard the click of a latch being bolted from the other side.

Cady rubbed her sore wrists and looked around her prison. A small window streaked with dirt allowed very little sunlight to filter into the room. The room itself was small and musty, the only furniture a narrow cot, covered with a thin blanket, and the small square table beside it. She tried to pry open the window, but it was sealed shut. She moved over to the cot and sat down, dropping her face into her hands with a sob.

She lifted her head at the sound of muffled voices. She raced to the door and pressed her ear against it, squeezing her eyes shut, straining to hear their words. She couldn't hear them all, but bits and pieces of their conversation were audible, bringing a renewed sense of terror.

"You can't just kill her!"

"Why not? I didn't get rid of the old man for nothin'."

"But—"

"The bitch is in the way. She has got to go…"

The voices trailed away as if they had walked outside. Cady slid to the floor and leaned her back against the door. She had heard enough to feel the sharp bite of fear. *Who would want me dead? And the old man they got rid of—was it Grandfather?* She drew her legs up, hugged her knees, and started to shake uncontrollably. After a time, she brushed her hair off her face, most of the pins having lost their hold long ago, and dragged herself to the cot. She lay down, pushed the filthy blanket aside, and stared at the ceiling, too exhausted to figure a way out of this mess. As the sun set, the room darkened and filled with shadows. Cady waited for her captors to return—and kill her.

Chapter 13

Cady opened her eyes. The room was cast in shadows, any moonlight thwarted by the dirt-covered window. She scrambled to her feet and stumbled to the door. It was locked. Did she honestly think to find it any other way? She slid to the floor and held her head in her hands. As her mind raced with possible ways out of her bleak situation, she threaded her fingers through her hair. Her eyes widened and she yanked one of the last remaining pins from the tangled tresses.

She located the doorknob and stuck the tip of the pin into the lock. She wiggled it back and forth until she heard a clicking sound as it unbolted. She eased the door open, flinching when it creaked in protest, the sound startlingly loud in the dark, quiet cabin. She cocked her head to one side, listening, and cautiously made her way to the door. Luck rode with her—she was alone. She crept outside and found dawn just a breath away, the sun barely beginning to lighten the dark indigo sky.

She picked up her skirt and ran, wanting to get far away from the cabin before the kidnappers returned. She slowed her pace only after it became apparent that no one was giving chase.

The sun was now suspended above the horizon, and still she walked. She had no sense of direction and prayed she was headed toward Ponderosa Pines. At the sound of someone approaching, she glanced over her shoulder in alarm, poised to run, and breathed a huge sigh of relief, recognizing the man atop the large black-and-white stallion. *Cougar.*

Even with the distance separating them, she could make out his grim expression. He reined up before her and slid from the stallion, the steed's hooves pawing the air. He clasped her shoulders, his fingers unconsciously digging into her skin.

"Are you all right?"

"Yes," she said, suppressing the urge to fall into his arms. No matter, he pulled her in and held her tight. After a moment, he loosened his grip and stepped back.

"Come on," he ordered, his voice gruff. His countenance was still stern but the hard lines around his mouth had softened. Swinging up on his stallion and lifting Cady into his arms, he placed her in front of him to straddle a fleece blanket while he grabbed the reins and wheeled the horse around.

"Cougar, how did you—"

"Later," he said. "We'll talk later."

Cady rode pressed up against his body, encircled by his strong muscular arms. His body heat burned through her blouse, igniting a slow flame. Her senses heightened by his nearness, she was filled with an excitement so intense it made her lightheaded. She tried to pull away, but he merely hauled her back against him with a whispered command to sit still. She suffered in silence.

After a few more minutes of quiet riding had passed, she felt something stir against her buttocks. She glanced over her shoulder, puzzled, and became further perplexed by Cougar's lopsided grin. It finally dawned on her just what was nudging her, and she gasped, mortified. She whirled around, face hot with embarrassment, and tried desperately to think about anything but the man straddled behind her and what he must be thinking.

They rode for several hours, neither saying a word, as the sun rose steadily in the sky. Cougar turned his horse through an opening in the mountains, the trail so narrow, Cady could reach out and touch the smooth stone. When they came out the other side, they entered a lush green valley with softly rolling grass-covered hills. Orange, yellow, and mauve wildflowers dotted the green carpet amid tall delicate grasses that swayed in the breeze. White puffy clouds, like pillows of cotton, drifted lazily across the azure sky.

Up ahead, Cady spotted a small cabin nestled in the foothills of the mountains. Surrounding it were cottonwood trees blossoming with clusters of cottony-fluff-covered seeds, their leaves fluttering in the breeze. A mountain stream flowed around the structure, sparkling crystal blue in the midday sun.

"I thought you were taking me home," Cady said in some surprise.

"I'll take you there in the morning. Looks like we're in for a storm."

Cady looked up at the sky. She was astonished to see that where moments before it had been cerulean, it was now slate-gray, with moisture-laden clouds threatening rain. Cougar dismounted and reached up to assist Cady to the ground. She placed her hands on his shoulders and slid off the horse, her body brushing along the length of his. She smiled shyly and stepped back into his horse.

"Whose house is this?" Cady asked, gazing at the quaint little cabin, ignoring the fluttering in her stomach.

It was one story high and made of weathered timber. Two narrow windows were set on either side of the front door, and a wide eave, running the length of the cabin and supported by wooden poles, covered the porch.

"Mine."

"You live here?"

"Yes," he answered, looking down at her with an arched brow. "You seem surprised."

"No. It's just that…I don't know. I didn't picture you living in a place like this." She shrugged her shoulders and followed him inside.

The cabin was larger than it appeared from outside and sparsely furnished. In fact, the only furniture was a wooden table and two chairs placed before a large stone hearth. Apparently, the colorful pillows strewn haphazardly around the room served as the rest. An object hanging from the rafters, above a mound of pillows piled on top of a fabric-covered mattress, caught her eye. It was fashioned in the shape of a spider's web, sculpted from suede, with long, soft leather fringes and wispy white, red and yellow feathers dangling from it. She touched one of the delicate, red feathers.

"What's this?" she asked over her shoulder.

"We call it a dream catcher."

"It's beautiful." Fascinated by the intricate design of feathers and suede, she gently pushed it until it swayed back and forth. "What does it do?"

"Legend has it that if hung over your bed at night, bad dreams become entangled in the web and only good dreams filter through and slide down the feathers to land in your sleep."

"What a wonderful story!" She gave it another little nudge and moved to a different mound of pillows and sank into the soft cushions with a contented sigh. Cougar crossed to the fireplace and struck flint to the kindling piled in the grate. When the tiny flames began to devour the twigs, he tossed several fat logs onto the growing fire, then moved to stand in front of her. He regarded her silently with an unreadable expression, his black brows drawn into a frown.

Cady, becoming uncomfortable under his scrutiny, averted her gaze and looked out the window, plucking at her skirt and becoming nervous with his continued silence. He surprised her when he squatted down in front of her and reached for her hands.

"Tell me what happened."

"What? Oh, yes, of course." How could she have forgotten her ordeal? "Randy and I were returning home from Fallen Tree. The Taylors had invited us over, you see. We had just reached Grayson land when we came upon a man with a lame horse. Or so he said," she added in disgust. "It was a trick! The next thing I know he knocks Randy out and another man jumps from the tree and grabs me." She looked worriedly at Cougar. "Did you find Randy? Is he hurt bad?"

"He's fine. I found him not long after it happened and took him back to Ponderosa Pines."

"How did you find me?"

"I followed your trail. Whoever took you didn't bother to cover their tracks. There were two men, right? Do you know who they were?"

"No."

"Were they the same men in your hotel room in Denver?"

"I don't know. I didn't look too closely at the one with the lame horse before I was blindfolded, and the other one wore a bandanna over the bottom half of his face."

He fell silent for a moment. "I doubt they were. I made certain they didn't follow us."

She pulled one of her hands free and reached for a lock of hair. Twisting it around her finger, she blurted out, "They were going to kill me!"

"Do you know why?"

"I didn't stop to ask them!" she cried hysterically.

"Of course, you didn't," he agreed, his tone calm. "I thought perhaps you overheard them talking."

"They didn't talk at all while we were riding. After I was thrown into a room, I heard them in the other room. All I could make out through the door was that I was in the way. And something about not getting rid of the old man for nothing." She began to shake, and her eyes filled with tears.

Cougar was about to question her further but stopped, tilting his head to one side.

"What?" she mumbled through her tears. "Why are you looking so…exasperated?"

"You."

"Me?"

"I seem to spend my life either rescuing you or protecting you."

"I escaped without your help," she reminded him.

"You did," he drawled in agreement. "But you would still be wandering around the territory if I hadn't come along."

"I would have made my way home…eventually," she insisted. "After all, I'm perfectly capable—"

"Of taking care of yourself. Yes, I know."

"Oh," she gasped, indignant.

He hid his smile, pleased that he had distracted her from her distress. He rose to his feet and spun on his heel, asking over his shoulder, "Are you hungry?"

"Yes," she answered shortly, still miffed at his arrogance. She looked around, studying her surroundings. The cabin was one large room with rough-hewn walls and wide wooden beams overhead. A huge stone fireplace with a wooden mantel took up one wall, and a pair of long, wide shelves that housed a variety of cans and bottles were nailed into a wall in one corner of the cabin, creating a makeshift kitchen. It was here that Cougar rummaged and after selecting a few items from the shelves placed them on the table.

Cady pushed herself to her feet, crossed the room, and plunked down at the table while Cougar prepared their meal. He nimbly mixed cornmeal and water in a cast-iron skillet and emptied a can of beans into a pot. He set both on a grate over the fire.

"I need to see to my horse. Try not to let the food burn." She nodded absently, ignoring his barb, and watched him leave. She stared at the closed door, thoughtful. She had found herself in many scrapes since leaving St. Louis and he always appeared when she most needed him, as if he could sense when she was in trouble. But then he would just disappear without a word. *After stealing a kiss or two.* She tapped her fingers on the table. What was he after? Or was he truly watching out for her because of a promise he made to her grandfather?

She shuddered. *And who would want me dead?* As far as she knew, she had never crossed anyone. But one thing was for certain—she would need to be more careful in the future. No doubt, there could be a time when Cougar just might not show up.

The odor of burning food filled the air and she looked over at the fireplace. The flames were engulfing the iron vessels of food. With a gasp, she jumped to her feet and ran over to the hearth. Without thinking, she reached in and grabbed the handle of the skillet, immediately yelping in pain and dropping it into the fire. She stuck her fingers in her mouth, trying to cool her burned flesh.

She heard the door open and felt a rush of cool damp air as Cougar rushed into the cabin. She quickly moved out of his way. He pulled the skillet from the fire and threw it on the stone hearth, shaking his hand at the hot sting.

"Nice going," he drawled, grabbing a towel, and lifting the pot of beans from the flames and placing it with the skillet on the hearth.

"I'm sorry. I was thinking about—" She blushed. "Well, you shouldn't have left while it was cooking," she muttered and sat back down at the table, blowing on her burnt fingers.

"I'll remember that." He reached for her hand and turned it over. The palm was red and tiny welts had already formed on her fingertips. She snatched her hand away and placed it in her lap, not knowing which was worse—the heat from the fire or the heat from his touch. Cougar grabbed a small bowl and plucked some leaves from a jar he took off the shelf. He mixed them with water, making a paste.

"What are those?"

"Herbs."

"Where did you get them?"

"In the woods. This will ease the pain," he told her, spreading a layer of salve on her fingertips and the palm of her hand with unhurried strokes. Her skin began to tingle, and the burning sensation abated almost instantly.

He fetched another jar from the shelf, grabbed a towel and, after wiping away the salve, opened the jar and slathered a thin layer of the emollient with the same slow strokes.

"What's that?"

"Aloe. It'll help your skin heal."

She glanced at her hand in amazement. The welts had vanished, and her skin was pink and cool to the touch.

"Thank you."

He went back to the hearth. Using the towel to shield his hand, he reached first for the pot of beans and then the skillet of cornbread. He placed them both on the table.

"Just scrape off the burnt part," he suggested with a half-smile. She made a face at him.

Before joining her at the table, Cougar reached for a ceramic jug from the mantel. He filled a tin cup with clear liquid, then pushed the jug across the table to her.

Cady filled her own cup and, thinking it water, swallowed it down in one gulp. She coughed and gasped for air, clutching her throat with one hand. Her face turned bright red and her eyes watered. "What the—" she sputtered.

"Tequila."

"Well, why didn't you warn me?" she demanded, rubbing her eyes with the heels of her hands.

"You didn't ask."

"Oh, of all the—" She attacked the skillet of cornbread and stuffed a chunk of warm bread into her mouth, trying to deaden the burn from the drink. Cougar just chuckled and set to his own meal.

The rain pounded on the windows and wind rustled through the trees. Flashes of lightning illuminated the inside of the room and answering rumbles of thunder shook the rafters. Inside the warm and cozy cabin, Cady felt safe, not only from the storm but from the kidnappers as well.

She refilled her cup with tequila, and sipping it, felt the warmth seep through her body. She eyed Cougar from beneath her lashes, her gaze drifting to his large, tanned hands, unwillingly remembering the feel of his touch on her skin.

His voice startled her from her musings. "Did you meet with Hank Doswell?"

She glanced at him in surprise. "How do you know about him?"

"Chas."

"Oh," she murmured, wondering how much he knew.

"Well, did you?"

Cady hesitated then decided to just blurt it out. "My grandfather wrote a codicil to his will stating that I had to marry in order to inherit the ranch."

"Who?" he asked, popping the last bite of cornmeal into his mouth.

"I don't know."

He gave her an odd look. "Didn't you read it?"

"Mr. Doswell can't find it," she said in annoyance. "His office was cluttered with paper. I have never seen such disarray. But that's not the worst of it! He can't even remember who it is!" She stared into her cup of tequila, then back at Cougar. "Renee and Webb think Chas wanted me to marry Terence. What do you—" She became alarmed at his expression. "What?"

He shook his head and took a drink of tequila. When it looked like he wasn't going to elaborate, she changed the subject.

"Do you know an Austin Taylor?"

"I do."

"I heard the most horrible story about him. Did you know he attacked Renee? Webb had him whipped and banned from Fallen Tree." Cady was fiddling with her cup, absorbed with her story telling and completely unaware of Cougar's now thunderous expression. "And Renee thinks he might have murdered Chas in revenge."

"And what do you think?"

"I honestly don't know," she said, reaching for the jug of tequila and refilling her cup. "There are some very good arguments." She looked up and fell back against her chair at the look of pure rage on his face. "Cougar, what is it?"

He stood up, throwing aside his chair. He reached out and dragged her to her feet, his fingers biting painfully into her shoulders. "Austin did not kill your grandfather," he said through gritted teeth.

"How do you know?"

"I just do."

"Well, that doesn't make any sense." She shrugged off his hands. Confident he would allow her to speak her mind, with no consequence, she demanded, "How can you be so sure this Austin didn't do it?"

"Trust me."

Cady stared at him in disbelief. *Trust* him? She didn't trust anyone! But before she could respond, he leaned down, his face mere inches from hers, and growled, "Do you think to get rid of me so you can marry

Terence?"

"What are you talking about? Why would I want to get rid of you?"

"You will never marry Terence. Do you understand me? Never!"

"Cougar—"

"You are mine. Don't ever forget that."

"Cougar, what is wrong with you?"

"Nothing," he snapped and turned away. Lifting the cup to his lips, he downed the tequila in one swallow, slammed the cup onto the table, and strode from the cabin, slamming the door shut behind him.

Cady stared at the closed door, her mouth open, her eyes wide. What on earth had she said to make him so mad? She dropped to her chair. She had never seen him this angry. And what was that about being his? A warm quiver shook her body. *His?*

She twirled her cup and mimicking him, drained it. Her thoughts by now had become fuzzy and she had difficulty keeping her attention focused. With a sigh, she pushed herself to her feet, grasping the edge of the table for support when the room started spinning. She lifted one hand to her forehead, awash with dizziness.

"I think I had better lie down," she said to no one. She stepped away from the table and swayed backward, saved from tumbling to the floor by a pair of strong arms.

She leaned back against his warm chest. She tilted her head back and giggled. Cougar's eyes were on the bottom of his face, his mouth on top. She blinked twice as a wave of nausea washed over her. After it passed, she reached out and touched his cheek. "I thought you had left," she murmured before her head fell back against his arm. She heard him chuckle and demanded, "What's so funny?"

"You're drunk," he whispered, and turned her around in his embrace.

She pulled out of arms and, tilting her chin stubbornly, muttered, "Am not." She started to turn, tripped over her feet, and would have landed flat on her face if Cougar hadn't grabbed her.

"What are you doing?" she asked him suspiciously.

"Seeing you to bed," he answered, hiding his grin.

"Oh, no, you're not," she retorted a split second before he hauled her up against him. Her mouth parted on a sigh as his head lowered and his mouth captured hers. She gave in to the magnetic pull and looped her arms around his neck as he deepened the kiss. She clung to him, her body pressed intimately against his, as stomach-tightening desire filled her with wanting more—more than just his kisses.

He stroked her back, he caressed her buttocks. When she moaned deep in her throat, clutching him tighter, his loins hardened in response, his body screaming for release. He knew he should stop—not only was she the worse for drinking spirits, but it would certainly complicate matters. But he ignored the voices in his head, too fully engrossed in kissing her to end this lust-filled ecstasy.

He slipped his tongue inside her mouth, searching for hers, and when he found it, the tip tentatively touching his, he growled and clinched her closer.

A clap of thunder shook the cabin, bringing him to his senses. It was probably the most difficult thing he had ever done—he stopped kissing Cady. He slipped his arm under her knees, cradling her against his chest, and stepped over to the mattress. He placed her on the mound of pillows beneath the dream catcher. She sighed, turned on her side facing the wall, and fell asleep.

Cougar gazed down at her, aching with his need. On the ride to his cabin, her nearness had fired him so, he had been close to surrendering to the never-ending lust hounding him. It consumed him to a point where he could think of little else. He was unable to stay away, craving her kisses, and sometimes wished he'd never met her. Ah, but she was lovely—she was sweet—when not upset with him.

He pulled off her boots and tossed them in the corner. After tucking a blanket around her shoulders, he moved back to the table and poured himself a healthy draught of tequila. Sipping the potent brew, he contemplated the sleeping beauty in his cabin, surrounded by a mound of pillows. Her soft, even breathing filled the room. He probably shouldn't have let her drink so much; she wasn't used to spirits. She would feel like hell in the morning.

He took a sip of tequila, recalling their conversation, and the anger began to simmer anew. She was being fed lies by that no-account family, and it pissed him off. He'd be damned if he'd allow her to marry that son-of-a-bitch! Marry Terence? No way in hell! He shook his head. And that Doswell! He was the most unorganized, inept man he had ever met. If he wasn't such an idiot, Cady would know her fate.

The codicil would be found if he had to search Doswell's office himself. The truth of the matter would become known, and Terence could go to hell. But more importantly—why hadn't she mentioned Chas's letter?

Chapter 14

Cady came slowly awake, her mind sluggish, her body aching. She opened her eyes and groaned. Gingerly, she raised up on one elbow and squeezed her eyes shut, grabbing her head with one hand trying to quiet the pounding in her temples. Opening one eye, she glanced around the empty room, waiting for it to stop spinning. When the pain in her head abated to a dull throb, she pushed herself to a sitting position.

"Cady?"

She looked over her shoulder and saw Cougar's tall frame outlined in the doorway. The sunshine spilled into the cabin behind him, streaking the wooden floor with long bright fingers of torture.

"What?" she whispered, squinting against the glare. "What are you smiling at?" she demanded, her voice hoarse.

"You," he said with a chuckle. "Are you hungry?" he asked solicitously as he stepped into the cabin.

"Lord—no." She hauled herself to her feet, swaying slightly and regaining her balance by holding on to the wall. She spied the ceramic jug on the table. *Tequila*! She turned on Cougar. He was watching her with heavy-lidded eyes and looking very pleased with himself. And why did he keep staring at her mouth?

"What exactly happened last night?"

"Nothing."

"Then why are you looking at me like that?"

"Like what?" he asked with innocent amber eyes.

"Cougar..." she said slowly, menacingly.

He ignored her and went to the hearth to pour two tin cups of coffee, before dousing the fire and stowing the supplies back on the shelves. He returned to the table, sat down across from her and sipped his coffee.

Cady sank into the chair, dropped her head in her hands, her mind racing furiously. She remembered burning her hand, drinking tequila, discussing Austin Taylor, Cougar's subsequent anger and... Her head popped up. That kiss! A wave of heat washed over her entire body, turning her cheeks bright red, as the memory pushed through the fog.

She reached for the cup of coffee and took a sip, eyeing him over the rim with narrowed eyes. He looked so smug! Setting the cup on the table, she rose to her feet, gripped the edge of the table for support, and asked, "Will you take me home now?"

She succeeded in tugging her boots on without causing further agony while he stowed their cups on the shelf and headed toward the door. She followed him outside a little more slowly, flinching when the sunlight struck her like a slap in the face. When Cougar handed her a wide-brimmed hat, she set it on her head and pulled the brim down low over her eyes, shielding her sensitive eyes from the sun, then made her way to Cougar's black-and-white stallion. He mounted first and reached down and lifted her in front of him.

She sat up straight, trying to keep from touching him, but the warmth of the sun and the steady motion of the horse lulled her to sleep. She slumped against his chest, his arm wrapped securely around her, holding her in his embrace. She drifted back into a memory, a happy memory. She was running through a field of wildflowers, the flora swirling around her legs in a sea of color. She squealed in delight when Cougar lifted her high above his head, then slowly lowered her, brushing against his body before he covered her mouth with his. The kiss had been thoroughly intoxicating and, surprisingly, he didn't pull away but continued kissing her for a very long time. She remembered the source of that memory. It was a good dream the dream catcher had let slide through its suede web.

When they arrived at Ponderosa Pines, Cougar reined up in front of the hacienda and nudged Cady awake.

"What?" she grumbled, rubbing her eyes with her hands.

"You're home, darlin'," he drawled and, lifting her clear of the horse, set her down on the ground.

She stepped back and looked up at him, shielding her eyes with her hand. "Would you like to come in?" she offered, oddly reluctant to see him go.

He looked over her head, scowled, and glanced back down at her. Without a word, he shook his head, swung the stallion around, and rode off without so much as a backward glance. Cady, perplexed by his abrupt departure, wondered what had caused his change in behavior. She watched him gallop down the drive and, with a heavy sigh, turned toward the house. She found Terence standing on the front porch gazing after Cougar, frowning.

He ran down the stairs to her side and grabbing her shoulders, asked anxiously, "Cady, are you all right?"

She flinched from his loud tone of voice and lifted

her hand to her throbbing temple. "Terence," she whispered. "What are you doing here?"

"Worrying about you. You look a little pale. He didn't—"

"I have a headache. But yes, I'm fine," she muttered, gazing back down the drive with an indiscernible look in her eyes.

Terence frowned. "Well, the important thing is that you're home, safe. Come on, let's go inside."

Cady readily agreed, exhausted from the earlier hours of terror and the warring emotions from her time with Cougar. Not to mention the lingering headache caused from too much tequila. She followed Terence into the house and met a frantic Maria in the hallway.

"Señorita Cady! You are home! Are you well, *niña*?" She clasped Cady's hands, peering at her anxiously.

"I'm fine, truly I am, Maria," she assured the housekeeper. "Cougar brought me home."

"Yes, then, of course you are," she agreed with a nod. "I knew he would find you and keep you safe."

"How's Randy?"

"He is resting in the bunkhouse. He has a nasty bump on his head."

"I will check in on him later." Cady moved into the parlor with Terence.

Maria brought in coffee and a plate of sweet rolls bursting with nuts and raisins. She left the room, closing the door behind her.

"I've spoken to Randy," Terence said, accepting a cup of coffee. "He told me what happened—to him, anyway. Are you able to talk about it?"

Cady nodded wearily and told him what had

happened, ending with, "Cougar found me yesterday and—"

"Yesterday? Where have you been all this time?"

"He took me to his cabin. The storm—" She eyed his expression. "Terence, what's wrong? Are you—mad?"

Terence reached for a sweet roll. When he looked up again, his face was composed. "No, Cady, just concerned."

"How did you even know I was gone?"

"I came over this morning to see how you had survived your visit at Fallen Tree. I was concerned we might have upset you with what had been said. When I arrived, Maria told me Randy had been found tied up and you had disappeared. I was livid when I learned she hadn't sent for the sheriff. She just kept saying that you'd be fine. I was just about to send someone for him when you rode up."

"No harm was done."

"Cady, do you think it could be possible that Austin was behind your kidnapping?"

"Why would you think that?"

"Well, if he was responsible for your grandfather's death, he must be after something. Perhaps you are in his way," he suggested, his expression filled with worry.

"I hadn't thought of that!" she exclaimed in dismay, suddenly remembering one of her kidnappers saying the same thing. Since she had not met Austin, it was entirely possible he had been one of the men who had taken her. She looked at him curiously. "Why do you believe he killed my grandfather?"

"I went to see Sheriff Bosler after you and Randy left Fallen Tree. He confirmed my suspicions."

"So, the lead he is following is Austin?"

"Looks that way."

"What can you tell me about him?"

"When my mother and I arrived at Fallen Tree, Austin still lived there. He was a few years older than me and mean as hell. He tormented me, but, of course, Ma and Webb knew nothing about it. I never said a word. Webb has the right idea about him. He's a cold son-of-a-bitch."

"Maybe, but that doesn't make him a killer."

"You don't know him like we do. He is capable of anything, including murder. It's rumored that he's killed before."

"No!"

"I'm afraid so." He grabbed her hands. "He is heartless. You must believe me."

"I believe you, Terence."

'You're all alone now and you certainly can't run Ponderosa Pines by yourself," he said with a touch of arrogance. "I can take care of you. Marry me, Cady!"

She shook her head. "I'm afraid I can't make any promises just now."

"But you will consider it?"

"Terence, my grandfather—"

"I know about the codicil. Webb told me after you left yesterday. I hope you don't mind."

Cady reached for her cup of coffee. "Not at all. It's bound to come out sooner or later," she said wearily. "So you can understand that I can do nothing until I have read it. It stipulates what I must do and whom I must marry."

"But it could very well be me. Webb and Ma seem to think so."

She shrugged. "That remains to be seen." To soften

the blow, she added, "I'm flattered by your proposal, but my answer is no. Besides, I'm not even sure I want to marry, despite the codicil."

"But doesn't this latest mishap prove that you need a man around to protect you?"

"If it had been you instead of Randy, the results would have been the same. I appreciate your concern, Terence, but I don't want to marry anyone. At least not now. As I said, I won't do anything until I have read the codicil. Anyway, I can take care of myself and the ranch," she stated with a toss of her head.

After she had convinced Terence that she was none the worse from her ordeal, he reached for his hat and reluctantly took his leave, with a promise to check in on her soon.

Cady climbed the stairs to her room and changed into a lilac-and-white striped nightdress. She crawled into bed and lay quietly for a moment thinking about Terence's proposal. She liked him well enough, but he didn't captivate her senses nor take her breath away with just one look. Only one man could do that—Cougar. He maddened her, true, yet she could not deny the attraction between them. It was electric. Just the mere sight of him sapped her strength, making her as weak as a newborn colt. She knew he felt the same—his kisses proved that. She just couldn't figure out why he always pulled away, stopped and disappeared.

She closed her eyes and drifted off to sleep, hugging a pillow to her breast and dreaming of Cougar. Day turned to dusk, the sun disappeared behind the mountains, and still Cady slept.

Chapter 15

As spring waned, Cady settled into life on the ranch. She put the kidnapping behind her after Randy informed her that Sheriff Bosler was looking into the matter. She had gone riding with Terence and not once had he mentioned marriage or the codicil. He had been charming, and she had enjoyed his company. She hadn't seen Cassie. She'd wanted to ask her about the scene in her parlor and the uproar over Austin Taylor. When Cady inquired after her, Terence told her that Renee kept her busy around the ranch.

Mr. Doswell had still not contacted her about the codicil, and she was beginning to wonder if he had been mistaken and was just too ashamed to admit it. Either that or he still couldn't find it in that mess he called an office. So, she did nothing. She knew she was being an ostrich by avoiding the issue, but she just didn't want to think about any of that right now. For the first time in her life, she was on her own and she wanted to relish every moment. All too soon she would be under another's control.

Randy taught her to shoot a gun. Despite his hasty denials to the contrary, she concluded that she was hopelessly inept. He had taken her to a secluded clearing amid a stand of piñon pines and placed several empty tin cans evenly apart on a fallen log. Taking out a small revolver, he demonstrated how to clean it, load it, and ultimately fire it. When he felt she was ready, he handed her the gun and pointed to the row of cans perched on the log.

"Aim for that one. That's right—hold it just so," Randy instructed patiently.

Cady lifted her arm and aimed at the can. She pulled the trigger and watched in dismay as the bullet sailed harmlessly past the row of cans and disappeared into the trees. She turned to Randy with a sheepish grin, but he merely smiled at her encouragingly and told her to try again. Her black brows drawn down in concentration, she fired again and, like the first, that bullet also flew past the log and into the trees. By the fifth try, she was thoroughly annoyed. She glared at the erect row of cans and handed the revolver to Randy.

"Don't be discouraged, Miss Grayson. It will take some practice to get it right," he said, laughing at her disgruntled expression. "You keep this," he said, giving her back the gun. "And practice."

With Randy's guidance, she learned about her grandfather's cattle business. She had already met most of the ranch hands and being Chas's granddaughter, she was assured of their respect. Their friendliness, however, was born from the instant affection they developed upon meeting her.

It was a busy time on the ranch and Cady was swept up in all the activity. It was time for the spring roundup and Ponderosa Pines would be used as the home ranch for sorting, counting, and branding the cattle. The nearby ranchers banded together to bring in the cattle from the open range where they had spent the winter grazing. Once collected, the herd was sorted and gathered by the men from each ranch, separating their own stock from that of the others. Randy explained that some cattle would be selected for the long drive to several of the Kansas cow towns, adding that her grandfather had long ago stopped handling the drive, instead turning the stock over to a drover who arranged cattle drives for a living.

It was also time for the new calves to be branded with each rancher's insignia. One day, Cady accompanied Randy to the branding of the calves. She stood off to one side, watching the procedure. Her heart went out to the little calf who was first roped then dragged over to a large fire pit where branding irons were heated crimson. There, two men grabbed the calf, one by the head and the other by the tail, holding it down. The brander then planted the red-hot iron on the flank of the calf, leaving behind the mark of its owner.

The smell of blood and scorched hair made Cady nauseous, the calf's mournful bellow tugged at her heart. She wandered over to another area where men were marking the cattle by cutting their ears in a certain shape, either notched on the side or cut off at the top, to also delineate between the different ranchers. When they began to castrate the bull calves, Randy came up and led her away.

"I think it best you not watch this, Miss Grayson," he said, having noticed her ashen complexion.

"Why are they doing that?"

"It makes then easier to handle," he explained. "However, not all of them are castrated. A few choice bulls are kept for breeding purposes."

"Oh," she murmured, blushing profusely. "I think I will head back to the hacienda."

Cady swung up onto the Palomino's back. "Next spring, I will stay away from this part of the roundup," she announced with a grimace.

"It happens again in the fall," he told her, suppressing his laughter at her horrified expression. "But there are fewer calves."

With a wave of her hand, she wheeled Dream around and headed back to the house. The sun hovered over the mountaintops, draping the jagged peaks with curtains of light. She was grimy with sweat and dust, and looked forward to a long, hot bath and a short nap before supper. She had risen early that day and now, late afternoon, she was bone tired. As she neared the hacienda, she spotted a horse tied out in front. She dismounted, looped the reins over the hitching post, and entered the cool foyer. She removed her dusty hat, allowing her ebony mane to escape and tumble around her shoulders. Turning into the front parlor, she found Terence lounging in a chair by the window. He had made himself at home, his long legs stretched out before him, a glass of whiskey in his hand. When she appeared in the doorway, he jumped to his feet.

"Good afternoon, Cady."

"Terence, what a nice surprise! What brings you to Ponderosa Pines?" She waved him back down as she sat on the sofa.

"I was on my way to town and thought I'd stop by for a short visit. So, you've experienced your first roundup?" he asked with a raised brow.

"Yes," she answered with a shudder.

Terence laughed. "It can be a bit daunting—for a woman," he said, a touch pretentious. "My foreman handles most of it for me."

"I saw Webb a few times."

"Yes, he still insists on participating."

"But why wouldn't he?"

"Pa's getting on in years and not as quick as he used to be."

"You don't say," she murmured.

"Yep, I pretty much oversee everything at Fallen Tree now. One day it will all be mine." He sighed and leaned back in the chair, crossing his legs at the ankle.

Cady was a bit put off by his conceit. Webb seemed as fit as any man half his age and not nearly ready to hand over the reins of the business. Terence's self-assurance was disconcerting, too, but she kept quiet. After all, he was a man, so it couldn't be helped.

"Have you heard from Hank Doswell?"

"No, he hasn't contacted me yet." She eyed him warily, preparing herself for a quarrel. He was becoming too persistent, and way too interested in her affairs.

"And what of you and me?"

"There is no you and me."

"But—"

"Terence, I still have not seen the codicil. And until I do, nothing has changed." She was fast becoming upset by his interference in a subject that was none of his business and one she'd just as soon leave closed.

"Fair enough," Terence agreed, not looking terribly happy. He rose to his feet and took her hand in his. "Until we meet again."

Cady walked him to the front door and watched him mount his horse. With a wave of his hand, he turned and galloped down the long drive. She climbed the stairs to her room where Maria had thoughtfully prepared a bath. Lord, she was tired of men. Cougar was infuriating, drifting in and out of her life, planting kisses on her whenever the mood struck him. Webb scared her into silence with his hair-trigger temper, and Terence was just too intrusive. Randy seemed to be the only sane man around, but he was so crazy over Cassie he paid Cady no mind, other than as her foreman and friend.

Cady divested herself of her dusty clothes and slipped into the tub. She sighed in pleasure as the wet heat eased her tired, aching muscles. When the water began to cool, she reached for a towel and quickly dried herself. Naked, she moved to the tall mirror in the corner of the room and, with a critical eye, studied her image. Twisting and turning in front of the looking glass, she marveled at the difference in her appearance since leaving St. Louis. Her skin had turned golden-brown by the sun, her body toned from the constant physical activity she enjoyed on the ranch. Her indigo eyes shone vibrantly against her sun-kissed skin and held a sparkle that hadn't been there before. She looked healthy and happy.

She pulled on a cherry-red robe and settled herself on the bed. Before sleep claimed her, she took a moment to reflect on her new life. She had come to love it here. The wide-open spaces, the fresh air and activity, all good for both body and soul. There was just one thing missing—the man she had started it with.

Chapter 16

Cady made her way to the dining room. The room was large and airy, decorated in a fusion of rust, gold and brown. One wall made entirely of glass afforded the view of the courtyard and garden beyond, bringing the outside in. She settled herself into a high-back tapestried chair and looked out into the courtyard to watch a bird swoop through the trees, its gay warbling filling the air with sweet sound. She envied its freedom as it flew from branch to branch on carefree wings. *It wasn't being forced to marry.*

She had just finished the last bite of her lunch when she heard the front bell ring and someone padding down the hallway to answer it. Maria entered the dining room a moment later and handed her a letter. It was from Mr. Doswell. Cady stared at it, her heart skipping a beat. Had he found the codicil? Did this missive hold her fate? Biting her lower lip, she slid her finger under the seal and opened it. She unfolded the note and read. Feeling nauseous, she read it again, then placed it on the table beside her plate, completely stunned. This could not be true! Fate could not be this unkind! The man she had to marry was—*Austin Taylor!*

She jumped to her feet, upsetting the chair and sending it crashing to the floor. She stuffed the letter into her skirt pocket and raced out of the house and down to the stables. She saw Randy conversing with several men outside the corral. His gaze shifted to her as she raced down the back lawn toward them.

"I need a horse!"

"Of course, ma'am." He peered at her stricken expression. "What's got you all flustered, Miss Grayson?"

"All hell has broken loose!"

Randy whistled for Raul, who came running from inside the stables. "Saddle up Dream for the *patróna*!" He swung back to Cady. "What can I do?"

"Nothing, Randy, but thank you."

"Where are you going?"

"To town—to see Mr. Doswell."

"Would you like me to go with you?"

"No, I can handle this myself!"

Raul came around the side of the stables with the Palomino. Cady leapt onto its back and swung out of the yard. Halfway to town, she pulled up on the reins.

What was she doing? The lawyer wouldn't be there. He had written that he had been called out of town and was on his way out that morning. He was probably already gone. She dropped her head in her hands, her breath catching on a sob.

She heard someone approaching and looked up to see Terence riding toward her. "Cady, what is it?" he asked after one look at her crestfallen expression.

She handed him the lawyer's letter. "I have to marry that blackguard!"

By the time he had finished reading the letter he was frowning darkly. "Cady, if this is true, it's disastrous."

"I know," she whispered.

"You haven't seen the codicil, right? Perhaps Doswell is wrong."

"But why would he tell me that," she pointed to the letter, "if he hadn't found it?"

"I don't know. But you can't be forced to marry that man!"

"If I want to keep the ranch, I don't have much choice. It was my grandfather's wish."

"You can't marry a murderer! What was Chas thinking? We'll have it changed," he declared vehemently. "We will fight this. No one in their right mind can expect you to marry Austin Taylor. When he is found guilty of Chas's murder, no law in the land will uphold the codicil."

"Yes, I will fight it."

"Cady, marry me. *Together* we will contest the validity of the codicil."

"Terence, I can't. If I marry you, I will lose everything, and he will inherit—" She sighed. "My grandfather had his reasons for leaving such a request."

"Do you think it's possible Austin coerced Chas into this before killing him?"

"I wouldn't know, but it's something to think about."

"Would you ever consider marrying Austin?" he asked, watching her closely.

"Of course not! How could you even think such a thing?"

"Well, you certainly don't want to lose Ponderosa Pines. And you say no to me—"

"That is absurd! I don't even know the man!"

Terence cocked his head, puzzled, but before he could reply, she held out her hand for the letter. "Thank you for your help, Terence. I will let you know if I need anything else."

"What will you do now?"

"Wait for Mr. Doswell to return."

Cady turned her horse toward Ponderosa Pines, deflated. She didn't want to marry a man capable of assault...and murder. She told herself firmly that she would do nothing until she read the codicil herself. Then, perhaps, some light would be shed on this catastrophe, for that's what it was fast becoming—a catastrophe.

Chapter 17

Someone continued to make Cady's life hell.

As her puppy's excited barking roused her from sleep, sounds of wild commotion pulled her awake. She looked around her room in confusion. The window was lit from outside as if the midday sun burned bright, but her room was cast in shadows and the clock on the bureau read midnight. The shouts grew louder, more frantic, finally moving Cady to action. She pushed her puppy aside, leapt from the bed and raced to the window. Brushing aside the curtains, she gasped in horror.

The stables were engulfed in flames, eerily bleaching the night sky. Wind-driven flames hungrily devoured the wooden structure as men rushed around, some urging horses from the burning building while others had formed a line and passed buckets of water to toss on the flames.

"Good Lord," she whispered, as she watched part of the stable roof crash in, sending a shower of sparks shooting into the air. Startled into action, she pulled on a pair of denims, tucking her white nightdress inside the waistband. She pulled on her boots and, seconds later, was racing from the bedroom and out of the house toward the raging inferno. The heat from the flames and the acrid smell of smoke nearly knocked her off her feet.

Cady spotted Randy off to one side, directing the chaos. She raced to his side and tugged on his sleeve to gain his attention. "What happened?" she yelled over the roar of the fire.

"Don't know, ma'am," he shouted back. He spared her only a quick glance, his face black from smoke and ash, and continued to shout instructions.

A horse-drawn wagon pulling a hand pump and reservoir came careening down the lane, stopping dangerously close to the fire. Two men jumped out and began pumping the levers, forcing water out of a cylinder and onto the flames. Several men stepped out of the line passing buckets of water to the fire, to instead keeping the reservoir attached to the hand pump filled.

Cady stood by his side, her heart in her throat, and watched the devastation in disbelief. Flames leapt skyward, swallowing the stables like a hungry beast. The frightened horses had been pulled from the stables and were now grouped in the far side of the corral away from the fire. They shifted nervously against each other, their ears pressed flat against their heads, their eyes rolling wildly with fright.

Cady glanced over her shoulder praying the wind wouldn't shift and endanger the main house. Even now, men were on top of the hacienda, wetting the roof while others tossed water on the lawn, hoping to deter any stray sparks from turning into another blaze.

After what seemed like hours, the men succeeded in extinguishing the fire. The stables were in ruins. Only one wall and two sections of a stall were left standing, like charred sentinels against the moon-lit horizon. Miraculously, no lives nor horses were lost.

Sheriff Bosler had arrived midway through the action, accompanied by two deputies carrying lanterns. They were now cautiously searching the perimeter of the glowing ashes looking for any clues to how the fire had started. Cady saw the sheriff straighten and listen intently to one of his deputies. He turned, and spotting Cady, hailed her to his side.

"Did you find something, Sheriff?"

He held aloft a metal container and, puzzled, she leaned over and sniffed.

"Kerosene?" she asked in alarm. At his nod, her eyes widened in disbelief. "Someone deliberately started the fire?"

"Looks that way, ma'am," he said, gazing out over the smoking debris.

"Who would have done it?"

"Don't know, ma'am. But I aim to find out." The sheriff shook his head, his lips drawn in a grim line. "Chas Grayson was a friend of mine," he said as if that was reason enough for his promise. He fingered his mustache and glanced down at her soot-covered face. "Go get some sleep. I'll let you know what I find out."

Cady nodded wearily, ready to drop from fatigue. She made her way to her room after first reassuring Maria, busy in the kitchen preparing shredded beef sandwiches and cool beer for the ranch hands, that no one had been injured in the fire. After pulling off her boots and denims, she fell into bed and pulled the blanket up under her chin, her mind in a state of turmoil.

She was afraid, deeply afraid. Someone was wreaking havoc on her life. Were they trying to scare her away or—kill her? She had not forgotten her kidnapper's words. They echoed eerily in her head. *The bitch is in the way. She has got to go...*

Her eyes filled with tears. She wanted Cougar— wanted to be wrapped in his arms, sheltered from harm.

He always appeared when she needed him most—rescuing her, holding her, kissing her. *Like the hero in a dime novel.* A girl could fall in love with a man like that—strong and handsome, larger than life. He could melt a girl's heart—if she weren't careful. A tear rolled down her cheek as she came to the sudden realization that she hadn't been careful. She had opened her heart, and he had slipped inside.

****

As the moon arced toward the horizon, its beams illuminated a man scaling the wall of the hacienda. His lithe form easily reached the second floor. He slipped through the window and into the room, crossed over to the bed and gazed down at Cady, asleep, one slim leg thrown over the side of the bed. Her chest rose and fell with her even breathing, stirring the few black tresses curled on her face. The tightness in his chest let up.

Cougar leaned over and brushed away the curls, feeling the strands slide through his fingers like silken ribbons. The acrid smell of smoke wafted from her hair, bringing back in full force the panic that had gripped him since he learned of the fire. He placed his palm against her cheek. She turned into his hand, murmuring softly in her sleep.

Cougar turned up the oil lamp on the bedside table, moved her leg aside, and sat on the edge of the bed, studying her sleeping form. Her hair fanned out against the pillow, her ivory skin was dusted with soot and one hand smudged with ash lay against the pillow. Her lashes rested on her cheeks like delicate black threads. He envisioned the vibrant color of her eyes, the color of the wildflowers scattered throughout the meadows near his home. Eyes he could lose himself in.

Cady shifted onto her back, trying to hold on to her dream. It was such a wonderful dream. She blinked against the light and her eyes fluttered open as the image faded. She gasped to find the vision of her dream perched on the side of her bed. She sat up, clutching the blanket under her chin.

"Cougar, what are you doing here?"

"I was worried about you. The fire…" He brushed his mouth against her slightly parted lips. They were soft and tasted faintly of smoke.

"Nobody was hurt," she whispered brokenly, and watched in helpless abandon as he leaned forward and captured her mouth. The kiss was tender, full of affection. His whiskers chafed against her skin, igniting a fevered excitement, and she leaned into him, kissing him back with all the passion her naïve body possessed. Her arms circled his neck, her fingers tangled in his hair. She craved his touch, his loving touch, and trembled in anticipation.

Cougar needed no more encouragement. He deepened the kiss as desire raged unchecked through his loins. He freed the buttons on the bodice of her nightdress and slipped his hand inside the folds to cup a breast. It was warm and filled his hand, the nipple hardening and pushing against his palm as he gently caressed it. He pulled his mouth from hers and pressed warm, unhurried kisses down her neck, sucking gently on her smooth skin as he travelled lower. His mouth replaced his hand.

Shaking from the powerful current flowing from his hands and mouth to every point of pleasure in her body, she arched her back as the delicious sensations surged through her body, leaving her trembling with want. She kneaded the muscles in his shoulders, feeling them bunch beneath her fingertips, and slipping her hands beneath his open shirt, she stroked his back, skimming lightly over the calloused ridges.

She clung to him, curious to know this intimate slice of life between a man and a woman. She wanted answers to the questions and knew Cougar could provide them. His heated touch, his manly smell, his delicious taste filled her senses. She surrendered to the moment—she surrendered to him.

Her heated response weakened his resolve—any second thoughts he'd had disappeared. He could think of nothing but making love to her, this most precious woman he held in his arms. His determination to not get involved, shouldn't get involved, knowing that shared intimacy would only further complicate matters, didn't seem to matter. His need for her suppressed any misgivings.

Cougar rose above her and stared deeply into her eyes—indigo eyes now expressing a sentiment that filled him with tenderness. He gathered her close, and in the blink of an eye, had both his clothes and her nightdress discarded and piled on the floor. He cupped her face as he planted kisses on her cheeks, her eyes, her forehead.

Shaking with emotion, his muscles taut with longing, he nudged her thighs apart with his knee and slid into her warmth, entering slowly so as not to frighten her. He pressed up against her maiden's wall and hesitated when she pulled back, her eyes wide with uncertainty.

"Do you want me to stop?" He sounded out of breath. "Cady, if you want me to stop, tell me now." He tensed, waiting for her to give him consent.

Christine Davies

She shook her head, never breaking eye contact. "No, Cougar. Please—don't stop," she whispered. She could no longer fight it. She was drawn to him body and soul and knew her heart was no longer her own. It belonged to him.

He covered her mouth with his, slid his hands under her buttocks, and with one powerful thrust, sheathed himself deep inside her velvet heat. His kisses muffled her cry of surprised pain as he made her a woman.

"Oh, darlin'," he whispered against her mouth. "I'm sorry I had to hurt you. But the pain will stop. No, don't move yet," he pleaded, his voice husky. He lay still, his cheek pressed to hers, his breath catching from the incredible sensation of being held inside her. The need to move taxed his endurance, nearly driving him insane. But he wanted her to be calm, wanted her pain to ease, wanted her to want him as desperately as he wanted her. When he thought he would perish from his need, he heard her quiet whimper and felt her shift against him.

Cady instinctively began to move in the age-old mating rhythm inherent to her as a woman. She clutched his back, her nails biting into his skin as he pulled back, then pushed deep. She wrapped her legs around his waist and matched him thrust for thrust, drowning in the waves of pleasure crashing over her body.

They soared to new heights, clinging to each other, as together they reached the peak and found sweet splendor. They drifted down, their desire quenched. Weak from emotion, Cougar collapsed on top of her, moved to his side, taking her with him. They lay entwined in exhausted glory.

Cady glanced shyly up at him, her eyes half hidden by thick black lashes. She blushed when he smiled down at her.

"There is nothing to be ashamed of," he said, his voice gentle.

"I'm not," she whispered. "It's just that—"

"I know… It was—" He cupped her chin in his hand, at a loss for words, and kissed her soundly. Gathering her close, he placed her head on his chest and stared at the ceiling. With the veil of passion lifted, reality shone through with blinding clarity, making him doubt the wisdom of his actions. Making love to her would complicate matters, make everything more difficult. Oh hell—consequences be damned! He would not change this incredible night despite the problems that would likely arise.

Cady listened to his heartbeat, the steady rhythm filling her with hope, as she landed from the incredible journey he had taken her on. Lying in his arms, overwhelmed with emotion and, trying but unable to ignore her future, she wondered if Cougar might help her out of the horrid situation she found herself in. Didn't tonight prove that he cares?

"Cougar?"

"Hmm?" His arm tightened around her.

"I—I have to marry another," she whispered against his chest. Tears spilled from her eyes, wetting his skin. "I have to marry that awful man!"

"Who?" he asked, his voice low and even.

"Austin Taylor," she said in revulsion. "I can't believe my grandfather wanted me to marry him. It's obvious he didn't know what kind of man he is."

"And what kind is that?"

"A murderer, a defiler of women—"

"He is none of those things.'

"Oh, I had forgotten. You know him." She sat up, draping the quilt over her nakedness.

"I do. And I can assure you he is not capable of what you accuse him of. What he's been accused of by others."

"Why are you so defensive of that horrible man? Why are you so adamant he hasn't done any of these vile acts?"

"Like I said, I know him."

"But Terence—"

"Don't mention that bastard's name to me! If it weren't for him—"

"What?"

"Nothing," he growled. He rolled from the bed, dressed quickly, and before she knew it, he had opened the door and left the room. She was staring at the empty doorway in confusion when suddenly he reappeared and, as sure-footed as a cat, made his way to the window. He slipped out before she could say a word. She jumped up, slipped into her nightdress, and hurried to the window. Throwing her leg over the sill and balancing precariously, she hung halfway out the window.

"Cougar!" she shouted, stopping him. "Come back here!" She lost her footing and slipped out the window, screaming as she sailed through the air. She landed in his arms with a whoosh and a small cry. He set her on her feet and glared down at her.

"Are you crazy? You could have killed yourself!"

"What do you know? What aren't you telling me?" She straightened her nightdress that had become twisted from her fall.

"I told you—nothing."

"Cougar, please, don't leave like this." He started to

turn away. She grabbed his arm and tugged, cringing beneath his quelling look.

"I should never have come here tonight. It was a mistake. It will never work." His words struck like stones, shattering her earlier hope that he cared. He pulled his arm from her slackened grasp and walked away, slipping behind a tree. After a moment, he peered around the trunk and watched her walk around to the front of the house. Her white nightdress billowed out around her like a specter, her anguished sobs drifting back to haunt him. He leaned his forehead against the tree and sighed. *What have I done?*

Cady rounded the side of the house, tears blinding her vision, and made her way to her bedroom. She curled up on the bed, her stomach twisted with shame, and wept.

Tears spent, she rolled over and stared blindly at the ceiling. She had let Cougar go where no man had ever gone. Worse than that—she had let him go where she had sworn no one would, ever again. She had allowed him into her heart. She found herself in love—in love with the frustrating, moody, yet magnificent man. But it was futile, this love, for it would amount to nothing. Hadn't he just said as much? *It will never work.*

Stifling a sob, she pounded the pillow with her fist, the scent of his skin lingering on the casing wafting around her. *You fool! You fool! You know love equates with heartache!*

Chapter 18

Through the open window, Cady listened to the sound of rain playing with the trees. Too exhausted to climb out of bed and close the window, she absently watched a puddle forming on the floor. Her eyes were dry, not another tear could she shed; they had all been cried. She had been left, again, but this time not only with a shattered heart but a loss of virtue.

Was she truly destined for unhappiness? Never to know love? Never to belong? She had found him, the man she'd been searching for, and now after taking her maidenhead he wanted nothing more to do with her.

She got out of bed, closed the window, and peered out at the thundershower sweeping the countryside. Torrential rain pounded the ground amid flashes of lightning and loud crashes of thunder. The weather matched her mood.

She made her way to the washstand and scrubbed her face and body with cold water until her skin glowed. She opened the wardrobe, absently studied the array of colorful outfits and settled on a blue-and-pink split skirt and a pink cotton shirt. She dressed quickly and, after pulling on brown leather boots, twisted her hair into a chignon at the back of her head, securing it with a pink ribbon.

She quit the room and the memories it held and entered the peaceful realm of the kitchen. "Good morning, Maria," she called out, planting a smile on her face.

"Señorita Cady! You're up early!" Maria wiped her hands on her apron. "I thought you would sleep late after last night."

Cady blushed before realizing Maria was referring to the stable fire and not her midnight activities. "I'm going into town. I'll be back later."

"But the rain!"

"It will stop soon. See, the clouds are already breaking up."

"You must eat first."

"I don't have time."

"*Si*, you do. Now sit," Maria demanded and herded Cady over to the table. Knowing she would not get out of the house until she did, Cady quickly ate a plate of pinenut pancakes, the food settling in her stomach like a rock.

"Okay?" Cady asked with a grin, wiping the molasses off her chin. She drank the last of her coffee, threw the napkin on the table, and rose to her feet.

"*Si*, Señorita." Maria turned away with a smile as Cady slipped on a leather vest and headed out to the stable ruins. On her way out, she grabbed a shiny, red apple from a ceramic bowl on the table.

The rain had indeed stopped, but the moisture-laden clouds lingered with a promise of more. She found Randy poking around the ashes with a stick.

"Morning, Randy. Find anything?"

"Morning, Miss Grayson. Nope, not yet."

"I'm going into town. Do you need anything?"

"No, ma'am. Would you like me to take you?"

"No, that's not necessary." She glanced around the

corral and spotted the Palomino on the far side of the dirt enclosure. She whistled sharply. The horse looked up and trotted over to her side. She rubbed her velvet muzzle and slipped her the apple.

Randy shouted for Raul, who came running from the other side of the corral. "Saddle up Dream for Miss Grayson," Randy instructed the boy. "If you can find a saddle," he muttered.

"*Si*, Señor." Raul smiled shyly at Cady and ran off, Dream in tow.

"Was everything lost?" Cady asked, looking around the stable ruins.

"No. We had some gear stowed in one of the bunkhouses. But we'll have to order more of everything."

"Will you take care of it?"

"Of course, ma'am. I've already made a list of what's needed."

"Good. Thank you, Randy." She pulled on her gloves when Raul came around with Dream. "I won't be gone long," she said mounting the Palomino.

"You have your gun?"

"Yes," she answered, patting the revolver he had given her, now tucked in her vest pocket. "Not that it'll do much good," she muttered with a frown.

"I'll take you out again." Randy laughed. "Remember, the more you practice, the better you'll become." His expression sobered. "Don't stop to help anyone."

"I won't."

"And if someone starts following you, ride like the dickens back here. Dream can outrun any other horse, if coaxed."

"I will."

Arriving in town a short while later, without incident, Cady entered the sheriff's office and found him enjoying his morning coffee. He glanced up in surprise when she pushed through the door accompanied by a gust of damp wind.

"Mornin', Cady. I would have thought you'd still be asleep after last night." He set down his cup and waved her into a chair.

"I'm afraid I didn't sleep very well after the fire," she murmured, hoping her face wasn't as red as it felt. "It worries me that it may have been deliberately set. Do you have any more clues?" She sat in a small wooden chair opposite his desk while he fetched her a cup of hot coffee. She accepted it gratefully and, sipping the strong brew, waited for him to resume his seat. He leaned back against the wall, tucked his thumbs in his suspenders, and sucked on his pipe.

"Not a one. Except for the kerosene can. My men were out at first light but couldn't find anything else. Course, the rain made things a bit difficult. I'm afraid it's a dead end," he finished in annoyance.

"Have you questioned Austin Taylor yet?"

"Can't find him." He glanced at her in surprise and arched a brow.

"Terence told me," Cady said, answering his unspoken question.

"Wish he hadn't," he said with a frown. "Nothing's been determined yet."

"Sheriff, if Austin is indeed guilty, I would hope that he will soon be behind bars."

"Of course, ma'am. Just as soon as I find him."

"Will you let me know if you learn anything further

about the fire?"

"Will do, ma'am. Now, don't you worry. We'll find out who was responsible. Justice will be served," he promised, rising to his feet.

"Well, then, thank you, Sheriff." She placed her cup on the desk and rose to her feet. She headed for the door, stopped, and turned back to face him. "Do you happen to know when Mr. Doswell will return?"

"Hank told me he had a personal matter that needed his attention. Said he'd be gone a month or two."

****

As Cady trotted up the back hill of Ponderosa Pines, she spotted a man atop a dark brown horse racing down the drive away from the house. She left Dream with Raul and rushed into the house, through the kitchen and met Maria coming down the hallway. She was frowning and muttering beneath her breath. She stopped when she saw Cady.

"Maria, who was just here?"

"Wiley Grayson."

"My cousin? What did he want?" Cady asked in alarm.

"He was looking for you. I told him you were not here, and he could not wait. He said he would come back. He is bad news, Señorita Cady."

A shiver of apprehension ran up Cady's spine. "Why do you say that?"

"He has been here before. Shortly before the *patrón* died. Your grandfather sent for his lawyer the next day."

Cady bit her lip, filled with a sense of impending disaster. *Both Maria and Mr. Doswell had referred to her cousin as trouble—what did he want from her?*

"Come, I fix your lunch," Maria offered, pushing

Cady into the dining room. She took a seat at one end of the long mahogany table as Maria brought her a small lunch of rice, beans, and tortillas, with a glass of wine.

She pushed the food around on her plate and stared blindly out the window. Did Wiley blame her for not receiving any inheritance? Did he hope to threaten her into getting his share? Well, there wasn't a thing she could do about it—she wouldn't even if she could. It's not what Chas wanted. She took a sip of wine trying to settle her nerves. She would just have to wait for him to resurface to discover his motive for coming to Ponderosa Pines.

Chapter 19

Twilight brought relief from the heat. Cady stood at the window looking out over the countryside. Her stomach fluttered in nervous anticipation of the upcoming party. It was not by choice, this gathering in her honor. Renee had insisted. She'd said that it would be good for Cady to meet the many people Chas had made a life with here in Santa Fe.

The fiery sunset caught her eye, and she gazed in awe at the panorama of color the sun created as it slowly disappeared behind the mountains, outlining the craggy tops in brilliant shades of yellow, orange, and purple. As it slipped away, the wide stretch of sky was streaked with bands of cobalt and periwinkle-blue.

She turned from the window and moved to the dressing table, where she sat on the tapestried bench and stared at her reflection in the mirror. Tiny lines had developed around her violet-blue eyes, now dull with worry. She was tense, and her stomach was perpetually knotted with anxiety. Life in Santa Fe was turning into a fiasco.

She couldn't believe her grandfather had been such an awful judge of character to want her to marry a man capable of attacking a woman, much less commit murder. Of course, while still alive Chas had no idea he would be murdered by him.

She picked up the silver brush and pulled it through

her hair until it shined. She pulled the jet-black curls off her face with a gold ribbon and allowed the rest to cascade down her back in a waterfall of ringlets. The color of the ribbon reminded her of Cougar's eyes. She had not seen him since the night of the fire, the night he had made her a woman, and she doubted she would ever see him again.

She trembled with remembered joy. She'd had no idea of the intimate pleasures shared between a man and a woman and had reveled in the discovery. She had become a woman under his tender guidance, his gentle touch. And she enjoyed it!

And then he abandoned her. She had given him her most precious gift and been left with nothing—except a wonderful memory and a broken heart. She stiffened her spine. She would not waste another minute thinking about him. He had deserted her when she needed him most, when she was at her most vulnerable. He didn't even offer to help with the Austin Taylor situation—he just got mad and left.

She crossed over to the wardrobe and opened the doors. Chewing on her bottom lip, she settled on a black, green, and gold floral-printed skirt that flared out at the waist and brushed the tops of her ankles. After donning a matching green blouse with a square neckline and short puffed sleeves, she wrapped a wide gold belt around her waist and slipped her feet into black leather ankle boots. She glanced in the mirror and smiled, pleased with her appearance. For the finishing touch, she pinned her mother's gold-and-pearl brooch to her blouse. On her way out, she grabbed a gold embroidered shawl, and after descending the staircase found Randy waiting in the hallway to take her to Fallen Tree. He had discarded his blue denims and collarless shirt for black trousers, a white ruffled shirt with a string bowtie, and a colorful brocaded vest. He was very handsome, and she almost envied Cassie her good fortune.

****

Randy escorted Cady into the courtyard at Fallen Tree. The soft glow of lanterns bordering the large brick patio illuminated the tables festively adorned with fresh-cut flowers and long, tapered candles. The sound of the musicians tuning their instruments drifted on the evening breeze.

Everyone in the county and many from Santa Fe proper had accepted Renee's invitation. Chas Grayson had been a favorite in the area, and they had shown up to meet his granddaughter, the new owner of Ponderosa Pines.

Renee glided through the guests like a queen. Dressed in a sky-blue silk dress, her hair perfectly coiffed, she made sure Cady met everyone, then moved on, flitting from one group to another and joining in the many conversations that swirled around the courtyard. Webb kept to himself, a full glass of whiskey in hand. His expression was impassive, his eyes uninterested as he watched the guests enjoying themselves.

Cady was conversing with Doc Flint, assuring him that her snake bite had healed with no adverse side effects, when Terence strode into the courtyard. An attractive woman held tightly to his arm as they moved through the guests to Cady's side. The woman's bright copper-colored hair, piled high on her head, clashed violently in color with the bustled burgundy dress she wore. As the couple reached her side, the doctor moved off to join Webb.

"Good evening, Cady. May I introduce Claudia Wright?"

Cady turned to the woman with a friendly smile. "It's a pleasure to meet you." Her smile faltered when she glimpsed the flare of hostility in the woman's brown eyes.

"Terence insisted I come," Claudia said with a giggle and tilted her head to peer up at him from beneath her lashes. "Didn't you?"

"That's nice," Cady murmured, looking around for a means of escape.

"How are you enjoying your little visit to Santa Fe?" Claudia asked, tightening her hold on Terence's arm, her smile not quite belying her unfriendliness.

"My visit?" asked Cady in some surprise. "But I'm here to stay," she continued pleasantly, a little devil urging her on. "You see, I am the new owner of Ponderosa Pines."

Claudia turned on Terence. "But you said—"

"Not now, Claudia," he said, patting her arm.

Cady looked at Terence with one brow arched. He smiled and dismissed the subject with a shrug. Over his shoulder, Cady spotted Cassie conversing with the butler. She too was wearing the flared skirt and colorful blouse the younger women favored, hers in colors of pink and black. After a few more minutes of strained conversation with Terence and Claudia, Cady excused herself and headed toward her friend. Accepting a glass of wine from Ebbitt, Cady turned to find Cassie staring at a group of men across the patio.

"Cassie?" Cady asked, glancing at the men, and wondering why she wore such a dreamy expression. When she spotted Randy in the group, she understood.

He seemed to be having a hard time concentrating on the conversation around him as well.

"Cassie, do you like Randy?" Cady asked, teasingly.

Cassie reddened and averted her gaze to stare wide-eyed at Cady, a small smile gracing her mouth.

"You do!" Cady exclaimed, laughing delightedly. "Does he return your affection?"

"Yes. But Pa doesn't know," she added quickly. "He wouldn't approve."

Cady nodded conspiratorially. "Your secret is safe with me."

Cassie smiled in gratitude and turned back to her admiration of Cady's foreman.

"Cassie, do you know Claudia Wright?"

"Unfortunately, yes," she answered, dragging her gaze back to Cady.

"You don't like her?"

"Not especially," Cassie replied, then paused when Terence appeared before them and extended his hand to Cady. "Would you care to dance?"

Ignoring Claudia's burning glare from across the room, Cady accepted Terence's offer and allowed him to lead her onto the area that had been cleared for dancing. The musicians were playing a lively tune and Terence whirled her around in time to the music. Cady concentrated on following the intricate steps and when the music came to an end, she smiled up into Terence's face.

"I hope I didn't break any of your toes."

Terence squeezed her hand. "Not at all," he said softly. The musicians altered the tempo and Terence moved Cady around to the slower tune.

"Did you lead Claudia to believe that I was only here

for a short time?"

Terence chuckled and his grin turned sheepish. "Well, yes, I did. You see, she was, ah, giving me a hard time—"

"What about?"

"You."

"Me? Why?"

He shrugged. "She got it into her head that I was smitten with you and well…"

The music ended and, without elaborating further, Terence escorted her back to the outskirts of the patio where Cassie waited. He excused himself and headed to the bar to join Webb and Doc Flint. Before Cady could blink, Claudia materialized, wearing a fierce frown.

"Are you enjoying yourself?" Cady asked politely.

"I would be if you would leave Terence alone."

Cady stemmed her rising anger. "Terence is a friend of mine. And, frankly, I don't care for your attitude. If you hope to keep him by your side, I suggest you soften your sharp tongue."

Claudia, face twisted and eyes flaming with jealous anger, looked like she was about to strike her.

"Claudia, how lovely you look," Cassie interrupted sweetly, drawing her attention away from Cady.

The woman turned on Cassie, and with a smirk, asked, "Heard from Austin lately?"

Cassie's smile remained fixed, but her brown eyes narrowed. "As a matter of fact, I have. And if I were you, I'd lock my doors at night."

Claudia paled and, with a toss of her head, spun on her heel and hurried across the patio to Terence's side.

"She is such a pill—the most spoiled woman in Santa Fe," Cassie said in disgust. "I swear, she can make me so mad. But I will not let her ruin my fun tonight," she vowed, casting a shy glance at Randy.

"She doesn't like me," Cady said matter-of-factly. "I wonder why."

"She doesn't like anyone—female, that it. She's mean and spiteful. Patsy Sapper told me that Claudia overheard Terence lauding your virtues. And that, coupled with the fact that he has been out to see you, has made her pea-green with jealousy. You see, she has had her cap set for Terence since the day she became interested in boys. She's also threatened by any girl who is prettier than she is—and you are."

Cady accepted Cassie's compliment with a smile. "I wasn't aware that she and Terence were an item."

"She thinks they have an understanding, but don't let her get to you. Her resentment sticks in her throat until all she can do is spit out her malice. She is quite proud of her looks, and she now finds herself with competition."

"I'm not competition!" Cady argued with a laugh. Then suddenly remembering Claudia's sneering question, she asked, "Why would she want to know if you had heard from Austin?" When Cassie didn't answer, Cady grabbed her arm. "Cassie, what aren't you telling me?"

"Please, not now," Cassie whispered, pulling her arm from Cady's grasp, her expression pained.

"Cassie, I'm sorry. Did I hurt you?"

"No," she answered quickly, straightening the sleeve of her blouse, but not before Cady spotted the livid bruise on her arm.

"Cassie, what—" Cady looked over her shoulder and saw Renee heading toward them. She turned back and saw panic reflected in Cassie's eyes. "All right, Cassie," she said calmly. "But you must promise to talk with me later."

"What are you two girls whispering about?" Renee teased cutting a sharp glance at Cassie.

"Oh, just how wonderful the party is going." Cady chirped, linking arms with Cassie. She'd table her concerns with Cassie, for now, but at the first opportunity would continue their discussion on both topics—Cassie's bruises and Austin Taylor.

"Have you had anything to eat yet?"

"No, we were just heading over to the buffet."

"Yes, we're starving," Cassie agreed and allowed Cady to pull her over to one of the long tables crowded with steaming floral-bedecked platters and bowls.

The two girls turned their attention to the appetizing array. Light-brown flour tortillas piled high on a platter; shredded beef and chicken, grilled trout coated with cornbread, chunks of red-chile marinated pork, mashed black beans, sourdough biscuits, and rice flavored with onions and green chilies, filled the other dishes. For dessert there were baked rolls sweetened with molasses and raisins, turnovers shaped in half-moons and stuffed with mincemeat, soft egg custards, and aniseed cookies.

They filled their plates with a sampling of each tempting food, then moved to a table covered with a white lace cloth. Between bites, Cassie whispered good-natured gossip about the other guests until Cady was sure she knew all there was to know about the residents of Santa Fe. After they had eaten their fill, Cassie excused herself and disappeared into the house.

Cady strolled through the courtyard to the back garden, leaving behind the chatter and laughter of the contented guests. Moonbeams covered the area in a blanket of soft light. Cady headed for the low brick wall that bordered the garden and sat down, fanning her colorful skirt around her legs. She gazed up at the full moon surrounded by twinkling stars in the pitch-black sky and sighed. This is heaven—heaven on earth. She breathed deeply of the flower-scented air, filled with a sense of peace. She had come to love Santa Fe, and life here would be perfect—if only that black cloud named Austin Taylor wasn't hanging over her head.

The gentle breeze caressed her mouth, bringing with it the memory of a pair of warm lips smothering hers in a fiery kiss. She rubbed her mouth with her fingertip. The image of Cougar's vivid amber eyes swam before her in the serene moonlit garden, and she felt a rush of heat steal over her body, a jolt of remembered joy.

She turned toward the sound of muted voices and saw the silhouette of a man and a woman against the high wall that encircled the entire courtyard. She looked away, dismissing them as lovers seeking a quiet moment together. Their words drifted to her on the evening breeze.

"I love you. I have always loved you." The woman sounded breathless, desperate.

"I carry the marks of your love," the man answered, his voice restrained.

Cady rose to her feet, embarrassed at having overheard them, and headed back to the patio where the merry sounds of guests enjoying themselves resonated. She joined Cassie on the outskirts of the patio, swaying to the music.

"Everyone seems to be having a good time. Are you?" Cassie asked.

"Oh, yes, it's a wonderful party. It was so nice of Renee to do this for me."

"Yes, she can be generous," Cassie answered, a touch of sarcasm in her tone. Cady looked at her curiously, but before she could comment, the musicians began a lively tune and Randy snatched Cassie's hand and swung her onto the dance floor. Red, the Taylor's foreman with bright red hair and sparkling green eyes, approached Cady and requested a dance. He literally spun her around the patio. She didn't have to worry about following the steps or fear she'd step on his toes. Her feet never touched the ground. When the music ended, Red escorted her, quite breathless, back to the edge of the patio where, grabbing Randy's arm, he dragged him away to join a group of fellow ranchers at the bar.

A young man approached, smiling shyly. Just a few inches taller than Cady, he was reed-thin with a full head of reddish-blond hair and a spattering of freckles across the bridge of his nose.

"I'm Sam Hathaway."

"Ah, yes," Cady replied politely, avidly searching her memory.

Cassie came to her rescue. "Sam owns Hathaway Haven. It's not far from Ponderosa Pines."

"Of course, you arrived with your mother."

"That's right," he answered with a grin, obviously pleased she had remembered him. "I understand you had a fire recently."

"Yes. The stables burned to the ground."

"Was anyone hurt?"

"No, fortunately, both man and beast survived without a scratch."

"That's good to hear." He cleared his throat. "Would

you care to dance?" he asked, a nervous twitch moving beneath his cheek.

"Yes, thank you." Next to Red, Sam was a flower. His hands barely touched her as he moved her around the patio, somewhat in time with the music. He didn't say a word, just gazed at a spot over her head and, when the music ended, escorted her off the patio and excused himself.

Cassie giggled and watched him run off. "I think he likes you."

"He's very shy, isn't he?" She turned to Cassie. "Now, about Austin—" Cady reached out and placed her hand lightly on Cassie's arm. "I have to marry him," she whispered.

"What?" A smile slowly stole over her friend's face.

"This makes you happy?"

"Yes."

"But everything I've heard—"

"Lies, all lies. Austin is a wonderful man. He wouldn't hurt a kitten."

"Cassie, I want to meet him. Will you take me to him?"

Cassie shot her an odd look, but before she could answer, a woman's scream rang out from the garden where Cady had just been enjoying the evening air. The two girls exchanged startled glances before picking up their skirts and racing toward the sound. Cady stopped in the shadows while Cassie ran into the thick of it. *What was he doing here*?

Webb and Terence had already arrived and stood side by side and face to face with Cougar, their complexions suffused with rage, both ready to explode. Renee stood off to one side, clutching her torn bodice.

Her hair was mussed, her clothing askew. In sharp contrast to the men's anger, Cougar appeared unmoved. Even in the dim shadows, though, Cady could sense he was alert, tense with the anticipation of danger. He was clad totally in black, his shirt open, and exposing his golden-brown chest. His long black hair was pulled back.

"So, it is like before?" Webb asked with an ugly sneer. "You cannot leave my wife alone."

"No!" Cassie shouted in alarm and ran to Cougar's side.

"Go back into the house, Cassie. This doesn't concern you," Webb said firmly.

"It most certainly does. I will not have you treat him like this—like you did before."

"Cassie, go," Cougar said in a low, even tone.

"But—"

Cougar shook his head when she started to argue. "I'll come to you later."

"Do not tell my daughter what to do!" Webb shouted.

Cady flinched at the pure rage in his voice. Her heart pounding, she clutched her hands together and struggled against the urge to rush to Cougar's defense.

"Webb, calm down. He's not worth the trouble," Terence said with a curl of his lip. "Other than molesting my mother, just what exactly are you doing here?"

"I came to see Cassie," Cougar said, ignoring Terence's barb.

"Cassie is fine. She doesn't need you."

"Is she?" Cougar turned his attention back to Webb. "I warn you, Webb. If you abuse her again, you will answer to me."

"Abuse her? What in the hell are you talking about?"

Webb sounded genuinely bewildered.

"I've seen the bruises."

"It's not what you—" Cassie pleaded but was interrupted by Webb's roar.

"Just what in the hell are you implying? I ain't touched a hair on her head!"

Cougar narrowed his eyes and cut a glance at Renee before saying slowly, "Consider yourself warned."

"Why you—" Webb took a step toward him. "Get the hell off my property. Chas might have been blind to who and what you are, but I'm not. You have just made the last mistake of your life," Webb threatened, taking another step toward Cougar, his hands raised in fists.

"Pa," Cassie implored. She turned to Renee and pleaded with her stepmother. "Please tell them it isn't true. That he didn't touch you."

"But he did, "Renee said, a glint in her eyes. "Just like before."

The entire group was a study of varying emotions. Webb was enraged, alarmingly so, Cassie was nervously biting her lip, and both Renee and Terence looked smugly satisfied. But it was Cougar who alarmed her—his expression was blank, his eyes inscrutable yet burning with hatred.

"The sheriff believes you killed Chas, you miserable son-of-a-bitch, and so does Cady," Terence sneered. "You won't have her, you know. I will," he crowed jubilantly. "Just as soon as you're thrown in jail!"

Cady stared at Terence in confusion. *What was he talking about?* Her thought was interrupted when Cougar smashed his fist into Terence's face, then spun toward Webb. "Your wife lies. She lies now like she lied years ago." His voice was deadly calm.

"Get the hell out of here, Austin! The sheriff will arrest you when he finds you. If you did kill Chas, you won't live to see a trial. I'll kill you before they have the chance to hang you," Webb said between gritted teeth.

Cady gasped and clamped her hand over her mouth. Renee heard the sound and, peering into the darkness, saw Cady hidden in the shadows. Cougar glanced her way before turning on his heel and, quiet and sure-footed as a cat, climbed over the wall to be swallowed up by the night.

Chapter 20

Cady allowed Renee to lead her from the garden, too stunned to do anything but follow her blindly into the house and upstairs to her bedroom. Renee pressed Cady into a burgundy velvet chair, then left the room, returning shortly with a small glass of sherry. She handed it to Cady.

Renee pulled off her torn dress and sat down at her dressing table, clad only in a silk chemise, to repair the damage done to her hair. She looked at Cady's reflection in the mirror, a face pale, drawn, and staring dismally into the glass of golden-yellow wine she held tightly between her fingers.

"My dear, you look positively unwell," Renee commented as she pulled a comb through her hair.

Cady looked up at her in confusion. "I don't understand. Why did Webb call Cougar *Austin*? I mean, Austin is the man who attacked you and may have killed my…" She swallowed back her tears.

Renee laid the comb on the polished surface of the dressing table and turned to face Cady. "Don't you know?" She peered closely at her. "You don't, do you? My dear, Cougar *is* Austin! Cougar is his—"

"What? No!" Cady shouted, raising a hand to her forehead, certain she was about to faint.

"I thought you knew," Renee purred, watching as clarity dawned in the young woman.

"Then that means that Cougar—I don't believe it!" Cady turned an even paler shade of white.

"It's true," Renee insisted. "There are scars on his back to prove it. And then there is tonight."

"But he is kind and—"

Renee grasped Cady's hands in hers and watched her closely. "Cady, are you in love with Austin?"

"Certainly not!"

"Good."

"It's just that my grandfather liked him. Even sent him to Denver to bring me here."

"Chas was blind when it came to Austin. He was always his champion."

"But I'm supposed to marry him!" Cady blurted out.

"Austin?" Renee echoed in disbelief. "You're to marry Austin?"

"The codicil to my grandfather's will. Mr. Doswell says it stipulates I must marry Austin Taylor. Didn't Terence tell you?"

"No, he did not," she answered with a frown. "I suppose he thought he could take care of it himself."

"Take care of what?"

"Nothing, child. Tell me, have you seen the codicil?"

"No, I haven't. Mr. Doswell is out of town. He sent word of the conditions before he left."

"What happens if, as he says, it is Austin Taylor, and you refuse to marry him?"

"I lose the inheritance."

Renee patted Cady's hand. "Well, let's not worry about it now. Perhaps Mr. Doswell was mistaken. Maybe you shouldn't mention this to anyone, especially to Webb," she added slowly. "Until, of course, we know for certain."

Cady stared miserably into her glass, brokenhearted. The wine reminded her of Cougar's eyes, and she swallowed back a small sob. He had tricked her into believing he was good when he was in fact bad. He'd made love to her, made her fall in love with him, just to make sure she wouldn't suspect him of such monstrous crimes. She was filled with such self-loathing she thought she might be sick. She set the glass of sherry on a nearby table and jumped to her feet with a small cry.

"I have to go," she whispered before fleeing the room.

"Of course, my dear." Renee watched Cady rush out the door, a small smile curving her mouth.

****

Cady shivered in the cool night air and pulled the blue-and-black checkered blanket over her knees. The full moon was bright, illuminating their way like a lantern. As Randy drove the buggy, she reflected on this latest turn of events, filled with humiliation. Cougar had listened to her accusations against Austin, at her lamenting at having to marry him, had kissed her, made love to her—all while knowing what she herself did not. She cringed. *How he must have laughed at me!*

And to think at one time she had hoped that he—Cougar—was the man she had to marry! Silly, childish dreams shattered. Once again, she had been proven right—no one was to be trusted.

Cady was startled out of her misery by the sharp report of a gunshot severing the night. She heard Randy grunt and felt the weight of his body slump against her. The reins slipped from his weakened grip and the horse, spooked by the sudden noise, took off at a gallop. Cady pushed Randy aside and reached frantically for the reins. When she was finally able to grab hold of them, she sawed on the leather straps until she brought the horse under control and the buggy to a stop. With a deep sigh of relief, she turned her attention to Randy. A scuffling noise drew her startled gaze to the front of the buggy. They were near a stand of trees that marked the beginning of Grayson land and the moonlight filtering through the branches touched on a man on horseback, his identity hidden by a bandanna covering the bottom half of his face.

Not again! Without a second thought and fear spurring her on, she dove for Randy's gun.

"Don't even try it, lady," the outlaw warned ominously, nudging his horse closer to the buggy. "Throw down the gun," he ordered, leveling his own on her.

The sound of a horse crashing through the trees drew the miscreant's attention behind him. He took one look at the huge man atop the equally large black-and-white stallion and took off in the opposite direction.

"Cady!" Cougar leapt from his horse and ran to her side, grabbing her arm and peering into her face. "Are you hurt?"

"No, but Randy has been shot!" She leaned over her foreman. "Randy, can you hear me?"

"Yes, ma'am." She could barely hear him.

"Randy, it's Cougar. Where are you hurt?"

"My shoulder," he whispered brokenly.

Cougar turned to Cady. "Can you handle the buggy?"

"I think so, yes."

"Take him to Ponderosa Pines. Have Maria send for

Doc Flint. I'll be there shortly." He swung up on his horse and went tearing off after the masked gunman. Cady grabbed the reins, clicked to the horse, and drove the buggy home.

When they arrived at the front stoop, Cady leapt to the ground and ran into the house, crying out for Carlos. He came sprinting down the hallway, Maria on his heels, and met her at the door.

"Can you help me get Randy into the house? He's been shot."

"*Dios mio*," Maria whispered, and hurried back down the hallway to the kitchen. Carlos lifted Randy carefully in his arms and carried him into the parlor, where he laid him on the sofa. Maria rushed in with a bowl of warm water and a towel, placing them within easy reach.

"I've sent one of the men for Doc Flint," she said as she stripped off Randy's blood-soaked shirt and gently cleansed the wound. She moved aside when Cougar strode into the parlor, knelt beside Randy, and examined the wound. The hole was red and frayed around the edges.

"The bullet went clean through," he announced as he reached into the pouch that hung from his belt. He pinched a few herbs into his palm and mixed them with water, making a sticky paste. He packed the salve around the wound, then instructed Maria to wrap it tightly with a strip of clean linen.

Cady watched him work, his large hands handling Randy with a gentle touch. Her glance landed on the heavy gold ring on his finger, and she frowned. *Where have I seen that ring?*

"He'll be fine until Doc Flint arrives to do whatever

else needs to be done." Cougar rose to his feet, grabbed Cady's hand, and pulled her out onto the front porch.

She grabbed his hand and stared at the ring. "Where did you get this?"

"It was my father's."

"I found it in my grandfather's room," she said, suddenly remembering where she had seen it. "It was under his bed." She looked up at him suspiciously. "How did it get there?"

"I was with Chas the night he died."

"You were? Why?"

"He needed me."

"But he was in a coma. He died in his sleep."

"He woke briefly before he…" Cougar shrugged. "Do you have any idea who shot Randy? I lost him in the dark."

"No. He wore a bandanna over the bottom of his face."

"It could be one of the men who kidnapped you," he said absently. He was watching Cady's face, and her expression was anything but worried. In fact, it was downright furious. He reached out but she took a step back, eluding his grasp.

"Don't touch me!" she cried, holding up her hand as if to ward him off.

"Cady, what is it?"

"I know your dirty little secret."

"What are you talking about?" His expression was guarded, as he waited for her to explain. She knew he was Austin Taylor, he had seen her in the shadows at Fallen Tree. But what else did she know?

"I know all about you—Austin."

Ah, his identity.

"Why didn't you tell me? You let me go on and on about Austin Taylor and all the while you were laughing at my ignorance. Making love to me—" Her voice caught, and she covered her mouth with her hand, swallowing the shame threatening to choke her. She looked away, hearing an awful sound—the sound of her heart breaking.

"You already believed their lies."

She turned on him, eyes wild with accusation. "How could you? The man loved you—even trusted you—and you killed him!"

"I did not kill your grandfather."

"You were seen riding away from here! Sheriff Bosler said so. He also has half of a bandanna." Her eyes widened and her expression became even more tortured. "A red bandanna," she said slowly. "I saw the other half in your saddlebags!"

"Cady—"

"Stop! I don't want to hear your lies! And what about Renee? I was in the garden at Fallen Tree tonight. I saw you! And before that I heard the two of you talking. She told you she loved you! She had already told me about that night—the whipping, the scars...on your back," she choked out. "And then tonight, the same thing?"

Cougar took a deep breath, trying to control the fury sweeping through him like wildfire. "Believe what filthy lies you want!" he said through gritted teeth. "But believe this—be wary of where you hear them."

"Did you kill Chas?"

"Believe what you will."

"Just tell me you didn't do it," she pleaded.

"I have told you I did not. If you have to ask again,

then nothing I say will change your mind." He shut down—his expression hardened, and his eyes became dark with resentment.

"I pray Mr. Doswell is wrong!" she cried. "There is no way in hell I will marry you! I would rather give up my inheritance!" She slapped him across the face, hard. "I hate you!" she shouted, and with an anguished cry ran into the house, the door slamming shut behind her, her heart shattered.

Cougar turned and left, his heart heavy, his thoughts dark.

Chapter 21

"She thinks I killed Chas. Or rather Austin did." Cougar was in his mother's tipi, sitting on the floor across from her, a small fire between them. The shadows from the flames flickered against the animal hide walls, the smoke spiraling toward a hole in the ceiling. In one corner, a bundle of cedar burning in a ceramic bowl purified the air with its fragrant smoke.

His mother looked into his eyes, eyes so much like his father's. "She knows you are the same man?"

"She does now. She had already been led to believe that Austin was guilty. Now that she knows I am he, she's mad as hell. She thinks I've made a fool out of her and won't listen to reason."

"But she knows how you felt about Chas."

"I thought she did. Either she has forgotten—or doesn't care. She believes all the lies she's been told." He scowled. "I thought she was different."

"Cougar, she doesn't know you." She reached for his hand. "What about the marriage?"

"I would say there won't be one."

"But the codicil—"

"It can't be found, but the lawyer told her she had to marry Austin to inherit Chas's legacy. But I doubt she will honor it," he added, a hard edge to his voice. "She'd rather give it up."

"You promised Chas," she reminded him.

"True. But I can't fulfill my vow if she is unwilling," he said sardonically. He sighed. "She hates me."

"Hate is a very powerful emotion," she said, studying her son's drawn expression. He usually had such a tight rein on his emotions, and to see him so utterly troubled gave her pause for concern. "She hates the man who killed her grandfather. Right now, she thinks it's you. She has listened to lies spewed by those who do hate you. Prove them wrong, her wrong, show her the man you are." She reached out for his hand. "Take her, marry her, fulfill Chas's request."

"She wants nothing to do with me. And I can't say I blame her," he spat out angrily. He was still so mad at himself for relaxing his hold on his convictions and making love to her, he couldn't see straight. Cougar recalled Chas's dying wish to take care of his granddaughter, and he sure as hell didn't think he'd meant in the biblical sense. How could he have been so careless? She was a virgin, alone in the world, and he had given no thought to the consequences of his actions. And then what had he done? He had abandoned her.

"Chas was not a stupid man. He knew what he was doing."

"I don't know about that."

"What about the letter?"

"I don't think she's read it. At least, she hasn't mentioned it to me." He stared into the fire. "I don't see how I can honor my promise to Chas. Especially under the circumstances. Besides, we come from two different worlds. It wouldn't work."

"Does she care?"

"I don't think she knows—yet. I haven't told her." He was pretty sure that when she learned, and she would, that he was half-Indian, she would no doubt shun him as everyone else had done. If not for Chas, Cassie, and of course his mother, Rose, he would have no contact with the white man.

Cougar rose to his feet and began to pace the length of the tipi. His stride was graceful, the hint of steel-muscled power in his measured steps. His movements stirred his long, black hair about his bare shoulders. The fire outlined his tall frame and highlighted the curve of muscle beneath his golden-brown skin.

"Why don't you talk with her?"

"It would do no good. After what happened at Fallen Tree, and then again on her front porch, she'd probably shoot me on sight rather than listen to anything I had to say."

Rose stood, wrapped her arms around his waist, and hugged him tightly. "Oh, my son, I wish there was something I could do to ease your pain."

"I'm afraid there's nothing anyone can do," he replied, drawing comfort from his mother's touch. "Terence and Renee are turning her against me. Just as they continue to vilify me to Webb."

"Webb is a stupid man. I am ashamed to call him my brother. Since Belle died and he married that awful Renee, he has turned mean, vindictive."

Cougar looked at his mother in surprise. "I've never heard you say a disparaging word against Webb. You know it's the liquor that makes him act this way."

"That's very generous of you, considering all that's happened. But, regardless, it makes me furious just thinking about what he's done to you. And now his rotten wife and her miserable son are getting to your Cady."

"She's not *my* Cady," he insisted vehemently. Then

softening his tone, he added, "I pray that she doesn't do something foolish. She can be a bit headstrong. She thinks she can take care of herself."

"Like someone else I know," she teased him softly.

Cougar smiled and turned back to the subject. "Webb is a mean-hearted son-of-a-bitch, and I couldn't care less what he does to me. What I do care about is that Cady has turned against me. And I blame them."

She studied her son's face. "Cougar? What is this Cady to you? Your face softens when you speak of her."

"Nothing," he scoffed. "A pain in the neck, really." He sighed. "But the more I'm with her, the more I want to be with her."

"Talk to her, tell her your side. Anyone my son cares for cannot be blind and stupid."

"I don't care—" He stopped, knowing he couldn't lie to his mother as easily as he could to himself. "She had a dream in the cave after suffering from the snake bite. It was disturbing at the time. I wasn't sure what to make of it. I didn't know her as I do now, how entwined our lives would become or what our future held." His expression was troubled, yet a glimmer of another emotion, a gentler one, was in his eyes.

"Why did it bother you?"

"I saved her, or rather a large black animal did, when she was being chased."

"A large black animal?" Rose's expression became thoughtful.

"I doubt she even remembers it."

"If she does, then you two are destined to be together."

Cougar shot his mother a curious look at her pronouncement, then kissed the top of her head. "I will visit again soon."

Rose watched her son stride from the tipi and thought about what he had said. More importantly, what he hadn't said. It seemed to her that he was in love with this "pain in the neck" and just didn't know it yet. And what about that dream? It had certainly moved him. She smiled as she reached for the young child tugging on her buckskin skirt, and rocked her gently against her breast, her mind searching for a solution to ease her son's pain. Although with the revelation of Cady's dream, her worry had lessened.

****

Cougar rode out of the village. As he headed to his cabin, his mind wandered back to the last time he had been with Chas. The conversation was still clear and played through his mind in one unbroken image. He had gone to Ponderosa Pines in the dead of night. Sliding open a window, he had slipped quietly into the house and made his way upstairs. Following a moonbeam that stretched across the floor, he had made his way over to the bed. After lighting the candle on the bedside table, he had gazed down at the wounded man. Deep lines were etched around his mouth, and his face was white and drawn from loss of blood. His white hair was twisted in clumps around the bandage that circled his head. Pain like an enemy's blade tore through Cougar's heart at the sight of the once-dynamic man now sallow and weak. It was indeed a heartbreaking sight to behold. He had sat on the edge of the bed and reached for one of the blue-veined hands that lay limp on top of the blanket. He had gently squeezed it, willing the man to wake. Cougar was not surprised when he did.

Chas slowly opened his eyes. "You'll get yourself

shot dressed like that," he whispered with a wry grin.

"No one saw me."

Chas smiled weakly. "I'm glad you came."

"You needed me," Cougar said simply, his voice hoarse with emotion. He leaned forward, his long black hair falling over his bare shoulders, and asked, "Chas, who did this to you?"

"I don't know. It was dark…" His eyes took on a sense of urgency as he struggled to sit up. Cougar leaned over and helped him to a sitting position, plumping the pillows behind his back.

"You have not forgotten? You will go for Cady?"

Cougar nodded, becoming alarmed by the circle of fresh blood that appeared on the bandage, staining the stark white gauze crimson.

"Just stay low. I should be hearing from Governor Thornwilde any day now."

"I'm not worried about that."

"I have complete faith in you." Chas sighed. "You must look after my Cady. She will want for nothing when I'm gone—except perhaps love. She's had precious little in her young life since her parents died." His complexion paled and he struggled for breath. "Please—promise me you will keep her safe."

"I will do my best."

"Marry her," he pleaded, his voice taking on a surprisingly strong edge.

"You know that's not possible," Cougar said with a frown.

"It is possible. To hell with their prejudices!" Chas took a deep breath that rattled in his chest. "I don't care what they say, and neither will Cady."

Cougar held his tongue and allowed the dying man

to continue. "I am leaving everything to Cady—provided she marries you. She will not understand this. She may even fight it. But you have to convince her of the soundness of my plan. She could be in danger otherwise. But with you by her side, he won't get all that I own."

"Who?"

Chas ignored the question, a frown marring his ashen face as he began to ramble. "I should never have allowed them to sway me from taking her in when her parents died. Said that a young girl had no place living with a man. Needed a woman's influence. With the kind of life she's lived, it's a wonder she didn't turn to a life of crime. I have to make it up to her—somehow."

"You haven't seen her in years," Cougar pointed out. "Why have you suddenly sent for her now?"

"I wanted to get to know her before too much more time passed. Who would have thought... She's my only heir, you know. Disinherited the others." He stared into Cougar's amber eyes and saw his pain mirrored there. "That miserable son-of-a-bitch, demanding to be put back in my will. There is no way in hell he'll get one red cent of my legacy. Not while there is breath left in my..." Chas gasped for air and slumped back into the pillows.

"Ssh," Cougar soothed, now understanding who he meant, and why it was so upsetting.

Chas coughed and a drop of blood appeared at the corner of his mouth. "I've told Doswell of my wishes. I also wrote a letter to Cady, just in case. I left it—" His forehead creased in concentration. "On my desk. I had this feeling." He looked up with indigo eyes dull with pain. "You promise you'll keep her safe?"

"Yes, Chas, I promise," he vowed uneasily. He slipped the heavy gold ring off his finger and placed it in the palm of Chas's hand. He curled the dying man's fingers around the ring and gently covered the weak fist with one of his strong warm hands.

Chas's eyes became misty with unshed tears. "You're a good man, Austin. You've been like a son to me. You know I love your mother? As I have loved you all these years."

Cougar swept his hand over his eyes and cleared his throat. After a moment, he felt able to speak. "I, too, have loved you all these years. No true father could have been as fine as you. You hold a special place in my mother's heart, as you do in mine."

Chas smiled, the tears on his cheeks glistening like dew in the candlelight.

"Is there anything else I can do for you, Chas?"

"Webb—he knows the truth. I think he believes you to be innocent but is just too stubborn to admit it. He hasn't been himself since Belle died." Chas coughed, his breath catching in his throat. "You two need to work it out. He cares for you—"

"Webb has never forgiven Rose for what he considers her ultimate indiscretion, nor has he stopped hating me for what I am and what he believes I did."

"Talk to him," Chas insisted weakly. "He just might prove you wrong."

"I'm afraid it's too late for words."

"How can you say that?"

'I have the scars to prove it," he drawled, a touch of sarcasm in his tone.

"Please, won't you try?"

Cougar started to refuse yet realized it would be futile. He had never been able to sway Chas from his convictions and he wasn't about to try now. If it would give him peace—he placed his other hand around Chas's fist and said with a sigh, "Yes, Chas, I will try…for you."

"Tell Rose—tell Rose I love her. Tell her she has always been in my heart." His eyes glistened with tears. "And I couldn't love you more if you were our son. Bless you, Austin, er, Cougar," he corrected himself with a small smile. Then closing his eyes, he followed the bright, loving light and crossed into the other world.

Cougar's eyes stung with unshed tears as he gazed down at the man who had been such a strong and loving ally. He slumped forward, the light from the candle touching his grief-ravaged face, accenting his hard, angular features. A lone tear rolled down his cheek.

I will find out who did this to you and hunt him down like the animal he is. But first I will bring your Cady home. He bowed his head and asked the Great Spirit for guidance. He did not see how he could possibly fulfill his promise to Chas. How could they merge paths, as dissimilar as they were? She would be shunned—just like he'd been.

He extinguished the candle, rose to his full height, and left the room, leaving a piece of his heart behind. He moved gracefully through the quiet house, descended the darkened stairs, and entered Chas's study. The room had not been touched since the shooting, except to clean away the blood. He made his way to the large oak desk and lit a candle, smiling to himself. Chas could afford the finest oil lamps yet still chose to use candles. More romantic, he had insisted with a wink.

Cougar searched through the papers that littered the desk but was unable to find the letter to Cady. He stepped back and frowned, wondering what could have happened to it. His gaze lifted to the portrait hanging above the fireplace. A portrait of Chas's son, Neil, his wife, Melinda, and their daughter, Cady. Even as a child, Cady was beautiful. He felt a presence behind him and spun on his heel, crouched low and reached for his knife. Recognizing the figure standing in the doorway, he straightened and sheathed his knife.

"He is gone?" Maria asked, a catch in her voice. She was clad in a voluminous white nightdress, her hands twisted in the material.

"Yes."

"I thought as much." Maria whispered a quick prayer. She stepped into the room and moved to the sofa, tears rolling down her caramel-colored cheeks. She dropped onto the soft cushions with a sorrowful sigh.

"It was peaceful," Cougar said quietly, moving to sit beside her.

"You were with him?"

"I was."

"Good. Then he was not alone. He had the one he loved most beside him." She sighed tearfully. "It is too bad he won't have time with his granddaughter," she said, dabbing at her eyes with a crumpled handkerchief.

"He was sad that he would not be here for her."

"You talked to him?"

"Yes. He woke for a few minutes."

"I'm glad you were with him." They sat in silence for a time. Then Maria asked, "You are going for her?"

"Yes."

"Then I will be sure to let her know how much the *patrón* wanted her here."

"Maria, have you seen a letter addressed to Cady?"

"No," she said. "Should I look for one?"

"Yes. But tell no one of it."

"*Si,* of course."

He enfolded Maria in a comforting hug, then stood and slipped out the window. He felt a whisper of material against his bare arm and, pausing, tugged at the piece of cloth stuck to a loosened nail in the molding. He briefly examined it, then stuck it in the waistband of his buckskins, thinking to approach the sheriff when he returned from Denver.

The outline of his cabin looming before him brought Cougar back to the present. His stomach tightened in misery. Chas had always been there for him. When he was a young man and had learned the truth of his birth, that his father was an Indian, Chas had encouraged him to not only accept his heritage but embrace it. When he had been whipped for a crime he hadn't committed, and then banned from his home, Chas had stood behind him and given him the strength to endure it. Chas had taken up the slack when the man who Cougar thought was his father had cast him aside. He could still remember the pain of being an outcast, of being branded a half-breed. It had taken him a long time to forgive his mother. But with Chas's gentle, guiding hand, he had not only forgiven her but had embraced her adopted culture as his own.

He owed Chas Grayson his life. Maybe not literally, but certainly spiritually. If it hadn't been for him, Cougar would have grown into a bitter man. Or a more bitter man, he amended with a grimace. It was for this reason, he would, against his better judgment, honor his promises to Chas. *All of them.*

Chapter 22

Cady gave the Palomino its head. They raced with the wind, chasing the white, puffy clouds that scurried across the azure sky. She pushed the mare to an even faster gait, the feel of the powerful steed beneath her exhilarating.

Lord, she had never been so angry. She had been betrayed by a black-haired, amber-eyed devil. She had lain with a man who was thought to have attacked a woman, killed her grandfather, and who knew what else? Perhaps he had been responsible for the stable fire and her kidnapping, as well. It was hard to believe the kind and decent man who had chased away the Indians, taken care of her when she had been bitten by a snake, and rescued her from wandering the countryside after being kidnapped could be the same vicious man portrayed by the Taylors.

She slowed her horse and trotted through a fragrant pine forest, stumbling upon a bucolic glade. In the heart of the clearing was a little pond fed by a mountain stream, the pine branches covering it like a leafy canopy, making it feel even more secluded. The air smelled of pine and earth.

A perfect place to sort out my jumbled emotions. She dismounted, leaving Dream to graze on the tender grass. She moved to the side of the pond and knelt, staring at her reflection on the surface. The gentle breeze rippled the water, distorting her image. *Exactly how I feel.* She sat back on her heels and idly dragged her fingers through the water.

The sound of a rider approaching brought her instantly to her feet, ready to flee. She relaxed when she saw it was Cassie prancing toward her atop a small bay mare.

"Cady! What are you doing here?"

"Seeking peace."

Cassie slid to the ground, plopped down on the soft green carpet of grass, pulling Cady down beside her.

"You have found my paradise," Cassie murmured, leaning back on her elbows, legs outstretched.

"It is beautiful." Cady looked around the quiet glade. It was early autumn, and a few late-blooming wildflowers lent a splash of vibrant color against the dark brown tree trunks. "Do you come here often?"

"All the time. It helps to relieve my tension."

"What tension is that, Cassie?"

She shook her head and stared off into the trees, her brow furrowed.

"Randy is fine."

"What?"

"Randy was shot last night, but—"

"Oh, no!" Cassie cried and rolled to her feet.

"He's going to be fine," Cady reassured her, reaching up and pulling her back down.

"What happened?"

"A man stopped us on the way back from your house. Cougar came to our rescue," she added bitterly. She looked over at Cassie. "It was a clean shot through his shoulder. Cougar bandaged it up."

"Then he will be fine," Cassie said, visibly relaxing.

"You have a lot of faith in him, don't you?"

"Austin? I mean, Cougar? Yes, I do."

"Cassie, I know they are one and the same."

"You do? How?"

"I heard Webb call him Austin last night in the garden. Then Renee took me to her room and told me the truth." Cassie gave an unladylike snort. Cady looked at her curiously before continuing, "She had already told me about him attacking her and being whipped for it."

"It was a lie. A filthy lie."

"But I have seen his scars."

"Oh, he was whipped, all right! But it was due to Renee's revenge. You know, a woman scorned..." she quoted with a grim smile.

"Cassie, I know family secrets are just that, secret, but—"

"I suppose you want to know about Austin."

"Well, yes," she said slowly. "Where did he get the name Cougar?"

"He just sort of—picked it up, I guess." Cassie averted her gaze to look out over the pond.

"Will you tell me about him? About him and my grandfather?"

Cassie leaned back on her elbows. "They were very close. Since Pa would have nothing to do with him, Austin would keep company with Chas. He offered advice, played the father figure, that sort of thing."

"What happened?"

"After Ma died, Pa was beside himself with grief. Up until then, he and Austin had always gotten along. Then, Pa married Renee. Terence and Austin took an immediate dislike to each other. Then, of course, Renee fabricated that story about Austin attacking her and had him whipped."

"I thought Webb had him whipped?"

"Is that what she told you?" Cassie shook her head in disgust.

"But doesn't Webb know that Renee lied?"

"I don't know. If he does, he's too proud to admit it. It's too late now."

"Why didn't Webb do something then?"

"Austin had already disappeared. By then, Webb was too set against him."

"Why?"

"I don't know. After Ma died, he found solace in a bottle of whiskey. Since Chas died, he has sunk deeper into despair. Terence has spent most of his life fanning the flames of hatred between Pa and Austin. Terence hopes to inherit Fallen Tree after Pa dies and wants to make sure that Austin receives nothing."

Despite her anger, Cady's heart went out to the little boy who had been shunned by his father. How well she knew the heartache caused by the careless, cruel actions of others. Hadn't she spent the better part of her life tossed between relatives?

"I know my grandfather loved Cougar's mother."

"You do?" Cassie stilled, watching Cady carefully.

"You'd think Webb would have hated Chas for that. Imagine, your best friend falling in love with your wife!"

"Who told you that?"

"Maria."

"She told you that Chas loved Belle, but she married Webb?"

"Not exactly. She said that Chas loved Cougar's mother. I just assumed Belle... I mean, isn't Cougar your brother?" Cady looked at Cassie in confusion. "I don't understand."

"Your grandfather loved Rose."

"Who is Rose?"

"Pa's sister."

"Chas loved Cougar's aunt? But why would Maria—" Cady finally noticed Cassie's pained expression. "What is it?"

Cassie took a deep breath. "There's something you should know. Rose isn't Austin's aunt—she's his mother."

"His mother? But where is she? Is she dead?"

"No, she's very much alive. Pa disowned her years ago."

"He did? Why?"

Cassie took a deep breath and looked Cady in the eye. "She married an Indian."

"No!" Cady whispered, shocked. Her eyes widened as the implication of what Cassie said pushed through her confusion. "Then that means—" She gasped. "Cougar is an Indian!"

"Half."

"What?"

"Half Indian," Cassie clarified. "His father was an Indian, his mother is not. When Austin learned the truth of his birth, he disappeared for a very long time. I was devastated when he left. We were very close. But I came to understand. His whole world had been turned upside down. It took him a long time to forgive Rose for the deception. Then Renee falsely accused him, and Pa turned his back on him."

"And what of Terence? Does he know?"

"Oh, yes! And he let everyone in town know, so that Austin is not welcomed by those with narrow minds."

"So, Cougar is his Indian name?"

"Yes."

Cady sat deep in thought, staring absently at the pond. The sun reflecting off the surface looked like little beads of glass. Well, that would certainly explain why he said those Indians by the river were his friends, and how he knew their language. She turned to Cassie. "This is why you were so happy when I told you I had to marry Austin. We would become family."

"Yes." Her smile lit up her face. "Have you told Pa?"

"Only that I was supposed to marry."

"Oh, yes, that day in our parlor when he agreed with Renee that he and Chas had always wanted you and Terence to marry." She looked sideways at Cady. "I know for a fact that Chas disliked Terence—immensely."

"I later told Renee that Mr. Doswell said it was Austin."

"And what did she say?"

"She agreed with Terence that perhaps Mr. Doswell was wrong and told me not to mention it to Webb."

"What are you going to do?"

"I don't know. But until Mr. Doswell returns, and I see the codicil for myself, I'm not marrying anyone."

Cassie studied Cady. "Does the fact that Austin is half-Indian shock you?"

"No," she answered truthfully. She had been reared on horrific stories about Indians. But Cougar had pointed out that, like in any walk of life, there was good and evil. Chas had to have been aware of his bloodline, yet it had not mattered to him. And, frankly, it didn't matter to her either. He was still Cougar.

"And you still think him guilty? Even knowing some of the facts?"

"Yes," she said without much conviction. She didn't know what to believe and was just too afraid to examine her feelings.

"He's not, Cady. He's a good, kind man."

"Well, that remains to be seen. Besides, he's your cousin and you love him."

Cassie stared thoughtfully at Cady, then stood up. "I want you to come with me."

"Where are we going?"

"You'll see," she promised, a bit vague.

They rode toward the mountains until they came to a narrow bridlepath. Following it through a pass in the mountains, they emerged on the other side into a lush verdant valley. They crossed the valley, the tall grasses brushing their knees, and through a dark cool forest. On the other side of the forest was a wide clearing. Large, cone-shaped dwellings were built around the perimeter of the cleared area. Small children chased each other, their spirited laughter filling the air, while dogs ran circles around them, barking excitedly. Women stopped their chores to stare in curiosity as Cassie and Cady made their way through the compound. The children ceased their play and ran to their mothers' sides, burying their faces in their buckskin skirts.

Cady's stomach tightened and she became increasingly nervous from the stares directed her way. Never had she seen so many Indians, and finding herself surrounded by them was a bit disconcerting. She nudged her horse closer to Cassie's, noting that she did not seem the least bit nervous. To her surprise, Cassie was even nodding to the women as if she knew them. And they were smiling back! In fact, on closer inspection, the looks directed her way were not hostile, they were merely curious. It made her once again rethink her initial opinion of Indians.

Cassie stopped in front of a structure like the others but larger, and after dismounting, she motioned for Cady to follow. She pulled aside the flap over the entrance and stepped inside. Cady ducked in behind her friend, tense with nervous anticipation. Once inside, she found the dwelling roomy and cozy with a small fire burning brightly, the smoke spiraling upward in gray ribbons. The sweet aroma of burning cedar and sage filled the air.

A slender dark-haired woman sat before the fire, a child cradled in her arms. She looked up as they entered and smiled. "Cassie! You came! I'm so happy to see you." She peered at Cady in curiosity. "You must be Cady. You have Chas's eyes."

"This is my Aunt Rose. Austin's mother," Cassie said, pulling Cady farther into the tipi.

Rose studied the lovely young woman, the granddaughter of the man she had loved so dearly, the woman who was now causing her son such mental anguish, the woman she was sure he was in love with. *Did she feel the same?*

Cady was just as avidly studying Rose. She was beautiful, with long, wavy black hair much like her own, intertwined with colorful beads. She wore a fringed butter-yellow buckskin dress, and matching moccasins decorated with intricate beadwork. She had large blue eyes and a kind smile and, except for the eye color, was the image of Cougar. If Cady hadn't already known the truth, she certainly would have suspected they were related.

"Welcome to my home. Please come in." Rose waved toward a pile of multi-colored pillows across the fire from her.

Cady sat down next to Cassie among the comfortable cushions and looked around with interest. Colorful blankets hung on the walls and a suede-and-feather object hung above a baby's cradle. A dream catcher. It was identical to the one hanging from the rafters in Cougar's cabin, except the feathers were red, blue, and yellow.

"How is the baby?" Cassie leaned forward and clucked the child under the chin receiving a delighted gurgle in response.

"Small Brook is growing fast," Rose said with pride, gazing down at the child. "You received my note?"

"Yes. I agree that Cady needs to know about you and Chas. As well as about Austin," Cassie added with a sideways glance at Cady. "You see, she thinks Austin is guilty."

"Of what?"

Cady blushed under the older woman's direct gaze. "Of murdering my grandfather," she said, lifting her chin a notch.

"Why, that's ridiculous," Rose said with a wave of her hand. "He loved Chas."

"Terence and Renee are trying to turn her against him," Cassie added.

"Ah, that Renee. She is a spiteful thing." Rose stood and crossed to the door of the tipi. Calling out to a young girl playing out front, she handed her the baby, whispered a few words to her, then returned to her place in front of the fire. She eyed Cady silently for a few minutes.

"I would like to tell you a story." She received Cady's nod before continuing. "Several years after my brother, Webb, and your grandfather moved here from Boston, I came for an extended visit. After your grandmother died, Chas and I became very close. In fact, we had even talked of marriage." She took a deep breath as if the memory was still painful. "One day while I was out riding, I became lost in the mountains. The sun was setting, and I became afraid of being alone in the mountains at night. A group of Indians found me huddled under an outcropping of rock. Of course, I was frightened, scared to death, really, especially when one of them decided to keep me for himself. But he was a kind and gentle man and showed he meant no harm. He took me back to the village and when the others saw that I was under his protection, I was welcomed. Ultimately, I fell in love with my captor. Tall Feather was magnificent."

Her eyes took on a faraway look as her memories took her back in time. Bittersweet tears shimmered in her eyes. "I became pregnant with his child and, soon after, we were married. We were very happy. Webb was not. I had contacted him, of course, and he insisted that I return home. But Belle came to my defense and convinced him that I had found love. She also informed Chas, who only wanted my happiness. He stood up for me as well." She brushed away a tear and rose to her feet. She crossed over to one side of the tipi and returned with a bottle of wine and three small glasses. She poured each of them a glass.

"One night, several months later, Tall Feather was killed in a hunting accident. I was heartbroken and thought my life was over. But to know that through our child a part of Tall Feather would live was indeed sweet."

"Cougar?" Cady asked softly, thoroughly engrossed in Rose's story.

Rose nodded. "Although I was welcome to stay in the village, I ultimately decided to go back and live with Webb and Belle. Belle had recently lost a baby, and we decided it would be best if everyone believed my baby was Belle's. The scandal, you see, would be devastating. So, for all concerned, we let it be known I was Cougar's aunt and Belle his mother.

"Webb was still unhappy with me for marrying Tall Feather and did not welcome me home with open arms. But he kept his displeasure to himself, for Belle's sake. He would have done anything for Belle. When Chas first learned of my circumstances, he offered to marry me. I loved your grandfather, but I couldn't push another man's child on him, especially an Indian's. He said that it would be no burden because he loved me and would love the child. But I still refused."

"Why?"

"The Indians are not readily accepted into society. Everyone knew of my marriage to Tall Feather and, therefore, by association, I was no longer accepted. They did not, however, know of my child."

"But if you and Chas loved one another, you could have weathered the storm," Cady insisted.

"Now, maybe, but back then times were different. Of course, on reflection, perhaps I should have trusted more in Chas.

"When Cougar was born, Webb accepted the little boy as his own. Belle and I were surprised because Webb had disapproved of the whole situation. But even though Webb cared for my child he was still not happy with me.

He thought I had disgraced the Taylor name. I became withdrawn and despondent, and missed my friends in the village. Cougar had a good home at Fallen Tree, had made a life for himself, even as a little boy, so I thought it best if I returned to the village. When I told them of my decision, Webb became furious. He told me that if I left, he would disown me. As you can imagine, I was in a quandary. Webb was angry with me for disgracing our family's name, yet he was livid that I wanted to leave. He would not speak to me, and I began to feel even more like an outsider." She stared into the fire, a frown marring her beautiful face as she remembered the pain of that time in her life.

"What about Chas?" Cady asked, intrigued by her story.

"He asked me to stay with him. I refused, of course. There was such scandalous talk about me already. I couldn't bring that to his door."

"But he loved you!"

"Yes, he did. Oh, it is so hard to explain! Chas said he understood, and of course we remained fast friends. I was lucky to have known such a wonderful man."

"I wish I had been so fortunate," Cady murmured sadly.

"When I returned to the village, without Cougar, I learned that Tall Feather's brother, Lightfoot, had lost his wife, leaving behind a newborn child. We came together and eventually married." Rose smiled warmly at her niece. "A few years later, Belle gave birth to Cassie. A beautiful, sweet little girl. When Belle died, Webb became lost in his grief and withdrew from his surroundings. Cougar was very young at the time and didn't understand why the man who he thought was his father had suddenly distanced himself. It was as if with Belle's passing, so did any love Webb might have had for Cougar. My son also missed Belle and didn't understand why she had left him.

"After Webb married Renee, bringing Terence with her, the situation turned bleak. They didn't need to be told that Cougar wasn't Webb's son. You'd just have to look at him and see no resemblance to Webb or Belle. They eventually learned the truth and in turn made Cougar's life miserable. Terence delighted in telling Cougar that he was in fact not Webb's son but the son of an Indian and a disgraced white woman.

"Cougar was so hurt and confused, he ran away and came to see me. I still don't know how he found me, but there he was outside my tipi one morning, demanding to know the truth. It was then I told him of his birth. I foolishly thought it would ease his pain. How wrong I was." She paused to sip her wine and brush away a tear from her cheek.

"Cougar was very angry with me. Not because of his background but because it had been kept secret from him. He firmly believed the distance Webb created between them was because he is half-Indian. I disagreed and said it was due to Belle's passing. Either way, I encouraged him to return home, still foolishly believing he would have a good life with Webb. I wasn't aware of the anguish Renee and Terence were causing him. He never mentioned it to me. He didn't stay long at Fallen Tree. He returned to the village, ultimately forgave me for my deception, and settled here with us."

"Then that messy business with Renee happened," Cady said with a frown.

"You know about that?"

"Yes, Renee told me."

"Then you can believe she told you lies," Rose said emphatically. "The truth is, that night Cougar went to visit Cassie. They would often meet secretly in the garden. Renee found them together and ordered Cassie into the house. Renee fancied herself in love with Cougar, and when he shunned her advances, she had him punished. To appease her own injured pride, and not let her feelings become known, she accused Cougar of attacking her and had him horsewhipped. When Webb returned from the range, he believed her lies and banished Cougar from his life."

"Renee told me that Webb had him whipped."

"Not true."

"Does Webb care that Cougar is half-Indian?"

"I think it might be a consideration but not a powerful one. Remember, it had never mattered before, that is, after his birth and before Belle's death. If he had any prejudice, he dealt with it. It didn't help when I returned to the village. Like a slap in the face. But despite Chas's insistence that Renee lied and his pleas to Webb to reconsider his actions, Webb stood firm. Perhaps he was jealous of Chas's relationship with Cougar." She glanced at Cassie. "I understand he drinks."

"Yes, but not nearly as much."

"Your grandfather loved Cougar like his own son. And Cougar returned the affection. Chas was the only one who really understood Cougar."

"Why does Cougar live in a cabin and not here in the village?"

"My son is a man caught between two worlds."

"I don't understand."

"When the circumstances of his birth became

known, Cougar had a difficult time because of his mixed blood. He proved himself here, so the village readily accepted him, but he is still shunned by the white community. For years he was ashamed of his bloodline. Especially with so many vile stories circulating about Indians. When he learned more about their customs, their beliefs, he came to embrace their ways with pride. But he is still torn, feeling not fully a part of either world. Therefore, he prefers to keep to himself."

"I know I'd like to see him more than I do, but it isn't wise for him to come to Fallen Tree," Cassie interjected, her eyes filled with disappointment. "Just look what happened the other night? Renee and her lies," she muttered, sullenly.

"Yes, it's probably best that he doesn't. For now," Rose agreed. She studied Cady's drawn expression. "Have you read your grandfather's letter?"

Cady looked at her in surprise. "What letter?"

"Then it still has not been found?"

Cady shook her head. 'I know of no letter. How do you?"

"Chas told Cougar about it the night he died."

"What does it say?"

"I don't know." She hesitated before continuing, "I understand you have learned what the codicil states."

"Yes."

"And does this displease you?"

"Well..." Cady paused, not wishing to speak ill of her son.

"What exactly have you been told?"

"The story about Renee as well as the likelihood that Cougar—Austin—committed murder. Terence claims he killed Chas because he covets Ponderosa Pines."

"I suspect he wants you to believe Cougar guilty so that he can move in and claim you for his wife, thereby inheriting the ranch."

"But he has Fallen Tree."

"Greed does not give someone more sense, merely more want. I'm sure he's afraid Chas might have left it to Cougar. He's not aware that Cougar isn't interested in material wealth. Being half-Indian, he lives off the land. Unlike that ungrateful wretch, Terence." Rose scowled. "I believe he would do anything to gain wealth."

"You don't like Terence, do you?" guessed Cady with a wry grin.

"I do not. How did you come to?" she asked, not maliciously but merely out of curiosity.

"He was kind to me and wanted us to be friends. He seemed to genuinely care for me. Then all I kept hearing about was what Austin had done and what a bad person he was. At the time, I had no idea that Austin and Cougar were the same man."

"Cougar is his Indian name."

"Yes, I know that now."

"He was named after the sacred black mountain lion that roams the mountains. It is solitary and elusive, and it's whispered that it protects those destined for true happiness."

"Truly?" Cady whispered her eyes wide. Then shaking her head, she suppressed a scoff, not wanting to hurt Rose's feelings. Not for one minute did she believe the myth. "There is no such thing as true happiness. You are lucky to get a slice of it in your entire life."

"You believe that?"

"I do." She gazed into the fire. A small seed of doubt had begun to grow as Rose's story unfolded. Now that she had heard it, she knew she had been too hasty in accusing Cougar, too quick to believe Renee and Terence.

"I am ashamed. How could I have been so stupid?" She shook her head. "To think for one minute that Cougar would kill the man who had not only loved him like his own son but who also loved his mother." She looked up at Rose, her eyes brimming with tears. "I'm so sorry, Rose."

"I forgive you, child. My son will too."

"Cougar hates me," she whispered brokenly. "I said such awful things to him."

"Cady, you need to rid yourself of anger and blame. It will only bring you sorrow. It will do no good to lament the past. Or the future, for that matter. It is already destined."

"The future," Cady echoed, seeing nothing but loneliness and desolation ahead of her.

"Go in peace, child. The Great Spirit willing, it will all work out as it is meant to be."

Cady rose to her feet and impulsively reached out and hugged Rose. "Thank you for telling me this story," she whispered. She turned on her heel and ran from the tipi. Cassie gave her aunt a quick hug and followed Cady outside.

Despite all the evidence to the contrary, Cady had made a terrible mistake in believing Renee and Terence. They said Cougar had killed her grandfather. And she had believed them. They said Cougar had attacked Renee. And she had believed them. Of course, in her defense, some of what Terence had said made sense, and the story Renee had told her had been very convincing. So much evidence had pointed to Cougar that she had readily believed their lies. But she should have known in her heart that they were not true.

Chas had trusted Cougar, had loved him, and Cougar had returned that love. So why would he kill Chas? What would he hope to gain? Ponderosa Pines, like Terence claimed? Not hardly, Cady scoffed, tending to believe Rose's version of the truth. She could feel her doubts melting away as quickly and surely as the snow in spring.

Chapter 23

When Cady returned home from her visit with Rose, she found Terence pacing the front porch. His blond hair was tousled as if he had continually run his fingers through it. When she reined to a stop, he hurried down the steps to her side.

"Where have you been?" he demanded, assisting her down from the Palomino. One side of his face was bruised, and the eye half closed, compliments of Cougar.

"I went for a ride. Why?" she asked, taken back by his brusque tone. She was not about to tell him of her visit with Rose, especially after everything she'd just learned.

"I've been worried." His tone softened.

Cady tossed the reins to Raul, who had come running from the corral, and started up the front steps to the porch. "Really, Terence, I'm perfectly capable of taking care of myself. I certainly don't need a caretaker." She glanced over her shoulder, lifting one brow. "Was there something you wanted?"

"Well, yes. I'd like to talk to you about Austin."

Cady leaned her hip against the wooden railing and crossed her arms over her chest. "Why do you hate him?"

'Who told you I hate him?"

"I was in the garden last night when you and Webb confronted him."

"Cady, he's absolutely no good."

"Why?"

"Well for one thing, he will do anything to get what he wants."

"And just what does he want?"

"Ponderosa Pines."

"I find that hard to believe."

"Is it?"

"Yes. He's never said or done anything conveying a wish to own my ranch."

"Cady, hear me out. I think he knew there was a codicil and was afraid it named me as the man you had to marry. So he decided to do something about it." He held up his hand. "Let me finish, please. The day after Chas was shot, I was in the saloon conducting some business. I overheard one of your men say that he had seen Austin ride away from the house that night."

"That doesn't prove a thing! Did anyone see him pull the trigger?"

Terence shook his head. "No, but it's pretty damning evidence, don't you think?" At her hesitation, he continued. "Austin has a lot of hatred built up inside him."

"Why does Webb dislike him?"

"Because of what he did to Ma."

"And you believe that it happened?"

"Of course! Don't you?"

She ignored his question and said instead, "My grandfather trusted him, even loved him."

"Your grandfather was a wise man, but he was blind when it came to Austin. He was in love with his mother."

"That still doesn't explain your insistence that he shot my grandfather."

"If you'd only think about it, you will see that I'm

right. Don't you want to see justice done?"

"Well, of course, but—"

"Cady, everything I've said makes sense. I don't want to believe it either. I mean, he is family—sort of. Listen, I can bring the sheriff here. You bring Austin here. The sheriff can question him. If he's innocent, then the subject is closed."

"No."

"No?"

"Terence, I don't believe he's guilty."

"What?" Terence cried. "Are you blind?" He paused and studied her set expression and rosy cheeks. "You're in love with him!" He grabbed her shoulders. "Are you in love with him?" he shouted in her face.

She jerked out of his grasp. "I'm tired, Terence. I'd like you to leave."

He stepped back. "Of course, you are. I'm sorry, Cady." He turned and went down the steps to his horse. "I will come back another time."

She went into the house, closed the door, and leaned her forehead against the cool wood, a maelstrom of emotions. She hated herself for believing their lies, believing Cougar guilty and refusing to listen to him. She was so thankful she'd visited with Rose and heard her story—the truth. No longer conflicted, she knew in her heart Cougar was innocent. But what did it matter now? Cougar was lost to her. She doubted she would ever see him again.

She pushed herself away from the door and went into the parlor and poured herself a short glass of sherry. Sipping the wine—and resolutely ignoring the color that reminded her of his eyes—she strolled to the window and looked out at the landscape. The cooler weather had begun turning the trees into a beautiful bouquet of golden-yellow, orange, and bronze, blending warmly with the green pine trees and the brown rugged mountains. The days were still warm beneath the early autumn sun, but the nights had a decidedly crisp edge to them.

She saw a rider galloping toward the house and watched in curiosity as it sped down the sloping hill. When the rider neared, she recognized Terence, a worried expression on his face. She set down her glass and ran to the front door and waited on the porch for him to dismount.

"Terence, what is it?"

"It's Cassie. She's been thrown from her horse."

"Oh, dear, is she hurt?"

"She's asking for Austin. Will you get him?"

"Me? Why me?"

"Do you honestly think he'll come if I go for him?" At her hesitation, he yelled, "Cady, just go! And bring him here." At her confused expression, he explained. "Randy is bringing Cassie to Ponderosa Pines. She was thrown just over the ridge," he said, jerking his thumb over his shoulder.

"All right, I'll go. Do you know where I can find him?"

"I'm not sure, but Cassie gave me general directions to his cabin. I'm hoping you'll remember from when you spent the night there." He hid his jealousy over that quite nicely.

Minutes later, Cady was pulling herself up onto the Palomino's back. She turned toward the mountains rising majestically in the distance and kicked her heels into the horse's sides.

Several hours later Cady pulled up in the shade of a group of aspen trees, their brilliant golden-yellow leaves looking like thousands of butterflies fluttering in the breeze. There was no doubt about it, she was hopelessly lost. As she looked around in dismay, it dawned on her just how much danger she was in—travelling around the countryside alone.

She thought for sure she had followed Terence's directions. She had travelled north through lush meadows, ridden though fragrant pine forests, and crossed several small streams, finally reaching the foothills of the mountains. She now needed to find the rock formation that signaled the entrance to the valley where Cougar's cabin was located. If only she hadn't slept the entire time Cougar had taken her home. She'd now know her way back.

She spied a trail through the mountains and clicked to her horse to head toward it. She rode down the narrow path praying she was headed in the right direction. A loud purring sound vibrated down the path at the same time the Palomino snorted and flattened its ears against its head. She pulled up on the reins as Dream began to prance and looked around for what was spooking her horse. She found it, high above the trail—a mountain lion crouched on a large boulder. Fighting to keep her horse under control, she told herself not to panic. When the Palomino finally calmed, Cady urged it slowly down the path, glancing warily over her shoulder. The large cat walked along the top of the rocks, following her, the sun glinting off its black fur. When it showed no sign of attacking, Cady urged her horse to a faster gait.

Without warning, her horse reared, its front hooves pawing the air and almost unseating Cady. She fought to stay on its back until it quieted and once again stood on all four legs.

She looked up and gasped in distress. *Not again!*

Two of the meanest-looking men Cady had ever seen, each sporting a rifle pointed at her, blocked the trail. She stiffened in the saddle, her heart plummeting to her stomach.

Their dark eyes shifted past her and, satisfied she was alone, they lowered their guns. One of the men pushed back his hat and leaned against his rifle, nonchalantly picking his teeth with a dirty fingernail. He was thin and wiry, with dirty blond hair that straggled past his shoulders. A jagged scar sliced his whisker-stubbled cheek, pulling down his right eye and leaving him with a permanently hideous expression.

"What have we here?" He winked at his partner. "Looks mighty lonely, don't she?" He swung his gaze back to Cady. "You lonely, little lady? Me and Harry can keep you company."

"Yep, Gus, we could have a real good time." Harry snickered. He was shorter than Gus and had a mop of curly black hair and a thick black mustache. He looked like he had never taken a bath.

They laughed in unison, the chilling sound sending shivers down Cady's spine. She inched her hand slowly toward her holster and, wrapping her hand around the butt of her gun, yanked it out. It caught on the clasp and tumbled to the ground. She stared down at it in dismay, cursing her clumsiness.

"Ain't too handy with a gun," Gus observed with a chuckle, still picking his teeth.

Squelching her fear, she clenched her fists to keep her hands from shaking. "What do you want?" she demanded, sitting up straighter in the saddle, and putting on her most menacing expression.

"Just a little fun," Gus replied with an evil grin.

At his smirk, her flesh crawled, and her throat became as dry as the desert. Her eyes darted around, desperately seeking a means of escape. She spotted the black mountain lion perched on the rocks, quietly watching the scene unfold. The men were unaware of its presence.

Gus straightened and edged closer. "You sure are a pretty little thing. I got me a hankering to taste you. You take care of me and Harry, and we won't hurt you none." He winked at Harry, who guffawed in response.

"Now git down off that horse," he demanded, his voice turning hard. He nodded to Harry. "Grab the reins," he said as she slid off the Palomino. She stayed next to the mare, pressed up against its warm sweaty side.

"Now start walking. That way," Gus ordered, pointing to a wide niche in the rocks.

She hesitated as her mind raced frantically for a way out of this predicament. "I have money. It's yours."

"Oh, we'll take that when we're done havin' fun," Gus said, poking her in the back with his rifle. She moved forward with feet dragging and knees shaking. She was fast losing her composure yet couldn't think of a thing to do to save herself.

Cady pressed up against the rocks, the sharp edges digging painfully into her back. Harry trained his rifle on her as Gus leaned closer, a lurid grin twisting his dirty, scarred face. His foul breath assailed her nostrils and just before his mouth touched hers, she ducked her head and screamed, pushing with all her strength against his chest.

Gus grabbed her arms and threw her to the ground, knocking the wind from her. She lay on her back in a daze, shaking her head to clear it of stars. Gus tossed his hat aside and straddled her body. Gripping the edges of her shirt with both hands he yanked them apart, tearing the material down to her belly. She frantically tried to cover her bare breasts.

"Mighty pretty, lady," Gus said, spit pooling in the corner of his mouth. He grabbed her flailing hands in one of his and yanked them over her head. She kicked out, bucking her body off the ground to rid herself of the repulsive man. Gus leaned back and with his free hand caught the hem of her skirt. He licked his lips in anticipation as he yanked on it. He grunted in frustration and peered over his shoulder.

"What the blazes? What you got on, girl?" he asked in surprised rancor as he stared down at her long slender legs and the skirt that wouldn't go past her thighs.

Cady kicked out at him as he sidled back to sit on her legs. He took his knife from his belt and sliced the material in two. He was so intent on his near conquest that he failed to hear Harry's grunt of surprise.

In the blink of an eye, Gus was dragged off Cady's body and spun around. A quick fist to his jaw knocked him out cold, and he collapsed to the ground beside his unconscious cohort. Cady jumped to her feet, pulled the edges of her torn shirt over her bare breasts, and glanced at the two men who lay oblivious to their surroundings. She breathed a sigh of relief. Her relief was short-lived, however, when her champion turned and faced her.

"You," she breathed, taking a step back at the look on his face, his amber eyes hard as glass. Her startled gaze swept him from the top of his long midnight-black hair over his strong, square clean-shaven jaw, down his bare chest to his tan buckskins and knee-high moccasins.

"What in the hell are you doing out here? Alone?" Cougar asked incredulously, struggling to keep his temper under control. He still hadn't collected himself since seeing her trapped under her attacker and that merely heightened his anger.

She stiffened at his tone, averted her gaze from his angry one, and ignored the question.

"What? No thanks?"

Riled by his sarcastic tone, she retorted, "I didn't ask for your help."

"Should I have let those men have their way with you?"

"I would have figured out a way to get away— somehow," she muttered. knowing she was being childish. She fingered a button on her blouse that had survived and quickly clasped it together.

He shook his head. "You can't do a damn thing without getting into trouble. You are always in need of my help."

She stood glaring at him, her eyes snapping indigo fire. He was right, of course. At least that's how it looked. And that rankled.

"Still no thanks?"

"Should I thank you for murdering my grandfather?" she retorted.

He grabbed her upper arms and pulled her toward him. "You ungrateful little—!" He swore, trying unsuccessfully to keep his composure. He glared down at her, his expression hard. "I loved Chas like my own father—"

"Your father was an Indian!" She jerked out of his

painful grip.

"How did...I suppose they told you." He sighed. He was so tired of arguing with her. She believed him guilty and now knew of his bloodline. Two strikes against him. There was nothing he could say that would change her mind. *So be it.*

His tone flat, he asked, "What *are* you doing out here?"

"Oh—I was looking for you." She had completely forgotten about Cassie. She felt her frustration evaporate.

"That's a good one, Cady," he said and turned away.

"Cougar, wait!" She reached out and stopped him. "It's Cassie. She needs you."

"What's wrong?" He became instantly alert by her tone.

"She was thrown from her horse. Terence sent me to get you."

"Terence?" His eyes suddenly filled with doubt.

"Yes, she's asking for you. Please you must come."

Cougar frowned, his eyes narrowing. She seemed to be sincere—he hadn't known her to lie. Nodding, he stepped over the fallen men and confiscated their weapons. "Get the rope from your saddle," he ordered over his shoulder.

"Why?" she asked suspiciously.

"To tie them up," he replied in exasperation. He twisted around to look up at her with one brow lifted impatiently. "Unless, of course, I should tie you up instead?"

With a haughty lift of her nose, Cady bent down to retrieve her gun, then ran to get the rope. She returned to his side and handed it to him. She watched him tie up the two men, fascinated by the play of muscles in his shoulders and back. She saw the long, jagged scars, the raised welts, that crisscrossed the broad expanse of his naked back and frowned. She felt anger at the injustice—she felt his pain. He had been punished for something he didn't do, she now believed that with all her heart. She had been wrong, so very wrong. Suddenly, any remaining doubt vanished into thin air.

Her gaze dropped to his legs where, crouched on his heels, muscles bulged beneath his tight buckskins. When he rose to his full height and turned around, her eyes moved to his chest. Not only was his jaw clean-shaven but the wide expanse of his chest was smooth as well, the nipples dark shadows against his bronzed skin. The sight made her giddy, her fingers aching to feel his skin. She lifted her gaze to his face, found him watching her closely, his eyes unreadable, and she quickly averted her gaze, blushing.

"Do I meet with your approval, darlin'?" he drawled, hoping to hell his manhood wasn't standing at attention under her blatant perusal. "At least you're not eating a biscuit," he remarked dryly, reminding her of one of her more embarrassing moments.

Her face as hot as the sun, she lifted her chin. "I'm just trying to get over the difference in your appearance," she snapped, trying in vain to excuse her obsession with his nearly naked body. She knew she had failed miserably when his shoulders shook with laughter. He acknowledged her appreciation with a jaunty nod of his head, disappeared behind the rocks, and returned with his stallion.

"Let's go," he ordered, swinging up onto the great black-and-white steed. His eyes travelled over her features. She was lovely, more so than in his dreams.

Desire swept through him, and he was hard pressed not to pull her onto his lap and kiss her until she begged for more. He tore his gaze away from her bewitching beauty and stared off into the distance while she mounted the Palomino.

He pulled on the reins, swung the stallion around, and started to ride away. Cady nudged her horse with her heels and jogged after him. She looked around for the mountain lion that had followed her earlier, but it had disappeared. It had been a *black* mountain lion. Rose's words echoed in her mind. She shook her head and scoffed. *It was only a myth.* An unfounded tale meant to give hope to those who had none. *She* was not meant to find true happiness.

****

The sun was grazing the tops of the mountains when Cougar and Cady rode up to the hacienda. Cougar had been skeptical when Cady told him Cassie waited for him at Ponderosa Pines, still wondering if she was playing him. She believed him to be guilty, her earlier accusations proved that, but she had assured him that Randy was bringing Cassie there, having been thrown from her horse on Grayson land.

Cady dismounted, stepped back from her horse and looked up at him, still astride the stallion.

"Cougar?" He was looking at the house, his expression thunderous. She turned, following his gaze, and frowned in confusion. Sheriff Bosler had stepped out onto the porch, two deputies by his side, his rifle trained on Cougar.

"You're under arrest," the sheriff said without preamble.

"May I ask why?" Cougar asked, his back straight,

his cold hard gaze swinging back to Cady. She was staring at the sheriff, looking bewildered.

"For the murder of Chas Grayson."

"What?" Cady gasped, a sickening feeling growing in the pit of her stomach. She looked at Cougar and wanted to melt into the ground. His eyes were filled with angry contempt as he glared down at her. Dragging her gaze away, she watched in disbelief as Terence stepped from behind the sheriff, a smug smile on his face.

"On what grounds?" Cougar inquired, lifting his gaze to the sheriff, ignoring her apparent confusion.

"We have witnesses who saw you ride away from the scene."

"Is that all?" He arched a brow and waited for the sheriff to continue.

"Don't bother to deny it!" Terence shouted triumphantly.

"Terence, where's Cassie?" Cady asked slowly, the feeling of unease rising, as the awful truth was beginning to dawn.

"She's at home, of course."

"But you said…" She looked at Cougar and took a step back at his fury, frightening in its intensity. "Cougar, I—"

"I don't want to hear your lies," Cougar growled.

"But I swear, I didn't know—"

"To hell with you."

"I'll take your gun, Austin," the sheriff demanded. "And your knife."

"I'll ask you again, Sheriff. What proof do you have?"

"Well, we found half a bandanna outside the window."

"So? I found the other half," he said, ignoring Cady's gasp. Sheriff Bosler disregarded his remark and stepped forward to relieve him of his weapons.

Cady was numb. It was obvious he thought she had betrayed him. If she were in his place, she would think the same thing. She felt him draw away from her, turn into himself, as a rock-solid wall was erected between them. She turned away from his animosity only to meet Maria's frown of disapproval. The housekeeper had followed Terence onto the porch and was now shaking her head, muttering under her breath.

With one last look at Cougar, Cady ran into the house. She couldn't bear to be near him, hating her as he did. His enmity was a beast, tearing her heart to shreds. She watched from the parlor window as Sheriff Bosler clasped handcuffs around Cougar's wrists and the men turned down the drive, the sheriff leading the stallion by the reins. The deputies fell in behind. The setting sun glinted off Cougar's midnight-black hair, his handsome profile made of stone.

She turned away from the window and watched Terence saunter into the room. He made his way to the sideboard and poured himself a whiskey. Resentment flared, burning brightly.

"You tricked me."

"I'm sorry about that."

"Damn it, Terence, you lied to me!"

"Austin is guilty! He has to pay for his crimes." He drained the glass and set it down. Clasping her hands in his, he said sincerely. "My offer of marriage still stands. I can give you protection and companionship."

"You've got to be kidding."

'No, I'm not." He dropped her hands and took a step

back.

"First of all, I don't trust you." She waved her hand toward the window. "And second of all, at this moment, I don't like you very much. I will not marry you."

"I wish you would reconsider. I think you will find it to be the wisest thing to do."

"Terence, I will never marry you! I wouldn't marry you if my grandfather rose from his grave and demanded it!"

"That's really too bad," he snapped, his expression turning ugly. "I have gone to too much trouble to have it any other way." Cady watched him stride from the room, her mouth agape in astonishment. He had never used that tone of voice with her. He'd always been pleasant, willing to help, albeit a bit persistent. A shiver of apprehension shook her shoulders. *What exactly has he done?*

Maria entered the parlor a few minutes later and planted herself in front of Cady. "This is a stupid thing you have done, Señorita Cady. Señor Austin loved your grandfather. Señor Chas would not be happy about this."

"Do you think I am?"

"Señor Austin is a good, honorable man. He did not do this!" Maria nearly shouted.

"I know that!" Cady did shout back.

"Humph," Maria snorted but shot her a curious look before leaving the room.

Cady sank to the sofa. The events of the past hours culminating with Cougar's arrest had sapped her energy, and she was suddenly exhausted. She laid her head against the back of the sofa and closed her eyes.

Raul came in a little while later with a small bundle of mail Carlos had picked up in town. Seeing his *patróna* asleep, he placed it on the table next to the sofa and retreated on silent feet.

Chapter 24

Cady rose with the sun. At some point during the night, she had made her way from the parlor to her bedroom. She had slept little if at all, and exhaustion coupled with guilt weighed heavy. She descended the stairs and went into the kitchen. The early morning sun streamed through the open window, illuminating the cactus-green and reddish-brown tiles. The aromas of baking bread and roasting meat filled the room.

"Good morning, Maria," Cady said, pouring herself a cup of coffee.

Maria turned from the kitchen fire where a cut of beef on a spit roasted over the flames, gave her a curt nod, and moved over to the table. She continued with her baking, expertly kneading the soft bread dough into rounds. Cady, uncomfortable beneath Maria's silent censure, left the room and sought solace in the parlor. If Maria didn't believe her, how could she possibly convince Cougar that she had been duped by Terence?

She dropped to the sofa, sipping on the coffee, and stared blindly out the window, her thoughts banging into each other. Every way she looked at the situation made her miserable. She absentmindedly stroked the head of her puppy, who sat curled in her lap. How easy it had been for Terence to trick her—as usual she had believed his lies. But he had shown his true colors by having Cougar arrested. His kindness had been a façade. She knew that now. He hated Cougar more than any of them, except perhaps Renee. The two of them were probably in on this together.

She reached for the bundle of mail, and idly rifled through it. A small brown envelope from Colorado caught her attention. She ripped it open and was surprised to find it from her cousin, Lucinda Grayson. What in the world could Wiley's sister want? She quickly scanned the letter. Lucinda wrote that she knew something about her brother that Cady needed to know, information she hesitated to put in writing. She begged Cady to travel to Silverhills to visit her.

What could Lucinda know? Cady was already aware Wiley was in town, or at least had been a few days ago when he came to Ponderosa Pines. She glanced back down at the letter. The ominous tone made Cady nervous. Could Wiley have something to do with all the mishaps that had occurred of late?

A commotion at the door drew her attention and she looked up in surprise when a tall, dark-haired man pushed past Maria and into the room.

"Señorita, it is him!"

"Who are you?" Cady asked the stranger who was leaning his hip against the wall watching her with heavy-lidded eyes.

"You don't know me?" he asked with a curl of his lip. "Tsk, tsk." He pushed his thumb arrogantly against his chest. "I'm your cousin, Wiley Grayson."

Cady's eyes widened in alarm, but she quickly hid her trepidation. She turned to Maria, who was wringing her hands in her apron and muttering an apology.

"It's all right, Maria," she said, trying to allay her housekeeper's worry.

"I just go and get Carlos," Maria said, turning on her heel and disappearing down the hallway.

"What do you want?" Cady asked, twisting her fingers nervously in Oro's soft fur and pushing Lucinda's letter beneath the sofa cushion.

"Just some friendly conversation." Wiley strolled across the room to the sideboard and helped himself to a glass of whiskey. He brought the glass to his nose and sniffed in appreciation. "Mighty fine stuff you got here, cousin."

"We have nothing to talk about." Cady moved the puppy off her lap, stood, and faced Wiley with her hands fisted by her sides.

"Ah, come now, Cady. We're family, ain't we?" he pouted, yet a glint hardened his brown eyes.

"Get out of here, Wiley. You were not welcome when Chas was alive, and you are certainly not welcome now."

"Is that so?" he sneered. "Ain't very friendly, are you?"

"I told you to leave," she said stiffly, hoping her fear didn't show in her voice.

"Fine, but you're coming with me." He placed the glass on the sideboard with enough force to cause the whiskey to slosh over the rim, dribble down the sides and stain the rug.

"I'm not going anywhere with you. Now get out!"

Wiley drew his gun and said through gritted teeth, "You bitch! So high and mighty, ain't you? Think you got it all!" he sneered. "You're coming with me. Now get moving!"

Cady's mouth turned dry as the barrel of his gun bore down on her like a lethal black tunnel. Oro, sensing her fear, began to bark, startling Wiley. He jerked his hand and with a muttered curse, leveled his gun at the puppy. With a nasty grin, he pulled the trigger. Oro yelped in pain and cowered on the floor, a small spot of blood staining his golden fur. With a cry, Cady fell to her knees beside her wounded pet and tried to soothe its whimpering.

"Get up, bitch!" Wiley demanded, glancing nervously over his shoulder at the sound of footsteps running down the hallway. In a panic, he faced the door as Carlos appeared, his gun drawn. Wiley swung his gun back on Cady.

"Get outta my way or she's dead!" he shouted. Helplessly, Carlos dropped his gun and raised his hands above his head. Wiley glanced back at Cady and spat, "The old man didn't die for nothin'. It will still be mine...all of it." He backed out of the room, his fist raised in anger. "This ain't over, bitch!" he shouted with an evil curl of his lip and then, shoving Carlos aside, he fled the room.

His words echoed ominously in the room, and Cady's eyes widened in horror. She had heard that before! She wrinkled her nose at the odor permeating the room, and her heart nearly stopped. She knew that smell!

Wiley had killed her grandfather! Wiley had kidnapped her! She was sure of it! The sound of rapid hoofbeats racing away from the house startled her back to awareness.

"Let him go!" she yelled at Carlos who had grabbed his gun and made to run after Wiley. "I don't need you hurt, too." She gathered the whimpering puppy carefully in her arms and ran to the kitchen, calling out for Maria, heedless of the blood staining her shirt.

"Maria, he shot my puppy!" Cady cried as she laid him on the table and stepped back. Maria bent over the little dog and quickly assessed the wound.

"It is all right, Señorita," she said reassuringly. "The bullet just skimmed his skin. I will clean it and he will be as good as new."

Cady peered anxiously over the housekeeper's shoulder, shifting from one foot to the other, flinching every time her puppy whined in pain.

While Maria tended to her pet, Cady worried over this new turn of events. She reached for a lock of hair and began twisting it furiously around her finger. Could Lucinda confirm what she herself already suspected?

It all made sense now, of course. With Chas dead, and if she, too, were out of the way, Wiley had everything to gain. Lord, if Wiley was indeed the culprit, she didn't have any time to waste. Her life was in danger.

She *had* to find proof that Cougar was innocent. He would never forgive her, she knew, but she had to at least try to get him out of jail, nevertheless. She shuddered, recalling his eyes—cold and unfeeling. No, he would never forgive her.

She needed to talk to someone, but who? Terence? No! Whether Cougar was guilty or not he would be all too happy to keep him incarcerated for the rest of his life. Webb? Good Lord, no! He would not lift a finger to help Cougar. Cassie? Of course! Between the two of them they would be able to figure out what to do.

Maria placed the puppy in Cady's arms. "You see, Señorita? Little Oro is all better."

"Thank you, Maria." She leaned over and kissed her on the cheek, then placed the puppy in his basket in the corner of the kitchen. "I'm going to Fallen Tree."

"*Si*, Señorita. But be careful. That awful man is out there somewhere."

Cady ran out the kitchen door and down to the stables. The work had been slow, but the building of the new stables had been completed. She found Randy in the tack room having just come in from the range. The foreman tipped his hat in greeting.

"Morning, ma'am."

"Good morning, Randy," she said as she pulled on her riding gloves. "How is your shoulder healing."

"Almost as good as new, ma'am."

"How are things going on the ranch?" she asked while Raul saddled Dream.

"We've had a spot of trouble lately. Some cattle are missing and one of the stations caught fire and burned to the ground."

"Was anyone injured?" she asked in alarm.

"No, ma'am."

"Is it normal for cattle to go missing?"

"Not usually, but they could have wandered off to better grazing land. I've sent some of the men to check on it."

"Randy, I know you heard about the sheriff arresting Cougar. Do you believe he could be capable of killing my grandfather?"

Randy shook his head. "No, ma'am. I know for a fact that he and Mr. Grayson were very close. Almost like father and son."

"Have you met Wiley Grayson?"

"Yes, ma'am. He came here and gave Mr. Grayson an awful time. Wasn't too long before Mr. Grayson was shot. Why?"

"He was just here…" She spotted a rider coming up

the back drive and recognized Cassie atop her bay mare.

"Cassie!" Cady called out as she rode into the yard. "I was just on my way to see you."

"Morning, Cassie," Randy said with a tip of his hat and a smile.

"Randy," she murmured, a pretty blush coloring her cheeks as she allowed him to assist her from her horse. "Who was that racing away from here?" Cassie asked, glancing over her shoulder at the lingering cloud of dust.

"My cousin, Wiley. He tried to take me with him. And he shot Oro!"

"Are you all right?" Cassie asked in alarm, grabbing Cady's wrist.

"Did he hurt you?" Randy asked, moving toward his horse.

"Randy, wait! Don't go after him. I'm fine, truly," Cady reassured him.

"Well, if you're sure." Randy didn't look too happy but obeyed her wishes.

Cady looked at Cassie. "I need to talk to you."

"Of course." She gave Randy one last look and followed Cady to the courtyard, where they sat beneath the scented branches of a pine tree. Maria had seen Cassie arrive and brought them a frosty pitcher of lemonade and a platter of aniseed cookies. Cady waited for her to leave before turning to Cassie.

"I need your help. But it has to be in the strictest of confidence." At Cassie's nod, she continued, "Are you aware that Chas disinherited his eldest son?"

"Cal? Yes, Pa told me the story."

"As I said, Wiley was just here. Apparently, he has been here twice before. Once, a few years ago, and the second time as recently as a few months ago. Both times he gave Chas a hard time about the will."

"I remember the most recent visit. I overhead Pa and Chas talking about it.

"Well, today he said some awful things, things that have got me thinking. And just this morning, I received a letter from Lucinda Grayson, his sister. She says that she has some important information about Wiley that I need to know. She wants me to visit her in Colorado, at her home in Silverhills."

"What do you think it is?"

"I don't know, but I aim to find out."

"Cady, what are you going to do?"

"Go to Silverhills, of course." Cady was tired of being a pawn in someone's sick game of revenge. It was her future at stake, and she was going to find out the truth. "Now, how do I go about getting there? Is there a stage?"

"Austin. He'll take you," Cassie said confidently.

"Uh, Cassie…Cougar's in jail," Cady said, reaching for a lock of hair and wrapping it around her finger.

"He's what?" Cassie stared at her in disbelief.

"He was arrested yesterday."

"Why?"

"For killing my grandfather." Cady took a deep drink of lemonade to moisten her suddenly dry throat. "Terence tricked me. He told me you'd been thrown from your horse and was asking for Austin. I, of course, went to get him, believing you had been injured. When I brought him here, Terence had the sheriff waiting to take him in. The next thing I knew, he was hauled off to jail."

"Oh, dear," Cassie whispered, biting her lower lip.

"Cougar thinks I was in on it and brought him here knowing the sheriff was waiting. But I didn't know! I swear!"

Cassie clasped Cady's hands. "I believe you, Cady. And I'm sure Austin will too—when you explain it to him."

"I'm afraid he will never forgive me," Cady said sadly. "He was so mad."

"Austin is proud but fair. He'll come around." She peered into Cady's face. "Do you still believe he is guilty?"

"No!" Cady cried vehemently. "I had already come to the conclusion I'd been wrong, so very wrong, when I was duped by Terence."

"Maybe you should tell Austin what you've just told me."

"I've tried. He will not listen." A tear slipped down her cheek. "The expression on his face nearly felled me."

"But—"

"Cassie, when Sheriff Bosler put the handcuffs on him—" She covered her face with her hands, smothering a sob. "It was awful."

"Cady, are you in love with Austin?"

"Certainly not!" She sat upright. "Everyone I've ever loved has deserted me, either by choice or by death. I shall never love again!" she added, a bit dramatically.

Cassie looked doubtful but held her tongue. The two girls sat quietly in the courtyard, each engrossed with their own thoughts. Suddenly, Cady jumped to her feet.

"Where are you going?"

"First, I have to get Cougar out of jail," she said. "Then I'm going to figure out a way to get to Silverhills. Even if I have to go there myself. Do you want to go into town with me?"

"No, I have to get back to Fallen Tree."

It was then Cady noticed a fresh bruise on Cassie's face, near her ear, almost hidden by her hair. "Cassie, who did this?" she asked, touching the discolored skin.

"This? Oh, it's nothing!" she said, clearly flustered, and turned away, trying to hide her face.

"Cassie—"

"Cady, please—"

"Is Webb hitting you?"

"Oh, heavens, no!"

"Terence? Renee? Don't be frightened. It's Renee, isn't it?"

"Yes," she whispered tearfully.

"Why, Cassie? Why does she strike you?"

Cassie slumped forward. "To keep me away from Pa. She never liked the bond we shared, at least until she arrived. I think she also resents me. She knows how close Austin and I are. Maybe she's jealous...I don't know. And if I so much as disagree with her—" She shrugged her shoulders.

Cady's mouth drew into a grim line. "We have to do something about this." She remembered Cougar's words in the garden the night of the party, warning Webb about the abuse. He was aware of it too, but had admonished the wrong person. She would set him straight. "I will speak to Cougar about it."

"No," Cassie said quickly, her eyes wide with fear.

"Why not?"

"He would kill her," she stated flatly. "Not literally, of course, but he'd find a way to stop her, and who knows what she'd do to retaliate!"

Cady thought that was probably true, she would most definitely strike back. Even so, she believed that those who abused did not value mankind and therefore were not entitled to enjoy the gift of life. "Cassie, go home. We will speak of this later." She touched her hand. "In the meantime, if she hits you again—hit back."

Chapter 25

Cady sawed on the reins in front of the sheriff's office, leapt from the Palomino, and rushed through the door. He glanced up in surprise and jumped to his feet, reaching for his gun when the door of his office flew open.

"Cady!" He relaxed and resumed his seat. "What brings you here?"

"I want you to release Cougar, er, Austin Taylor."

"I can't do that," he said with a shake of his head.

"But his arrest was a horrible mistake. He did not kill my grandfather."

"Sorry, ma'am. He stays in jail until the trial."

"But it was Terence—he tricked me into bringing Cougar to Ponderosa Pines. I had no intention of turning him over to you." Her pleas did not budge him. She eyed his stony expression. "Sheriff, do you know Wiley Grayson?"

"Ain't never met him. Heard your grandfather talk of him, though. Not very kindly, I might add." He tucked his thumbs inside his suspenders and leaned his chair back against the wall. "Why?"

"I want him arrested."

"What for?"

"I believe he is responsible for Chas's murder."

"Do you have proof?"

"No, not yet."

He waved his hand. "Talk to me when you do."

"He tried to make me go with him against my will. I also think he kidnapped me once before." She placed her hands on his desk. "And he shot my puppy."

"Sounds like you're a magnet for trouble."

"It's not my fault, Sheriff. Someone obviously wants me out of the picture. I think it's Wiley," she added with a firm nod of her head.

"Why would he want you gone? What would he gain?"

"He'd get Chas's inheritance."

The sheriff pursed his lips. "Let me get this straight. First you want Taylor arrested because you think he killed your grandfather."

"I did *not* want him arrested," she clarified.

"Now you want him released. And now you want me to arrest your cousin because you think he did do it *and* that he's trying to kidnap you—"

"*Did* kidnap me."

"And he shot your dog. Really, Miss Grayson, I can't go around arresting everyone on your half-baked suspicions." He stood up. "Besides, in addition to your grandfather's murder, I arrested Taylor because there is another matter under investigation." He tilted his head to one side. "Is your dog dead?"

"No, Maria fixed him." She put her hands on her hips. "What about Wiley?"

"I'll look into it."

"Sheriff, why are you being so unreasonable?"

"I'm a busy man. I'm sorry if I sound brusque, but this is exactly why I didn't tell you who we suspected in the first place. Women tend to muddle things up."

"But—"

"Good day, Miss Grayson."

"So you won't release Cougar?"

"No. Besides, I'm waiting for a wire from Colorado."

"Very well." Cady spun on her heel but paused at the door. She thought to remind him of the fire in the stables and Randy's gunshot wound but didn't care to be further insulted. "If any harm comes to me, Sheriff, you have no one to blame but yourself."

****

As Cady neared the hacienda, she spied a horse tied out front. She didn't recognize it, but it was a beautiful animal—gray with dark spots over its entire body. She dismounted and made her way up the front steps. Maria met her in the foyer.

"You have a visitor," Maria said, her face wreathed in a smile. "Rose has come to see you!"

"Cougar's mother?" Cady swallowed past a lump of uneasiness and made her way to the parlor.

"Hello, Rose."

Rose turned from the window where she'd been admiring the view. She was dressed differently from when Cady had first met her, now wearing blue denims, a bright blue shirt, and leather boots.

"Hello, Cady." She held out her hand in greeting. Noticing her curious appraisal, she explained, "I dress differently when I leave the village, alone." They moved to the sofa, sitting next to each other. Rose placed a burlap bag on the table and turned to Cady.

"So—my son is in jail."

Cady ducked her head in embarrassment. "Yes. I…"

"I know you weren't responsible. It was Terence up to his old tricks."

"True, but Cougar thinks I betrayed him. I was just in town to see Sheriff Bosler. I tried to get Cougar released, but the sheriff won't budge."

Rose patted her hand. "Cougar can take care of himself." She clasped Cady's hands and took a deep breath, as if searching for her next words.

"You are destroying my son."

"I…what—?" Cady fell silent.

"He cares for you."

"Cares for me? He barely tolerates me." But Cady's heart did do a funny little flip. "Unless, of course, he's kissing me." Cady slapped her hand over her mouth.

Rose smiled to herself. How she treasured honesty! "The part of him that is his father keeps his emotions on a very tight rein. It's amazing the control he has over them. He's afraid of getting too close, concerned you will be ostracized if you're coupled with him, despite my advice to the contrary. However, desire for someone is hard to deny, regardless of one's beliefs. He cannot deny how he feels, and because he thinks he cannot act on his feelings, he's torn." She watched the rosy blush stain Cady's cheeks. *Or would he?*

"Well, that may be true, but why does he always get cross with *me*? He shows up whenever he feels like it, and after a spell, he'll get mad and abruptly leave."

"He's unable to decide what he thinks is right and what he wants to do," Rose reminded her.

"And if he's not angry with me, he's poking fun at me, ridiculing me—"

"He teases those he loves, Cady. Although there aren't many of us."

Love? Cady's heart did another little flip. "He said it would never work."

"Do you want it to?"

"I don't know. Everyone I have ever loved has left me with a broken heart."

"A heart that hasn't been broken, hasn't known love."

"Well, that may be true, but I will never love again."

She patted Cady's hand. "Give it time. And please do not shut yourself off from love. It's too wonderful." She reached for the burlap bag and handed it to Cady. "A gift for you."

Cady opened it and pulled out a pretty little ceramic bowl and two small pouches.

"You admired mine when you and Cassie came to the village. One pouch is sage, the other cedar. When burned, sage dispels negative energy and cedar cleanses the house and pulls in positive energy. You may burn them separately or together. Wherever sage or cedar burns, no evil will enter."

"What a beautiful belief. Thank you."

"I will take my leave now." She rose to her feet. "Remember, Cougar is a man of few words. His actions speak louder than anything he could say."

"Well, maybe—unless he's scolding me. Then he has plenty to say."

Rose laughed. "That I can agree with!"

"Well, it doesn't matter now. When the sheriff took him away, his fury was directed solely at me. I doubt he'll ever speak to me again."

"Not to worry, Cady. Give him time. He'll come around." She patted her hand. "You'll find your happiness."

Cady doubted that but didn't voice it. She escorted Rose to the door, then returned to the parlor to contemplate her visit and examine her gift. Maria entered, her apron covered with dust, her hair a mess.

"Rose has left? She is a lovely woman, that one."

"Yes, she is very kind." Cady looked up and laughed. "You look like you've been through a scuffle."

"I've been cleaning out your grandfather's study. You know, I have not been in there since—"

"I know."

"I understand you tried to get Señor Austin out of jail."

"Yes."

"That is good. I misjudged you. I am sorry."

"It's all right, Maria. I was thoroughly taken in by Terence's and Renee's lies. I will do everything I can to get Cougar free."

"You are just like the *patrón*. He believed in justice and wouldn't rest until it was carried out."

"What's that?" she asked, pointing to a brown envelope Maria held in her hand.

Maria handed it to her. "It is for you. I believe it is the letter Señor Chas wrote. Señor Austin asked me to look for it. I found it under the shelves in the *patrón*'s study."

The letter.

Cady turned the envelope over in her hands. Her name was scrawled across the front in bold black lettering. She brushed away the dust and cobwebs and ran her finger across her written name. She heard Maria leave the room yet continued to stare at the envelope. With a deep breath, she slid her finger under the flap and opened it. A single sheet of paper fell into her lap. She lifted it, found it covered with the same bold handwriting, and began to read.

My dearest Cady,

If you are reading this letter, then I am no longer on this earth. I hope you are not mourning me but rather getting on with your own life. I remember you as such a sweet and loving little girl, and my heart will always be filled with love for you.

I am sorry I did not have the chance to get to know you better. I was foolish to let the others sway me after your parents' deaths and should have insisted that you live with me. You must believe that I have always wanted you with me. Unfortunately, wishes do not always come true.

As you should know by now, you are my sole heir. I have, however, added a codicil to my will. In order for you to inherit my property, I ask that you marry Austin Taylor. You may think me as crazy as a loon for making such a request, but please try to understand that I do this for your own protection.

There are those that will go to any lengths to take what isn't theirs to have. I've done what I could to thwart them, but it may not be enough. With Austin by your side, he will protect you and keep you safe from harm.

You may hear some unsavory things about Austin. Let me assure you that they simply are not true. He has never wronged anyone. He has a kind heart and a gentle soul. There are those who have and will continue to spread lies about him. My dear, please, do not believe them. You can trust Austin with your life, as I have with mine. He is a good man. I am confident that you will come to love him as I do.

I can assure you that this is not done under duress. Austin does not desire, nor has he ever coveted, what is mine. He is only complying with my wishes. I hope you will find it in your heart to follow them as well.

There is one other thing I would ask of you. Perhaps you could find a way to bridge the gap between Austin and Webb. If you don't yet know the story, you will. There is love there, but it has been buried for so long I fear it may be lost forever. If you could do your best to see it done, I would be forever grateful.

I love you, child. I would not entrust your welfare to Austin if I did not believe it was for the best.

Your loving grandfather,

Chas

By the time Cady had finished reading the letter, tears were streaming down her cheeks. She could better understand why he had made the request. It was not blackmail, as she had railed at the lawyer, but a way to keep her safe.

She would never allow Wiley to inherit the ranch, knowing how much her grandfather did not want that to happen. But she couldn't keep the ranch without marrying Cougar, a man who probably didn't like her very much, despite what Rose said, and would most likely never even speak to her again. Sadness enveloped her like a well-worn blanket. She had always wanted a marriage like her parents'—a union filled with love. But it didn't look like that was her future—what a sad thought. In order to keep the ranch, she must marry a man who didn't love her. That thought was the saddest of all!

Chapter 26

Cady sat on her bed, fully clothed, tense with nervous excitement. When she heard the downstairs clock chime her appointed hour, she rose to her feet, strapped her holster around her waist and, after fitting her revolver into it, reached for the saddlebags she had packed earlier.

She made her way through the dark, silent house to the stables, where she led the Palomino from its stall and quickly threw a saddle over its back. She was pulling on the cinch when the hair on the back of her neck stood on end. She stiffened and jerked around. Seeing a shadow outlined in the doorway, she reached for her gun. It tumbled to the ground.

"Who's there?" the shadow asked, lifting the rifle it had clutched in its hands.

"Carlos?" She sighed in relief. "It's me, Cady." She bent to retrieve her gun.

"Señorita Cady? What are you doing?" He lowered his rifle and stepped inside.

"I'm going to Silverhills," she said, leading Dream from the stables.

"To Silverhills—Colorado? Alone?"

"Cougar is going with me," she assured him with the lie.

"Señor Austin is out of jail?" he asked skeptically, watching her mount the Palomino.

"Yes. I'm meeting him at Fallen Tree," she said, hating to lie but knowing Carlos would try to stop her if he knew she was traveling alone. She was afraid if he tried, she'd allow him to sway her. As it was, it took every ounce of courage she had to make the trip alone.

"Señorita, are you sure?"

"Of course. I have to hurry now. He's waiting for me." She waved at Carlos. "See you soon!"

"Well, if you are sure…" He stepped aside to allow her to pass.

The night was clear and cold with a myriad of lights twinkling in the ebony sky. A star streaked across the black expanse, falling slowly to the horizon, and out of a childhood habit, Cady impulsively whispered a wish.

She left Santa Fe behind, traveling north and following the base of the mountains. Night melted into morning and dawn brought with it a burst of color that splashed against the slate-blue sky, highlighting the wispy clouds. As the sun rose, the temperature climbed as well. Cady removed her jacket and freed the top buttons of her shirt.

She passed through a kaleidoscope of terrains. Flat, grassy plains became auburn-colored deserts with dry riverbeds and towering rock formations. Cacti dotted the desert among sand dunes sprinkled with sagebrush and prairie sunflowers.

She rode steadily throughout the day and by late afternoon had come upon a wide river that snaked down the mountains and flowed through a forest of cottonwoods, their leafy branches spread wide, affording desired shade. She dismounted and moved to the water's edge, leaving Dream to graze on the sweet grass. She knelt, cupped her hands with the cool water and splashed her face, licking the drops of water that trickled from her lips. She filled her canteen, then sat back on her heels, eyeing the seductively cool river. The surface rippled with white foamy peaks, swirling around rocks rising from the surface like fists of stone. How wonderful it would be to immerse her entire hot, clammy body in the sparkling water. She gave in to the urge, stripped down to her undergarments, and waded into the water, shivering as its cool fingers caressed her fevered skin.

She dipped below the surface to just above her breasts. The sun warmed her shoulders as the refreshing water swirled around her body. She spent unhurried minutes relishing the bliss until, without warning, her feet were snatched out from under her. She stumbled, trying to regain her footing in the turbulent undercurrent, but it was too powerful and proceeded to carry her downriver. She tried frantically to gain a foothold on the rocky river bottom, the sharp stones cutting into her skin as she desperately tried to keep her head above water. Through a watery haze, she spotted a huge boulder jutting from the river. She was helpless to avoid it with the current swiftly carrying her toward it, and she slammed into the rock, barely retaining a hold on the slippery, mossy surface. She hauled herself up, managing to pull half her body out of the rushing water. It pulled relentlessly, trying to take her with it downriver, and she held on to the rock for dear life. She wasn't far from shore but, surrounded by the turbulent water, she'd never make it.

She screamed for help, foolishly believing someone would hear her, though she had not seen a soul since leaving Ponderosa Pines. After several long minutes, exhausted, she laid her head on the boulder and closed her eyes.

Unbidden, her parents' image flashed before her. How she missed them! They had truly loved her, unconditionally. She had been so angry after their accident, blaming them for leaving her alone. They had not chosen to die, they had not decided one day to leave her, it had just happened, an unfortunate accident. Rose was right—she had to let go of her anger and blame. They hadn't wanted to leave her—just like her grandfather hadn't wanted to leave her either.

She had blamed everyone for her loss instead of taking what life handed her and making the most of it. She had created her own unhappiness and made sure everyone around her knew it. The world owed her nothing. *I am pathetic.*

She thought of Cougar and her heart surged with love. There was no denying it, no pretending it wasn't true—to the depth of her soul, she loved him. But in her stupidity, she had probably ruined that too.

Feeling her strength weakening as the river continued to suck hungrily at her body, waiting to devour her if she relented at all, she prayed for a miracle.

"Cady!"

She lifted her head, wondering if her mind was playing tricks on her. *Cougar!*

"Are you really here?" She felt a rush of joy and her heart soared as she drank in the sight of the magnificent man she loved.

"I am."

"But—you're in jail."

"Not anymore."

Crouched on the riverbank, a length of thick rope in his hands, he was busy fashioning a loop at one end. His expression was outwardly unruffled, expertly hiding his inner turmoil. The scare he had experienced when first seeing Cady clinging to the rock had not yet dissipated.

"Here—grab the end of the rope," he instructed calmly as he threw it out to her. The rope landed in the water. "Cady, you have to catch it," he said, pulling it in and tossing it out again. "Good," he said after she had grabbed the end of the rope. "Now slip it over your head. Tuck it under your arms. That's right. Now let go of the rock."

"I can't," she whispered, her voice trembling, her eyes wide with fright.

"It's all right, darlin'," he assured her. "I've got you."

She shook her head, lips pressed together.

"Cady, you must let go so I can bring you in." He noticed the stubborn set of her jaw even as it trembled. His sigh was dramatically loud. "For someone who claims she can take care of herself, you sure do get into a heap of trouble. And here I am, once again, coming to your rescue. You make a sorry wanderer, Cady."

He smiled inwardly when she glared at him then clenched her lips together in a determined line and, with a little cry, released her death grip on the rock. As soon as she did, she was drawn into the swift current, pulled beneath the choppy surface. She swallowed mouthfuls of water as Cougar reeled her in like a hooked fish. When her feet were once again on solid ground, she climbed up the riverbank and straight into Cougar's arms. He wrapped her in his strong embrace, while his heartbeat returned to normal.

She clung to him, trembling, soaking up his warmth. Too soon his body heat penetrated her chilled body and she pulled away, suddenly unsure. Now that she was safe, would he turn on her? Would his eyes be filled with hatred? She peeled wet strands of hair from her face and smiled uncertainly up at him, but all she saw was his concern.

"How did you find me?"

"You leave a trail a blind man could follow."

Cady sniffed and wiped her hand under her nose, his lopsided grin tugging at her heart. Confused by his attitude, she waited for him to light into her, certain he was still angry at her for her part in his arrest. But he said not a word, his eyes resonating with an emotion unfamiliar to her, one she couldn't name, as he untangled her from the rope. The wind caressed her body, rippling her skin with goose bumps. She rubbed warmth into her arms using brisk strokes of her hands. Feeling bare flesh beneath her fingers, she realized with a start that she was practically naked. She found Cougar studying her scantily clad body with interest.

"Turn your head!" she shouted in embarrassment. "I'm not dressed!"

"So I noticed," he drawled, removing his shirt and handing it to her. "Where are your clothes?"

She pointed upriver and quickly donned his shirt, instantly becoming warm from his body heat in the material. He strode off and, closing her eyes, she raised her arm and breathed in his scent. Watching his return, she appreciated the view as he walked, with the grace of an animal, with long purposeful strides, each part of his body in sync with the rest. He carried her clothes under one arm, her horse in tow. When he handed her the clothing, he took a moment to look her over, from her tousled wet hair to her legs bare from the knees down.

She ducked behind a tree to dress while he tied Dream beside his horse. She limped from behind the tree, tossed him his shirt, and sank to the ground, thankful he had not given her a hard time. Her relief was short-lived.

As soon as her bottom hit the ground, he lit into her, berating her for her foolish behavior. "What made you think you could make it to Colorado on your own? And *don't* tell me you are perfectly capable of taking care of yourself! We just witnessed that you are *not*!"

"It's all your fault," she told him, rubbing her sore foot, cringing at his reproach.

"My fault?" One brow arched incredulously.

"Yes."

"If you'll remember, darlin', you had me thrown in jail."

'No, I did not. Terence did. I was merely a pawn."

She ignored Cougar's derisive snort. He knelt on the ground in front of her and, brushing aside her hand, picked up her slender foot and turned it over, searching the cut and bruised sole for the source of her discomfort. A small stone had imbedded itself in the soft skin, and he began to gently knead the instep until he had worked it out. He continued to massage her foot, working his way up her calf, sliding under her pants' leg.

Fingers of fire shot through her body, and she became uncomfortably warm, dangerously hot. She jerked her leg from his hands and straightened her pants.

"I did try to get you out," she added in her defense, trying to calm her erratic heartbeat.

"Why?"

"I thought perhaps I was wrong about you," she conceded. "But you could have defended yourself."

He threw her a look of disbelief. "What do you think

I tried to do? You would have nothing to do with the truth. You listened to an embittered old man, a spiteful woman, and her devious son."

"It was an honest mistake," she muttered. "There seemed to be so much incriminating evidence. The description of the man riding away from the house, your ring, and—what about the torn bandanna in your saddlebags?"

"You should have asked me about it instead of assuming the worst. You could have listened to me just as easily as listening to them."

She blushed and lowered her head. He was right, of course.

"How did you come by the bandanna?"

"I found it the night I visited with Chas. The night he died."

"Why didn't you tell me this before?"

"You didn't ask."

"Why didn't you tell me you were Austin? You let me go on and on about what a horrid man he was."

"I don't know," he answered, sounding genuinely bewildered. He sat on the ground and crossed his legs.

"Well, you should have told me. None of this would have happened."

"Let's not veer from my initial question, darlin'. Why did you set off by yourself? Imagine Carlos's surprise when I showed up at Ponderosa Pines. He was under the impression that you were travelling with me."

"I thought I could make it alone. I would have, if I hadn't stopped to cool off in the river."

"If I hadn't come along, you'd be dead," he pointed out. "Or halfway across New Mexico."

"I know what almost happened, and, well, thank

you."

"You're welcome."

"How did you get out of jail?"

"That's not important. What changed your mind about my guilt?"

"A couple of reasons," she hedged, not wishing to share with him just yet the reasons for her change of heart—her newfound love! "I tried to convince Sheriff Bosler to release you, but he wouldn't until the trial. He was also waiting for a wire from Colorado."

Cougar swore under his breath, and when he didn't comment further, she gazed out over the river. Another thought came to her, and she swung back to him. "If you've been following me, then why didn't you show your face sooner?"

"I wanted you to see how difficult it would be to go it alone."

"Oh, of all the—" She stuck her nose in the air. "If not for the river, I would have managed perfectly well on my own. As you know, I'm—"

"Yes, I know," he drawled. "Let me see," he said holding up one finger. "I scared off the men who invaded your hotel room." Another finger went up. "I interceded with the Indians by the river." Another finger shot up. "I sucked out the snake venom." A fourth finger went up. "I found you wandering the countryside—"

"After I escaped the kidnappers on my own!"

"And let's not forget the first time. I helped you get a hotel room in Denver," he finished with a self-satisfied grin. "Well, look at that! I've run out of fingers!" He chuckled. "Should I start on the other hand?"

"That won't be necessary," she grumbled. "Besides, I didn't need your help in Denver. The clerk had already recommended another place for me to stay."

"Where?"

"Fannie Morrison's."

Cougar uncharacteristically flopped on his back and rolled on the ground, roaring with laughter. "I had forgotten about that!"

"What's so funny?"

"Fannie Morrison's is a whore house," he told her, nearly choking on his laughter.

"Don't hurt yourself," she muttered, highly insulted by his unbridled display of amusement at her expense, not to mention the idea of being sent to a whore house by a total stranger.

He struggled to a sitting position and grinned, the smile making her heart flutter.

"Now do you appreciate my company?"

"Oh, of all the conceited, arrogant—" She lunged at him, wanting to scratch the smug look off his handsome face. The fact that he was right was harder to admit faced with his arrogance.

His grin faded and he rolled to his feet, gaping at her in astonishment. "Me? You are the most infuriating, stubborn woman I have ever met. You're not only blind to reality, you are willful, ungrateful—" Cougar let out a heavy sigh and with a shake of his head, turned on his heel, and disappeared into the grove of cottonwoods.

Looking back at the river, she thought about her close call with death and began to shake uncontrollably. He was right. If he hadn't come along when he did, she would be dead—or drifting aimlessly across the territory.

Chapter 27

The sun was setting, and Cougar still hadn't returned. Cady was about to start looking for him, wanting to apologize for her awful behavior, when he emerged from the trees, carrying an armful of kindling. She breathed a sigh of relief. The thought had occurred to her that he just might not come back.

"We'll make camp here for the night," he said, dropping the wood on the ground. He started a fire, then stood and faced her. "I'm going to wash off the trail dust. Make yourself useful and rub down your horse. But stay away from Wind Runner. I'll take care of the stallion when I return."

Cady was a bit put out by his cool attitude but really couldn't blame him. But did he have to torment her at every turn? She was quite capable of making a fool out of herself without his help. Rose's words echoed in her mind. *He teases those he loves.* Again, her heart did a little flip.

After she finished currying her mare, she turned to the stallion, a thoughtful look in her eyes. Ignoring his growled dictate to stay away from his horse, and wanting to do him a favor, she stepped up to the stallion, avoiding looking into its wary black eyes. Taking hold of her trepidation, she whispered softly to it and bent to its back with the currycomb. She could barely reach the top, but she did her best with the areas she could.

Cougar took his time in the river, washing off the trail dust as well as cooling his anger. That woman was the most maddening one he'd ever met. She showed no gratitude, was willful, obstinate—he would do well to wash his hands of her. He scoffed. And always insisting she could take care of herself. Couldn't she see that she needed him?

He had to admit, though, she was resilient, able to bounce back from anything thrown her way. She possessed enough fortitude and know-how to handle just about any obstacle that popped up. Given enough time, she could probably get out of any difficult situation. That realization, however, made his anger resurface. *Damn it! She needs me!*

He concentrated on catching their dinner from the fish-laden river. Having succeeded in nabbing several fat trout, he rose from the river, drew on his buckskins, and made his way back to camp. Twilight had fallen and the setting sun had stained the sky with smudges of red, orange and yellow. When he broke from the trees, he stopped short, stunned at the sight of his stallion standing as docile as a lamb, allowing that small slip of a girl to rub its glossy coat. He shook his head in amazement and leaned his shoulder against a tree to watch.

She was beautiful—and he was hot for her. Growling in frustration, he tamped down his lust. He could not get involved with her—period. It was bad enough he had already slipped once, which he still felt deep in his soul. And he needed to stop kissing her, it just made it harder to stay away. He pushed away from the tree and approached her, his steps quiet. When she leaned into the stallion, he stopped. Good Lord—she was whispering in its ear! He chuckled to himself and ambled up behind her.

"Do you always talk to horses?"

She jumped at the sound of his voice. "When they're the most intelligent thing around, yes," she replied flippantly.

She spun about to comment that it wasn't nice to sneak up on someone, but the retort died on her lips. Her eyes widened in shock and a wave of excitement flowed through her body. Why he was practically naked! His long black hair was wet and the tiny drops of water clinging to his broad, naked chest trickled down his flat belly and disappeared inside the waistband of his buckskins.

Cougar watched her quietly, becoming aroused. Her gaze lifted to his face, he read the desire there, and it broke his resolve. He hauled her up against him and dipped his head to capture her mouth with his. The contact sent a jolt of electricity between them. He wrapped his arms tightly around her body and bent her over his arm, slanting his mouth demandingly over her supple lips. His body was drawn, aching with his need for her.

Cady, swept along by his powerful allure, moved her arms up and around his shoulders. Her hands circled his neck, and she threaded her fingers in his long black hair. She sighed deep in her throat, and clutched him tighter, pushing away reality lurking on the edge of her mind. She pressed into him, kissing him enthusiastically, savoring his river-sweetened taste.

"Cady, my Cady," he whispered almost to himself. He rained soft kisses on her brow, her cheeks, her chin, before once again settling on her mouth. They were enveloped in a cloud of passion, unaware of their surroundings. The moon could have fallen from the sky and still they would have held on to each other, oblivious.

The stallion nudged Cougar's shoulder, bringing him to instant awareness. He pulled away and, setting her aside, settled a frown on his face.

"What's wrong?" she asked, still drugged from his kisses.

"I will not ruin your life."

"Cougar?" she asked in bewilderment, placing her hand lightly on his arm. "How could you possibly ruin my life?"

He ignored her question. "I thought I told you to stay away from Wind Runner," he snapped, masking his intense longing behind anger.

Cady flinched at his tone of voice. "I just wanted to thank you for…" Her words trailed off under his piercing, smoldering glare.

"There is no need. In the future, please do as I ask." He turned his back on her, knowing if he didn't, he would grab her again. And this time, he would not let go.

Cady smothered a gasp and ran blindly into the forest, brushing away the tree branches slapping at her face and arms. She plunked down on a fallen log, totally at a loss. Even when infuriated, his touch—his kisses— kindled a flame that was all consuming. Then, lost in a maze of passion and wanting more, he withdrew and became cross. It seemed their kisses always made him cross.

Cady knew she couldn't sit in the forest all night, that she eventually had to go back. Besides, she was hungry, and the smell of frying fish and roasting cornbread drifted to her on the breeze. She pushed herself to her feet and walked slowly back to their camp. She swept by him, her nose in the air, and sat down on the other side of the fire. He handed her a plate of fish and cornbread and a battered tin cup of coffee.

She nodded her thanks, and, despite her inner turmoil, she devoured the savory meal. When her plate was empty, she licked her fingers clean, then sipped her coffee, eyeing him from beneath her lashes. Drops of water still clung to his hair and glistened like stars in the firelight. She ignored the fluttering in her stomach and averted her gaze to stare at a point just over his shoulder.

His deep voice pierced the quiet night. "We'll leave at first light." She tilted her chin at a stubborn angle. "Cady?"

She nodded, turning her back on him to lay down on her bedroll. She moved onto her side, trying to get comfortable on the hard ground, and pulled the blanket up around her shoulders.

Cougar poured himself a liberal amount of whiskey and by the soft firelight watched over Cady. The nocturnal sounds of forest creatures scurrying in the woods and the nightbirds' sweet songs were soothing ones for him. Surrounded by the comforting sounds of nature, he felt his taut muscles begin to relax.

He finished the whiskey in one swallow, then moved his bedroll near Cady's. He lay on his back, folded his arms behind his head and gazed up at the sky. The moon hung low, suspended in the diamond-studded sky. His gaze followed one of the bright lights as it streaked across the dark expanse.

His thoughts turned to Chas. He missed him more than he thought possible. Chas had understood him better than anyone, even his mother. He wondered how different his life would have been if his mother had married Chas all those many years ago.

He heard Cady murmur and glanced over at her sleeping form. Soft moonlight illuminated her features making her seem almost ethereal. He breathed a heavy sigh, ignoring the stirring in his heart. Ever since he had met Cady Grayson, he hadn't had a moment's peace.

What am I going to do with her?

Chapter 28

Cady slapped the hand shaking her shoulder. "Go away," she grumbled, rolling over and pulling the blanket up over her head.

"Time to get up, darlin'," Cougar whispered in her ear. "Unless you want me to join you?"

Cady pushed back the blanket and looked up at him. His face was dangerously close to hers and she wondered wildly if he was going to kiss her. Her lips parted and her heart did a little skip. He chuckled and jumped to his feet, slapping her on the buttocks.

She threw off the blanket and stood. "You may be innocent of killing Chas, but you are still a cad." She flung her long ebony mane over her shoulder and stomped off into the trees with a decidedly angry stride.

Cougar chuckled again. *What a woman!* Her temperament, however, needed a bit of softening around the edges. He supposed he was partly to blame—with his unpredictable moods, his pulling her in and pushing her away. He wasn't happy about it either.

He moved to the fire and poured two cups of coffee. When she reappeared, he handed her one and gestured for her to sit. Dropping to the ground in front of her, he stretched his long legs out, leaned back on his elbows, and arched one black brow at her. She eyed him suspiciously. *What now?*

"Tell me about the fire at Ponderosa Pines."

"What?" she asked, startled by his question. She certainly wasn't expecting it.

"The fire—the stables," he prompted patiently.

"Oh, well, the sheriff thinks someone deliberately started it. He found an empty kerosene can near the back entrance."

"Does he know who did it?"

"No. Do you?" she asked with one arched brow. She ignored his shout of laughter. "You know, Cougar, a lot of strange things have happened since I arrived here. I've been kidnapped, my property's been damaged. And poor Randy—he could have been killed!"

"I have a feeling the bullet was meant for you."

Cady gasped in alarm. "Do you really think so?"

He nodded and studied her in silence. Most women would have fainted or become hysterical after the ordeals she'd been through. Yet she consistently landed on her feet, for the most part unruffled. She had changed these past months. She had always had backbone—he had learned that upon their first meeting in the hotel lobby in Denver—but the haunted fear and anger had disappeared from her eyes. Or had it been unhappiness? Quite a change from the young lady he had escorted to Santa Fe, he surmised with a touch of admiration. Although, she was still too obstinate, by far.

"Why don't you tell me about the letter you received from Lucinda."

"How did you know about that?"

"Cassie."

"She wasn't supposed to tell anyone."

"Cassie can't keep a secret—at least from me."

"Oh," she murmured, filing that bit of information away for future reference. "Lucinda wrote that she has information about Wiley she wants me to know. Do you know who Wiley is?"

He nodded. "The thwarted heir."

"She asked me to travel to Silverhills—"

"And off you go," he muttered beneath his breath.

"I heard that." She arched a brow in annoyance. "What am I supposed to do? Just wait for Wiley to strike again?"

"What do you mean—again?"

"He came to Ponderosa Pines. He tried to kidnap me—again."

"So you think he is one of the men who took you to that deserted cabin?"

"I do. I also think he's behind all these dastardly deeds."

"Hmm, you may be right," Cougar agreed, thoughtfully.

"Do you think he could have killed Chas?"

"He has plenty of reasons. It bears looking into." He looked at her, his gaze intense. "Is there anything else you want to tell me?"

She looked away, suddenly uncomfortable. Folding her hands in her lap, she took a deep breath. "Chas wrote me a letter. I understand he told you about it."

"Yes, but I couldn't find it. I asked Maria to look for it."

"She found it the other day. Do you know what it says?"

"I didn't read it."

"I'm supposed to marry you!" Cady blurted out, blushing hotly.

"I know."

"I thought you didn't read it."

"You have already told me that Doswell said you had to marry Austin."

How could I have forgotten that?

"And I was with Chas the night he died. We had a long talk and one of the things he told me was that he wanted us to marry."

"But why didn't you tell me this before?"

"You wouldn't have believed me."

Cady started to argue but stopped. He was right. She would not have taken his words as truth. Lord, she had believed him guilty of murder on hearsay, hadn't she?

"He wrote that he thought I might be in danger. Do you suppose he had a premonition, or did he just worry about me being alone?"

"I think he was genuinely concerned for your welfare. I suppose he thought marrying me would keep you safe."

What do I do now? Ask him to marry me?

She bit her lower lip and waited for him to say something—anything. When he didn't, she asked, "And what of Terence?"

"What about him?"

"Why does he hate you so?"

"You'll have to ask him. I never did understand him."

"Could he be involved in any of this?"

"Other than having me arrested, I doubt he had anything to do with Chas's death or the other incidents. It's not his style. Terence's ways are much more underhanded."

"He tricked me," she said bitterly, still angry at him for using her to get to Cougar. "I honestly believed Cassie was hurt. I did not help him arrest you—at least not intentionally."

"I know. That had Terence written all over it."

Silence fell. Cady stared into the fire, the unspoken question standing between them like an invisible wall. She just couldn't gather up the courage to ask him if he'd marry her. She glanced over at him.

"Will you take me to Silverhills?"

"Looks like I don't have a choice. Every time I turn around, you're in some kind of trouble. But let's get a few things straight. I am in charge—not you." He held up his hand to stem any argument. "I know you think you can take care of yourself, but this latest incident begs to differ. You are placing your welfare in my hands, and you must do as I say."

He waited for her to explode. During the course of his edict, her eyes had turned stormy, but she just tossed her head and lifted her chin.

"Why my grandfather trusted you, or even liked you, is beyond me. You are the most egotistical man I have ever had the misfortune to meet. I—"

"Can you shoot a gun?"

"Of course." At his skeptical look, she informed him, "Randy taught me."

"Well, just stick close to me." He rolled to his feet and kicked dirt on the fire. Ignoring her defiant expression, he strode to their horses throwing a curt demand over his shoulder, "Let's go."

She grabbed her saddlebags and followed Cougar, wanting to kick him in the shins for his superior attitude. While they rode, Cady's anger simmered just below the surface. How dare he just order her about? *Why, he treats me like a child!* The more she thought about his overbearing attitude and list of demands, the more incensed she became. So she had encountered a few mishaps? It could happen to anyone!

Cougar was fighting an unexpected feeling of disappointment. She had made no mention of whether she would marry him. He had seen a host of emotions cross her face ranging from embarrassment to misery. What had she been thinking? Was she sorry she had to marry him in order to inherit Ponderosa Pines? Was the idea so repulsive?

They rode in relative silence, each lost in their own thoughts, until late afternoon when they came upon a small town, a weathered wooden sign welcoming them to Trapper's Junction. The tree-dotted mountains rose majestically beyond it, ablaze with red and golden color. Cougar pulled up on the reins and surveyed the sleepy town.

"We'll stop here and get some supplies," he said, lowering his hat over his eyes and urging his horse forward.

Cady looked around the small drab town. The main street was a narrow strip of dirt with ramshackle buildings on either side. It was nearly deserted save for a few people milling around with no apparent destination in mind. A group of scruffy-looking men stood outside the saloon openly watching them ride down the street. Cady instinctively nudged her mare closer to Cougar.

They pulled up before a building bearing a faded sign proclaiming it the general store. Cady dismounted and stretched the kinks from her back. She pushed her hat off her head and looked up at Cougar who was still astride his stallion.

"Aren't you coming in?"

"No, I'll stay with the horses."

Cady nodded and walked up the two steps to the door, pushed it open, and entered, a little bell heralding her arrival. An old man with gray hair and a thick gray beard and mustache came out of the back room. He was dressed in denim overalls and a flannel shirt, a pipe clamped between his teeth.

"Good day, ma'am. What can I do for you?" he asked politely.

While she rattled off the list of needed supplies, he rummaged through the shelves and placed the requested items on the counter. She counted out the necessary coin from her pocket, thanked the man, and gathered up the provisions. At the door, a board plastered with wanted posters caught her eye, some yellowed with age, others newer and white. Curious, she scanned the faces staring at her from the notices. She started to turn away but stopped. Gasping in alarm, she found herself staring at the unmistakable image of—Cougar! *Austin Taylor Wanted for Armed Robbery and Murder,* it read in bold black letters. The words jumped out at her, and she flinched as if struck. She left the store with a decidedly heavier step.

Cougar immediately noticed her distraught expression and swore under his breath. *Those damned notices must still be posted.*

"Cady?"

She ignored him and stuffed the supplies in her saddlebags. She mounted her horse and pulled on the reins, wheeling the horse around. As she headed out of town, Cougar came abreast of her and rode thoughtfully by her side.

Cady's head was spinning with all sorts of grisly images. Cougar was wanted for armed robbery and murder. Lord, every time she turned around, she learned something new about him. And not altogether good!

Cougar watched her out of the corner of his eye. She looked like she might bolt at any minute. How in the hell was he going to convince her of his innocence? She only recently believed he didn't kill her grandfather. The task ahead would not be easy.

"There's a river up ahead. We'll make camp there for the night." He kicked his heels into his horse and shot forward. Cady had no recourse but to follow him, and she did, reluctantly and with a wary eye. They rode into a small clearing, and after Cougar dismounted, he reached up to help her down. She ignored him and slid off the Palomino's back unassisted. She pulled her bedroll and saddlebags from the back of her horse and moved to the center of the clearing and sat down. She spotted the sparkle of water through the trees but had no interest in running to its edge, as she would have if heavy thoughts weren't weighing her down. The cool water would soothe her hot tired body, but it would do nothing for her troubled mind. Instead, she watched the sun set, the last of its rays reflecting off the water.

Cougar stripped the horses and left them to graze. He gathered kindling to light a fire and soon had a small blaze burning.

"You hungry?" he asked, squatting beside the fire and watching her carefully.

"No." Her stomach was knotted so tight she feared she wouldn't be able to keep anything down even if it did make it past the lump in her throat. She lay back and rested her head on her bedroll and stared up at the dusky-blue sky, awash with uncertainty. Every time she believed in him something would turn up to make her doubt all the good things she did know about him.

"Cady, did you see something in the general store that upset you?"

"No," she lied, refusing to look at him.

"Cady—talk to me."

"You're *wanted*!" she blurted out, sitting up and staring at him with eyes wide with accusation.

"It's not what you think." Faced with her silence and expression of doubt, he continued, almost pleadingly, "Cady, you have to trust me."

"*Trust* you?" she cried in disbelief. "How am I supposed to trust you?" She lifted her hand toward the direction they had just come. "A wanted poster—"

"Would Chas have trusted me if it were true?"

"Maybe he didn't know about your sordid past."

"He was trying to get my name cleared when he died."

Cady eyed Cougar's bottle of whiskey and held out a tin cup. He obliged by pouring her a small draught.

"So you're saying he knew about it?" She swallowed a large gulp of whiskey, wheezing as it burned down her throat.

He nodded. "It was a set-up. A man was killed at a bank in Denver, during a robbery."

"Who set you up?" When he ignored her question, she eyed him suspiciously. "So you are guilty of the robbery?"

"No. That was a set-up too."

"And you have no idea who was behind it?" she asked skeptically.

"Oh, yes, I have a very good idea. I just can't prove it," he said in disgust. "Before Chas died, he was waiting for my pardon from the Governor of Colorado. To my knowledge, it has not arrived." He arched a brow, and she shook her head.

Cady was silent, listening to the furies in her head hounding her not to trust him. Their warning to not let her attraction blind her echoed over and over until she thought she would scream. She lay back on her bedroll, racked with uncertainty. What was her grandfather thinking to link her to a man like Cougar? She squeezed her eyes shut, trying to block out the voices.

After a moment, she peered at him from beneath her lashes, studying his drawn expression, and wondering if he was telling the truth. Had he truly been set up? Was he innocent? She had been so quick to judge him on Chas's murder, on the assault on Renee. She had been wrong then, so very wrong. And, too, everyone seemed to like him, except, of course, the Taylors, excluding Cassie. And frankly, other than Cassie, she didn't think too highly of any of them.

More importantly, how could she be in love with a man supposedly guilty of any of these crimes? She may be a novice at love, but affairs of the heart were true.

She decided to give him the benefit of the doubt— for now. But if just one more disreputable issue surfaced, she would leave him and Santa Fe altogether.

Even with her inner turmoil somewhat resolved, she was still wary of falling asleep. She concentrated on the night sounds to distract her. That was a mistake. As soon as she closed her eyes, they lulled her to sleep. Relinquishing the tight rein on her control, she succumbed to her exhaustion.

Cougar sat across the fire from her, his back against a tree, and smoked a cheroot. From beneath lowered lids, he watched the play of emotions cross her face and wondered what conclusions she had come to. He observed her fight to stay awake and, for some reason, the act wounded him. She didn't trust him—would probably never trust him. Could he blame her? Since they'd met, he had not been shown in a very positive light.

He studied her through the blue smoke curling around his head. She had one hand tucked beneath her cheek, the other resting on the ground. He tossed the cheroot into the fire, rose to his feet, and walked quietly to her side. He stared down at her peaceful countenance. Her chest rose and fell in gentle sleep, her face soft in slumber, and to look at her now, one would never know the scared, lonely girl underneath. She had had a hard life—unloved, full of doubt and mistrust. He wanted her trust—he needed it. He knelt beside her and reached out to gently brush away an errant lock from her cheek. He rubbed the silky tress between his fingers, releasing the subtle powdery scent of violets. Careful not to wake her, he lay down beside her and gathered her in his arms. She sighed and instinctively turned toward his warmth.

He held his breath as she murmured in her sleep and gently brushed his lips against her hair. He felt himself stir but tamped down his desire. This was a time for emotional stroking, not sensual. He was suddenly overcome by a feeling of protectiveness so overwhelming it took his breath away. He pulled her close, hugging her against his chest, and closed his eyes. He drifted off to sleep to dream of a black-haired, indigo-eyed beauty.

Chapter 29

Cady burrowed beneath the blanket, instinctively cuddling closer to the heat. Her eyes fluttered open, and she blinked in confusion. Her face was pressed against a warm, muscular chest, the entire length of her body flattened against his, encircled by his strong arms. His leg was thrown intimately over her thighs, trapping her beneath him. She steadied her initial shock and listened to his heartbeat.

She pulled back and studied his face. Slumber had erased his infuriating grin, and he looked almost angelic. She scoffed. Angelic, indeed! She knew better. Her gaze wandered from his handsome face down to where his open shirt exposed his neck and smooth chest. Her hand, resting lightly on the wide expanse, looked pale against his golden-brown skin. A tingling sensation started radiating from her fingers to her toes. She squelched the urge to kiss his chest and lifted her gaze back up to his face. She caught her breath and turned pink. Cougar was watching her, a steady flame burning in his amber eyes.

"Morning, darlin'," he murmured huskily, tightening his hold when she tried to pull away.

"What are you doing here?" she demanded indignantly, sounding more breathless than stern.

"Taking you to Silverhills," he drawled lazily.

Her eyes narrowed. "You know what I mean. This!" She poked his chest with one finger.

"You looked cold."

"Well, I'm not cold now." She brought her other hand up and pushed, to no avail.

"Yes, you are," he whispered before hauling her up against him and capturing her mouth with his. Ignoring her struggles, he deepened the kiss, wanting her response, needing it. His kiss became more demanding, kneading her lips before slipping his tongue inside to mate with hers.

Engulfed in a wave of longing she was helpless to stem, she found herself kissing him back. A low moan escaped from the back of her throat, and she slipped her arms around his neck, molding her body as close as she could to his. She could feel the hardness of his arousal nestled between her legs and unforgotten passion flared anew.

Cougar caressed her body with long even strokes. Deftly unbuttoning her shirt, he cupped a warm breast, kneading the soft skin, rubbing the crest with his thumb. She threaded her fingers through his hair as his touch wove magic threads around her senses.

He rose about her, completely besotted. Her taste— like honey. Her feel—like velvet. Her face was softened by passion, her eyes cloudy with desire—and something else. He smothered a sigh. It was fear. Was she afraid of *him*? Or did she not trust herself *with* him?

A whisper of lucidity murmuring in her ear, she rolled from under him, jumped to her feet, and ran blindly into the trees. She tripped over a dead log and landed flat on her face, her fall cushioned by a blanket of pine needles. She lay still, trying to gather her thoughts.

She was drawn to him, to his magnetism, almost against her will. But it was strong, this attraction between them. A tear slipped down her cheek. She could not lie with him—not again. She couldn't bear it if he set her aside afterwards, especially now—now that he had her heart. She just might not recover.

Cougar's first instinct was to go after her, demand to know what was wrong, then make mad passionate love to her. But he held himself back, swearing under his breath at this turn of events. He had always been the one to stop their kisses before they went too far—again— acutely aware of the consequences. But this time she had pulled away and run off. *Why?* She was now aware of his bloodline—was that the reason? Did his mixed blood disgust her? Despite her denials to the contrary? He vehemently hoped not—for there wasn't a thing he could do about it.

Cougar nudged the dying embers into a small blaze and set the black coffeepot above it. He knelt and stared into the fire as if seeking answers in the blue and gold flames. He heard Cady come back into the camp, and said without looking up, "We'll leave in ten minutes."

"I'm not sure I want to continue on with you," she stated, planting herself across the fire from him.

"Have you forgotten what happens to you when you venture out alone?"

He did have a point. "What about the wanted poster?"

"I explained that."

"What am I supposed to believe?"

"Believe what you will. I'm tired of defending myself," he said, his tone flat.

She rested her hand on her gun. "All right, I'll go with you. But remember, I'm a crack shot."

"Yes, I will," he drawled, his expression inscrutable.

"And I would appreciate it if you would keep your hands and your mouth to yourself," she said between gritted teeth.

"Don't worry," he promised, feeling her rejection like shards of glass cutting into his heart.

"I mean it."

He shot her a look of pure exasperation and poured himself a cup of coffee, moving to sit cross-legged by the fire.

Cady strode over to her saddlebags, located her brush, and sat down to work the tangles out of her hair, fully aware of Cougar's smoldering gaze on her. Her fingers fumbled as she tried to plait the unruly tresses into some semblance of order.

Cougar's mind wandered erotically at the sight of her sitting among the trees, the sun reflecting off her raven-black hair. Berating himself for behaving like a lovesick boy, he threw his coffee on the fire. It hissed and died, a cloud of smoke billowing from the wet ashes. She was nothing to him, he told himself firmly, nothing but an irritating thorn in his side. What rankled him was that he had agreed to stick her there.

"Come on, we've got a lot of ground to cover."

"Is there anything to eat?"

Wordlessly, Cougar tossed her a biscuit. She caught it with one hand and munched on the hardtack while he loaded their gear. He was dressed in sand-brown buckskins that hugged his muscular thighs and a dark brown shirt left open at the neck. He had not yet tied back his hair, and it stirred around his shoulders as he stowed the saddlebags and bedrolls on the horses. She turned away with a silent curse and reached for her canteen of water to wash down the dry biscuit.

"Ready?" he barked, with an irritated lift to one brow.

She nodded stiffly and allowed him to help her mount the Palomino. He strode to his stallion, swung up into the saddle, and pulled him sharply around. She followed Cougar out of the clearing, staring morosely at his rigid back. She sighed. Why were they always at odds with each other?

****

Early that afternoon, they rode into Silverhills, a small prospecting town situated on a river in the foothills of the mountains. Cady gazed at the shabby little town as they trotted down what she assumed was the main street. Although it was a sight better than Trapper's Junction, it did not compare with the grander cities of St. Louis or Denver and had a long way to go before it reached their lofty status.

They rode quickly through the underdeveloped town and drew up before a house badly in need of repair and a fresh coat of paint. They dismounted and ascended two broken steps to the sagging front porch.

Before they could knock, the battered door creaked open and a female voice inquired meekly, "Cady Grayson?"

"Yes," Cady answered, peering into the gap between the door and the house. The opening widened and a young woman with short curly brown hair and timid brown eyes appeared in the doorway.

"Lucinda?" At her nod, Cady gestured to Cougar. "This is Cougar. Ah, may we come in?" she asked when Lucinda made no move to let them in the house.

"Yes, of course." She stepped back and allowed them into the hallway, then showed them into the parlor.

The entire room showed signs of poverty. The faded floral paper peeled away from the walls and the furniture was tattered and worn. The olive-green rug was threadbare, allowing a spot of wood to peek through here and there.

"Thank you so much for coming," Lucinda said as she walked a wide circle around Cougar and sat on a green-and-white striped chair. She waved them toward a matching sofa before clasping her hands in her lap. Cougar waited for Cady to sit before taking a place beside her, immediately sinking into the middle.

"What information do you have?" Cougar asked, without waiting for small talk.

Lucinda looked startled and glanced uneasily at Cady, who was patiently waiting for her to answer. "It's about Wiley. I'm afraid he might have been responsible for our grandfather's death," she answered nervously.

"Why do you say that?" Cady asked, sharing a quick glance with Cougar.

"He left for Santa Fe in early spring—with another man." She took a deep breath. "One night, before they left, I overheard them talking. Their words frightened me."

"What did they say?"

Lucinda appeared shaken by Cougar's sharp tone and leaned back into the chair away from his forbidding presence. Cady understood and sought to ease her mind. "It's all right, Lucinda. He's not angry at you."

Lucinda nodded and took another deep breath. "I couldn't hear anything specific, mind you. But it had something to do with someone having to die in order to get it."

"Do you know who they were talking about?"

"No, not for certain, but I think it was Chas. You see, a couple of years ago I came across my mother's diary. She hated our grandfather, you know, ever since he disinherited my father, Cal. And she did her best to make us hate him, too. I do believe she only married my father for what he could give her. After he was disinherited, she made his life miserable."

She looked timidly at Cougar, then back at Cady. "I don't think Wiley knew you were coming. Several weeks after he left, I received a wire from him. He said that something had come up and he would be gone a while longer. He's very protective of me, you see." Lucinda shook her head as tears welled in her eyes. "I'm so sorry about Chas's death. I wanted to warn you because I'm afraid your life might be in danger, too. If Wiley did do it, then he wants the inheritance bad enough that he won't let you stand in his way."

"I see," Cady murmured, frightening certainty sinking in and twisting her stomach in knots. Cougar grasped her hand tightly in his. She looked up at him in surprise but did not pull her hand away. They shared a long look, only glancing away when Lucinda spoke again.

"I didn't know anything about you until I read Grandfather's obituary. My father never talked about his brother, Neil." She looked helplessly at Cady and said in simple explanation, "Wiley feels cheated."

"Why didn't you tell me all of this in your letter? Why ask me to come?"

"I was afraid Wiley might find out I warned you. He'd be very upset with me." She smiled shyly. "I also wanted to meet you."

Cady rose and clasped Lucinda's hands while

Cougar struggled to his feet. "I'm glad we've had this chance to meet. Thank you so much for telling us. I know it took a lot of courage." She gave her a quick hug and stepped back. "Please know that you are always welcome at Ponderosa Pines."

"Bless you both."

Cougar drew Cady to the front door and after bidding Lucinda farewell, they rode back through town, each lost in their own thoughts. This news pretty much confirmed Cougar's suspicions about Wiley, although he seriously doubted the simple fact Cady was married to him would make the least bit of difference. He would just kill them both. How could Chas have thought that marriage between the two of them was wise? It might save her from immediate harm, but it could cause far worse damage.

He would not live in her world, and he couldn't imagine her living in his. Even if she did agree, she would never be able to bear up under the snubbing she would receive being married to an Indian. But how tempting it was! For her, he could almost live in the white man's world.

"I think we should get married," Cougar announced, startling himself with the declaration that completely contradicted his earlier mindset. It was one thing to think it, quite another to say it out loud. He didn't dare look too closely at his reason for coming to this conclusion, and therefore elected to ignore it. His feelings for her tended to throw him off balance anyway.

"Your grandfather wanted us to marry," he continued. "And the codicil stipulates it. We might as well do it now. Perhaps it will deter Wiley."

"Cougar, I—" Her heart sank. In the blink of an eye

she had gone from elation, when he'd first mentioned marriage, to dejection. *He is only complying with my wishes.* Isn't that what her grandfather had written? Cougar was only doing what he had promised her grandfather. That realization made her even more miserable.

"Cady?"

"Is that the only reason?"

"Of course, why else?"

Why else, indeed?

Chapter 30

It was done. A couple of questions answered, a chaste kiss to seal the bargain, and she was Mrs. Austin Cougar Taylor. She had been surprised when Cougar had insisted on using both his given names, especially considering his dismal view of the white man, at least those with narrow minds. They had been lucky enough to find a magistrate who did not know Cougar was a wanted man. The ceremony was quick, and they were out of the small courthouse within minutes.

Cady looked down at her left hand, at the heavy gold ring encircling her middle finger, branding her Cougar's wife. It was too large for the traditional place on her fourth finger and even now fit loosely. She traced the outline of the mountain lion etched into the smooth gold surface of the ring. She had been startled when, during the short ceremony, Cougar had pulled it off his finger and placed it on hers.

From beneath her lashes, Cady stole a peek at her husband, wondering what he was thinking. He hadn't uttered a word since they left the courthouse. He looked straight ahead, his expression closed, his profile hard. She sighed in dismay. She should have thought of another way to keep the ranch without marrying Cougar. It was obvious he was not happy about it. The bond he had shared with Chas must have been strong indeed if he was willing to sacrifice his freedom, his happiness, for marriage to her.

Cougar was thinking he had lost his mind. He was torn between doing what was best for Cady and fulfilling his promise to Chas. They were not one and the same. A white woman married to an Indian, despite the fact he was only half-Indian, was not looked upon kindly and would only bring a wealth of problems to her door. His mother had been mistaken. Times had not changed. Perhaps he could keep it quiet, allowing only the lawyer to know. That way she might be spared ostracism. That idea did not necessarily sit well with him. In fact, it made him furious.

By the time they made camp that evening, Cougar's expression had become so ominous that Cady thought it best to steer clear of him. They had stopped near a small tributary, and after finishing a small meal of roasted rabbit and biscuits, they sat by the fire and watched the flames, each lost in their own thoughts. Cady absently twisted the gold ring around her finger, trying to keep her tears at bay. Her dream of a love fulfilled didn't seem any closer to being realized. She knew if the roles were reversed, she would be as bitter as Cougar. She started at the sound of his deep voice cutting through the silence.

"I have fulfilled Chas's wish. And I will try to keep you safe." He lit a cheroot. "I suggest we tell no one. When Doswell returns, I will let him know that the conditions of the will have been met. There is no need for anyone else to know. And don't expect me to live with you at Ponderosa Pines. I don't like being tied to one place." He watched her face in the fire's glow, it was expressionless.

"That's fine," she said, hiding her pain at his blatant rejection. "At least we have prevented Wiley from stealing it away from me."

"Don't be too sure he won't continue to try."

"Well, it no longer concerns you, does it? You have married me. You need do no more." She averted her gaze and stared into the trees, trying desperately not to cry. She had lied—it mattered a great deal to her that their marriage would be in name only. She was so uncontrollably drawn to him that his rejection was a knife twisting in her heart. The fact that she was married to him did not change a thing. He had given her his name and protection, but she was still as alone as ever. To be a yoke around someone's neck was humiliating. That it was around the neck of her husband, the man she loved, was just plain cruel.

Cougar had seen the pain in her eyes despite her flippant remarks, and his heart broke. But it was for her own good; the censure she would receive married to him might break her spirit. And that was one of the things he admired most in her. She was exasperating, stretched his patience to the limits, and drove him to distraction, but her spirit was never-ending. He dragged on his cheroot.

Oh hell! Truth was he loved her. He was in love with the most maddening woman he had ever met, and his heart was hers, if she wanted it. Trying to convince himself otherwise was foolish. And he was anything but foolish. He could not easily set her aside—didn't want to set her aside—and that was the basis for his quandary. If he was smart, he would take her directly home and never set eyes on her again. He looked up at the heavens. *Well, Chas, I did what you wanted. Your Cady is now my wife. Let's just hope it's enough to keep her safe.*

He tossed his cheroot into the fire and rose to his feet. "I'm going for a swim. I won't be gone long."

Cady nodded and watched him disappear into the trees. When he faded from view, she turned back to her contemplation of the dancing flames, her hand weighed down by the ring on her left hand, a heavy reminder of her loveless union.

It was dusk, the sun hovering over the horizon, and the evening air had a decidedly crisp chill. Cougar undressed to his loincloth and dove into the river, splitting the water with his lithe form. His strong arms sliced the water as he tried to swim off his frustration. After several minutes of hard exercise, he rose from the river and reached for his buckskins. He stilled, every muscle stretched taut, every sense alert.

"Hold it right there, Taylor," a menacing voice warned from the trees.

"Make one move and you're a dead man," another threatened.

Cougar cursed his stupidity. He had been so occupied with thoughts of Cady he had uncharacteristically let his guard down. In the deepening dusk, he glanced up and saw two men step from the trees, their guns pointed directly at his heart.

"May I at least put on my pants?" Cougar drawled, one brow elevated.

"Okay, but any sudden movement and we shoot. Makes no difference to us if we take you in dead or alive. We still collect the reward," one snickered, nudging his cohort with an elbow.

Cougar reached for his buckskins and the gun hidden beneath them. An owl hooted, startling one of the men and in a panic, he squeezed the trigger. The shot echoed sharply in the crisp night air. Cougar stiffened in pain and slumped forward, feeling a warm liquid flow down his arm.

Cady heard the shot and glanced around, her heart in her throat. She grabbed her gun and headed toward the river. Instinctively keeping her steps silent, she moved through the trees, stopping behind a large trunk on the edge of the forest. She peered around it and her breath caught in her throat. Cougar, clad only in a loincloth, stood at the river's edge, blood streaming down his arm from a hole in his shoulder. Two men stood before him arguing together and waving their pistols around.

Cougar heard the faint rustling in the trees and his keen gaze spotted Cady's pale face among the shadows. He nodded surreptitiously and swung his attention back to the men.

Cady didn't think twice. Despite everything, her first instinct was to protect Cougar. She snuck from behind the tree and stopping several yards away from the men, raised her revolver. It did not tumble to the ground.

"Drop your guns." Clearing her throat, she said louder, "Drop your guns or I'll shoot." Her hand shook so hard the gun wavered uncontrollably.

The men jerked around in surprise and hooted with laughter, apparently finding the sight of the delicate-looking girl wielding a gun vastly amusing.

"You can only get one of us, girly," one of the men said with a loud guffaw.

"But *we* can get two," Cougar said, his tone almost conversational.

The men spun around and cursed. In their amusement, they had made the moronic mistake of turning their backs on their captive.

"Had enough fun, boys?" Cougar's voice had become low and deadly. "Drop 'em!"

One of the men threw his gun to the ground and reached his hands toward the darkening sky. His partner threw his gun at Cougar and made a hasty retreat. A moment later they heard his horse crashing through the trees. The man left behind looked furtively around for a way to escape.

"Tell your partner you got the wrong man. Understand?"

"You mean I can go?" he asked incredulously. He stood rooted to the ground, as if unsure it if was a trick or not.

"Get the hell out of here—now!" Cougar demanded, his tone edged with ice.

The man backed slowly into the trees, but as he passed by Cady he lunged for her gun. Startled, she stumbled back and automatically pulled the trigger at the same time Cougar fired his weapon. The man grunted and crumpled to the ground, dead.

Cady stepped back in horror, her revolver slipping from her numb fingers, and covered her mouth with her hands. Cougar strode toward them and with his bare foot rolled the man onto his back.

"I killed him," she whispered, staring at the dead man in sick disbelief.

"No, Cady, you didn't," Cougar reassured her. "I did." He looked at her. She was as white as the moon, her eyes dark circles against her pale skin. Her lips were trembling, and she looked like she was about to faint.

Cady looked up at Cougar, wanting desperately to believe him. She had never killed another human being, and the thought made her sick. It didn't matter that he could have just as easily killed them both. She looked into Cougar's eyes and, seeing the tenderness there, ran straight into his open arms. He wrapped her in his strong embrace and, with his uninjured arm, held her head against his chest as she shook with emotion. She felt the wet warmth beneath her cheek and pulled out of his arms. With her sleeve, she gently wiped away the blood that seeped from the wound in his shoulder.

"You're hurt."

"You'll have to get the bullet out." He pushed her toward their camp. "Let me take care of him and I'll be along shortly. You'll find bandages in my saddlebags. And get the whiskey while you're at it," he added, his voice husky.

Cady nodded and made her way back to camp. She threw more branches on the fire until she had a roaring blaze. She rustled through his saddlebags, gathered the necessary items, and placed them near the fire. Kneeling on the blanket, she anxiously awaited his return, her nerves stretched taut, every small nocturnal sound making her jump. She envisioned the dead man at her feet and skittered away from the image like a frisky colt. She reached for the bottle of whiskey, uncapped it, and took a long swallow. She pulled a lock of hair over her shoulder and unconsciously wound it around her finger. When she heard Cougar approaching, she turned to watch him. His face was drawn from pain and the stream of blood oozing from his wound had widened. His hands and buckskins were covered with dirt, and she correctly assumed he had buried the unfortunate outlaw.

Cougar sat down on the blanket beside her with a loud sigh and stuck his knife into the fire. From his canteen, she poured water over his hands and washed away the dirt. She handed him the whiskey, and after taking a long pull, he doused the bullet wound with the liquor.

He pulled the knife from the fire, the end painted scarlet, and handed it to her. She looked at him wild-eyed and paled a shade whiter.

"What?" she nearly shouted.

"Use it to find the bullet."

"I don't think I can," she whispered brokenly.

"Yes, you can," he insisted calmly. He moved slightly so the fire illuminated his shoulder.

She hesitated, her whole being tense with nervousness.

"I trust you, Cady."

Upon hearing that, she took a deep breath and concentrated on her task, knowing that if he so much as moved a muscle, she would run screaming into the trees. She grimaced at the scraping sound of metal against metal. "I think I found it," she whispered. After several attempts to pull it free, she cried tearfully, "I can't get it out!"

"You'll have to use your fingers," he said, his voice strained.

She looked at him as if he had lost his mind. "What?"

"Your fingers, they're small. Here," he took a pull from the bottle of whiskey before handing it to her. "Clean them first, then reach in and pull out the bullet."

"Won't it hurt?"

'No," he lied.

Cady, looking like she was in more pain than he, splashed whiskey over her fingers, then tentatively reached for his shoulder. Gnawing on her lower lip, she pushed her fingers gently into the wound, feeling the wet warmth close around them.

"Cady, you have to move a little faster." She glanced quickly at him. He was motionless, the only outward sign of any discomfort was a fine sheen of sweat beading his brow.

Stomach churning, she searched through blood and sinew for the bullet. Just when she thought she would lose her fragile hold on sanity, she found the metal slug. She tried to grasp it, but it slipped through her fingers. She whimpered and tried again, this time succeeding in pulling it out of his shoulder. Blood gushed from the wound. She dropped the bullet and quickly pressed Cougar's bandanna against the hole, stemming the crimson flow. He handed her the roll of bandages, which she wrapped tightly around his shoulder, crisscrossing it around his chest and back.

"Aren't you going to put some of your magic plants on it?"

"I need to wait until it stops bleeding." He reached for two tin cups and poured them each a liberal amount of whiskey. Cady sat back on her heels and accepted a cup, feeling as weak as a newborn colt.

The flames sought out his face, highlighting the lines around his mouth, his lips drawn tight, his eyes inscrutable. He had sat stoically throughout the entire ordeal, and he had to have been in unbearable pain. She was amazed at his control. She was ready to pass out from just the emotional turmoil alone.

Cady looked up at him and smiled weakly, too exhausted to speak. She drank half the contents of her cup and felt her tension begin to ease. After several long, silent minutes, she asked, "What did they want?"

"The reward." He licked his finger and used it to wipe away the smear of blood on her cheek.

"Oh," she whispered and started to cry. Suddenly, everything came crashing down around her. All the pent-up emotions she had kept locked inside since first meeting Cougar rushed to the forefront, all the events that had happened since arriving in Denver broke through her protective wall. This last act had been the one to break her tenuous hold on her control. Cougar lifted his good arm and without hesitation she fell into him. He wrapped his arm around her as she sobbed out her emotional trials. He caressed her hair, whispering calming, nonsensical words in her ear.

He felt her small body shaking, heard her weeping echo in the quiet glade. Her tears soaked him, their warm drops trickling down his bare skin. Cougar was emotional but for an entirely different reason. *I owe her my life.*

That thought didn't scare him—it brought him peace. She had defended him against two glory seekers, even though moments earlier he had left her with harsh, angry words hanging between them. If not for her, he'd either be dead or thrown in jail for a crime he hadn't committed. When her trembling subsided and her tears had dried, she straightened out of his embrace, but not from his side.

"I'm sorry," she whispered, her eyes lowered.

"For what?"

"For this," she said, indicating the tears lingering on her cheeks.

"Cady, you have nothing to be sorry for. Tell you the truth, I'm surprised your tears didn't start long ago," he said with a soft chuckle. "What you did tonight was very brave. And I thank you."

They sat in companionable silence, watching the

flames undulate in the breeze coming in from the river. The peaceful sounds of nature settling in for the night began to chase away the grisly images.

"It could go hard on you," Cougar said softly.

"What?"

"Your marriage to me."

"Why?"

"Because I'm an Indian."

"Oh, I don't care about that."

"No, but others do."

"Well, I don't care. They're not so bad."

"No longer afraid?"

"I'll admit that, at first, they scared me. But from what I can see, they're not at all like what I've read."

"And what other Indians have you met?"

"Well, your mother, for one."

"You met Rose?"

"Yes. She's very nice."

"Cady, she's not an Indian," he pointed out with a lopsided grin.

"Well, true, but she was dressed like one and she lives like one."

"When did you meet her?"

"Cassie took me to visit her after I, ah, after Randy was shot. After I—"

"Accused me of killing Chas?"

"Well, yes," she admitted, embarrassed.

"What did she tell you?" he asked curiously.

"A little story."

"Is that why you decided I was innocent of Chas's murder?"

"Well, partly. The rest was common sense."

"I didn't think you had any," he muttered under his

318

breath.

"I heard that." Her heart did a little flip at his grin. "She also came to Ponderosa Pines."

"She did? Why?"

"She brought me a gift." Cady wasn't willing just yet to share their conversation. After a minute, she cocked her head to one side, and asked quietly, "Who do you think set you up? In Denver."

"You believe me?"

"Well, yes, I do. You don't seem the type of man to do something like that. Besides, I couldn't be in—" She stopped abruptly, appalled at what she was about to say. "So who do you think did it?" she asked again, hoping desperately he wouldn't guess what she'd almost revealed.

"Webb."

Cady glanced at him in surprise. "Are you sure?"

"I can't prove it. Call it a gut instinct."

"I can't believe he would do that."

"Believe it."

Recalling a portion of Chas's letter, she wondered how she would ever begin to heal the rift between Webb and Cougar. She could start by dispelling one belief.

"Are you aware that someone is hitting Cassie?"

He glanced at her sharply. "How do you know?"

"I asked her about it—"

"I swear, I'll kill him if he lays another hand on her."

"Who?"

"Webb."

"It's not Webb. It's Renee."

"What? Are you sure?"

"Yes. It took a while to get the truth out of her, but Cassie finally admitted it to me. I wasn't supposed to tell you. Apparently, Renee is jealous of your love for Cassie. She also wants to keep her away from Webb. Renee rules her with an abusive hand."

"Why didn't she tell me?"

"She was afraid of what you might do." She paused at his dark countenance before continuing, "Maybe I shouldn't have told you."

"No, you were right to tell. Damn! I should have known," he growled.

"There's something else, Cougar. Renee was responsible for your whipping."

"I know," he replied bitterly. "She told Webb I had attacked her, and he saw the job done."

"That's not true." She nodded at his look of disbelief. "Renee ordered it. Webb didn't know about it until after the fact. Chas told him."

He shrugged. "What's done is done. Makes no difference to me who ordered it."

She stared at him searching for any hidden pain, but his expression had closed. Seeking to lessen his angst, she asked conversationally, "So you're an Indian?"

"Half-Indian," he muttered, still seething from the knowledge of Cassie's abuse. He didn't want to even touch the startling news that Webb had not ordered the whipping.

"What's it like?" she asked with genuine curiosity.

Cougar glanced at her with one arched brow, then simply said, "It's peaceful."

"Peaceful?"

"Yes, peaceful."

"I like your mother. She told me how she met your father, Tall Feather. It's a shame you didn't know him," she finished, stifling a yawn.

Cougar watched the undulating flames. How many times had he thought the same thing? When he looked back, he found Cady curled on the ground, sound asleep. He slipped on his shirt and reached out, gathering her close before he lay back on the blanket, resting her head against his good shoulder.

He wondered, not for the first time, what he was going to do with her. This time, however, there was no anxious tightening in his belly, no disagreeable thoughts. He believed Fate had already taken care of their future.

Chapter 31

Cady awoke cradled in Cougar's arm. One arm lay across his chest, and one leg was thrown quite intimately over his thighs. She glanced up at his face and found him awake and staring at the smoky-gray sky. It was not quite dawn, and they were nestled beneath the widespread branches of a cottonwood tree. The fire had dwindled to a pile of glowing embers.

"How's your shoulder?"

"Hurts like hell."

"Shouldn't we change the bandage?"

"Later," he growled, disengaging himself from her limbs. He rose to his feet and threw a couple of fat branches on the embers.

Cougar was adamantly fighting the desire raging through his blood. He had been awake for hours, listening to her breathing, feeling her soft body snuggled up against his. *He had to keep the marriage in name only!* It had become a litany—a chant he had begun to despise. But, oh, how he wanted her!

Cady raised up on one elbow and stared at his rigid back. "Cougar?" she whispered. He turned and faced her. "What's the matter?" she asked. His gaze was hot, caressing her body, and she started to tremble with excitement.

"I want you." He sighed in disgust as soon as the words left his mouth. Instead of explaining to her the need for them to stay uninvolved, he had voiced aloud the longing that haunted him.

"I want you, too," she answered shyly, a light blush smudging her cheeks.

"We must keep our marriage in name only."

"Why? When we both want each other?"

"We come from two different worlds."

Ah, so that *was* it. Could it be then he cared for her? A spark of hope flickered. She didn't give a fig about his bloodline—she only knew she wanted him, her body hungered for his, and she was tired of denying it or thinking she was less of a lady because of it. And if he left her afterwards, so be it. It was time they both acted, again, on what they wanted—each other.

"Cougar—come here," she demanded gently, her voice soft but unyielding.

He glanced at her in surprise but did as she asked. He knelt in front of her.

She scrambled to her knees and placed her hands on either side of his face. She leaned forward and touched her mouth to his, tracing the fullness of his lips with the tip of her tongue. When she heard his groan of surrender and felt his arms close around her, she knew she had succeeded in breaking down his silly barrier.

They knelt on the blanket, clutching each other, the flames of the fire outlining their impassioned embrace as they both gave in to what they wanted, what they needed.

Cougar rained soft kisses on her face and neck. She tasted like dew and the autumn wind, the scents filling his senses. He forced himself to slow down, not wanting to frighten her, nor make her run away. But Cady would have none of that. She wanted her man—and she wanted him now.

She loved the feel of his lips on hers and was surprised anew at their softness, for his mouth usually possessed a hard edge. She spread open his shirt and ran her hands over his smooth chest, carefully avoiding his injured shoulder. His muscles bulged beneath her inquisitive fingertips, inciting her already frenzied desire to a higher level. She marveled at the difference in their bodies. Where she was soft and smooth with gentle curves, he was firm and muscular. She could feel his strength in every inch of his body.

A very thin line of black hair sprouted on his lower belly and disappeared into his buckskins. Boldly, she reached out a slender finger and traced the hairline, her finger catching on the waistband.

Cougar drew in his breath. "Don't."

"Why not?"

"Because I'm on the edge."

"The edge of what?"

"Cady..." He sounded almost pained.

She obeyed his command, but her grin was naughty.

With a growl, he divested himself of his clothes before quickly removing hers, flinging her pants over his shoulder. He gathered her close, pushed her back against the blanket, and covered her body with his own. The hiss of the fire and subsequent sparks went unheeded as their passion reached a higher plateau.

His mouth travelled down her throat, stopping to kiss one breast, circling the crest with his tongue, before moving to the other, and brushing his tongue over the pink nub. She threaded her fingers in his hair, every nerve alive, tingling beneath his touch, and soared to new heights of sexual longing.

Cougar rose above her, hardly able to contain

himself, and knew if she wasn't his soon, he would perish from the need. He nudged her thighs apart, his arousal seeking her heat. He entered her with one powerful thrust, sheathing himself deeply and completely inside her, making their bodies one. She fit him perfectly, as if they had been made for one another. Her silken legs wrapped around his waist, and she matched him thrust for thrust.

They came together, oblivious to their surroundings, aware only of each other. Nothing else mattered at that moment except they were united, their bodies joined, and riding the wave of pleasure cresting over them with a force so powerful they shuddered from the sheer breathtaking size of it.

This was different from their first time. This time their unspoken love made it more intense, more rewarding, binding them closer together. When they found their release, and drifted slowly back to earth, their bodies trembled with unspoken yet fully realized love.

Cady fell asleep wrapped in Cougar's arms.

****

The sun filtering through the trees touched Cady awake. She stared up at the bright blue sky, her gaze following a lazy white cloud drifting by. She rolled over and looked around for Cougar, spotting him over by the horses. She blushed, remembering the early dawn hours spent in his arms. As if sensing her awake, Cougar turned and smiled. She returned his smile and, still blushing, sat up, brushed the hair from her eyes, and slipped on her shirt.

"Good morning, darlin'," he said with a grin, and leaned over and kissed her soundly.

"Good morning," she responded breathlessly,

studying his face. "You look awful," she observed candidly. His face was pale and drawn and blood spotted the bandage wrapped around his shoulder. "And your wound—it's bleeding!"

"No, it stopped a while ago. Our early morning activities disturbed it," he said with a lazy grin. "But you'll need to apply the poultice and a fresh bandage."

After she finished blushing at his remark, she pushed the blanket off her legs, preparing to rise. She gasped, realizing she was naked from the waist down. She looked around for her pants.

"Your pants burned."

"They—what?" she asked in confusion.

"They, ah, landed in the fire and—" His grin turned into an out-and-out smile.

"Oh," she whispered.

"Do you have another pair?"

"Yes, in my saddlebags."

Cady rummaged through her saddlebags and found a pair of blue denims. After asking him to please turn around, ignoring his shout of laughter and raised brows, she donned the denims and reached for her vest and boots. While she dressed, he opened the pouch hanging from his belt, pinched a few herbs into the palm of his hand and mixed them with water from his canteen.

Once fully clothed, she went to work on his shoulder. After unwrapping the bandage, she examined the wound. It looked angry—purplish red with thick, yellow pus around the ragged edges. With a clean damp cloth, she wiped away the messy discharge and gently applied the poultice, packing it carefully around and over the frayed hole.

As Cady worked, Cougar stared into the forest of

trees. *Just what am I supposed to do now?* She seemed to want to stick around. Why would a lovely young girl like her want to be stuck with a man who had nothing to offer her except misery? It was more than the inheritance—Cady was no more materialistic than he. So, what was it? He slanted a look at her while she worked on his shoulder. Her face was set in a determined line, her lips clamped tightly together. Could it be she cared?

She finished tending his wound and sat back on her heels, wondering at his thoughts. She had heard his muttered curse and guessed it had something to do with her and him and their different worlds.

"Rose told me about the past. About Chas. She had the same doubts as you do now."

He glanced at her, wondering where she was going with this. "And what are those?"

"About you being Indian and me not. You know—"

"The same holds true now as it did then."

"Times have changed."

"Not that much."

"Cougar, I don't care!"

"You will," he said ominously. Her expression was set in stubborn lines, and a small seed of hope started to sprout. Maybe, just maybe it would work. They could—

"She also thinks that Webb doesn't care about your bloodline either."

"She is wrong."

"Maybe if you talked to him… perhaps you two could work out your problems."

"No."

"Won't you at least try?"

"I said no. End of subject."

"But—"

"Damn it, Cady! I have had enough nagging for one day!"

He stood up and stepped back. "Let's go," he snapped. "I don't want to be here if the other man decides to come back with a posse."

The rest of their ride to Ponderosa Pines was uneventful and made in an uneasy silence. Cougar looked completely unapproachable. Gone was their earlier comradery, now replaced by uncomfortable silence, brought on by her thoughtless demands. She should have known that a man as proud as Cougar would not simply concede. There was too much bad blood between him and Webb. Oh, why couldn't she have left well enough alone?

When they arrived at the hacienda, Cougar followed Cady into the parlor and stood stiffly in the doorway.

"Cougar, I'm sorry. I should never have brought up the subject. It's just that Chas—"

"I have to go now."

"Where are you going?"

He raised a brow and said, "I told you I would not live here."

"But after this morning—"

"This morning has not changed my mind. I will keep you as safe as I can, but we will not set up house together."

"Go on with you then! I don't care if I never see you again." She presented her rigid profile to him, lashing out at his rejection. When he didn't respond, she turned to find him gone.

She ran to the window and watched him ride off into the sunset, hot tears burning her eyes. She sniffed loudly and turned back to the empty room. She sank onto the sofa and stared miserably at the floor.

"Señorita Cady! When did you arrive home?" Maria padded into the parlor, startling Cady from her misery.

"Just now," she muttered.

"We were so worried, Señorita. But when Señor Austin came here looking for you, we knew he would find you and keep you safe."

Cady glanced up and replied sullenly, "Yes, he found me. And, Maria, it's *Señora* now." At Maria's look of puzzlement, she explained, "I married Cougar a couple of days ago."

"You did!" Maria beamed and bustled over to her side. "But that is good, no?"

"No. But I believe he will be an absent husband, so it doesn't really matter."

Maria patted Cady's hand. "I think not, Señora."

Cady turned to stare out the window. Her puppy bounded into the room with an excited bark and jumped into her lap. She stroked the soft fur, her thoughts centered on her dark, brooding husband.

The object of her musings was just as occupied with thoughts of his new bride. He was obsessed with her, the vision of loveliness he had left behind—the girl who had crept into his heart and stayed.

He pulled his stallion to a stop and glanced over his shoulder at Ponderosa Pines. The setting sun cast the hacienda in smudges of orange and red. He ran a hand though his hair, angry at himself. He imagined her alone in the house, astounded by his rudeness and abrupt departure.

He was not happy about the way he had acted but reminded himself that it was for the best. Despite her words to the contrary, he knew it would never work. Their marriage would make her an outcast and she would eventually end up hating him for it. He couldn't let that happen. He could withstand just about anything—but that.

Chapter 32

Cady couldn't stand the silence. It was eerie, like the calm before a storm. She knew it was only a matter of time before Wiley struck again, regardless that she was married. She was tired of having no say in her life, no control over the events shaping it. *Well, that was about to change.* Deciding to call on Cassie, she dressed in denims and a black cotton shirt and took off astride Dream, the sun warming her face, the wind tugging at her hair.

She reined up at Fallen Tree and dismounted. Cassie had apparently seen her coming and was waiting for her on the front porch.

"Cady, you're back!" she exclaimed, rushing down the steps. Taking in her distraught expression, she asked in alarm, "Are you all right?"

"No—yes, I'm fine."

Cassie looked confused. "Did Austin find you? He came here demanding to know where you'd gone. I'm sorry. I had to tell him."

"Not to worry, and yes, he found me. In a river, clinging to a rock." At Cassie's nonplussed expression, she said with a heavy sigh, "It's a long story." She decided against telling her of their recent nuptials. She just couldn't bear her enthusiasm over the union.

Cassie pulled her into the house and closed the parlor doors behind them. She sat Cady on the sofa and sank down next to her. Lowering her voice, she asked, "Did you find Lucinda?"

"Yes. She had quite an interesting story to tell. She thinks Wiley could have killed Chas."

"No!" Cassie breathed, clasping her hands together. "What about the fire and Randy's injury?"

Cady shrugged. "She didn't say, but I wouldn't put it past him."

"What are you going to do now?"

"I am going to find Wiley. I have to get to him before he gets to me—again."

"But how? Cady, I don't like that look in your eyes. What are you planning?" she asked, alarmed by the gleam in her friend's violet-blue eyes.

"I have an idea. Come on!" She jumped up and pulled Cassie to her feet.

"Where are we going?"

"To Ponderosa Pines. I'll explain on the way."

Once at the ranch, the two girls ran up to Cady's room. Cady pulled a linen sheet from the bed and tore it into long strips. She handed several strips to Cassie. "Tie these around your chest."

"Why?"

"To flatten your breasts," she responded matter-of-factly, removing her own shirt.

"Cady, what are you up to?"

"I'm going to find Wiley and stop him once and for all. And you're going to help me."

"How?" Cassie asked, becoming nervous.

"I don't know yet."

"Maybe we should get Randy—or Austin," Cassie ventured timidly.

"No. They will only try to stop us."

"For good reason," Cassie muttered. "What exactly are we going to do?"

"We're going to the Buckhorn and see what we can find out."

"We're not!" Cassie exclaimed, her brown eyes beginning to sparkle with guarded enthusiasm. *The saloon!* "But Cady do you think we should? I mean—"

Cady laughed as she wrapped the strips of linen around her breasts. "We'll blend in with the others, so there's nothing to worry about." She glanced at Cassie, who was simply holding the strips in her hands and looking at them with a frown.

"Hurry, Cassie, before Maria comes looking for us."

Cassie held up the strips with a wry grin. "I don't think these will be necessary." She laughed as she gestured to her rather less-than-endowed chest.

Cady smiled and, with a nod, took the strips and stuffed them in the bottom of her wardrobe. She grabbed a pair of pants and a flannel shirt and handed them to Cassie. "Here, put these on," she instructed as she slipped her shirt back on. "We can't have you wearing gingham to the saloon."

Cassie quickly changed. They braided each other's hair and stuffed the heavy plaits under their hats. "But how do you know he'll be there?"

"Where else would he be? He doesn't work and he's not here tormenting me."

When suitably disguised, they descended the stairs, pausing on the bottom step. Cady knew if Maria spotted them, dressed as they were, she would not let them out of the house until she had heard their explanation. Upon hearing it, she would most definitely not let them leave. Hearing sounds of Maria moving about in the kitchen,

Cady placed her finger over her lips and gestured to Cassie to follow her out the side door, into the courtyard, and out the back gate to the stables.

Luck was on their side. They made it from the house undetected and found the stables deserted. They quickly mounted their horses and took off at a gallop. Upon arriving in town, they pulled up outside the saloon and hitched their horses to the wooden post.

Sounds of men's voices and raucous laughter drifted to them over the swinging double doors. Cady took a deep breath and turned to Cassie, who was staring at the saloon, a panicked expression on her face.

"Ready?" Cady whispered.

"Ready as I'll ever be. Oh, Cady, do you think we should?"

"Yes," Cady said firmly, stifling the nervousness threatening to take away her courage. "Remember, we're dressed like men, so act like one," she instructed, watching a man stumble from the saloon and stagger down the sidewalk.

Cassie looked at her helplessly. "How?"

"I don't know." She turned back to Cassie. "Swagger a lot and—spit."

"Spit? For heaven's sake, I don't know *how* to spit!"

"Well, then don't spit. Just swagger." The boisterous sounds became louder as they ascended the wooden steps to the sidewalk. Cady took another deep breath and pushed open the doors to the saloon.

"Just act like we belong," she whispered before stepping across the threshold. She paused on the landing to look around and was bumped from behind by Cassie. She pulled her up alongside and surveyed the room. The saloon was larger than Cady had imagined and smelled of smoke, liquor, and sweat. A long wooden bar occupied one side of the room where several small groups of men were gathered, talking among themselves. Behind the bar were rows of bottles arranged beneath a large mirror that covered most of the wall. Paintings of scantily clad women hung haphazardly on the other walls. Kerosene lamps hung from the ceiling over tables, some of which were covered in green cloth and encircled by men playing cards. Sawdust was strewn on the floor and brass buckets were situated around the room. The clink of glasses mingled with chatter and laughter, and tinny music from a piano resounded throughout the room.

Cady was surprised to see women in the saloon, and she eyed them with interest. There were perhaps six of them, all dressed in bright jewel colors. Their skirts were short, exposing a good deal of black silk-clad legs. They were laughing and talking with the men.

"Follow me," Cady whispered to Cassie. She stepped into the saloon and swaggered up to the bar. After catching the barkeep's attention, Cady lowered her voice and called out for two whiskeys. The barkeep eyed them curiously, then poured them each a shot. Cady sipped the whiskey, encouraging Cassie to do the same, and surreptitiously scanned the room.

"There he is." She nudged Cassie with her elbow and nodded toward her cousin. Wiley sat at one of the back tables with another unscrupulous-looking man. They had their heads together in conversation. *Obviously hatching another plot to do me in.*

"Come on," Cady whispered and sidled down the bar, stopping just a stone's throw away from the men. She leaned casually back against the bar and strained to hear their conversation. Their words were muffled, and she was nearly bent over their table in her quest to hear what they were saying.

"Ah, Cady—" Cassie nudged Cady sharply in the ribs with her elbow.

"What?"

"Look."

Cady followed Cassie's gaze and groaned in frustration. "Lord, he's going to ruin everything."

Cougar stood in the doorway of the saloon, a dangerous expression on his face, and swept the room with an amber gaze of steel. She felt her trepidation rise when his gaze passed over the girls only to swing back and settle on them, his eyes widening in disbelief. His expression turned murderous as he moved into the saloon and stalked them like an animal.

Cady's stomach knotted in fear, and she shrank back against the bar as his measured steps came closer. He stopped in front of Cady and leaned down into her face.

"What in the hell are you doing in here?" he whispered furiously. He turned on Cassie. "And you? You're a part of this—this crazy scheme? When Maria told me she had seen the two of you sneak out of the house dressed as boys, I could imagine Cady doing something this stupid. But you! I would have thought you smarter than this, Cassie," he admonished.

Cassie cringed under Cougar's recrimination and whispered, "But, Austin, it's important. Wiley is responsible for all that has befallen Cady. She's trying to stay one step ahead of him."

Cougar ignored her, having already turned back to Cady. "I ought to—" he started in a dangerously low voice.

"Ssh, I'm trying to hear what they're saying," Cady mumbled, deciding to stand her ground. His unleashed fury scared her witless, but she wasn't going to show it. This was too important.

Cougar glanced over at the table that was occupying her attention, then back to his wife. He rested both hands on the bar, one on either side of her, trapping her in place. He'd already opened his mouth to reprimand her when she ducked beneath his arm and sidled farther down the bar. His expression turned incredulous at her defiance, and he reached out to grab her arm.

"You lookin` for trouble, mister?" a surly voice asked from behind Cougar.

Cassie gasped in dismay and stared wide-eyed at the stranger. He was nearly as tall as Austin and carried almost twice his weight. Cady was so intent on her cousin that she at first didn't know what was happening.

Cougar turned slowly around. "This doesn't concern you," he told him, his voice deadly.

The man pushed his hat off his forehead and peered closely at him. "Hey, you're that savage fella, ain`t ya?"

Cassie edged out of the way, down the bar to Cady's side. Cougar's face darkened, and faster than the eye could follow, his fist connected with the man's jaw. The man flew across the room, crashing into a table and chairs along the way. Talk was suspended as all eyes were glued to the fight. The man staggered to his feet and lunged at Cougar. Cougar neatly sidestepped him and clipped the back of his neck with a swift, powerful blow of his hand.

When the man lay unconscious on the floor, Cougar glanced around daring anyone else to challenge him. When no one moved, he grabbed the two girls' arms and escorted them from the saloon. Cady looked over her shoulder and found Wiley watching her with narrowed eyes. She turned quickly around and stumbled alongside Cougar.

Once outside, he turned on them. "What in the hell were you thinking? You could have gotten yourself in serious trouble."

"We were doing just fine until you got here," Cady muttered, averting her gaze from his stormy one. "If you hadn't shown up, none of this would have happened."

"What in the hell were you doing?" Suppressing the urge to shake her, he spat out, "You little fool! You could have ruined everything."

"I merely wanted to find out what Wiley was planning next so I could be prepared." She looked at him suspiciously. "What do you mean? I could have ruined *what*?"

"Never mind," he growled, itching to shake some sense into her. Without looking at Cassie, he snarled, "Go home. I'll deal with you later."

Cassie needed no further encouragement. She jumped on her horse and, with a last woeful look at Cady, dug in her heels and took off toward Fallen Tree.

Cougar threw Cady onto his stallion and swung up behind her. She tried to jump off, but he wrapped his arm around her waist and held her in place. Pulling the Palomino behind them, he galloped out of town. She struggled against the arm wrapped securely around her waist, but he merely tightened it until she could barely breathe. She crossed her arms over her chest, her back as straight as an arrow, and ignored him.

When they reached Ponderosa Pines, Cougar jumped from his horse and turned to help Cady down.

She slid from the stallion and swept by Cougar and into the house. She stomped into the parlor, clearly disgruntled, and stood defiantly in the center of the room, her back to the door. She heard Cougar enter and close the door behind him.

"If I ever catch you doing anything this foolish again, I'll—"

"You'll what?" she shouted, spinning on her heel. "I am not a child to be ordered about! You have no say over me, no right to tell me what to do! You said so yourself, our marriage is in name only." Her eyes were afire with anger, her chest rising and falling with each breath.

"Regardless of the conditions of our marriage, you are still my wife, and you will do as I say. I demand that you not leave this house again without me."

"You *demand*—how dare you!"

"I'll dare anything. Every time you venture out you get into trouble. And, frankly, I'm tired of saving you."

She gasped. "I never asked you to watch over me! And besides, you only married me to fulfill Chas's request. Well, I release you from that promise. I refuse to be married to someone like you or to someone I've been forced upon. I have spent my entire life forced on people."

"Do you think the world owes you? Is that it? You were left an orphan and had a miserable life because of it? Because of your nasty attitude, you most likely alienated everyone around you. You have brought on yourself all the misery you think you've endured. It's a wonder Chas loved you. But then again, he hadn't seen you since you were a child."

Cady stared at him, her mouth agape. She had already come to the same conclusion. But to hear the words spoken aloud—and from the man she loved no less—wounded her deeply. In her pain, she struck out.

"I hate you!" she shouted and slapped him as hard as she could across the face.

Cougar hesitated but a moment before he grabbed her arms and yanked her up against him. He smothered her mouth with his, the kiss hard, unfeeling, and resembling nothing like his earlier ones. She pushed at his chest with her fists and pulled her mouth from his.

"How could I have ever dreamed you were my protector? That dream was probably the most foolish one I've ever had! You are nothing but an arrogant bully!" She pointed toward the door. "Get out," she hissed between gritted teeth.

He looked into her eyes, his as hard as glass. "I knew it was a mistake to seek you out. I should have kept a tighter rein on my emotions. But believe me, darlin', I won't make the same mistake again." He turned and left without another word.

Cady fell to her knees, covered her face with her hands and wept.

Chapter 33

Cady was miserable. She soaked in the tub and tried desperately to forget about Cougar since that crushing scene in her parlor. He had said aloud what she herself had come to realize, and dislike, about herself. And out of shame she had struck out in anger. There was absolutely no doubt now what his feelings were for her. He had made it blatantly obvious.

And now she had to gather her scattered wits and attend the Taylors' small dinner party. It was the last thing she wanted to do in her exhausted mental state, but Cassie had insisted she attend. Cady had finally agreed, thinking that perhaps once there, surrounded by other people, and free of the disturbing image of her husband, she would find some calming normality. She was also curious about Terence. What would his manner be tonight? When she saw him last, he had been less than kind.

When the water began to cool, she quickly finished her bath and towel-dried her body. She donned a long, ruffled black skirt and a lavender blouse with a high neck and long, tight-fitting sleeves. She pulled her hair back with a purple ribbon, leaving it to cascade long and full down her back. She slipped off her wedding band, looped it onto a piece of yellow ribbon, and tied it around her neck, hiding it beneath the blouse. She grabbed a black knitted shawl before joining Randy out front where he had brought around the buggy. With a shared smile, they each took out their revolvers and placed them in their laps within easy reach if the need should arise.

The evening air was cool and clear, the moon a silver crescent smiling in the ebony sky amid a smattering of twinkling stars. Tall pine trees swayed in the breeze, stark silhouettes against the darker backdrop of the mountains.

Ebbitt, the Taylors' butler, escorted them into the formal parlor where the guests had gathered to enjoy libations and conversation. Cady knew most of them from her welcoming party and spent a few minutes reacquainting herself with them. Renee came up and slipped her arm through hers.

"I'm so happy you're here. Oh dear, Cady, are you unwell?"

"No." She smoothed back her hair.

"You look a little pale, dear. You must take better care of yourself. Have you spoken to Mr. Doswell?"

"No, he's still out of town."

"I see. Perhaps—" She glanced over Cady's shoulder. "Will you excuse me, dear?"

Cady's gaze followed Renee across the floor as she made her way to her husband's side. Webb was leaning against the wall, a tall glass of whiskey in his hand. Renee leaned over to whisper in his ear. He nodded curtly and swallowed half the contents of his glass.

Sam Hathaway approached her, holding out a glass of red wine.

"It's good to see you again, Miss Grayson."

"Hello, Sam, and please call me Cady," she said with a smile, accepting the glass.

"All right—Cady. How are things at Ponderosa

Pines?"

"Fine," she answered absently, her gaze traveling to the door where Terence was entering the room with Claudia Wright clutching his arm.

Her attention was drawn back to Sam when he asked hesitantly, "Would you like to go with me to the Humbletons' dance next week?" he asked, his head tilted, his smile shy.

"I'm sorry, I can't. You see, I'm ah, not able to just now. But I do appreciate the invitation." She flinched at his crestfallen expression, but just then Terence and Claudia approached, silk dress swishing, saving her from further wounding the kind, shy man.

"Hello, Cady. I'm glad to see you could attend our little party. You remember Claudia?" Terence's sincerity was belied by an artificial smile.

"Of course. How do you do?" Cady asked, not really caring.

Claudia nodded her head haughtily, then turned to Terence and pulled his head down to whisper in his ear, rudely ignoring Cady and Sam. Cady looked over Claudia's red brocaded shoulder and turned back to the group.

"Cassie is waving to me. Will you excuse me?" Without waiting for an answer, she escaped and made her way to Cassie's side.

"Thank you, my friend," Cady said, grasping Cassie's arm and squeezing lightly.

"I'm here to help," Cassie said with a small laugh. "Have you seen Austin since the fiasco in town?"

"No."

"He was so angry. Why, he was acting like he owned you."

Cady shrugged. "Well, it's over now. I just hope Wiley doesn't have any more surprises up his sleeve," she muttered, explicitly implying that if he did it would be Cougar's fault. She had not yet told Cassie of their marriage and wondered when and if she should.

"Let's not think about it now. You're safe here."

"What's going on between Renee and Webb? They appear to be arguing."

"Pa confronted Renee." Her voice dropped to a whisper. "He threatened to kill her if she laid another hand on me."

"Good."

"It's time to go into dinner. I hope you're hungry," Cassie said, leading her into the dining room. With a grin, she placed Cady next to Sam at the long, elegantly decorated table and moved to sit on her other side next to Randy. Cady suffered through a stilted conversation with Sam and thought the dinner would never end.

****

Cougar stood outside his cabin and watched the sun set, only vaguely aware of the play of colors against the cobalt sky. By the time the sun had slipped below the mountain ridge, he had come to a decision. It was time to collect his wife.

He had visited his mother that morning. She had begged him not to make the same mistake she had made all those years ago with Chas, afraid of the consequences married to a woman pregnant with another man's child—an Indian's child. *If you love Cady, take her, keep her by your side. Do not worry about what others may think. Your love will overcome any obstacles, including ostracism*, she had counselled.

He was certainly capable of protecting her from

anything, whether it be outlaws or narrow minds. Why had he kept denying that? And Cady—she was one hell of a strong woman. If confronted with prejudice, she could handle it.

Cougar didn't want to live without Cady. He couldn't live without her. He had guarded his heart fiercely, and love was something he'd avoided, but it had found him. She had found him.

He thought about the dream Cady had in the cave and, though it had disturbed him at the time, he embraced it now as the truth.

As a young man he had learned a great deal about dreams and their significance from the holy man in their village. All dreams had deep and profound meanings, he had been told, and should always be taken seriously. The holy man had added that at first glance dreams are elusive, but at some stage in one's life the meaning becomes clear.

Is that what her dream had meant? That they were destined to be together as his mother had decreed? Despite all the obstacles they faced? He was beginning to think it was so. *And the fact that she had remembered it was telling.* He grimaced. Even though it had been thrown at him in anger.

He had also been lying to himself. He had not married her merely to fulfill his promise to a dying man. No, he had married her because he wanted to—because he wanted her. But he knew it was something more— much more. He was truly and madly, deeply in love with the girl.

Yes, he loved everything about her. From her annoying habit of running off blindly to do whatever the hell she thought needed doing, frustrating him no end, to her caring nature and sweet loving kisses.

Oh, Great One, I do love her. But I'm afraid—afraid I might not be able to shield her, afraid that she will end up hating me because of it. Please, I ask for your guidance.

A feeling of peace came over him. He knew what he would do—what he had to do. But first he needed to convince Cady that she loved him as he loved her.

A rush of happiness welled up and he felt like he could conquer anything. But could he conquer Cady's hurt and anger? Would she forgive him for the shameful way he had behaved?

He desperately hoped it wasn't too late, that he had not driven her away by his foolish beliefs and even more foolish behavior.

Chapter 34

At Fallen Tree, Ebbitt answered the summons at the front door. He stepped aside as Cougar pushed his way into the foyer. He tried to usher him into Webb's study, but Cougar, ignoring the butler's flustered request, made his way to the dining room where he heard the murmur of voices. He paused in the doorway and surveyed the room. Perhaps a dozen people were seated around the elegantly clad table, among them his wife.

Webb looked up at the commotion. "What in the hell are you doing here?" he shouted, his face beginning to darken with rage.

"Hello, Webb," Cougar drawled and leaned his shoulder against the door frame. He was dressed in pale tan buckskins, matching shirt, and knee-high moccasins. His whole demeanor was one of indifference, looking completely at ease, but he was, in fact, not. He had no idea how Cady would react to his presence. If she shunned him... He looked away from Webb, his gaze sweeping the entire gathering, finally settling on his wife. Her expression made Cougar even more uneasy. Had he waited too long?

"Well, well, what brings you to Fallen Tree?" Terence asked, placing his napkin on the table, and leaning back in his chair.

"I've come to collect my bride," Cougar answered, his gaze never leaving Cady's face. The gasps of surprise rose as one as Cougar moved toward her. They locked gazes—amber and indigo—and she saw the look in his eyes, daring her to defy him. They also conveyed a depth of emotion she'd not seen before, and her heart skipped a beat.

Cassie leaned over and whispered to Cady, "What is he talking about?"

Cady didn't have time to answer, for Cougar was now standing behind her chair, one hand resting lightly on her shoulder. It was like a dead weight pinning her down, challenging her to decry his startling announcement. She sat rigid in her chair trying to restrain her resentment at his audacity. Still, she quivered from his touch.

Webb jumped to his feet, upsetting his glass of wine, the red liquid staining the white table linen like blood. "What in the hell is going on here?" he shouted, turning to Cady. "What does he mean his *bride*? You married this—?"

Terence jumped to his feet. "You married him? Are you crazy?"

Cougar gripped Cady's shoulder to keep her silent. "What's it to you, Terence?" he drawled with a lazy quirk of his brow.

"She said she would marry me!" he shouted. Claudia's gasp of outrage filled the ensuing silence. She bent a murderous glare at Cady.

Cougar gazed down at Cady with one arched brow. "That true?"

"I never said I'd marry you, Terence. In fact, I distinctly said—"

"Chas would be rolling over in his grave if he knew about this!" Webb shouted to no one in particular.

"But he was the one—" Cassie tried to interject.

"Chas wouldn't be in his grave if it wasn't for him!" Terence cried, pointing accusingly at Cougar.

Throughout the uproar, Renee had remained silent, her eyes narrowed thoughtfully on Cougar. She patted her mouth delicately with the corner of her napkin and sat back to watch the scene unfold.

"Well, I for one think it's wonderful news," Cassie declared, at once drawing her father's wrath upon her head.

"Oh, you do, do you?"

"He killed your grandfather!" Terence shouted above the din. "Good Lord, Cady, you even had him arrested!"

"No, *you* had him arrested. I was merely a pawn in your game of revenge," she said with a meaningful glance.

"We will have it annulled," Webb said in a voice that brooked no argument. "I will not have the granddaughter of my best friend shackled to the likes of this—this savage for the rest of her life. He's a damn half-breed, for God's sake!"

"I knew it!" Claudia shouted triumphantly. Terence motioned her to silence.

"We will have it annulled," Webb repeated with a wave of his hand.

"Yes, annulled," Terence echoed in agreement.

"It's too late for that," Cougar drawled, the meaning of which took a moment to sink in.

"You—you laid with him?" If possible, Webb's outrage rose to new heights.

Cady blushed and looked down at her lap.

"Regardless, you can't expect to hold Cady to

marriage vows now that she knows the truth about your bloodline," Terence said, hiding his jealousy with a satisfied grin.

"I knew the truth when I married him, Terence."

"What?" he said in disbelief. Then his face hardened. "Then he forced you."

Cougar drew Cady to her feet. "It's time to go." He felt her body stiffen and looked into her eyes, afraid of what he would find. His heart sank. It was too late. He had driven her away by his callous behavior.

"You are no longer welcome in this house, Cady. Get out of here and take that no-good bastard with you!" Webb roared.

Terence stood beside him, just as furious. Renee had a slight smile on her face. The other guests just looked stunned.

Cady turned to Cassie with a stricken expression. "Cassie—?"

Cassie jumped up and hugged her friend. "Go with him. It will be all right," she whispered encouragingly.

Cady clutched Cougar's arm and allowed him to lead her from the dining room. She kept her back straight, knowing all eyes were upon them. They made their way to the front door and outside to his horse.

"Get on," he ordered brusquely.

"Go to hell." She turned to walk away. Cougar grabbed her arm, staying her. She glared up at him. "I believe we have said everything there is to be said." She pulled her arm free. "Now, if you don't mind, I'm going home...alone."

"You belong to me!"

"In name only! You refuse to be my husband."

"You told Terence you would marry him?" he

asked, his voice incredulous.

"Of course not. He asked but I refused. You knew that!"

"Why would he ask you?"

"How should I know? I suppose he wanted to."

"Did you want to marry him?"

"No. If I had wanted to, I would have."

"But then you wouldn't inherit Chas's property." He was fury personified, thrown completely off guard by her casual attitude about Terence, and being totally unfair.

"Oh," she screamed in frustration. "You *are* a bastard!"

"And you, darlin', are a—!"

"Fine," she shouted, pulling the ribbon from around her neck and slipping off the gold ring. Throwing it at him, she cried, "If I'm so awful, then just keep it! I never wanted to marry you anyway!" She spun on her heel and ran around the side of the house.

Cougar watched her run away, his heart heavy. He bent down and picked up the ring. His resolve to gather Cady in his arms and love her madly had disappeared when Terence had declared that she had agreed to marry him. Jealousy had gotten the best of him, and he had lost his self-control. He sighed. Where Cady Grayson was concerned, he had no self-control. And now it looked like he had nothing at all.

****

Her eyes filled with tears, Cady peered around the side of the house and watched Cougar pick up the ring and place it in the pouch hanging from his belt. He swung up on his stallion and rode off, his whole being carved from stone.

"Miss Grayson?" a voice whispered from behind.

She jumped clear off the ground. "Randy!" She gasped. "You startled me."

"Sorry, ma'am. Are you ready to go home?"

"Yes, thank you," she replied, wondering how much he had heard and appreciating his tactful silence.

Cady climbed into the buggy, her heart broken. She hated their shouting matches, their hurtful words. *What is wrong with me?* She didn't give two hoots about Terence and yet she'd let Cougar believe she did. He had entered the lion's den, and she had thanked him by shouting and throwing his ring at him. *How he must hate me now.*

When they arrived at Ponderosa Pines, Cougar was pacing the length of the front porch, his strides graceful, his powerful muscles working in sync. He stopped as they pulled up and waited for Cady to climb out of the buggy. She walked slowly up the stairs and straight into his open arms. Over her head, Cougar nodded to Randy, who gathered the reins and tooled the buggy around back.

"You didn't desert me, even after all the horrible things I said," Cady whispered against his chest.

"*I* said such awful— I didn't mean a word." He buried his face in her hair. "I'm so sorry for the way I acted. I've behaved badly. Can you forgive me?"

"There is nothing to forgive."

"I was hurt—"

"Ssh…" she whispered, laying her fingers over his mouth.

"Jealous—"

"Of what?" She looked at him with interest.

"Terence. When I heard him announce you'd—"

"How can someone so smart be so stupid? I don't

want Terence. I have never wanted Terence. I want you!"

He gathered her in his arms and kissed her, unlike any other kiss they had shared. She pulled back to look into his eyes, eyes glowing with a sentiment she'd not seen before this night.

"It's you I love. It's always been you," Cady whispered, tears in her voice.

"Cady, my Cady—I love you, with all my heart." He pulled the gold ring from his pouch, lifted her left hand and placed it back where it belonged.

The familiar weight of the ring was comforting. "There is something I don't understand, Cougar. Why did you keep rejecting me? After kissing me, you'd get mad and leave."

He dropped to the porch divan and pulled her onto his lap. "I have wanted you since the day I saw you in the hotel lobby in Denver. Every time I wanted to act on it—or did—I was furious with myself. I couldn't make a life with you, even though we needed to honor Chas's request, which is why I made that asinine declaration that we wouldn't set up house together. Your kisses were torture, but making love to you made it even harder to stay away."

"Because we come from two different worlds?"

"Yes. I couldn't bear it if you suffered what I have since it's become known I'm half-Indian."

"Well, that's just silly. First of all, I have complete faith in you. Faith that you would deflect any unkindness directed at me. And second, you know that I am perfectly—"

He leaned in and kissed her mid-sentence, hearing her murmur against his mouth, "But how wonderful it is to be taken care of—by you."

He chuckled, moved her off his lap, and kissed her soundly. "There's something I need to do. I'll be home in a little while."

Home! He had said *home*! She waved as he mounted his stallion, turned, and headed down the drive.

Chapter 35

Cady strolled into the parlor to wait for Cougar. She poured herself a small glass of wine and sank to the sofa. *What a night!* Before she could form another thought, the front bell sounded.

She pushed herself to her feet and went to the door to find a stranger on her porch. "May I help you?" she asked, taking a step back, ready to bolt at the first sign of danger.

"I'm looking for Cady Grayson. That you?" He squinted at her from beneath his wide-brimmed hat.

"Yes."

"Here." He handed her a thick brown envelope. "The postmaster asked me to deliver it to you."

"Thank you," she replied, and stepped into the hallway and closed the door. She opened the envelope and read the letter, her eyes widening in amazement. It was from Governor Thornwilde of Colorado, informing her that Austin Taylor's pardon had been inadvertently misplaced, and he was therefore enclosing another copy. She scanned the official document. *Austin Taylor has been found innocent of all alleged charges levelled against him in the territory of Colorado. He is no longer wanted by the law; he is a free man,* it read.

When Cougar had proclaimed his innocence, she had doubted him. Like every other charge levelled against him, she had not believed him. She was ashamed.

She continued reading the governor's letter. Apparently, his agent had been waylaid near Ponderosa Pines, knocked unconscious, and woke to find his satchel, containing the pardon, gone. The governor went on to write he had been unaware of her grandfather's death until his agent had reported back to him. He extended his sympathy for her loss and, in closing, offered his assistance if she should need it.

Cady went into her grandfather's study and placed the envelope on his desk. Who would have stolen the pardon? It was something to think about and most definitely tell Cougar.

She glanced up at her family portrait and smiled. "I belong," she whispered. "For the first time since the accident took you away, I belong." The once familiar anger and resentment were gone. Now just a bittersweet sadness remained.

She spotted her dime novel where she had left it on the desk. She picked it up, flipped through the pages, and with a poignant smile, opened the desk drawer and put it away.

The cool autumn night enticed Cady outside. She sat on the front porch listening to the chirp of crickets, trying to wait patiently for her beloved to return. Restless, she walked down the front steps and wandered around the side of the house. Although the sun had set, lights from the kitchen window kept her from total darkness, and the moon was high in the sky, further brightening the yard. A rustling noise startled her, but before she could react, a hand clamped over her mouth, stifling her scream.

A gun poked her in the ribs and a man's voice hissed in her ear, "One wrong move and you're dead. Got it?"

She nodded, terrified. She was dragged across the

lawn to a row of shrubs where a horse was hidden. The man tossed her onto the back of the horse before he jumped up behind her, tied a bandanna around her eyes, and kicked his heels into the horse's sides. They took off like a shot, vanishing into the night.

****

When Cougar arrived back at Ponderosa Pines, Cady was nowhere to be found. He ran down to the stables thinking she was biding her time with her horse, but Dream was in her stall contently munching her oats. There was no sign of his wife. He sprinted back up to the hacienda and into the kitchen and found Maria at the table, her head in her hands, weeping. She looked up when Cougar raced into the room, her eyes swollen from her tears.

"Where is she?"

"She is gone! I looked out the window before heading to bed and saw her riding off on a horse."

"Alone?"

"No, there was someone with her. It looked like a man. He tossed her on the horse and they disappeared into the night."

"Who was it?"

"I don't know."

"I do," he muttered darkly. "I'm going after them."

"Vaya con Dios," she whispered, her voice wracked with pain as she watched him stride from the room.

Chapter 36

Cady hadn't seen who had taken her, but she could guess, experiencing a sinking feeling in her stomach when assailed by the cloying scent she'd come to know.

After a long stretch of riding, they stopped. The bandanna was ripped off her face and she blinked, trying to focus on her surroundings. The sun had not made an appearance but was just beginning to lighten the sky. She looked over her shoulder.

"Wiley," she said in disgust. Struggling from his arms, she slid to the ground. "I knew it."

"Hello, cousin dear," he said with a smirk, sliding off his dark brown horse. "We meet again."

"What do you want?"

"You got more lives than a cat." His eyes narrowed. "I'd kill you now, but you're worth more to me alive."

"Just what are you planning to do this time?"

"Sell you. Then, with you gone, I will inherit what is rightfully mine."

"You'll never get Ponderosa Pines. It will go to my husband." Her false bravado was becoming more difficult to maintain. *Sell me?*

"You got yourself married? To who?"

"Cougar."

"Who?"

"Austin Taylor."

"That savage fella?"

"He is not a savage!"

Wiley laughed, an ugly sound that sent a chill down her spine. "Did you honestly think that by marrying Taylor you'd be safe from me?" He shook his head. "I'll just have to get rid of him too."

She stared at him in alarm. "No! You can't! Wiley, this is crazy," she cried, her heart pounding with fear.

Wiley's gaze shifted over her shoulder, and he grinned. She turned and her heart stopped. An Indian atop a large brown-and-white speckled horse was coming toward them. He was dressed in buckskins and moccasins and had wild designs painted on his arms, bare chest, and face. His head was shaved save for a strip of black hair extending from his forehead and disappearing down the back of his head. He watched them impassively with black unblinking eyes.

Cady knew instinctively he was not a friend of Cougar's. He looked different from the ones by the river and in Rose's village. His menacing aura reached her across the space separating them, and she panicked and spun on her heel. Wiley reached out and grabbed her arm before she had taken a step and, with his other hand, signaled to the Indian to approach.

Cady watched in horror as the Indian dismounted and walked toward them. She cringed when he reached out and grabbed her chin firmly, moving it from side to side, studying her features. He grunted once and nodded. Pulling a leather bag from his belt, he threw it at Wiley. Then taking her by the arm, he pulled her along to his horse.

Cady glanced back over her shoulder. "Wiley! You can't do this! Please, don't leave me with him," she pleaded, hating the pathetic sound of her voice.

"I thought you liked their kind. After all, you married one," her cousin sneered.

A loud crash exploded in the trees. All three of them looked to see Cougar erupt from the forest atop his stallion. He pulled sharply on the reins and the horse reared up, its powerful hooves pawing the air.

The Indian dropped her arm and eyed Cougar warily. Cougar let out a blood-curdling scream and leapt off his horse. Cady didn't hesitate—she darted out of the way. The Indian crouched with his arms outstretched as if waiting to embrace Cougar. In one tackle, Cougar had him pinned to the ground. The Indian grunted and flipped Cougar onto his back, holding a large knife to his throat.

Cady held her breath, watching in horror as they battled, hand to hand. Wiley came up from behind and grabbed her arm. She struggled against him, but he easily overpowered her and dragged her into the trees. He pushed her ahead of him, his gun digging into her back.

"Move!" he hissed and shoved her harder.

"No!" she cried, stumbling, trying to look over her shoulder. Dear Lord, she prayed, please keep Cougar safe.

Wiley swore and, grabbing her arm again, dragged her through the forest heedless of the branches that brushed past him and slapped her in the face. She saw a sparkle of water through the trees and a spark of hope flared. A river! It would stop their flight and give her time to think.

The sound of someone running toward them sent Wiley ducking behind a tree, pulling Cady with him. Wiley peered around the side of the tree and pulled back, swearing blackly. Without another word, he pushed her out from behind the tree. She stumbled upright, feeling

Wiley's gun trained on her, and her eyes filled with tears at the sight of her magnificent husband striding toward her.

Cougar rushed to her side, his expression softening in relief. He started to embrace her but hesitated when something in her eyes alerted him to danger. Before he could react, Wiley stepped from behind the tree and smashed the butt of his pistol against Cougar's head. Cougar crumpled to the ground with a groan.

Cady gasped and fell to her knees. With a loving hand, she brushed a lock of hair off his forehead and caressed his cheek. Wiley grabbed her arm and yanked her to her feet.

"Get up, bitch."

She struggled, but he only tightened his grip painfully.

"Let me go! You've hurt him!"

"I'll do more than that," Wiley threatened. He threw her aside, grabbed Cougar's feet and dragged him toward the river.

"No, please don't! You can have Ponderosa Pines."

"Since when?"

"I want my husband!"

"Too bad," he said with a curl of his lip.

She ran after him and grabbed his arm, her nails digging into his skin. "Take me! Wiley, please, let my husband live!" she begged tearfully.

He knocked her down, sending her sprawling to the ground. She scrambled to her knees and watched in horror as Wiley waded into the river, pulling Cougar behind him. The water was studded with rocks and crested in furious whitecaps.

"No," she whispered, her fingers digging into the

soft earth. She watched helplessly when, with a shout of laughter, Wiley released Cougar's feet. He was quickly carried away on the swift current, his dark head disappearing beneath the surface. She heard the distant roar of a waterfall and froze with fear.

Wiley ran back to her, a self-satisfied sneer twisting his face. She snarled like an animal, jumped to her feet, and began to beat him with her fists, hot tears blinding her vision. "You bastard! I hate you! I'll kill you, I will!"

Wiley cursed and, raising his fist, hit her upside the head. Her ears ringing, she looked over at the surging river and something inside of her died. Her beloved was lost to her—forever. She ceased her struggles and preceded Wiley from the area, deflated of all emotion. She no longer cared what he had planned for her now.

****

Cassie rode over to Ponderosa Pines to see how Cady was faring after yesterday's disastrous dinner. The shock of the evening had worn off and been replaced with happiness at the glorious news that Austin and Cady were married. She found Maria puttering around the kitchen, doing nothing really except weeping.

"Maria! What is it!"

"Oh, Señorita Cassie," she cried, "Señora Cady is missing!"

"What?"

"Someone took her last night. I saw a man throw her across his horse and gallop off."

"Oh no!" Cassie's heart began to thump wildly. "Where was Austin?"

"I don't know, but when he came home, I told him what had happened, and he raced off on that big black and white horse of his."

"Then she will be found," Cassie declared, having complete faith in her cousin. She bit her lower lip. "I need to let Pa know. Despite how mad he is at Cady, she is still kin." She hugged Maria. "Stay strong, Austin will find her and bring her home safely." She ran from the room, leapt onto her horse, and took off toward Fallen Tree.

Cassie ran into the parlor where Webb was seated with Terence and Renee, all enjoying their morning coffee. "Cady has been kidnapped!" she exclaimed, dropping into the nearest chair. They all stared at her, mouths agape.

"Kidnapped? By who?" Webb asked, setting down his cup.

"I don't know. Probably that nasty cousin of hers. He's tried it before."

"Who? Wiley? He's taken her before?"

"Well, he tried."

"And where was Austin?" Terence sneered. "Now that they're married, perhaps he arranged it so he'd get Ponderosa Pines."

"Oh, shut up Terence!" Cassie spat. "I am sick and tired of you criticizing Austin."

"Cassie, please don't speak to Terence that way. It's most unbecoming," Renee admonished with a frown.

Webb jumped to his feet. "I'm going after her." He turned to Terence. "Go get the sheriff and meet us at Ponderosa Pines. We'll pick up Randy—he knows how to track."

"I'm coming with you," Cassie declared, rising to her feet.

"No, you stay here. This is men's work."

"Well, I'm going if my son is going," Renee

declared. "Let me change first, I'll be down in a minute."

After the men, and Renee, took off on their horses, Cassie didn't waste a second. She mounted her bay mare and headed toward the mountains—to Rose. When she arrived at the Indian compound, she dismounted and rushed into Rose's tipi. Rose glanced up in surprise.

"Cassie! What is it?" Alarmed by her distraught expression, Rose set aside the child she'd been nursing and jumped to her feet.

"It's Cady. She's gone!"

"What do you mean *gone*? She's left Santa Fe?"

"No, she's been kidnapped! Most likely by her wretched cousin."

Rose sat back down, pulling Cassie with her. "Tell me everything,"

"We had a dinner party yesterday—what a fiasco! Austin came to collect Cady—his *bride*—and took her home. Pa was furious. I'd never seen him so angry. He ordered Cady out of the house, told her to never come back. I went over to see her this morning, I was worried about her. That's when Maria told me what had happened." She quickly told Rose of her conversation with Maria. "Pa gathered up Terence and Randy— Austin taught him how to track—to find Cady. He wouldn't let me go. Renee, of course, intruded and went with them."

"Oh, dear," Rose whispered, her hand on her throat. "I'll gather Lightfoot and a couple of other men to help find her."

"May I go with you?"

"Of course. After all, she's family now, isn't she?"

Chapter 37

Cougar was dead. A fresh spasm of pain swept over Cady as in her mind's eye she saw him swallowed up by the mighty river. The strong current had carried him downriver, his body disappearing under the whitecaps.

A gust of wind blew over her thinly clad body, covering her with its icy breath, and tossing her midnight-black curls around her shoulders. It whistled through the trees, the eerie sound making her shudder with a sense of impending doom. The sun sneaking through the trees dotted the forest floor with puddles of light, yet the air stayed chilly from the autumn wind. She had long since lost the shawl she had donned earlier last evening. She clenched her bound hands in her lap to stop them from shaking from cold, from fear.

Her wrists were slick with blood, oozing from deep cuts caused by the tight ropes binding them, and her struggles to escape. Her temple, where Wiley had struck her, throbbed a painful tattoo.

She ignored it all. What did her discomfort matter? Cougar was gone. If she ever got out of this alive, her life would never be the same without the man she loved. Squeezing her eyes closed against tears of grief and pain, images of their time together ran through her mind. The list of his kindnesses was long, and at every turn she had shouted she could take care of herself. Choking on the lump in her throat, she realized she would never have the chance to tell her proud, magnificent husband how much she needed him.

Please bring my Cougar back, she prayed fervently. Like a litany, she chanted—*if only I had one more chance.*

A shout of laughter interrupted her prayers and drew her attention to the two men huddled by the campfire. She and Wiley had ridden for hours until meeting up with a man in a small, secluded glade. It was the same man she had seen Wiley with in the saloon. He was short of stature, thin and ugly. She stiffened when they looked at her and grinned. *No doubt discussing my demise.*

She eyed Wiley. No wonder the sheriff had said the description of Chas's murderer resembled Cougar. Wiley was nearly as tall, had shoulder-length black hair, and rode a dark horse. But there the resemblance ended. For where Cougar was breathtakingly handsome, Wiley was ugly. Where Cougar was kind and loving, Wiley was an odious cur.

Cady's chest tightened in remembered shock. While Wiley trussed her up with the thick rope, he had gleefully told her how easy it had been to kill Chas. Like killing a duck on a pond, he had boasted.

Cady had stared at him, horror-stricken. "How could you? What had he ever done to you?"

"Left me and my family penniless," he sneered.

"But—"

"I aim to get what's rightfully mine."

"Why did Chas disinherit your father?"

"Don't know, don't care." He leaned over, securing the rope around the tree. She took a breath and almost retched from the sweet, cloying odor. "You shot Randy and kidnapped me!"

"Yep," he said almost proudly. He peered at her curiously. "Still can't figure out how you escaped from the cabin."

"And the fire in the stables?"

"Thought to scare you away."

"And in the hotel room in Denver?"

"Don't know nothin` about that."

"And Cougar's pardon—did you steal that, too?"

"Don't know nothin` about that neither." He waved his hand. "No more talkin`." And then he'd rejoined his companion by the fire.

And now he had killed her husband.

Her heart began to pound when Wiley rose to his feet. With only a cursory look at her, she heard him announce to his cohort, "Watch her. But leave her be." Grabbing his rifle, he disappeared into the tall pine trees encircling the glade.

Cady closed her eyes, exhausted. A small noise snapped them back open. The other man was approaching, his lips twisted into a lewd grin. She stiffened, a shiver of apprehension running down her spine.

"Don't touch me," she warned, recoiling against the tree.

"And just who's gonna stop me, little lady?"

"Wiley," she said with a jerk of her head in the direction he had disappeared. "He told you to leave me alone, remember?" she said, praying he would heed the threat.

He hesitated and appeared to be considering her words, his brow furrowed in thought. He glanced over his shoulder and swung back to her with a shrug of his shoulders.

"We got plenty of time. And if you're a smart girlie, you won't tell him neither," he threatened. He took another step toward her, his eyes glazed with lust. She opened her mouth to scream but only a hoarse croak escaped, scratching her dry throat. She struggled against the ropes, the heavy cords slicing deeper into her soft skin, while rivers of revulsion trickled between her breasts.

Her captor leaned in closer, his face twisted with lust. She shrank back against the tree as he reached out and grabbed a handful of her blouse. He stopped, distracted by the horses. They had begun to move restlessly against each other, stamping their hooves and snorting loudly, their ears pressed flat against their heads. He looked warily over his shoulder, his hand inching toward his knife but, seeing nothing amiss, turned back to her, eager to sate his itch.

"Ready for me, little lady?"

Cady flattened against the tree, the ragged bark cutting through the thin fabric of her blouse. He reached down again with his grubby hands, but jerked back as if burnt, rooted to the ground, paralyzed with fear. Cady had heard it too, a low growl reverberating in the glade and mixing eerily with the wailing wind. Her startled gaze swept the boulders piled on one side of the clearing. Her breath caught in her throat. A black mountain lion crouched above them, perched on the edge of the rocks, its long tail slapping rhythmically against the shale. It was watching her, its unwavering amber gaze glowing with an eerie light. Then, without warning, the large cat emitted a bloodcurdling hiss. He reared back on his haunches, sprang gracefully through the air, its huge front paws outstretched, its sharp claws bared, its sleek body elegantly elongated. *I have lived this before!*

The man fumbled for his knife at the same time the mountain lion grabbed his shoulders and dragged him to the ground. Its powerful jaws sank into his neck, its teeth sundering his spinal cord. The man's horrified scream ended in a sickening gurgle, as blood gushed from the severed life-sustaining veins. Alas, he was no match for the beast's steel-muscled strength.

The mountain lion sheathed its claws, gave one powerful shake of its head, and released its victim. The man crumpled to the ground in a gory silent heap. Cady stared at him in morbid fascination, then lifted her gaze to the mountain lion. The black beast swung its head toward her, its muzzle stained dark with blood. Yet Cady felt no fear, for it was her savior.

As if sensing her gratitude, the mountain lion blinked its amber eyes once, then turned and leapt over the boulders, disappearing behind the rock wall.

Cady stared in disbelief at the spot where the large cat had disappeared. When she finally snapped back to the here and now, she looked around, avoiding the man crumpled on the ground, and studied her situation. Glimpsing a glint of metal among the pine needles, she spotted the knife. She stuck out her bound feet, caught the handle with the heel of one boot, and dragged the blade toward her. Grasping it with both hands, she quickly sliced through the rope around her waist, her cold fingers making her clumsy. Then bending over, she sawed through the ropes around her ankles, and that done, she clamped the knife between her knees and moved her wrists up and down the blade until she had sawed through those bindings.

She heard someone approaching and glanced up

with a cry of dismay. Wiley came running into the clearing. With a shout of surprise, he bent over the fallen man, then slowly looked up at her. His expression changed from incredulity to rage when he saw the knife clenched between her knees. He ran over, grabbed the knife, and tossed it aside. He grasped her roughly by the shoulders and pulled her to her feet.

"Come on," he snarled. "We're getting out of here."

"No," she hissed, kicking out at him. Her knee landed in his groin, and he fell to the ground, yelping in pain and curling into a ball.

"You'll die now, bitch!" he cursed through gritted teeth and rose slowly to his feet, still slightly bent at the waist. He drew his gun and pointed it at her heart. An almost maniacal light glowed in his eyes as his finger curled around the trigger.

Cady backed into the tree, her gaze darting around for a means of escape, when something whizzed past her ear. She flinched when the knife stuck in Wiley's chest. He gasped and, grasping the hilt, pulled it out. Dark red blood spewed from the wound as he crumpled to the ground with a loud groan, stilled, his unseeing eyes open.

Cady didn't wait to see who had thrown the knife. She picked up her skirt and ran.

"Cady!"

She stopped and turned slowly, unable to believe her eyes. Happiness such as she had never known felled her and she sank to her knees with a whispered prayer of gratitude. She watched her beloved stride toward her with the grace of an animal, his face battered and bruised, a huge gash across his forehead. He was bare-chested, his arms and chest sliced with a profusion of smaller cuts, his bullet wound, secure. He dropped to his knees and held out his arms.

"Cougar," she breathed and fell into his embrace with a sob. She felt his arms close around her trembling body and she laid her head on his chest, wrapping her arms tightly around his waist. Her heart was so full of love she thought it might burst.

"You're alive," she whispered tearfully. "My dream—it came true. You are my mountain lion," she murmured, "my black mountain lion. You protected me, just like in my dreams."

"It's over, my love. You're safe now," he murmured against her hair as he rocked her gently in his arms. He kissed the top of her head, inhaling the subtle scent of violets that still lingered in the silky strands.

She touched his battered face with a gentle hand. "I thought you were dead. I prayed for one more chance. You came back to me."

"The cold water must have revived me. I got pretty beat up by the rocks, though. And the tumble over the waterfall didn't help," he muttered under his breath.

"How did you know where I was? How did you find me?"

"I will always find you, darlin`," he avowed, love shining brightly in his amber eyes.

"I love you, Cougar."

He brushed his mouth lightly over hers and whispered against her lips, "I love you, Cady." He tightened his arms around her as if afraid she might vanish. "You are mine. I protect what is mine."

The thunder of horses shattered their loving reunion. They turned to face a group of riders reining up before them, clumps of grass flying through the air from the horses' hooves. Webb was in the lead, Terence, Renee and Randy behind him. Sheriff Bosler brought up the rear.

Cougar stood, bringing Cady with him. He pulled his knife from Wiley's death-strengthened grip, wiped the blood off in the grass, and stuck it down his moccasin. Putting his arm around Cady's shoulders, they faced the group as one.

"Are you all right, girl?" Webb asked, his face creased with concern. "Cassie told us what happened."

"Yes, Cougar found me."

Webb glanced at Cougar, noted his arm around her, and immediately his anger resurfaced. "Get your hands off her!" He pulled out his rifle and laid it across his lap.

"Go to hell, Webb," Cougar responded in a deadly voice.

"Cady, step away from him!" Webb ordered. "I'm not too happy with you, young lady. But you're my best friend's kin and I won't do you no harm."

Before Cady could respond, another group of riders came galloping into the glade. Cassie with Rose, and a handful of Indians, pulled up alongside the others. Cougar acknowledged the tribe with a nod of his head and one hand lifted in greeting.

Webb stared at his sister, his face registering disbelief. "What in the hell are you doing here?"

"We came to find Cady. And to stop you from blowing off my son's head," Rose added, cutting a glance at his rifle. At the sound of Webb's angry tone, a huge Indian urged his horse forward positioning himself next to Rose. Rose held out her hand and spoke aside to him and he relaxed yet kept a sharp eye on Webb.

"This ain't none of your business, Rose."

"The hell it isn't," she retorted, looking at Cady.

"Are you all right, Little Cat?"

Cady nodded, clinging to Cougar's arm. She could feel his taut muscles, his body prepared for any threat. Her own heart was slamming in her chest.

"You gone and dubbed her some Indian name?" Webb sneered in disgust. "Chas would be spitting mad if he was alive!"

"My husband is half-Indian, Webb, and I'm proud of it!" Cady shook her head. "You should be ashamed of yourself."

"Chas approved of their marriage, Webb. Even knowing of his heritage," Rose replied calmly.

At Webb's look of disbelief, Cady stepped forward. "It's true, Webb. The codicil. He stipulated that I was to marry Cougar."

"But we talked about you and Terence—"

Cady glanced at Cougar to see his reaction. He was stone-faced.

"Then he only married you for your money," Webb sneered.

"No, that was Terence's intent," Cady replied.

"Now, Webb," Rose interjected softly. "We both know Cougar better than that. He's not interested in Ponderosa Pines—nor Fallen Tree, for that matter. Chas knew Cougar would protect Cady with his life, as Chas would have himself if he were still alive. Chas loved Cougar and accepted him as he was. Unlike some people," she said, her glance skimming over Renee and Terence.

"It doesn't matter how it came to be! I will not have my best friend's granddaughter married to a no-good bastard! He'll ruin her!"

"I think the most important issue here is that our

Cady is safe. If we must, this discussion can be continued at another time."

"No," Cougar stated, his voice resolute, his expression impassive. "Cady is my wife, by her own consent and her grandfather's blessing. Nothing and no one will take her away." His hard amber gaze swept the group, daring anyone to defy him.

"What about Colorado?" Terence shouted. "He's still wanted there—for murder!"

"He's been pardoned," Cady and Sheriff Bosler said in unison.

Cady looked at the sheriff in surprise.

"Got the news this morning, over the wire."

"I received a letter from Governor Thornwilde. It seems the man he sent here with the pardon was waylaid and his satchel stolen. The agent described the two men he spoke with at the Buckhorn," she said to Terence with one brow arched.

"I had an appointment in town and left him with Sam," Terence asserted, his face riddled with guilt.

Webb stared at Terence in disbelief. "That true? You had something to do with that, boy?"

"No! It was—"

"Quiet!" Webb roared. "I've had enough of your lies!"

"Governor Thornwilde has investigated the incident in Denver. It seems they were after the wrong man," Cady explained.

"Were you in on that too, Terence?"

Cougar sighed in exasperation. "Webb, you had me framed."

Webb looked at Cougar in genuine surprise. "I did no such thing. I may not have cared for the likes of you, but I certainly wouldn't have you arrested for something you didn't do."

Cougar looked skeptical, but Cady's hand tightening around his wrist kept him from commenting aloud. Webb slumped forward as if the weight of the world rested on his shoulders. "Seems we've been at odds for such a long time, I've forgotten how to behave. But no longer," Webb vowed and turned to Terence. "You miserable son-of-a-bitch. I never want to see your pathetic face again."

"What about what he did to Ma?" Terence cried, looking at Renee for support. She merely lifted a brow and watched Webb.

"Pa, she lied," Cassie cried out. "Austin never touched her."

Webb looked at Renee, one brow arched, and asked, "That true?"

"She told me you had ordered the whipping," Cougar muttered darkly.

Webb turned back to Renee. "You did what?" he roared. "Chas tried to tell me you lied about that night. But in my drunken haze, I believed you. By then, the damage was already done. It was too late to make amends. How could you?"

"You take that savage's word over mine? Your wife?" Renee finally found her voice, screeching in disbelief. Her face was twisted, her beauty buried beneath her wrath.

Webb nodded his head, a look of long-lost acceptance lighting his face. "Yes, I do. You see, Chas tried to make me see the truth. But I was so grief-stricken over Belle's passing I couldn't see what was going on around me. He even tried to dissuade me from marrying you."

Cassie started to dismount, wanting to go to her father. A resounding slap reverberated, startling the gathered group. Everyone turned to stare first at Renee, then at Cassie, her hand covering one side of her face that even now was turning red. Cady held out an arm and Cassie slid from her horse and ran to her side. Cady could feel her trembling like a frightened bird. She smoothed her hair, whispering softly to her.

"You bitch," Webb said through gritted teeth, sliding from his mount. "I told you I'd kill you if you touched my girl again."

Renee paled at the fury in Webb's voice. She pulled on the reins and her horse skittered backward, bumping into one of the Indians.

"You'll be sorry, Webb!" Terence shouted. "I've stood by your miserable side and endured your nasty remarks for years. I may not get Ponderosa Pines, but Fallen Tree will be mine! No one will take it from me!" He grabbed his gun and leveled it at Webb's heart.

Before anyone could react, Cougar drew his knife and with a flash of light, the blade embedded in Terence's shoulder. The gun fell from Terence's numb fingers and dropped harmlessly to the ground. He grabbed his shoulder and with a stricken look tumbled to the ground. Renee slid off her horse to rush to her son's side. She knelt beside him and cradled him in her arms.

Webb stared down at Terence without emotion, then turned to Cougar, breaking the deafening silence. "It seems I've been hoodwinked. I should never have let this young whelp and his mother sway me like they did. I am ashamed."

Cady felt Cougar relax. She looked up at him and

smiled. They shared a long look before he turned back to Webb and nodded.

"Thanks to Austin here, I discovered the identity of Chas's murderer," Sheriff Bosler announced. "It was Wiley Grayson, all right."

"How did you find out?" Cady glanced curiously at Cougar. "Wiley just today admitted everything he's done."

"One of my men, posing as an out-of-work gunslinger, met up with him in the saloon. Grayson was bragging about it." The sheriff nodded to Cougar. "It was his idea. Told me of his suspicions—and produced the other half of the bandanna we found outside Chas's window."

Cady looked at Cougar with a questioning lift of her brows. "His cologne," Cougar said. "After you were kidnapped—and escaped—" he added for her benefit, "I went back to that abandoned cabin. The odor filled the place. I did a little digging around, learned he was in town, and put two and two together."

"No wonder you were so angry with me for going to the saloon," Cady said. "I could have ruined your plans."

"You—what?" Webb roared. "You went to the Buckhorn?"

"Relax, Webb. I got there before she and Cassie could get into trouble."

Webb turned on his daughter and roared again, "*You* went into a saloon?" At her slow nod and sheepish grin, he slapped his forehead and groaned. "Do I have no control over my family?"

"Still can't figure out how you got out of my jail," the sheriff muttered, looking at Cougar with a pensive gleam in his eyes. "I'll need to check those locks when I get back." He nodded to the other fallen man in the center of the glade. "What happened to him?"

"Mountain lion."

Rose's eyes widened and she exchanged looks with the impressive Indian next to her. He turned to Cady, his black eyes narrowed in speculation.

"Was it—" Rose's question stumbled to a halt.

"Black."

Rose clasped her hands together in wondrous joy. Cady looked past her at the group of Indians who had stayed silent, but vigilant, throughout the family discord. Most wore smiles on their faces, all of them were looking at her with awe. Even Cougar was looking at her with something close to reverence.

"I see you two have finally found each other," Rose said softly. "True happiness." She clasped the hand of the magnificent Indian by her side. "It is truly a beautiful day."

Cougar smiled and looked down into Cady's indigo eyes ablaze with love. She leaned into his side, wrapping an arm around his waist, and holding him close. They truly belonged together, nothing would keep them apart—not any one person, not her fears nor his. Cougar was her protector, her soul mate, her love—for life.

Epilogue

As preparations continued for the wedding, the sun began its daily descent, the last of its orange and yellow rays streaking the slate-blue sky like strokes from a painter's brush. Outside, the women were busy preparing the wedding feast, the men were keeping Cougar company—doing what, Cady didn't know.

Though Cougar and Cady were already legally married, Rose had insisted on a traditional Indian wedding. Cady had enthusiastically agreed. Fascinated by her husband's heritage, she was eager to learn more about their customs. Cougar had been more than pleased to find her so readily embracing his culture.

Earlier in the evening, Rose had helped Cady dress for the ceremony. She had donned a traditional wedding dress of snow-white buckskin with hundreds of multicolored beads sewn around the bodice, the fringed hem, and down the long, belled sleeves. On her feet, she wore matching white moccasins also accented with colorful beadwork. Her long black hair was parted in the middle, left to hang loose down her back, and adorned with more of the brilliant beads, with a posy of violets pinned behind one ear. Rose had gifted her with turquoise-and-silver jewelry which now adorned her ears and throat.

While Cady dressed, Rose had told her that she'd had a long talk with Webb. "There has been one misunderstanding after another. It all started when Cougar left home. Webb thought Cougar had turned his back on him, that he had shunned him when he learned of his heritage."

"But that's what Cougar thought Webb had done!"

Rose nodded. "I know. It didn't help that Renee and Terence fed them both lie after lie." She sighed. "It will take time for them to fully reconcile. Neither one is entirely sure about the other, and there have been too many years of hatred and mistrust. Not to mention their pride," she added with a roll of her eyes. The two women shared a smile.

Now, Cady waited with Rose in her tipi. She glanced nervously out the door at the deepening dusk. The village was cast in shadows, the full moon waiting to make its ascent. "Has Cougar arrived yet?"

"No, Little Cat. He will not appear until the ceremony begins."

"Why do we wait until sundown?" she asked, turning from her vigil at the door.

"Darkness covers the couple like a blanket—a blanket of peace and harmony to begin their new life together." Rose began to fill the white wedding basket with mush made of ground white cornmeal and water. "And corn is the symbol of life."

Cady turned back to the door. "Oh, I think I see Cougar," she exclaimed just as Rose's husband, Lightfoot, appeared in the doorway. Cady stepped aside and allowed him to enter. Lightfoot was a tall, handsome warrior. When Cady had first met him, she had been awed by his size and strength. Tonight, however, there was a definite sparkle of warmth in his eyes.

"It is time." Rose handed Cady the basket of mush

as Lightfoot preceded them from the tipi, carrying a ceramic jug of water and a yellow hollowed-out gourd. Cady walked beside Rose, carefully carrying the white basket.

The tipi was crowded with guests. Bright, colorful shawls adorned the plain walls, adding to the festive atmosphere. A large multi-colored shawl hung outside the entrance in honor of the wedding. A bundle of sweetgrass burning in a ceramic bowl perfumed the air.

Webb stood with Cassie, her hand clasped in his. Maria and her family were in attendance, along with Randy and Red. Sam Hathaway stood off to one side with a young woman holding onto his arm. The others present were from Cougar's Indian family. Terence and Renee of course were absent, having left town right after the confrontation in the glade. No one in Santa Fe expected to see them again.

Cassie pointed to a saddle heaped in one corner of the tipi. "Pa, what is that doing there?"

"It's Austin's. Rose told me it symbolizes that he will not leave his wife once they're married." He looked down at Cassie. "If he does, he'll answer to me," he threatened with a mock growl.

"Oh, Pa, you know Austin loves Cady. He will never leave her." She glanced at Randy and smiled shyly.

Randy sidled over and grabbed her other hand. Webb saw the gesture and arched a brow. Taking in his daughter's blush, he could easily guess what was happening between them. After a moment, he shook his head in resignation and smiled at the two of them, silently giving them his blessing.

He nodded toward Sam and the young woman who had a death grip on his arm. "Who's that girl with Sam?"

"That's Lucinda Grayson. Wiley's sister. When Cady was in Silverhills, she told her she was welcome any time at Ponderosa Pines."

"Looks like she took her up on it rather quickly."

"Yes, she showed up a few days after Cady was kidnapped by Wiley. Cady introduced her to Sam. Seems they fell instantly in love. They haven't been apart since."

Just then Cougar ducked into the tipi, his large frame filling the opening. He walked around the small fire in the center of the floor and sat cross-legged on one side of the tipi, facing the door. He was dressed in white fringed buckskins and matching knee-high moccasins. His white buckskin vest was sewn with blue-and-gold beadwork. He wore feathers of blue-and-white in his long black hair, and around his forehead was a strip of white buckskin with gold beads sewn into the image of a mountain lion. The firelight played across his face, a face full of peace.

All eyes were riveted to the door as Cady entered followed by Rose and Lightfoot. She, too, walked around the fire and, bestowing a brilliant smile on Cougar, who had not taken his eyes off her, sat down beside him and placed the white basket on a small pile of sand between them.

Cady poured water from the ceramic jug into the gourd and proceeded to wash Cougar's hands. Cougar did the same. For the benefit of those not knowing the custom, Rose said aloud, "This ritual washes away the past." She gazed at the couple, her eyes shining with unshed tears. "From now on, your life is as one."

Cougar took a pinch of cornmeal mush from one side of the wedding basket and fed it to Cady, and she in turn did the same. They continued this ritual until they had taken a pinch from each side of the basket, finishing with a pinch from the center. When the basket was empty, the ceremony was complete. They were married. Cougar handed his mother the basket to keep as a keepsake of the ceremony.

Before the feast was brought in for the celebration, Webb, acting on behalf of Cady's family, gifted Rose and her family bags of food. Rose in turn presented Cassie and him with dream catchers, the enchanting little objects that ensured only good dreams.

When the guests had finished the lavish wedding feast, it was time for Cougar and Cady to receive advice on their upcoming life together. Cougar drew Cady to her feet, whispering in her ear that because Indian culture was based on respect for the elders and their knowledge, it was an essential part of the ceremony.

Rose stepped forward and clasped Cady's hands in hers. "You have captured the elusive mountain lion. He will no longer roam the earth alone. You will travel by his side on your journey through life. He will never desert you. He will protect you. The Great Spirit willing, your journey will be filled with true happiness, with only beauty surrounding you."

She reached for Cougar's hand and placed it over Cady's. Curling her cool fingers around their clasped hands, she looked deeply into her son's eyes. "Your solitude has come to an end, my son. Protect her with your strength, with your love. It will conquer all obstacles." She kissed them both. "Let nothing but splendor surround you as you begin your life together, indeed, throughout your life. You are twin flames of the same candle. You two are truly blessed."

Tears spilled forth as she gazed at her proud, handsome son, his amber eyes filled with the love he held for this beautiful woman he had finally found.

After the elders had spoken, Webb stepped forward and faced Cougar. "I have wronged you. I know Chas loved you like his own and I wish I had heeded his advice. No longer will I hold hatred in my heart." He held out his hand. "I know you will take care of her."

"Always." Cougar clasped his hand, accepting his offer of peace.

Webb turned to Cady and kissed her on the cheek. "I wish Chas were here to witness this moment. He loved you so very much. He was a wise man—he saw what I couldn't. I'm sorry about that. If you'll let me, I would like to act in his stead."

Cady stepped up and hugged Webb. "I would like that. And I believe he is watching from above, witnessing that his request has not only been fulfilled but quite happily so."

Cady and Cougar turned to face each other, their hands clasped together, their fingers intertwined. Cougar looked into his bride's moist indigo eyes so clearly full of the love they shared.

"You are my love. You are my life. Through your eyes I have seen the beauty in my existence. You are the sun that wakes me in the morning, the moon that covers me at night. Your eyes are the stars in the ebony sky that shine with love when they gaze upon my face. You are my first love—you are my last love. I treasure you as I treasure no other. I belong to you, and will stand by you, always. You are my true happiness."

Cady's eyes filled with tears as she gazed at her husband's tender countenance, at the words he imparted, exposing his vulnerability.

"You are my love. You are my life. Through your eyes I have seen the beauty in my existence. Your arms are branches cradling me with love and security. With you, I have not only learned to trust in love but have blossomed in it. You are my first love—you are my last love. I treasure you as I treasure no other. I belong to you and will stand by you, always. You are my true happiness—my black mountain lion."

Cougar leaned down and brushed his mouth against hers. Then slipping one arm beneath her legs, he lifted her up, cradled her against his broad chest, and carried her from the tipi amid cheers from the guests. Without breaking stride, he swung up on his stallion, settled Cady on the fleece blanket and, with a slight pressure from his knees, turned the steed around and headed for his quiet cabin nestled in the mountains.

Cady laid her head against her husband's chest, listening to his heartbeat, as, guided by the moonlight, they galloped down the narrow trail to the lush valley beyond.

A mountain lion reposing on top of the rocky ridge, bathing its glossy black fur with its pink tongue, paused long enough to watch Cougar and Cady disappear into the valley, a twinkle in its amber eyes.

A word about the author...

Christine has a passion for love stories. When not weaving romance and mystery to create her own, she enjoys floral film photography, watching classic movies, and chocolate.

She resides in Virginia with her dog, Apache.

christine-davies.com

Thank you for purchasing
this publication of The Wild Rose Press, Inc.

For questions or more information
contact us at
info@thewildrosepress.com.

The Wild Rose Press, Inc.